Desire's Tempest Journey

THE SAGA OF BRIGA OF CYMRU AND THE WOLF-WARRIOR

AUTHORED BY ALAN ROY JOHNSTON
WITH CONTRIBUTING AUTHOR ENA BRENNAN

Celtic Romantic Fiction
© 2012
© Revised 2014

Desire's Tempest Journey:
The Saga of Briga of Cymru and the Wolf-Warrior

Book One of the Long Journey Home series

Category: Romance, historical fiction

Cover art created by

Emily Balivet
Beltane Reunion—Pagan God and Goddess
http://www.emilybalivet.com/

Published by
Alan Roy Johnston
ISBN-13: 978-0615956565 (Custom Universal)
ISBN-10: 0615956564
Library of Congress Control Number: 2014901916
Alan Roy Johnston, La Grande, OR

Printed in the United States of America

CreateSpace, North Charleston, South Carolina

Books of the Long Journey Home series:

Book 1: Desire's Tempest Journey: The Saga of Briga and the Wolf-Warrior
Book 2: Desire's Depths: The Saga of Briga and the Birth of the Sea-Wolf
Book 3: Desire Fulfilled: The Return of Briga and the Rebirth of Caswallon the Druid
Book 4: Desire's Eternal Flame: Cylch Mawr, the Great Circle of Life and Love

Dedication

To my wife, Rebecca Ellen, whose patience and support
allowed me the time to complete this journey.

To my mother, Beverly Theresa, and my grandmother, Eva
Maria, whose stories set me in the direction of seeking truth
and wisdom in the feminine.

And to Ena Brennan, my contributing author, whose good advice and help I have cherished.

I also dedicate this book to all the women in this world.
Without womankind, there would be no humankind.
You are the star gate through which all human life
enters the earth from the *Cruthadair*, the "Creators."

You are the sacred feminine.

Introduction

When I was a young child, my mother would often tell me, "You are descended from the kings of Ireland and Wales." At the time I thought she was telling me another family fable, and as I grew older and my life became complicated with raising a family, I forgot my mother's words. With idle hours on my hands once I retired, and with the help of my older brother, Don, I began researching our ancestry on Ancestry.com. What we found changed our lives and thinking forever. We are related to the ancient kings of Ireland and Wales, and our ancestors include the Norse men who founded and settled Dublin and Cork. My mother was telling us a truth, and that truth sent us researching and digging deeply into the history and people of Wales, Ireland, and the Nordic countries.

We discovered people and great stories that had never made it into our contemporary education here in the United States. These were sagas equally as great as the Greek and Roman legends we had been taught in our literature classes—with an important difference, as these were the stories of my ancestors and my children's and my grandchildren's ancestors. As I learned about the people of my ancestry and their sagas, a strong desire to tell their stories grew inside me. I had a deep yearning to let the sagas, forgotten for generations, grow into legends once again; the stories I write are fiction, filled with the dreams of past lives and the imagination of an old Irish/Welsh-American storyteller.

The first book of the Long Journey Home series, titled *Desire's Tempest Journey: The Saga of Briga and the Wolf-Warrior*, takes a look into the lives, culture, and beliefs of early Iron Age Celts in Wales/Cymru and Ireland/Erin at the end of the pre-Christian era and the beginning of Christian history. I and my coauthor, Ena, attempt to reveal to our readers myths, legends, and a way of life that have been hidden for centuries. Most storywriters avoid the so-called Dark Ages, but we wanted to weave story lines that are fictional yet heavily woven with historical places, people, and events. We hope to open the minds of our readers to searching and investigating beyond the known and the accepted—to look into their own ancestries and the historical events surrounding them so that we, their descendants, might live. We hope our readers will view the world of the pagans differently, discovering that it was filled with passionate heroines and heroes, many of them our blood ancestors.

The book contains the authors' insights and imaginings as well as the best possible reconstruction of the era and its people, along with their religious practices, moral values, and teachings as they might have appeared before the introduction of Christianity to the people of Cymru. The story attempts to open a window into a pagan world altered forever first by the Roman Empire, and later by the empire of Roman Christianity.

Alan Roy Johnston

Opening of the Oak Door of Cymru:

⊣ Duir/Dair (rune letter for *door*)

The old druid Caswallon, a seeker of truth, held the small boy
with the light-red hair

and the blue-gray eyes on his knee as he taught him.

The child was his son, a child of Beltane.

Only the old druid and the mother of the child

knew that the Ard Druid of Cymru was the father of the boy.

Smiling, with eyes filled full of pride, the old man said,

"Remember, Conall, a brave and honorable death

is the only pathway to opening the oak door

that leads to our rebirth."

Prologue

Banished in tidal waves of misery, Briga said, "I don't believe in the gods anymore! How could they let this happen?" Briga's heart had sunk into the deepest anguish as she sputtered through clenched teeth and the taste of her own blood. The Luti raiders had killed her companions and brutally murdered Conall's cousin in front of her. She alone had escaped death, only to survive and be kept alive as a *thrall* for the old hag, Freya.

The only world she knew had been ripped away from her. "Where are you, Conall? If you had been here, none of this would have happened. As for the gods, from now on you and I are strangers. I will never trust my life to you again." The path of resentment was easier for her to travel than the road to hope.

The darkness of her fears surrounded her as images and memories of the last few days flooded into her mind. So many had died, and she feared Conall's failure to rescue her meant only one thing: he was among the dead.

Exhausted, she collapsed and lay in the fetal position. She lifted her head to face the ocean as she watched the men struggle to float the beached ship. Tears of fear, confusion, and abandonment welled in her eyes until they could hold no more. They stung as they burst from her eyes and rolled down her cheeks. She was pregnant and alone.

As she looked out at the distant horizon, she felt as cold as the chiseled and carved face of her stone god. The waters of the vast ocean that lay before her only amplified her loneliness and isolation. Briga had little knowledge of the world beyond her beloved Cymru, and her ignorance of that world only added to her anxiety. Her breathing was fast and shallow. Only one thought entered her head: "I have to survive."

Bound with ropes of despair and held captive by fear for her child, she was defenseless, on a storm-swept beach looking out into the Celtic Sea. She was far from her people. Pain from bruised limbs and a broken nose seared her body. "Life is cruel and unfair," she mumbled. "It's all so senseless. Everything dies. Men shred each other, and women are left alone. No one cares... There is always warring...always mothers crying and living a darkened, depressed existence. This isn't what I was promised by the gods." What little hope she mustered was a fragile seed that refused to take root.

Before her in the inky black that was the color of her misery appeared an image of a very old man, a druid; it was Caswallon, her great-grandfather and his instructive words drifted to her from out of the mist—and the past.

> Brave hearts fade when darkness comes
> and those with strong arms become weak.
> Boldness sets with the sun
> as the bright light is replaced by the darkness.
> Doubt and fear fill the hearts of the meek.
> With every star that appears,
> those of weakened soul and spirit become afraid.
> Filled by the gloom, their strength disappears
> and is replaced by panic.
> Darkness and death are the same for the weak.
> Be strong; be filled with the light of truth and the
> radiance of hope,

for those who carry within themselves the light of the
creators
never see the darkness.

She whimpered into the surrounding darkness, "Grandfather
Caswallon, please help me."

Chapter One

The early-morning bite of the cold made him feel as exposed as the charcoal-black darkness that surrounded him. Snow crunched under each step, and his breath was labored, wanting, devoid of the strength of spirit that seemed to fade at every step. Hope of seeing the sunlight again was beginning to slip away. Dawn's pale glow was nowhere to be seen on the horizon, as the sun still battled with darkness to return to the sky of Cymru.

"I'm so tired," Conall said with a sigh into the gloom that caged him. For days he had been walking alone in the silent wilderness. All he felt was a penetrating numbness that began inside his head and slid down his spine. He ceased thinking as his legs moved him along, propelling his body forward as he tried to make his way back to all he loved most in the world. The will to live was beginning to erode from the great Conall Cearnach of Clan Diahad.

Just above the mountain ridges that made up the distant eastern skyline, he could see *madainn rionnag*, the morning star, and it was shining brightly about eight fingers above the horizon. Toward the south and above the madainn rionnag was the thin, silver crescent of the waxing moon. Conall knew it would be at least two hours before sunrise, and he was cold, hungry, and exhausted.

He stopped moving and squinted into the thick darkness that surrounded him. "There," he said out loud as he made out an outline of an even greater darkness. He slowly moved toward the obscure shape that showed itself against the lighter gray of a cloud-covered sky.

He tripped over a tangle of tree roots and caught his fall with his shoulder, slamming against a large Saracen bluestone. He spoke his words out loud, piercing the surrounding cold with an attitude of annoyance and pain: "*Damn* all the foreign gods!" Then, with a resigned whisper, he said, "Danu, please, help me. Come to me and sit down beside me. Hold me and watch over me as I rest and restore my body and my strength."

In the darkness he reached out and fingered the cold rock wall that was barely visible as he hesitantly inched toward it. It was not the shelter he'd hoped for, but it would do until the morning light appeared. Drawing runes on the rock with his finger, Conall dared not give in to slumber until he saw the sun rise again; besides, it was still too cold to fall asleep, and if he did, perhaps he wouldn't wake up. The freezing breath of Cailleach, the Hag of Winter, hunted in the long, dark nights, seeking to choke the life from a man. "Danu, help me stay awake," he voiced to himself. Conall continued shivering in order to conserve what warmth he had. Later the next day, when the sun was high in the sky, he would find a sheltered, south-facing rocky nook, warmed by the sun and protected from the wind; it would be in such a place that he would lie down and sleep.

For now he sat down in the still darkness against the Saracen stone that faced east. As he closed his eyes, he could see madainn rionnag through the thinning clouds. The morning star was clear and bright on the horizon. "So cold," he thought, and closing his eyes, he turned his attention to the warmest place he knew—the place he was fighting cold and death to return to, his *Mo Anam Cara*.

He smiled into the darkness that clutched him as intimate memories of the woman he loved flooded him with warmth. No longer numb and on a hillside far away from her, his mind journeyed back in time, across space, to a memory that was filled with summer sun, warm breezes, and the sweet fragrance of her scented body.

Conall was making his way home to his beloved Briga. He thought of her and all the time that he had been away from her—the long, six years of training required to be in the order of the wolf-head, the *Cunobarrus*. He had walked with her at their first Beltane following his return. They had held a hand-fasting ceremony at *Alban Hefin*, the summer solstice, and now, after only a few months of marriage and living together, he was once again far away from her arms and her love.

Conall was thinking only of her as his pain melted away, and his fingertips warmed at the thought of touching her bare skin. His breathing became more rapid as he played over in his mind the memory of how her soft, silky inner thigh felt as he caressed his beloved Briga. Conall's flesh began to thaw as he focused on how she pleased him and how he loved to please her...

He uttered a sigh as his fingers slowly walked from her waist, up along her ribs until he found the warmth and the round fullness of her breasts. Conall's two callused hands found their mark below her beautiful neck; hands that had been cold for hours warmed quickly as blood from his pulsing heart pumped stronger and harder while he remembered the woman who gave him inconceivable pleasure.

His nostrils flared, and his breathing grew rapid as he imagined the way she smiled, the cadence of her voice, and the sensual way her body moved. Into the cold darkness, Conall declared out loud, "I love you, Briga!" Pounding rapidly, his heart pushed his blood into all of his extremities, warming him completely and shoving the cold from his body back into the darkness that surrounded him—back to the cold, barren place it belonged.

Hours had passed as his mind continued its journey into gratifying memories with her. The magic of their love was still working on his body, and he groaned in pleasure as he thought of her pheromones wrapping themselves into every cell of his being. He could taste her syrupy kisses on his lips. He kissed her on the forehead and gently ran his rough, manly hands through her hair, away from her scalp.

As he sat against a cold *cròmleac* in the darkness of late winter, he chuckled at the thought of himself glowing with heat. Conall was aroused by passionate thoughts of her. He whispered her name into the darkness. "Briga," he called out into the shadows, "*is tu m' annsachd!*" ("Briga, thou art my best beloved!")

He spoke the words three times so that they would be heard and sealed forever in the world of flesh, in the mists of the spirit world, and in the center of the *Cruthadair*. He wanted them all to know that he loved Briga.

Cold and exhaustion slowly crawled their way back to Conall. By the movement of the stars across the sky, he knew hours had passed. The magic of his love for Briga worked in his body so that he was able to shake off the cold and exhaustion before it could consume him. With renewed vigor and fresh energy, he mustered his strength to continue moving eastward. He had been traveling east to confuse those who had been following him, and he knew he would soon have to turn north toward his beloved Briga.

Rested and energized, he opened his eyes, and to his delight, the clouds had parted on the eastern horizon. A thin, dim, pale line of sunrise showed its first fruit of promise. East had been the direction that his numbed feet and weary legs had carried him, and now the spine of darkness was finally broken. With new life,

Conall stood up and faced the approaching sunrise. "Thank you, Danu," he said, and turning to face north, the direction toward home and the woman he loved, he added, "Please, Danu, give me the strength to return to my Briga."

Druuos was still visible, the motionless star in the northern sky, the home of his ancestors and all the generations of the people of Cymru. As he looked upon the North Star, Conall lowered his head, placing his chin firmly against his chest, exposing the back of his neck. He assumed a posture of humble respect and submission. With eyes closed, he spoke gently, with great respect.

"Grandfathers and grandmothers, I am Conall of your clann. Ancestors and blood of my blood, please hear my prayer. Help me. Give me your wisdom and strength as I journey back to Llyn Tegid and y Bala, to the *crannog* of Briga, my wife, and Mo Anam Cara." He opened his eyes as he raised his head and looked out at the horizon. "Finally, the Sky Father returns." He spoke in a voice loud enough for the whole world to hear as he said, "I thank the Cruthadair for the gift of another day."

He rejoiced at the return of dawn—the sun would soon join him on his journey. His voice seemed foreign to his ears, harsh and raspy from the long hours of breathing the cold air. Thirsty, he bent at his waist, holding his left side as he reached down to scoop up a large handful of ice-crusted snow. He began sucking on the snow to release its water. His lips were blistered from the cold and the wind that seared his parched throat; the moisture and cold of the snow relieved both his thirst and the dryness that blanketed his lips.

Standing upright, he looked for the bright and brilliant star on the horizon that seemed to dance and flicker in the cold early-morning dawn. He had been following madainn rionnag, the morning star, ever since it had first appeared on the eastern horizon hours earlier.

He shook off the reality of exposure and the pain from being wounded. The Great Mother Danu was guiding him home to his beloved Briga. He felt Danu's presence swirling about him as he struggled to return. He instinctively knew she would always be with him, as it was her energy, and her unfailing strength, that filled his soul and gave force to his life.

Once again he began moving down the hillside toward home, but now he turned north, and finally he would move west, across the mountains to the lake that was home. "Not far now," Conall uttered confidently.

As the dim light grew more intense on the horizon, so did Conall's hope. As he walked, he thought, "So much has happened since I left Briga and those I love. So much of my life energy has been spent in the effort to just survive."

New threads had been added to the tapestry of Conall's life story as woven by the goddess Danu on her great loom. These were threads that didn't include Briga, and that made him frown, creating new worry lines that etched deeply into his face.

Each step was forced and echoed with pain. Yet as painful as each step was, it moved him closer to her, as it was the hope of touching her again, of being held close to her that kept him moving forward. The day had turned to rain and wind, and as both stung the inside of his ears, he could hear no other sounds. Like an unfaithful friend, the rain stuck to him, clinging to his cloak and dripping from his hands as he made his descent. The miserable hours dragged on like the dreariness of the weather, and the surroundings he walked through became a blur. The crunching of ice-crusted snow under his feet and his labored breath were the only signs that he was still alive. He smiled as he thought, "Briga will be happy that I haven't yet returned to the oak grove in the land of my ancestors."

Conall fingered the talisman that hung around his neck just below his father's *torc*; his father had died in battle. Briga had given this prized gift to Conall before he left on his journey. She had placed inside the white doe-leather bag a locket of her hair, dirt from the shoreline of their home at Llyn Tegid, three acorns, thirteen dried blossoms of the purple centaury flower, and a piece of the sacred blue stone from *Carn Goedog*. As he fingered the talisman, he thought, "Don't worry, my Briga. My fate will not be my father's fate. I will not die at the hands of these raiders that defile our Mother Cymru."

It had been many hours since he'd last seen any sign of those who followed him. He traveled in and out of darkness and cold for what seemed like an eternity. The combination of cold, rain, and the gloomy shadows of the thick forests had left him numbed not only in body but also in mind. He had walked for days by sheer willpower. His strength now ebbing, he used what was left to fight the pain. Bitter cold and gloom lingered like a tormented memory that would never end. His ice-cold fingers touched the deep wound in his left side, and he smiled into the darkness as he did not feel the sticky warmth of his own blood.

"Good," he muttered, breaking the silence of the cold and dark winter sky. Silence had been his only companion for hours. "At least the dried yarrow and this damn cold have stopped the bleeding." His mind wandered in and out of certainty as he thought of Briga again. As her image filled his thoughts, warmth once again began waxing into his body.

His breath quickened and deepened at the memory of her touch. He envisioned the last time her hands had danced on his bare skin, her fingers twirling lightly in the dark, reddish curls of hair that grew thick on his burly chest. He could feel her fingertips on his chest, her nails softly writing rune marks on his skin that told him, "You are my beloved, and I am yours." ("*Is tu m' annsachd*" in his native tongue.)

His heart pumped stronger, and the blood in his veins warmed. Just the memory of her was enough to give him resurgent strength and hope. The pain, the cold, and the darkness were all swept away as he mind-journeyed away from his body and the suffering.

Trained by the druids, Conall was able to detach himself from present reality. He was able to travel into the memories of days before the current moment. Time, place, and space held no limits for him; he journeyed into the past, far away from the aching cold and the pain that spiraled down into his bones. He couldn't decide if it hurt more to be injured or to be absent from the other half of his soul. He had to conquer the fatigue somehow. He went to the place he knew best and loved above all others; he returned to Briga…

Chapter Two

onall's mind wandered, moving further and further from the suffering of his body. He felt his energies whirling as his soul moved away from the present, far away to the past, to the summer camp in the mountains above the lake valley he called home. He could see the waterfall pool at the place of the talking rocks—the waterfall of the *còmhradh carragh*—and he smiled as he thought to himself that this was where Briga had anointed the talking pillar with their love. Into the cold he warmly whispered, "*Mo Briga, far an d'ung thu an còmhradh carragh le ar gràdhaich*." His Briga had given the place its name, the Còmhradh Carragh, which later became Pistyll Rhaeadr (spring of the waterfall). The Celtic tribes Ordovices and Silures were honored in naming many such landmarks. As teenagers playing, Briga and Conall had discovered the cave hidden behind the falls.

The waterfall only had a voice in the spring, when the water in the stream reached its greatest volume. It fell over the cliff's rocks in three stages, with great force and grace, before crashing against the massive flat rocks scattered at the base of the falls. Silky strands of water exploded into a fine mist as the droplets sailed, floating on the air, only to be caught by the morning sunlight that turned them into luminous rainbows.

The hollow voice seemed to echo from deep within the water, loud enough to be heard over the sound of the falling water crashing on the rocks. Briga had wanted to know why it talked. She wondered what this mystery was. Her mind was like a water-wheel—always turning, always thinking, always wondering why things were the way they were. She was never satisfied with accepting things as they were. She wanted to know why.

Briga always had a taste for the fruit of knowledge—deep in her soul was a seeker of truth.

Why had her ancestors always believed the headwaters and wells were sacred gifts from the goddess? She had stared in amusement at the headwaters—the chief nursery, the cradle of life, the womb that rested inside her waiting to be opened and bring forth life.

She knew that within her dwelt the numinous necessity...

In his soul's mind, Conall was there now, standing and watching Briga deep in thought, as she stared and pierced the unknown with her keen mind. Then Conall's mind imagined her undressing.

They were both still very young, still almost children. She had been only twelve, and he had just seen his sixteenth summer solstice. It was the first time he'd seen her without clothes. He smiled as he remembered.

She was unshapely and thin as a boy. The goddess hadn't touched her body with her moon blood yet, and she wasn't yet a maiden. The only clan tattoo she wore was the birthing tattoo on the bottom of her left foot. She was just a child, and he had looked at her nakedness as one looking at a childhood friend.

"She is fairer and whiter than the ninth wave of the sea," he thought as he looked upon her nakedness.

"Come on, silly, undress, and let's find the fall's voice." The distant words filled his mind. He remembered watching her. Even at twelve, she had moved with the grace of a woman much older and wiser in the ways of a woman's body and the force of its pleasure. Her movements were both teasing and inviting; without knowing, she already knew how to catch his eye. Truth was, she'd always had that way about her, and he'd always been attracted to her.

She had climbed high on the rocks and bent over to peer into the deep shadows behind the waterfall. "Conall, come up here!" she shouted as loud as she could. "There's something behind the water!" As she bent at the waist to peer past the falls and into the darkness beyond, Conall could see that she was no longer just a child. It was the first time he had looked at her differently. It was on that summer day long ago that he'd first noticed that her hips were beginning to find an inviting roundness, and he'd thought that it wouldn't be much longer before the goddess visited her.

No man ever touched a young maiden until the goddess visited her with the circle of her moon blood; after her first moon blood, every young maiden waited eagerly for her first Beltane. Each maiden would choose the man who would walk with her down the Beltane path into the oak forest—the path that was her journey of transformation into womanhood. That first Beltane's fire festival would be her first experience with a man. It was the most sacred journey from young maid to woman, and the journey was made within a ceremony that proclaimed to the whole village that the maiden was taking the path to womanhood as she walked off into the forest with her *Cernunnos.*

A man could not refuse the request of a young maid who selected him to take her first sacred walk; refusing her at Beltane would be turning your back on the goddess Brighid. It was on the day they discovered the secret cave at the talking falls that Conall first began hoping he might be the man whom Briga named as her horned god of Beltane. Looking up at her, Conall said, "All right, Briga, I'll follow you on your quest." She shouted back down to him, "Be my warrior, Conall!" He quickly undressed and took off everything except the thick, massive, gold wolf-head torc he wore around his neck. It was the torc that had been given to him by his mother—the torc his father and his father's father had worn.

Now that he was standing there naked, she turned to give him her full attention. It was the first time she had seen him naked as well. At sixteen he was already very manly, almost ten hands tall and weighing fourteen stones. His shoulders were already broad and his arms and chest well muscled. At the age of six, he had been fostered with the druids, and years of exercise, training, and daily practice with the weapons of war had formed strong, defined muscles upon the frame of the man he had become. She smiled and liked what she saw. Something twirled and whizzed inside her head. She felt warm all over, as if someone had just poured warm goat's milk over her entire body. Briga trusted Conall completely; she had no reason not to—he was training to be a *convel.*

He wore the clan's tattoos, and he had an armband on his right arm of two defiant wolves fighting together as one; this was to let the world know that Conall's life had been given to Cymru, and he was a convel, a "wolf-warrior." His upper left arm and the left side of his chest already had scars. Blades in battle had already tasted his flesh, and he had killed and taken the heads of the men who had blessed him with the marks.

She watched as he turned to place the last of his clothes on a rock.

"What a fine form he has," she thought to herself as she looked at the defined shape of his body, at his broad shoulders, his narrow waist, and the wonderfully strong muscles of his torso. His legs were also muscled and strong, and Briga was sure Conall could run faster and farther than any man in Cymru. The only defect about him was a slight limp when he walked.

Suddenly she remembered her grandfather Caswallon telling her that Conall had fallen as a young child from a very tall *derw ynn*. Conall, the young boy dressed all in white, had climbed high into the oak tree on the sixth day of the moon to gather mistletoe for the old druid. Stretching awkwardly, he had reached out to an outgrowth of mistletoe that he cut with a golden sickle, and as it fell toward the ground to be caught by two druidesses holding a white cloak, Conall had slipped and fallen, breaking his leg. Caswallon had repaired the broken bone, but Conall still walked with a slight limp.

Looking at him with renewed respect, she noticed he had no scars anywhere on his backside. Among the men of Cymru, there was one goal, a driving hope that moved each warrior: no warrior ever wanted to receive a wound to the back. A scar on the back was a sign of cowardice or treachery. Conall always faced his enemies in battle, and his enemies would never by treachery or act of violence leave such disgraceful wounds on his back. He turned to face her again. She took in the full view of him as a man, and what she saw forever changed her thinking and her desires from a little girl's to that of a woman waiting for the day of her blessing and emergence.

"How very manly he is, and how perfect," she thought to herself. "He seems to pulsate with the heartbeat of the stars." She could hear all creation whispering his name. Even at the age of twelve, feelings stirred deep within her, and on that day she made up her mind that it would be Conall who would receive her gift on Beltane night.

"Please, Conall, come up to me." Without hesitation he began to climb up the rocks, and soon he was standing next to her on the ledge. He was only one hand away from her, and he trembled. His knees weakened. It was the first time of many that she'd have that effect on him. He didn't know the meaning of it then, but he would learn later that he had experienced the combined soul energy of the Mo Anam Cara as they'd come close to each other.

Already blooming within Conall's soul was the rarest flower in Cymru, the purple centaury (*dréimire mhuire*), which only the goddess Danu would cause to grow at the moment Briga and Conall blended their souls and became one living flame. He knew he would live and die for her. As he watched her, he trembled, and as he looked at her face, he noticed that she also had a strange look. Her blushing smile told all. Many years later she would share with him how her body had trembled that day, and how for the first time in this body-life, she had ached to be filled by a man—by her Conall of Cymru.

He remembered that the mist from the falls had been so thick, it had been hard to breathe. The water was so cold, they turned blue and began to shake, but she insisted they keep moving. They found the entrance to a very large cave hidden in the cliff behind the falls. When Briga's curiosity was satisfied, they climbed down to the pool, and on the moss and maidenhair ferns at the edge of the water, she stood in front of him, shaking with cold.

"I'm so cold, Conall," she said. Without even thinking, he took her into his arms. She melted into him, and they stood together while the warmth of a late spring sun reached down from high in the sky and began massaging their naked skin. The light breath of a gentle breeze softly helped them dry. He held her tightly way too long, but he loved how she smelled and the way her body had melted into his. He couldn't decide what it was that sent his mind spiraling and swirling to another world: the warm aroma of a forest floor mixed with her loveliness, or her own special essence, her phenomenal signature that wrapped around him to hold him like silk ropes. Whatever it was that day, he'd discovered the only woman he had ever and would ever love.

At sixteen, Conall had already been introduced to the pleasures of the goddess. When a young boy reached the age of thirteen, he was counted among men with special rites and ceremonies, but it was at the fire festival of Beltane when women would share with him their sacred ceremonies. At his first Beltane after reaching the age of accountability, the older and experienced women of the clan, usually widows introduced him to the goddess and taught him the secrets of pleasuring a woman. He'd already become skilled in finding the many pathways on a woman's body that would take her to the stars. It was a man's duty to make love to a woman, guiding her with intimate touch until she stood in paradise, in the very center of the circle of creation—at the source of new life with the good god and goddess.

As he held her in his arms, his soul flew into the open door of her emerald eyes and he knew what she was thinking; like him she had been overcome with the energy that flowed between their bodies. He decided at that moment he would end his pleasuring at the fire festivals. After that day he swore an oath to Danu that he would love no other woman until he could love Briga. He swore that after loving her, he would love no other with his heart and soul. She was and had always been his Mo Anam Cara, his twin flame, the other half of his soul.

From that day on, the azure pool, the enchanting waterfall, the talking rocks, and the hidden cave became their secret places. They formed a private hideaway where he and Briga spent many wonderful, long summer and fall days together that year, growing closer in their love and desire. Conall the wolf-warrior had grown into a man, but he never touched her. He waited for the gifting at Beltane; because of his love for Briga, he had made a promise in his youth to never again touch another woman. Conall realized the great value of the gift he wanted to receive from Briga—he wanted to be her first lover, and he offered his abstinence to the goddess as a sign of his intent to honor Briga.

It was in the winter of his sixteenth year that Conall was initiated into the Order of the Cunobarrus, the "wolf head." On the first full moon following the winter solstice, called the wolf, the men and warriors of Cymru always held a great gathering. It was during this wolf-moon ceremony that young Celtic warriors were initiated into the Cunobarrus, the next step in becoming a convel, the wolf-warriors of Cymru. He would now train with a group of young warriors; these young men wore wolf skins for six years, running in packs of eight. They survived in the forest during this initiation phase by hunting the enemies of their clan. The young men who survived the long, arduous journey were accepted as full wolf-warriors during the full wolf moon six years later. Due to the elite nature of this warrior class, the legend of the wolf-warriors inspired fear and respect into the souls of others. The wolf-warrior was feared and elevated above all other warriors in Cymru.

Standing by the ceremonial fire and covered by the skin of a great male wolf, Conall had recited in the presence of his elders and wolf brothers, "I will draw my wolf skin over my back, placing the beast's gaping jaws around my head. I fasten the forelegs to my wrists, his legs to mine, and I will mimic the four-footed wolf gait that is so hard for foes to spot. I will learn the way of the wolf with my brothers. I will hunt the enemies of my people."

It was at the wolf moon that Conall had left Briga, ending their days at Còmhradh Carragh, the talking falls. He journeyed east with the warriors of Cymru to wage war on the raiders of the North, the Luti from Jutland. These mercenaries were employed by the Romans to explore the coastlines of Alban and Cymru for weaknesses and for locations to land the invading armies of Rome It had been decades since the invasion of Julius Caesar and his success in defeating Cassivellaunus in the battle at the Thames crossing.

Follow the battle at the Thames crossing, Caesar had been forced to return to Gaul to defeat and crush the armies of Vercingetorix, and even after the emperor was long dead, the Roman Senate looked with greed toward Britain. They wanted the rich tin and gold mines and natural resources of the island, and always hungry for slaves, they also wanted the men and women of the lands they called Britannia, Caledonia, and Hibernia. Conall battled in the east, fighting against the raiders from Jutland for six full years before he returned. He grew to manhood during his absence from Briga, and he received many more scars and took many more heads in battle. His fierceness in battle earned him the name Conall Cearnach (Conall the Victorious).

It was his very name, Conall Cearnach, which became a powerful war cry, bringing fear into the hearts of his enemies as well as strong sword arms and brave hearts to those that fought with him. For those who allied themselves with the sword and shield of Conall Cearnach, victory was guaranteed; his was the strength of a warrior who had never tasted defeat or known fear in battle, and within his heart was the deep conviction that the goddess Danu watched over and protected him.

Conall grew into the mightiest of the wolf-warriors, a *Conry*, which means 'King of the Wolves'—before he left on that day of the wolf moon to become a hero among his people, he'd made a promise to Briga, an oath sworn by blood, that the pool of the talking rocks would be their secret place. If the time ever came that they needed to hide, or if they ever became separated, they would come here to find each other again.

Chapter Three

So it was that now, with his soul in trouble, he kept returning to the azure pool and the enchanting mist-covered waterfall. As he journeyed back to the present, he was very much aware of the blinding pain, the cold, and the suffering of his battle-worn body. With much mental distress and agony, he was trying to find his way back to her. He had been trained from an early age to endure bodily pain and all kinds of suffering in his flesh; nevertheless his soul moved out of his body, past time and space, toward the one he loved. He continued to return to the azure pool and the talking falls where he'd been first consumed by her devotion. He'd become her willing slave even before the moment his soul flew into the open door of her emerald eyes.

He stumbled in the predawn darkness, more falling than walking down the mountainside. Time after time his mind returned to the peace and safety where Briga anointed the talking pillar of water with their love. "*Mo Briga, far an d'ung thu an Còmhradh Carragh le ar gràdhaich.*" The memory of her brought healing to his torn body and peace to his troubled mind.

He saw her standing up to her waist in the water as she bathed. Her back was to him. She was washing her hair in the clear, living water. He watched in wonder at how beautifully the muscles of her back moved as she reached up to take her long, flowing black hair into her hands. She bent at the waist to rinse her hair. Every graceful movement unchained his emotions, and every movement of the feminine muscles of her arms and back emphasized her womanliness.

He loved her very much, he thought as he silently watched. She stood back up and began squeezing the water from her hair. Her right hand held her bunched hair close to her scalp as her left hand pulled the water down the long, jet-black strands. Her hair cascaded down her neck and across her shoulders, flowing gracefully down her back like the delicate falling strands of water that fell from the heights of the talking falls. He was so grateful that she had chosen him over all the other men in the village. They all wanted her, but she had willingly given herself to him. Her moon blood had come on her thirteenth year, but she'd waited for five years to give him her gift at the fire festival. When he had returned from his six-year training as a wolf-warrior, Conall had attended Beltane. It was his first festival back home since he had left to become a fully initiated convel, and now he looked for Briga, hoping she would pick him to dance with and to be her stag.

She had seen him walk into the light of the Beltane fire, and she had immediately jumped up and moved toward him and said, "Conall, I choose you to walk with me." Looking into her eyes, he had smiled and said, "I would be honored, My Lady Briga." As he walked into the forest with Briga, he thanked Danu for having accepted his offering of celibacy.

She had waited for him, and she gifted Conall that night with the honor of teaching her the ways of pleasure. Only he would be her fountain of living flame. Only her wolf-warrior would show her the path to the stars and teach her how to be one with the good god and goddess. He was her first, and he would be her only Mo Anam Cara.

Far from the snow and rain, far from the punishing cold and pain, he watched as she turned and saw him standing at the edge of the pool. She smiled at him. When she spoke, the sound of her voice and the words were carried away by the force of the falling water and the hollow speech of the rocks, but he knew the movement of her lips.

She said to him, "*Is tu m' annsachd...*"

With much warmth and deep affection, her words danced into his mind, now tingling with life: "Thou art my best beloved."

Now, thinking to himself, he remembered that he had said out loud, "Her voice seems so timeless—a simple maturity, as if it were there a thousand years ago, and it is here now, and it will still be here for a thousand years to come." Briga was the voice of the earth, and the earth was the voice that came from Briga. He heard her voice and saw her beauty everywhere throughout the land of Cymru. She was the valleys between the mountain peaks, the curve of the rivers that gently meandered in the lowlands, and the mountain peak hidden by the fog. She was as wild as a she-wolf appearing out of nowhere. She thoroughly captivated him.

She came out of the water and walked toward him. The shining droplets of water that covered her naked, porcelain skin caught the sun's reflective light and exploded like diamonds.

She was the moon, that golden orb of rarified beauty, he thought—so very perfect.

She was the luster of his soul, the prism of purity that showered rainbow colors over his life. He felt her love inside his heart, and the spirit that dwelled there welled up with warmth in response to her presence in him. Distance could not separate the memory of her and the love they shared. He loved her, and his heart was hers and her heart his, forever. Conall knew that even death would not separate them as lovers.

She moved her head at the neck in a seductive wide circle; her long hair danced a flowing circle and rested across her shoulders.

She stopped to stand in front of him, as if for his inspection. Her hair, having come to rest on her shoulders, now covered her arms down to her elbows. Amazement was stamped upon his face.

Her full, firm breasts were uncovered, and they flashed with the water that still dripped from her nipples. They rose with each long, deep breath she took as she looked at him. His own breath caught in his throat with a gasp as he looked at her. She was so beautiful, and he was filled with passion and desire at the sight of her standing before him. He realized with red-faced embarrassment that his desire for her was clearly visible beneath his rough-hewn garment.

Her voice was filled with the sparkle of laughter. Looking at him with the same flaming desire, she said, "Are you my captive bird, with a trembling heart, my dearest?" She smiled again, and her full lips parted slightly. As she moved toward him, the look in her emerald eyes changed.

Her hungry eyes took on the look of a wild she-wolf as she stepped in close. Her right hand reached up to rest on his bare chest, touching his *treskelle* wheel tattoo as her left hand found the opening in the side of his garment. Sliding her hand into his warmth, she found what she wanted. She held him as she stretched upward on her tiptoes and placed a warm, moist kiss on his lips. Pulling away slightly from his embrace she smiled and said, "I can feel by what I am holding in my hand, evidence that you are happy to see me my beloved."

Immediately the pleasure of the memory of her touch faded, when along his path, he was struck across the face by a frozen branch.

His hand went to the burning pain on the side of his face that now replaced the pleasurable thoughts of his Briga. He swore as the word *cachi* escaped his lips. He stopped to lean against a huge oak tree. The warm thoughts of Briga had been enough to ease the numbing cold of the dark, black world he walked in, and now the cold once again left his hands and feet as he began to think of the touch of his Briga. Resting against the male strength of the massive derw ynn, Conall felt his energy begin to grow as he went back to remembering pleasure and warmth. In his mind he traced the curves and lines of her body as his large, callused hands journeyed over her shoulders to her back. The very memory of her filled his world with happiness.

Conall began moving downhill again, this time a little slower, a little more cautiously; his mind continued to replay memories of his times of pleasure with Briga. As he walked, he remembered lifting her up off her feet, bending his knees slightly as he rested her on his lap. He leaned his back against the warm, hard rock of the cròmleac that had been set deep in the earth at the edge of the water. As his body supported hers the two became one flesh; the warmth of her sacred valley surrounded his phallus and overpowered his senses, his mind journeyed to the center of creation, where the pleasure goddess lives. His hungry mouth found hers. Their kisses became intense and ravenous, and for a moment, as he moved in the dark and cold, he was no longer in a land of ice and snow.

As beautiful and warm as her memory was, the shock of a hidden and very sharp tree branch piercing into his leg brought him back to the world. "Damn all the foreign gods," he growled, his deep voice loud and angry.

That same voice echoed back to him in the darkness, resounding off the cold stone of the mountain cliffs that now lay behind him. It seemed to him that the very rocks of the earth mocked him, that they had joined together in laughter at the thought that he, a mere human, would attempt to overcome the dark and cold just to return to the one he loved.

The deep charcoal black of night had given way to the gray of early dawn. He had been feeling his way down the mountainside all night, but now, with the coming light of day, he was able to see, and he quickened his pace. "Not much farther!" he shouted back to the rocks. The valley lay below him, and he knew that if he continued down, he would soon be out of the snow. Already he'd moved far enough down the mountain that he no longer struggled through knee-high snow and even deeper drifts. The snow was less than a foot now, and easier to walk through.

"I will not be killed by winter, you sons of godless filth!" he yelled at those he'd left on the other side of the mountain. The anger in his voice shattered the silence, and living things that heard him stirred uneasily in their nests.

Even the spirits in the rocks and trees shuddered at his determination. Only a man intent on returning home is invincible to trickery and magic. As Conall moved forward in the darkness, he remembered the words of the druid Caswallon: "Love is stronger than all the ancient blackness of the time without light." The old man's words strengthened him as he thought, "My love will carry me home."

Into the cold Conall spoke loudly through clenched teeth. "When I die, is this what it is like to cross the western sea to the place of the Blessed Isle? Does my mind just think of the pleasant and good until my body fails, and I am taken by the hand of the goddess Fand to Tír-na-nog, the land of the young? Or is this what it's like walking through the fire of Cernunnos—moments of pleasure overpowered by hours of pain and suffering?"

He knew that the steepness of the slope was the only reason he was able to continue in the darkness with no chance of becoming confused or moving in the wrong direction—down was home. He was going home.

Nothing that lived, flesh or spirit, was going to keep him from returning to Briga and the child he knew was growing inside her. No! There was no power, human or spirit, that would keep him from her welcoming arms. He would kill anything that made an attempt to stop him. He wore the evidence of that conviction in his side—the large, gaping wound in his left side, inflicted by the three dead men who had tried to stop him from reaching her.

Amid the darkness he stumbled, his toe hooked under a surfacing root, and he fell, landing hard on his injured side. He groaned loudly in pain, and the echoing cliffs mocked him in his anguish. Her name was ripped from his soul as he called out, "Briga!" The cliffs mocked him again by calling her name back to him, but at a lower pitch. The thought of her was all that kept him alive.

The vision of her in his mind kept him moving down the mountain. In the darkness her image had become the light that guided him—his white radiance, his star of love. His rationale told him each pain-filled step brought him closer to her and their unborn child.

They were the only two things in creation that kept him from sitting down against a tree in the cold snow to rest and sleep—a sleep he knew he would never awake from. He would arise with resurgent strength because he had been blessed by the magic of his name, Conall, which meant "mighty" and "strong wolf." Conall didn't fear death. He didn't believe in death. In Conall's mind and heart lived the sayings taught to him by the druids in their sacred words: "Death marks the beginning of new life."

He just wasn't ready to leave his body yet, to move into his next life. No, he wasn't ready to leave Briga, and he was not leaving this bodily life until he'd held in his own hands the child they had given life to at the center of life's formation. No, not yet...not this day.

"I must get up," he said aloud to the cold and surrounding darkness.

"I must get up," the cliffs mocked.

He growled like the animal that was part of his soul, and he tried to rise up from the earth that wanted to claim him. The earth wasn't concerned that the soul dwelling in him wasn't ready to leave his body lying on the ground—a body that would return to the earth as his soul returned to the stars. The earth pulled at him, and the darkness held him fast as the cold attempted to crush the last of the spirit breath from his lungs.

He'd die here if he didn't stand up and continue moving down the hill. His side was burning as new warmth flowed down from the region of his last rib. In the darkness he touched his wound; his fingertips came away sticky with fresh blood. He was bleeding again, and fresh agony tortured him to the bone with hopelessness.

His strength faded fast as he tried again to rise up from the deathbed that waited to swallow his body back into the earth. "Danu, please give me strength," he whispered. "Mother of all created things, please hear my pleas. I'm not ready to make the journey to your side while holding the hand of the goddess Fand. Please, Mother Danu, let me return home to Briga."

Chapter Four

He lay in the snow as its cold hands attempted to pull the little remaining warmth from his body, but he saw hope on the horizon at the edge of the sky; he could see the morning star. The horizon was growing a pale gray line against the black. In his soul he felt Danu's presence, and her words softly filled his spirit with the promise, "Soon, my son. Soon the sun will join you in your journey. Take the Sky Father's hand and continue your journey back to Briga. The Sky Father will give you warmth and strength, and he will chase his brother, the darkness, from the sky. You are a son of the light of Cymru—the priceless gift of freedom."

Lifting himself off the ground and certain death, Conall rose to his knees—softly, like a warm shawl, he felt her spirit surround him. It tingled and danced on his face and hands. It reached into his heart, giving him strength and filling him with peace. "Thank you, Danu."

Still on his knees, he faced the distant, bright light of the morning star. In his mother tongue, it was called madainn rionnag. He bowed his head. In the ordeal of pain that had become his journey, he paused to pray. He moved his left arm to his injured side as his right hand found the dirk under his cloak. Holding the hilt of the dirk, he raised his left arm, bent at the elbow, across his chest, and with a clenched fist he struck his chest slightly off-center and to the right side, three times.

Once again he softly, gently uttered the words from deep within his heart and soul: "Thank you, Danu."

Conall bowed to no man, nor would he ever bow to any of the false male gods of the raiders or the Romans. He followed his internal code, written on his heart, and he followed the living word of life that issued from the goddess, burning brightly in his soul; he deeply loved and worshiped the feminine—*bainionnach* or *caithe beatha* in his mother tongue.

To him, they weren't just words when the druids of his clan told him, "A man is never as strong as when he willingly kneels before a woman in respect and honor." This was his truth, and the worship of the goddess was all that mattered to Conall; in doing these two things, respecting every woman of the clan and honoring them in all things, he protected Briga and all the women in Cymru.

As a warrior of the old way, he served the Cymru, the earth that had received the bodies and the red blood of his ancestors— the old ones called her *Y Ddraig Goch*, the Red Dragon. His worship, honor, and protection were oath-sworn and would be given to the great Earth Mother; the goddess Danu; his birth mother, Epona; his wife, Briga; and all the women of the clan.

He would honor each equally as long as his heart beat and he drew breath from the earth. His life was dedicated to providing for and protecting the women of Clan Dia and those who served the *mamaidh* Cymru.

From birth he was oath-sworn to carry the sword and provide the shield, to live and die for Cymru. Born into the line of the *Bona Na Croin*, the "unconquered wolf," he was a wolf-warrior— *madadh-allaidh mìlidh*, according to his mother tongue—and he would live and die with honor.

Conall remembered clearly being taught by Caswallon and the words he said: "Remember, Conall, a brave and honorable death is the only pathway to opening the oak door that leads to our rebirth."

He was one of the few left who still carried within them the seeds of the "once-ones," those who had come to these islands when the land of the ancients sank beneath the rising seas. His mother was from the island of Erin, and her hair was the beautiful blush-red of the ancient ones. Her name was Epona, and her ancestors had served the *Ard Righ* of Tara from the time they had arrived with the Hebrews of Israel and the scholars of the Avdei Hashem. They had traveled to Erin with Jeremiah and the Princess Teá after the destruction of the temple in Jerusalem, and they had helped found the dynasty of the High Kings of Tara.

Like all his clan, he traced his lineage through his mother's people, and so he received his birthright from Epona, in the form of a birthmark on his forehead and in the red that showed in his beard and long hair.

Among the people, the red birthmark was recognized as the mark of the Cymru, the Red Dragon. His mother and grandmother carried the same mark, and both had been inducted into the mystery of the druids, who would later become *Ceile De'*, servants of the one god who became many, the good god Daghda. Conall's mother and her mother before her had come to Cymru from Tara as chaste maidens, serving on the Hill of Afallach until the Ard Druid of Ynys Mon and the *penarddun* Ard Righ of Cymru married them to lesser kings for allies.

Epona and the other women who served Daghda and Danu also served the Cymru, the living lands of Danu and Esus, her son who walked on the earth. All the women serving Cymru carried the birthing seeds of the ancient mothers of his people—the ones who had come to this island from the distant lands far to the west or from the lands to the east and Jerusalem.

Some of these ancient women and men from the west had landed on the shores of this island many generations ago, when their land had sunk below the waves to the bottom of the ocean. Only a few had survived, but they brought with them all the teachings of the star gods. They came to *Y Daearen* from *Y Saith Seren Siriol*, the "seven cheerful stars of the sisters" of the great star god *Caomai*, the armed king. These ancient ones brought with them all the knowledge of truth and wisdom known to the star gods.

Chapter Five

In very ancient times, the people had made a choice to protect the ancient ones, and they in turn taught the people the secrets of all things created, and they shared with the people the knowledge of wisdom and the meaning of the code of truth and the word that issued from the goddess.

The land was made whole in that time, and the ancestors became the "seekers of truth"; together, the people and the ancient ones became the "keepers of the truth." The great oak door was opened to the people, revealing the secrets that dwelled deep in the earth and high in the heavens, at the very place in which the stars and souls became one: *Anam Rionnag*, according to Conall's ancient language.

It was the mother goddess herself, Danu, who had planted the first acorn seed that grew among the people of Cymru and became a mighty oak tree, or *duir*, reaching upward to connect earth, sky, and stars. Her roots were pulled downward, where living waters formed—at the very source of life. These roots of the duir tree were tucked deeply into the womb of the earth to receive nourishment, which traveled to every part of the tree of life and in turn nourished all who came in contact with her. When the tree was complete in its growing, the darkness was replaced with moving, ineffable light and love. It was from this tree that acorns tumbled to the ground, and from this tree that Cymru and Esus would spring forth from the earth.

This is why Conall's life was devoted from birth to service and faith. He was to be a guardian and defender for the people; it was his *annsachd*—his greatest calling. His sword cut deeply into the hearts and bellies of the men who would harm any woman or child. The enemies who faced him on the battlefield rarely lived to tell about the day they fought him. The few who did survive with their wounds avoided tempting death again, and they fled in terror at the sight of Conall.

It was one thing to go into battle, thinking that in combat, one may die and return one's soul to the stars; it was another thing to walk into certain death as if committing suicide. Those who saw Conall in battle and survived knew he was certain death in a man's body when he held a sword. Those men would certainly avoid him on the battlefield if ever they met again.

What gave him his great skill and strength was his belief in Danu and the old ways. His faith in the "mother of all life," the *màthair-beatha*, was as great as the strength of the arm that held his sword, and as deep as his love for Briga.

It was that profound sense of service, love, and faith that had brought him to his knees on a cold, dark morning on a snow-covered mountainside, so many miles away from his home and all those he loved.

As he knelt and prayed to Danu, his mind walked with his people, but now the world of the present began to surround him once again as he faced the east and the soon-rising sun.

He was renewed and ready to defeat his enemies again, just as he'd always done with the help of Danu. With a great shout that shook the earth, he yelled out in defiance, "No, I will not die yet—not today, not here in this place, not now!"

He paused and roared again, "No, not today!"

The earth shook from the force of the mighty outburst that erupted from deep inside Conall's body. Frightened by this man, death released her hold on him. The crushing weight of the cold fled from inside him—fled from the anger in his voice.

Even the darkness withdrew as the sun, promised by Danu, quickly brought the white radiance of light back to the forest. It forced the darkness to return to its place on the other side of the world.

He rose from his knees, and like the wolf-warrior he was, he howled. His voice carried a challenge across the face of the earth, from the lowlands to the mountaintops. Conall would live!

$$\dashv$$

Chapter Six

ar off in the distance to his left, in the direction of the *Druuos*, the firm North Star, Conall heard his call answered by the howls and calls of a pack of wild wolves. He steadied himself on his feet and smiled.

In a voice raw and raspy from the cold and thirst, he said, "This was a good sign."

The distant call of his wolf brothers had to be a good omen. North was the direction of the unmoving star that stands firm in the night sky. North was the home of his ancestors. It was the direction of the Hall of Souls, the place souls returned to when they no longer desired a bodily life.

"Yes, it was a very good sign," he thought. His ancestors had heard him and let him know they were with him.

Conall stepped forward in the stillness, onto the white ground. Thick snow crunched under each step as he again began his journey home. The sky brightened quickly, expanding his view as the sun moved steadily higher above the horizon and into the world of humanity.

The old saying was very true; he muttered to those who could hear his voice, "It is always coldest before the dawn."

The temperature dropped rapidly as he continued downhill. It was bitter cold, and he did what he could to preserve his warmth. He covered his face and mouth, and he began breathing his own warmed breath through the coarse weave of his wool cloak. Yet even with his entire head covered, the cold still entered, and he suffered as he walked and waited for the sun.

With each step the sky became a blaze of a flickering flame, and the first colors appeared in the clouds. Streams of light began appearing in shafts of rays through the breaks in the clouds low on the eastern horizon; they exploded, streaming into the sky, announcing that the Oak King was coming—the light that defeats the darkness of winter. The intense rays refracted to dark grays, turning white as the sky lightened. Then the sky itself turned the soft blue of a robin's egg, while the clouds appeared to turn to a light and then brilliant pink, dancing through the spectrum of color—a beautiful prism of purity.

He stood in awe at the contrast of the vibrant pink against the full depth of the blue, but the color only lasted a short time. This daily announcement of the Oak King was always breathtaking to him.

Conall always viewed the sunrise with the excitement of a child. Each morning he marveled at the wonderful living image of changing colors that the Creators made; he rarely missed a sunrise.

He smiled to himself, thinking of Briga. As if he were describing her to the rising sun, Conall said, "My Briga loves the comfort of her fur blankets and the warmth of her bed." He watched in awe as the sun moved darkness to the other side of the earth.

As he watched, he also remembered his mother. She'd taught him that each day was made new; yesterday was gone, and tomorrow wasn't yet made. "Each day is made new for us by the Cruthadair, the Creators, and it is made good," she'd said to him. "The Cruthadair give us new days because they don't hold against the children the mistakes they made yesterday. So go, fill this new day with good works and love. Go be useful, my little warrior. Go and help the people. The good god Daghda never hands his family judgment, but only freedom. The goddess Danu only pours out her abundance. In the darkness of her womb, she is impregnated and gives birth to all living things. She is the ever-fulgent font of creation. Through her love she nurtures all her offspring. And through her wisdom she sustains all living things, hovering over them in watchful care, like a mother bird. By her sacrifice the wonders of creation are made new. She replenishes the face of the ground forever, flowing into the world she loves. She is mother of the living.

"Together, the Creators provide opportunities to develop our individual personhood, parentage, and purpose by following their example in the development of goodness for all peoples of the land of the Red Dragon. Their love gives the gift of balance and order to the universe—like the unbroken circles of ripples in the water, raindrops falling to the earth, the earth circling the sun and the moon, and even what the old bard called the great standing stones of the circle of life. It is at these great circular dolmens during the summer solstice that the sun flashes light at the center of the circle—a reminder that all is one. We leave the earth and come back to rebirth. This is the *cylch mawr*, the great round circle that reflects the rhythm of the cycles of the earth: fertilization, gestation, birth, death, and rebirth into a new bodily life. The *cylch mawr* always comes back to its point of beginning."

Judgments handed down by gods of everlasting torment and death didn't exist in Conall's beliefs, nor in those of the people of the ancient ways of Cymru.

He had always wondered why the new religions of the Roman armies, who now attempted to conquer the lands near the Ladies of Afallach, were so filled with fear of death and the judgments of their gods.

Only the constantly renewing circle of life, given to creation through the love of Daghda, the masculine life force, and Danu, the feminine life force, gave the people of Cymru purpose and their daily reason for living. Loving and accepting all created things was how the people had lived long before the coming of the Roman armies and the Luti raiders they employed.

The warriors in Conall's clan learned from nature. For example, they spent long hours observing and watching wolves. Conall had noticed that wolves alter their voices when they howl, so two wolves can sound like a pack of twenty. This keeps other neighboring packs away from their hunting territory. He'd also noticed that they howl both before they hunt, to rally the pack; if they get separated; and when a mate dies. Wolves usually mate for life, and the nurturing of pups is the responsibility of the pack. They move in quietly and cautiously for the kill, and they can run long distances without tiring. Conall's band of men had spent many years training in this type of ambush warfare, learning from nature's deadliest and slyest creatures.

These same warriors also spent long hours learning from *neidr*, the snake, or from *morgrugyn*, the forest ant; all the creatures of Danu's world shared life with us to teach us wisdom and understanding.

As Conall walked, he remembered the stories his mother had told him of the time of his father's father, when the people of Cymru had fought alongside Cassivellaunus against the armies of Rome.

Fighting the Romans had been costly, with the loss of many lives on both sides. Many men and women of Cymru hadn't returned home to their families; the wolf torc that Conall wore around his neck had been handed down to him when his father died, just as it had been handed down to his father when his grandfather died fighting the Romans who had come with Julius Caesar.

Following the first Roman war, there had been many orphans and widows among the people of Cymru. It is in the heart of the goddess Danu and the law of the druids that no child of Cymru, no woman or man, be left alone, without a family. Orphaned children were adopted into new families and cared for by the clan, and the widows or widowers of fallen warriors entered into marriages as sister-wives or brother-husbands one year after the death of their spouse. No one in Cymru was ever left alone; everyone was to be cared for and loved.

It seemed that death and destruction had once again come to visit the people of the land of Cymru. Rumors of invaders had traveled north, and for this reason Conall had left to make the journey south, toward the sea and the bay at three rivers.

A rumor had come to the people of the highlands that a great army had landed by sea on the southern coast, at the mouth of Afon Tywi, and that it was beginning to move north along the river valley. Word had come to the druids that it was the intent of this horde of foreign raiders to march inland and destroy everything in their path, taking as many slaves as they could keep alive and plundering metals from their mines.

Conall had gone south with a dozen warriors, including himself. He was the most experienced wolf-warrior in the clan and had been assigned their leader—their Conry. He led eleven good men toward the southern sea and three rivers. They had fought the raiders and freed some of their slaves; Conall knew that some of his convel had been killed in the raid on the Luti camp.

He had stayed with the women and children whom he had freed until he was sure they were safe. When he left them, he had changed direction often in an attempt to conceal the direction of his village. Now he changed directions and moved steadily northeast, back toward his village. He had begun to have a feeling of dread—a feeling that if he made it back, he would be the only one of his convel to return.

Driven as he was by his desire to see Briga, he was also compelled to return by his duty to the ard druid Caswallon, carrying with him the news of the strength and numbers of the raiders. This information had to be received by the *Cyngor*, the Council of Elders, and the Ard Righ Caradoc ap Bran. He fought cold and death to keep his promise to Briga and to the Cyngor; he would not let them down.

It was up to him to survive and return to Briga and their unborn child, and to all the people of Cymru. They had to be warned of the terrible storm of death and destruction that was sweeping toward them.

He had to survive...

He was not ready to die—not yet.

He pushed himself harder and moved as fast as his injuries would allow. He moved with a determination and purpose that could not, or would not, find rest until he was among his people.

As he struggled on, his body moving automatically on its own, his mind wandered to thoughts of the past few days of outrage he had witnessed. His anger was rekindled, driving much of the cold from his body as thoughts of revenge filled him.

He knew he would not rest until his revenge was satisfied and the invaders had been driven from his lands. They had violated the lands of Danu and her people.

He wanted to deliver death and destruction to the raiders and those who led them; he would return, and this time death would come with him, and many of the raiders would never return across the sea to their homelands again.

Chapter Seven

hey were coming. Luti raiders from Jutland had found the southern shore of Cymru and the great bay at three rivers.

As Conall moved toward Briga and home, he began to think about his first encounter with the Luti; it now seemed like it had happened a very long time ago. The cold and darkness and the pain from his wound had distorted time and distance, but he had a vivid memory of lying on a ridgeline, bathed in warm sunlight as he looked down in the river valley below.

It was impossible to count them all, but they numbered in the many hundreds; there were so many of them that they easily swarmed out over the land and destroyed everything within their filthy reach. Their polished metal shields, helmets, and swords caught the sun and stung Conall's eyes. Everywhere he looked below, he saw flags flying in the light breeze and what looked like a forest of spears. He stood up, outraged, his heart racing, as a mixture of anger enclosed in a shield of hate covered him; disgust for his enemy coursed through his veins.

"This is not going to continue," Conall roared out to his men. "This outrage on the body of Cymru and her people stops now. By the gods, we won't let this happen." Conall's heart beat steady and strong, deeply in his chest, its spiritual energy burst out past his horsehair-twilled tunic, beating like the drum of war, its strength joining with those that stood with him. In the next heartbeat, he said to his convel warriors, "We must do everything to stop these men." Such was the heart of Conall Cearnach of Clan Diahad.

Conall and his wolf-warriors watched from the ridge above the river valley that was formed by Afon Tywi. A mass of men had swept inland, killing, taking captives, and burning everything in their path. The lives and property of the people in the path of this horde were swept away. All the living souls, the children of Danu, lay dead or dying, or were captured by the invaders to become slaves in some far-off lands.

The raiders' lust was only partially satisfied once the people were dead. After all the living souls had been destroyed, they began stripping the dead of their knives, swords, and any valuable gold or silver jewelry, copper pots, and household goods made of metal. It was known that the lands of Cymru contained deposits of copper, tin, and silver and rich deposits of gold that came from the mines found in the mountains of Eryri in northern Cymru. Gold from these mines was beautiful and very rare in its purity, and it was prized throughout the lands of Gaul, even to Rome. The raiders had come to Cymru for gold and slaves. Nothing moved after they passed through. The soul of the great Conall of Cymru had been thoroughly insulted. There was only one place for his anger to go: his animal nature. With all his great strength, he howled an animal like pitch of bereavement and loss, and then he let out a howl of human vengeance. All around him his convel joined him, howling like a pack of wolves, voicing the cry they used to alert the wolf pack to come to a kill. The wild wolves of Cymru answered, and soon the valley below echoed with the sounds of hundreds of howling wolves.

Conall and his men caught up to the invaders and studied them at close range. The raiders had stopped their advance, occupying a small farming village in the valley of Afon Tywi; they'd taken over the dwellings and set up camp. Soon, great fires and feasting were taking place below them as Conall and his men watched from the ridgetop. Sounds of anger and strange words floated up to the men lying in the deep grass at the top of the hill, while the men below ate, drank, and fought one another like crazed animals.

"They look like maggots devouring a dead corpse," Do'nal said as they observed the raiders. Looking down upon the men, it didn't take the wolf-warriors long to notice a dozen men who dressed differently, standing apart from the other raiders. They wore helmets, armor, and red wool tunics, and they were heavily armed with both swords, short thrusting spears, and round shields. One of the men in this group stood out even at this distance, as he was dressed in a white tunic made of white linen, with a golden woven trim running vertically along its length; the gold caught and reflected the sun's light, creating a reflection that was easily spotted by Do'nal.

As they all began looking at these men, Do'nal hissed a single word from between clenched teeth: "Romans!"

"Are you sure?" asked Conall.

Do'nal turned to face Conall and said without hesitation, "Yes, I am very sure. When I went to Gaul to the city of Beauvais, the city of my mother's family and the Bellovaci tribe, we fought many Romans dressed like these men. The man in the white tunic is important, a leader, and if the Romans are here with the raiders, it is bad, very bad for Cymru. Rome is always hungry for precious metals and slaves, and this means they are once again turning their attention toward Cymru."

All the men fell silent and watched the scene below.

As the men below became inebriated with the mead they had looted, the fighting between them became intense. Their loud voices carried upward on the gentle breeze that blew from the valley to the ridgetop. Angry voices spoke in words the convel could not understand. One of the raiders drew a long dagger and lunged toward the man standing in front of him, and with a quick thrust, he sank the dagger blade deep into his chest. The loud arguing fell into silence as the body fell to the ground.

"Look, Conall," Do'nal said, "the maggots are beginning to devour themselves. That's too bad. There will be fewer of them for us to slaughter if they keep this up. Maybe we should hurry down the hill before there are none left to sacrifice to the goddess."

The other men with Conall snarled and sneered in disgust, and a few laughed softly as they watched the animals below fight among themselves. What they'd seen was already enough to make them want to bathe in the blood of these destroyers of peace; the convel were filled with a rage that could only be abated by attacking and tasting the raiders' blood on the metal of their swords.

Conall's journey south had been made as winter moved toward Imbolc, the festival of the emergence, and he was under instruction from the Ard Druid Caswallon. Reports had made their way inland, brought by those fleeing the coast of Cymru— rumors of ships landing and large numbers of foreign raiders moving inland, attacking and killing everyone they encountered. These reports were brought to the attention of the Ard Righ and the Ard Druid Caswallon of Cymru. The Cyngor had been asked to send a reconnaissance group of wolf-warriors toward the coast under the leadership of Conall. Their mission, as declared by the Ard Righ and the Ard Druid, was to observe and report back what they discovered. What was happening below was forcing Conall to modify their plans.

The leaders of the raiding party appeared before their captives. The calls and screams of women, young girls, and boys who had been captured, tortured, and used could be heard unmistakably by Conall's men watching on the ridgetop.

One by one, the leaders of this human filth could be seen dragging women and children out into the open. Now that the leaders had finished using these poor souls for their own perverse pleasures, they began handing them over to the rest of the men to quiet them. Shouts went out from the leaders, and the mass of men below turned their attention from fighting among themselves to abusing the poor innocents, whose flesh was to be tormented for the brutal pleasure and cruel lust of the raiders.

The men of Cymru watched as the men below began to fight over the bodies of the women and children. The screams of terror and fear, as well as the anguished cries of children, were hurled up like spears to the men on the ridge. The cries of the innocent washed over them like an angry ocean wave, and it covered them with the suffering of those below.

The mixed cries of anger and fear drowned out all other sounds that came to the ears of the men above the encampment. The sound of women and children in a state of terror was too much for a wolf-warrior to silently endure.

Conall could stand no more.

He stood up in full view of the Luti, and from deep inside his life force, he voiced a howl that caused the men below to stop their acts of violence. All his convel stood up with Conall and joined him in the wolf howls that announced a hunt. The voices of twelve good men roared and howled their rage over and over again. Their howls echoed back from the surrounding hillsides and were joined by hundreds of wolves. It deceived the men below into thinking there were hundreds of wolf-warriors on the hillsides around them. The camp below became silent; even the women and children made no sounds. The men below could see a group of wolf-warriors standing on the ridgetop just above their camp. The raiders had no way of knowing how many wolf-warriors were in the area. They now feared that men moved in the forest and on the ridges above them, intent on delivering to them the deaths they all deserved, in revenge for these savage abominations they'd committed.

Even the godless know when they've outraged the good god and goddess.

Panic could be seen below as screams and shouting returned; but this time it was not the cries of women and children that filled the camp, but the panic of men who feared for their lives. The men began running about in confusion while their leaders shouted orders. The prisoners were returned to a place of confinement, and the mass of men below spent the rest of that day and the night on watch as they waited for the attack that never came.

As dark covered the camp, the men from Cymru began making a new plan, and as it began taking shape, it rapidly moved away from the directions given by the Ard Righ and the Cyngor.

The plan was now a wolf-warrior's plan, and it would involve removing from Cymru all of the invaders that had brought death and destruction. The blood of raiders was now the only thing that would return honor to the land and the people of Cymru— and it would be the wolf-warriors that would make sure that the raiders blood soaked deeply into the earth, restoring honor to Cymru. From birth Conall was oath-sworn to carry the sword and provide the shield, to live and die for Cymru. This oath was his greatest calling, his *annsachd*; born into the line of the *Bona Na Croin*, the "unconquered wolf," he was a wolf-warrior, a Conry, and if needed, he would die with honor as a Convel.

Honor would demand that Conall's men attempt to rescue the women and children below, and slaying as many of the invaders as possible would be the sport of wolves.

"Our mission has changed, and tomorrow we hunt," Conall said into the darkness that surrounded him and his men.

Some of the men around him growled like angry animals—low, rumbling growls—as others spoke loud words of approval and support. The spirit of the words and the growls of these good men filled the darkness and floated upward, to be caught in the wind and carried to the raider's camp. Like stinging hail, the curses of the convel poured down on those sleeping in the camp, and that night many of Luti warriors dreamed of their deaths.

As wolf-warriors, Conall's group had long ago pledged to provide their blades and lives to protect all women and children. None of the men with him would question his decision or doubt his resolve; they just listened intently as he told them how they would save the ones below held prisoner, as well as how they would make great sport out of hunting those who held them captive.

Chapter Eight

Now, as he walked north toward Briga and his clan, Conall relived the last seven days and nights that his wolf-warriors had terrorized the raiders' camp. The anger he felt at thinking of those seven days filled him with resolve and strength.

A warrior is trained, very early and very young, to walk outside his body's pain and anguish. Certain thoughts can move him away from pain. Anger toward his enemy will remove the pain from his body and fill his flesh with magic, giving him renewed strength of both will and body. The ability to shapeshift was one of Conall's weapons, and the wolf was his metamorphosis animal. The druids of Conall's clan had taught him this skill. From them he'd learned that all physical matter is from a primal, mysterious energy source, and that energy can be transformed and transferred from one form into another. He'd learned that there are two worlds that mirror each other. When they come together, through energy alignment and special chants sung in the form of a *Fonn*, these energies dancing together form the energized soul of a powerfully spoken word, there is a transformation that takes place: the body of flesh disappears and is replaced by the new form of an illusionary spirit, usually animal—and in Conall's case, always fierce and deadly.

In the fading light of twilight, the physical form becomes a shadow, and in the mind of the enemy, what was human will now appear far different.

As Conall continued walking towards the valley below, towards home and everything in this life that he loved, his mind found comfort in thinking of the crushing revenge he had showered down on those who had hurt the innocent.

Yes, he and his wolf-warriors had delivered a great deal of justice on the other side of the mountain, and they had shown no mercy.

As Conall sat down in a hollowed-out duir tree seeking shelter from the rain, his mind began to recall the actions of the last few days. He soon found himself dream-walking in a deep, self-imposed lucid trance; his physical body sat with his back against the duir tree, but his mind remembered and relived the past.

The men of Cymru had set about bringing confusion and death to their enemies as soon as the first light of dawn made it safe enough to begin hunting the adversary. Like a wolf pack, Conall and his men knew that the first dim light of early morning or the evening twilight was the best time to hunt.

Shadows play tricks on the mind. The light was just right for Conall to make use of sunlit rays to shapeshift into an illusionary yet realistic animal form.

Distance is never certain in the twilight between dark and light, as form and shape seem distorted. The human eye's depth perception does not function well in dim predawn light. This advantage is enough that the animal hunter will have an edge over the hunted, and the prey, confused, often panics. If the prey runs in the dim light, he often trips and falls, making the death-blow easy for the hunter.

A wolf-warrior is trained to fight in a pack of four. Both men and women are trained to fight in groups, and forming a pack, they will forage, fight, and defend one another as one strong unit. Wolf packs of warriors were made up of both men and women, but Conall's group of convel wolf-warriors was only made up of men. If the danger was too great and the warriors faced great odds and likely death with the possibility that they might not return from the situation—a wolf pack was sent out with only men. Like wolves, they never fight alone.

They fight to survive and only when it is required to protect one another.

Conall remembered well the words of his druid, spoken many years ago as he trained to become a wolf-warrior. It was a lesson that had saved his life many times. The druid who taught their class had told them to memorize this adage: "The strength of the pack is the wolf, and the strength of the wolf is the pack."

He'd gone on. "Always fight together, never alone! The power of the convel pack is in learning the wolf's hunting technique and the effectiveness of the wolf pack. You must fight to outwit your opponent, and this requires thinking as a synchronized unit of strength. You must never attack an enemy that is larger than your pack. The sum of all parts contains more wisdom than each one alone, but never endanger the one, and never waste the life of even a single convel."

Conall knew they must now separate into smaller units and harass the enemy at every opportunity. He divided his men into three groups of four, knowing that even fighting as three separate groups, they would fight as one. Conall's warriors had grown up together. They knew one another's combat strengths and weaknesses, but more than anything, they knew the territory of Cymru like their own bodies.

"Three," he remembered thinking, "a very good number."

On the hilltop above the river, in the dark, a plan of action was beginning to take shape. As his men spoke about the coming exploit against the invaders, Conall wondered to himself how many of his friends would die in battle. "Who among my men," he thought, "will be taken by the hand of the goddess Fand to be gently held and led to his death, from this bodily existence into the Hall of Souls, to there become a divine echo, the purest resonance of the soul's vibration?"

These twelve friends, warrior-brothers, formed a circle, and they raised their swords toward one another as the last waning beam of a fading full moon danced lightly on their blades. Conall shouted, "For the children of Danu and the people of Cymru!"

He was joined by the eleven wolf-warriors who would follow him anywhere—even back to the stars, back to the portals of rebirth if necessary. In one voice, they all shouted, "*Cymru am byth!*"

Chapter Nine

It was now time. The raiders became the hunted. At every opening and chance encounter, the wolf-warriors attacked and slaughtered the enemy. Conall's men lay hidden in the bush, silently waiting hours along trails leading away from the encampment, just to strike out in ambush and terrify the enemy.

Screaming wildly in piercing death wails and howling like wolves, they appeared before the enemy with bodies painted with the blood of the slain and the blue of woad; with stiffened, white-limed hair, they glowed like evil spirits.

Like hornets exploding from a nest that had been kicked, they burst into the middle of the adversary, hacking and killing their way back into the woods, only to silently disappear deep into the shadows, taking with them the heads and other fleshly trophies claimed from the bodies of their slain enemies.

The raiders soon believed that ghosts and spirits stalked them and that death waited for them each time they left the safety of the camp.

The leaders began losing control of their men and were forced to follow them into what was quickly becoming an evil and dangerous land.

It was one thing for strong men with weak souls to wage war on farmers and families full of women and children; it was another to face the men of Cymru and the warriors of the wolf from the *madadh-allaidh* clan.

The inland advance of the raiders was stopped.

Twelve wolf-warriors had blocked their progress in just three days. Again and again, Conall's men stalked and ambushed the enemy. They killed them in great numbers, only to then fade like apparitions into the tree-covered hillsides and the unknown darkness of woodlands, which the raiders feared and the wolf-warriors called friend and home.

They never stayed in one place long. They rarely slept. They were constantly moving, hunting, killing, taking food, stealing weapons, and removing anything else they needed from their enemies' bodies before fading into nothing, just like the ghost spirits they'd become to the raiders. The terrified raiders began to think of them as evil spirits or ghosts that lived in the forest.

When they could, they took the heads of their enemies and other trophies.

On the fourth night of death and fear, one of the wolf packs slipped quietly into the raiders' camp, cutting the throats of all the sentries they could find. These four moved soundlessly into the camp, and there they stood together defiantly in a circle at the very center of the enemy's stronghold, near the leaders' thatched roundhouse.

Here in the center of their enemies' perceived safety, they poured out onto the ground four large, heavy bags of heads, an assortment of hands, and other body parts. The dying firelight of the raiders' camp cast the men of Cymru in deep shadows, and for all those who saw them that night, they looked like great shadowy giants dancing around the fading firelight at the edge of darkness.

With their arms stretched up to the stars, and with one voice, they yelled out with all their strength the war cry of the convel and ran off into the darkness.

As they disappeared, they yelled, "Cymru forever!" Running into the darkness, their voices sounded as loud as thunder as they continued calling out, "*Cymru am byth!*"

On both sides of the camp, spread out around the perimeter, the other wolf-warriors joined in with their shouts of "*Cymru, Cymru am byth!*"

The hillsides and even the mountains joined in with echoing that rolled across the camp, until the twelve voices sounded like the calls of hundreds of wolf-warriors.

Once again, the encampment was thrown into chaos and panic. The wolf-warriors taunted their enemies with shouts and laughter as they ran from the center of the camp past men paralyzed with fear of death and the unknown.

The convel killed men as they left the camp, and the wolf-warriors on the outer edge of the camp made sure that no one running into the darkness lived.

For the *madadh-allaidh*, the wolf clan of Cymru, it was great sport. They enjoyed spreading fear and death among the raiders.

For the raiders who survived, it was a frightening story that they told around campfires for years to come. Over thirty men died on that night when the giant wolves of Cymru struck their camp from the dark woods of the evil land of the people of Daghda and Danu.

Death had come to stalk those who dared to enter Cymru with evil intent.

Chapter Ten

The raid of the giant wolves of Cymru deeply struck fear into the hearts of the Luti, and again the raiders spent a sleepless night watching and waiting for death to visit and claim them. The chieftains of the raiders also waited for their demise at the hands of their own panic-stricken men. Talk of mutiny was whispered throughout the camp and action by the frightened men could not be far away; they wanted to return home to Jutland.

The raiders had grown weak from the terror of the death that surrounded them; they could smell it everywhere, in the stench of the corpses that lay rotting all around them, in the flies that constently filled the air when not landing on them—they could even taste death in the air when they opened their mouths.

Conall now waited for the moon. It was waning, and it would soon be at its darkest. Men do not fight well when they are forced from their homes and taken to lands foreign to them; inexplicably, every shadow becomes an enemy, and every unknown sound fills their squeamish hearts with anxiety and their souls with apprehension.

If fright is great enough, and the danger surpasses what is possible for men to endure, at that juncture warriors often turn on their leaders and revolt, wanting only to return home. These men did not want to die in some unknown land filled with evil demons.

Conall knew this, and he used it to his advantage. Darkness and sound became his allies. Fear became the spear he used to pierce the enemies' hearts, and terror the sword he wielded to cut the spirits from those who had dared to come into his people's lands.

He knew the will to fight and a man's effectiveness were diminished when terror poured over him like heavy rain; then he became nothing but an empty stalk of grain, void of any potency. Men will often take their own lives rather than face the uncertainty of a dark death filled with demons that have grown in their minds. These demons explode out from the darkness, shrieking in terror; they are so horrible that they rip flesh and inhale the breath, blood, and life from the enemy, laughing as they melt back into the darkness.

When the men of Cymru weren't hunting the raiders, they rested, lying on the hillsides among the tall ferns or in the thickets, watching, covering themselves with leaves and moss. They blended in so well that even the deer couldn't see them. Waiting, they watched to learn all they could about their prey, as the wolf had taught them—silent, unseen, and ready for when the time came to kill.

They'd observed the layout of the enemy's encampment below, and they'd identified all the locations where the captives were held in the complex of roundhouses, farm buildings, and pens. They watched carefully as food and water were taken to each location.

They also identified each of the makeshift dwellings housing the leaders of the marauders. They noted where sentries were posted, and they memorized the pattern of sentry changes. Campfires, buildings, and ground features were committed to memory, and the safest routes into and out of the encampment had been determined.

As they lay on the hillside, the men closed their eyes and took turns mentally moving in and out of the camp. They made a game out of challenging one another to have the most detailed recall of the camp's layout. Now they were ready for the blackest night.

Even hampered and limited by darkness, these wolf-warriors would be able to see into the most sinister of spaces. They would swoop down like wolf demons as the camp finally fell asleep in exhaustion, and in near total darkness they'd assassinate as many of the leaders as they could find, meanwhile freeing the poor captive souls.

So far Conall had lost none of his comrades, which is how he wished it to remain. He'd told his men, "Kill as many as you can, especially the leaders, and free all those who can still run, but put a blade of mercy to the captives who cannot run, putting an end to their torment. Do not sacrifice yourselves. Cymru will need you, for this fight has only just begun, and we must return to protect our homes."

Conall's men ate, talked, and prepared themselves together for the victory or the death that awaited them. They conversed among themselves as they planned their attack; the words of each man and his opinions were as important as the next man's. The attack on the enemy below would be an effort of individual war-riors working together under the authority of their own hearts. No warrior was commanded or forced to face death, and so it was with these convel; the wolf-warrior always had a choice in placing his life before a wall of certain death.

Conall had decided on what action needed to be taken, but it was now up to the individual wolf-warriors to decide on their own to join in the battle against the invaders, and it would be up to all the men with Conall to commence the plan of attack.

Soon they all came into agreement, having received the same vision of the preparation within their hearts and minds.

Now they only waited for a sign from Danu...

Chapter Eleven

Danu delivered her sign with the next morning's light. Those observing had brought Conall very good news. By the sixth morning, fear had done its work. His men reported that dozens of corpses had been removed and thrown into a gully near the camp.

The corpses were the bodies of faint-hearted men who could no longer endure their nightmares; they'd ended their wretched lives by their own hand. Conall's men reported to him that fights were breaking out all over the camp.

It didn't take long for the report to come to Conall that he most wanted to hear: a large group of angry men had gathered at the center of the camp, and they appeared to be turning on one of their leaders.

Conall moved into cover above the camp, and as he watched, a heated and boisterous argument broke out between one of the leaders and one of his men; without warning, the man pulled his sword and cut down the leader, like barley at harvest time, leaving him to lie dead and alone on the blood-soaked earth. The crowd of men who had gathered melted away into the shadows and the buildings of the village. This fallen man would soon be the feasting place for the ravens, as they would first enjoy his eyes and then rapidly reduce his face to gristle-like particles of bone.

Conall smiled as he watched the men below. He thought of the druid Caswallon's lessons and words: "The war is only over when Bran the Raven feasts on the eyes of your enemy." Conall intended on giving his friend "Bran" a great feast. These men were the vilest, like incurable sores on the innocent tongues of children; they needed to be cut out of Cymru.

Turning to the men around him, he said, "Yes, our time is nearly here. Tomorrow night the moon will not appear until early morning, and then we'll have only a very thin sliver of a moon. We attack tomorrow with the approach of midnight, when the moon approaches Caomai, the constellation of the armed king."

With their plans made, they spent one more day hunting the raiders. Good fortune was with them as they found small parties of terror-filled men deserting and moving outside the camp, back toward the coast.

Soon they had slaughtered over a half-dozen men. The long, narrow blades of the convel pierced deeply into the enemies' chests, and they could hear the blood at every jolt as it came gurgling from the froth-corrupted lungs. The warriors cut off their enemies' hands and heads and soon had several fine bags of gifts for that night and the next morning.

That night, at the time when most of the raiders ate their evening meal, the wolf-warriors used slings to cast the severed hands into the middle of the camp.

Men shrieked. They stood trembling, and some lost control and wet themselves. The look of terror on their faces told all. A few, struck by a severed hand, were overtaken by madness and lost all control—they ran shrieking into the darkness outside the camp, only to find their own deaths on the wolf-warriors' blades.

Conall planned one more act of violence. Very late that night, his men crept down to the encampment. Having identified the areas that the raiders had made into latrines, and knowing their morning routines, they placed the heads in the filth of those trenches.

That morning, as the enemy rose from sleep and moved slowly toward the dugout latrines, screams of terror vibrated off the hillsides as men found the rotting heads of their comrades staring back at them from the filth-filled ditches of human waste and camp refuse.

For days the camp commanders hadn't been able to send out patrols. Now, men just lay on the ground. A few cut their own throats and watched with glazed-over eyes as their once-potent life force trickled red onto the earth. They'd lost the will to fight. They'd lost the will to live. The leaders of the invaders sheepishly sauntered back into their dwellings, not stirring outside again that day for fear of mutiny. They felt defeated.

Confident, Conall and his band of brothers found a resting place on the hillside, near a grove of oaks and a small spring of living water that bubbled up from underground into a small pool, forming a stream that tumbled clear, cold water into the farmland below. The living water was another sign from Danu that victory was imminent; the sacred goddess was birthed from the spring of living water.

Two men kept watch as two men slept. They did not fear discovery by the enemy, knowing that their adversary, paralyzed by fear, would not leave the camp. Men at the helm, men at the post, men always at their stations—this was the way of the wolf-warrior. No matter how safe one seemed, two men always watched as two men slept.

All that day, they rested.

It was now the beginning of the seventh night, and the men of Cymru had planned a special evening for their enemy. Just before sundown, the men gathered together and prayed to Daghda and Danu. Some said prayers of thanks as they asked for the strength they would need that night.

As the men prayed, they whispered songs in the form of *fuinn*, rejoicing and thanking the goddess Danu for life and rebirth.

Each man held their *paidreans* draped across both wrists, their fingers counted down the one hundred fifty beads of amber and jet that formed the beaded loop. They recited the virtues of the warrior and the old law. Then they ate and drank by the small pool of living water and took turns keeping watch as each man cleansed himself completely. They washed from their bodies the stench and the days of filth, blood, and splattered brain matter.

Tonight, when they entered the enemy's camp, they didn't want to smell foul or have dirty and matted hair. Once clean, many of the men spiked their hair high and upright with pine pitch, adding lime so that the tall spikes of hair shone white in both moon and sunlight. They also added new painted symbols on their bodies and faces with woad—blue symbols of great magic, protection, and power. The blue dye was extracted from the yellow flowering plants of the woad. The druids had held tightly to the secret of how to collect the plants' blue dye magic. Briga had told Conall that once she had gone with Caswallon to collect the woad to make the magic blue dye. All around them the plants grew tall and full of yellow flowers, and Briga had shouted, "Here, Grandfather! Here they are growing so tall!" Caswallon had smiled and taught Briga the secret: "The woad plant takes two years to grow, and only grows tall and flowers in its second year. This two-year-old plant is worthless, as it will not produce much dye. We must find the first-year plants that form a low-growing cluster of long narrow leaves; these leaves, my darling granddaughter, will be rich in dye and in woad magic. Also remember, Briga, that these first-year leaves contain a powerful antiseptic that can be used to prevent infection in battle wounds."

When the warriors finished preparing their bodies for war, they rested, and as it is among men about to go into combat, they began telling stories about one another. Each warrior attempted to tell the most outrageous tale he could about his comrades.

Each of the single men boasted about how many of the beautiful young maids held captive below would want to return home with him and reward him with kisses for his bravery and valor.

They laughed and joked, and as men do before they go to certain death, they all became quiet. The stillness cut through the thick darkness like a jagged blade, unevenly splitting their emotions in two. This moment became deeply personal. Suspended at a level above mortal men and outside the world of physical form, their thoughts were completely naked, and some men felt shame.

The wolf warriors remembered the stories of their ancestors; generations of past wars and death spread over their minds and rage filled their hearts as they felt the agony of their ancestors—they knew the hearts of the Creators as the sacrifice they would be required to make was revealed into their souls.

Within the circle of unity, they were collectively feeling untold generations of anger at the lives that had been robbed from their ancestors by past invaders. The convel were filled with dìoghaltas, blood vengeance, at the men who had robbed the sons and daughters of Cymru of their lives and the glories of spiritual wisdom and happiness.

Conall felt hot tears of anger and sorrow stream down his face as he thought of his own father and grandfather. All of the Convel recognized this as an extraordinary sacred moment—a sacred flash from the lives of their ancestors and the men of Cymru remembered the prophecy that their land was to be the dominion of wisdom—and they remembered that some of their ancestors had failed to carry on that charge. The Convel must not let this happen again.

This vision accelerated into the minds of the other men, and simultaneously they all began to cry, dropping to their knees one by one to do obeisance toward the east. Suddenly Conall had a vision of himself in the future, in a *corricle* on the raging sea.

The small boat was tossed about fiercely as huge waves seemed to cover it up completely. As the *corricle* disappeared under waves, the vision gradually dissolved. He did not have time to think about the mighty waves that crashed over the sides of the small animal-hide *corricle* he was in, nor did he think again of the full moon that brightly shone on the crest of the waves.

Their thoughts and souls moved into a deep meditation as pieces of themselves traveled out of their bodies. They returned home to their loved ones who waited for them—to their mothers, wives, and children. Conall looked down at his feet, and as he did, he saw the *Ogham* rune symbol for oak, the duir, written in the dirt.

At his feet was drawn the symbol ⊣ and as he looked up, the druid Caswallon stood there in front of him. The old man frowned, and worry lines deepened on his face as he said, "Remember, Conall, a brave and honorable death is the only pathway to opening the oak door that leads to our rebirth."

That night every man sent home the better part of his soul— his divine echo, patterned after Danu. He would entrust his soul to be held by his loved one until he returned; tonight he'd only need the animal combined with the human when he entered the raider's encampment. The druids taught all the convel that there were three parts to the nature of man—the animal, the man, and the god—and that these three parts were demonstrated by the *triskele*. At the center of the triskele is the point of the moment of our action, a point that is connected directly to the Cruthadair, and around that center rotates three sweeping arms. One is the animal, one the human, and one the divine god, and every time a man makes a choice and takes action in this world, he must choose one of the three arms. Will he choose to be godlike, man-like, or animal-like? Tonight the convel chose only to be animals.

As the darkness came and the light was swept away to the other side of the earth, the men began saying their good-byes to one another. They all embraced, some with the knowledge that this would be their last night in this bodily life.

Each asked the other if he had an offense that had injured or hurt his comrades. Each asked forgiveness for any offense, and they all prepared themselves to enter the Hall of Souls as friends and comrades-in-arms.

If they should die this night, they wanted to make sure that they would not take anything into the great hall of the ancestors but valor, honor, loyalty, and experiences they'd had with one another.

As the final parting came, a few kissed. They embraced one another as soul friends, and a couple embraced each other as lovers. Then, with a sadness that comes over men as they move into a battle promising death on both sides, they said their final farewells. They shouted into the gathering darkness that was growing before them, "Kill or die!"

Men who are warriors have the ability to combine the human intellect with the craftiness of the predator. They were trained to shapeshift, and each warrior now entered another dimension; through the portal of his thoughts and the control of his animal energy, each one morphed into beast-men. These men chose to move around the three-part treskele and find the arm that was pure animal; each awoke the wild wolf-spirit that was within him.

They had crossed over, and now only the wolf-man remained—only an instinctive killing beast that felt no mercy. And that beast felt virtually no pain. These lethal predators now moved into the forest toward the camp, intent on bathing in blood and leaving the raiders in a sea of carnage.

As they moved slowly and silently into the darkness, they had no thought of tomorrow or the sunrise; they thought only of revenge and setting free the hostages, and only death would stop them.

Chapter Twelve

nce their attack began, the night's silence turned to screams, shrieks of terror, and the sounds of dying men. Fires broke out everywhere in the camp as the wolf-warriors torched anything that would burn. The houses of the farming village and the wooden storage barns soon blazed like torches, providing light for the convel's attack. The entire encampment soon became filled with scorching heat and thick smoke. The loud cracking and popping of burning buildings, joined by the screams of frightened men, were now heard every-where, and as the thick smoke filled the lungs of the Luti, panic soon followed.

Most of the enemy reacted as Conall's men had hoped: in-stead of taking up positions and fighting, they ran from the wolf-warriors when they saw them approach.

As the men of Cymru moved through the camp, they soon became drenched in blood—their faces, arms, and garments covered in the blood of cowards. Sweeping through the panic and chaos, the wolf-warriors killed any Luti raider they encoun-tered, and soon dozens of the enemy had fallen, cut down by the sharp blades of the warriors of Cymru. They even managed to locate and slay a few of their leaders. The camp was now totally ablaze, and the air began to fill with swirling clouds of thick, black smoke that carried with it the strong, acrid stench of burn-ing flesh. The combination of fire, smoke, and the repulsive smell of burning hair and flesh was enough to make the strongest of men run in fear as an instinctive reaction. It was natural to want to save their own lives, especially when they had no real vested interest in the camp.

But not all the raiders ran crazed by fear; by the time the wolf-warriors began to free the first of the hostages; they'd lost two of their own. Some of the captives recognized them as wolf-warriors and willingly joined them, including some of the women, who picked up knives and swords and joined the wolf-warriors in fighting the raiders. Others could no longer fight or run; their will and the spirit of freedom had departed, only to have been replaced with paralyzing fear—these poor souls were freed with a slashing cut to their throats so that they would be taken by the hand of the goddess Fand home to their ancestors.

It was one thing for Conall's men to fight an enemy as the *madadh-allaidh*, as wolves; it was a far different thing to try to herd sheep as wolves. Most of the hostages had become just that—sheep, too terrified to fight and barely able to run, herded by a pack of wolves.

It took some doing, but finally the wolf-warriors managed to herd three groups of people into a body willing to move as one; nevertheless, they moved slowly. The delay had cost them another life of one of their own. It had also given the enemy time to reorganize under the authority of their remaining leaders.

Even those filled with terror could count, and it didn't take the leaders and their bodyguards long to figure out just how few of the wolf-warriors had entered the camp.

Conall saw the group that Do'nal was attempting to lead out of the camp. With only one of his warriors left, Conall could only watch as over thirty raiders surrounded Do'nal and his one remaining wolf-warrior. Terribly outnumbered, the two comrades soon fell to the blows of ax, sword, and arrows. Once the two

convel were dead, the raiders killed every woman and child attempting to escape. Conall vowed an oath of revenge for Do'nal
and for those who had fallen with him.

Conall managed to get his group moving but soon found himself blocked by three raiders; one of them seemed to have authority, as he was yelling out what sounded like orders. The other two
seemed to be his bodyguards, and they were standing between the
large red-haired man and Conall, the three were now blocking
his route of escape. There was no hesitation as Conall's big frame
burst into a full running attack; his charge was so swift that the first
man was still falling to the ground as Conall's sword cleaved the
head from the body of the second warrior. The large red-haired
man turned and tried to run, but was sent crashing face-first onto
the earth by a tremendous blow to his back from Conall's sword.
Looking down with contempt at the man lying at his feet in the
dirt, Conall said, "If I didn't kill you, coward, you will always carry
a scar of disgrace hewn into your back by the sword of the Conry
Conall of Cymru."

Looking around him, Conall saw confused, frightened men
running in panicked disarray amid the smoke and flames. As he
turned to gather his group of women and children, he saw that
not everyone was in a state of fear. Standing off to his right was
the group of Romans, intently watching him.

They stood with swords and shields at the ready, in an assem-
blage that formed a wall around the man dressed in white. As
Conall watched, the man stepped past his guards to face Conall.
The distance between them was only a few yards—in a quick
charge, Conall could have easily been upon him. He was young,
his hair wavy and black, and his features sharp and handsomely
cut. As Conall looked at him, he smiled, like a man who knew a
deep secret. He turned to his men and spoke, and as he did, the
men sheathed their swords.

Turning back to face Conall, he raised his right arm high, his hand open and his fingers spread far apart, and shouted, "*Salutis!*"

Dropping his arm, he turned toward his men, gave a command, and was once again surrounded by his guard. As they all walked away, the Romans had once again drawn their swords to be at the ready.

Conall watched them withdraw only for a moment, and then he returned to gathering the women and children who had followed him. For now he could only turn and push those with him out of the raiders' camp. In minutes that seemed to progress like slow hours, they made it out of the encampment and into the forest beyond.

He yelled to Da'ire, "Take half and head south and scatter; get back and warn the Ard Righ!" He wasn't sure, but he thought the third group had scurried away. They had all disappeared into the darkness together.

It was one thing to memorize the enemy's enclosures and enter as an attacking wolf-warrior by the covering of night; it was totally another to run blindly into the woods, over rough terrain in the dark, with women and children.

It didn't take long for the Luti to reorganize, and as soon as morning's first light appeared, large parties of raiders dashed after them like packs of hounds to find and take them down. The raiders' profound, paralyzing confusion had turned to the deepest depths of hate and revenge.

All that night and the next day, Conall stayed with his group, moving them through the woodlands as far from the Luti as possible. He learned from a young maiden that the raiders came from a place they called Jutland, which was far to the north, and their leader was a large red-haired warrior named Healtholaf. Conall knew the Luti and had fought them once before, when he had gone east at the age of sixteen. He remembered all too well the six years he had spent away from his people and Briga, having gone east to fight raiders as a Cunobarrus, along with the seven other members of his wolf pack. The raiders had been attacking along the eastern coastline of Britain, sometimes called *Baratanac,* which meant land of tin. The last time the Luti invaded, they had just explored only the coastline for the Romans.

This time it was a deeper penetration into the mainland. One of the women Conall had freed was from Gaul and learned the words spoken by the Romans. She had warned Conall that the Romans wanted to find a weak place along the coastline with a safe harbor—a place to land their legions and build a fortress. Rome was planning an invasion of Britain and Cymru, and they wanted to establish footholds to support their legions.

Now Conall knew that the Luti had come inland from the sea and had chosen this village as the place to begin deeper raids into the interior of Cymru; it would be from here that they would send out raiding parties to test the strength and resolve of the people of Cymru. The raiders soon went out in strength, bringing back livestock, grain, metals, and slaves. Conall learned from the women he had saved that the Luti shamans, the *seidre,* had prophesied by augury that Cymru was ripe for the taking; they believed the people of Cymru were weak and could easily be enslaved.

Conall herded the people southeast, then doubled back toward the northwest, and finally north. The women and children Conall had rescued were farmers, familiar with the forest and the countryside. As they moved to safety, they foraged for the wild plants that grew along their way. The children, half-starved, overturned fallen logs to find fat grubs that they quickly ate; the women looked for the dried seeds and fruit left over from last summer that were still good to eat. When dusk fell, they all settled in to rest, and Conall them he would have to leave them in the morning.

"I have to get back to my people and warn the Ard Righ that the Romans are here with the Luti." He told them to follow the ridges up into the mountains. "The *Ordovices* of Cymru will give you protection. You will find them in the hills and mountains to the north."

The women wept and pleaded with him to stay as the younger children clung to his arms and legs. Tears formed in the great Conall's eyes as he explained why he must leave and move as rapidly as possible back to his people.

In the end the women and children were persuaded. They understood and thanked Conall for saving them. Softly sobbing, they all held one another as they fell asleep among the ferns and trees.

The next morning, as the sun rose, Conall woke the women and children and told them to hurry, move off into the woods, and wait. He would make a trail that the raiders would surely follow, leading the Luti away.

"Travel only at dawn and dusk. Move without making any sound, and move in small groups—close but not too close— and do not talk. Use hand signals only until you are safe in the mountains with the people of the Ordovices. Rest only during the darkest part of night and hide quietly during the brightest part of the day. Conserve your energy, and drink the dew of the early morning if you cannot find water. Eat as you walk and share what you find. When you stop and rest, cover yourself with leaves, moss, and brush, anything you can find. Hide and blend in," he cautioned, and those were the last words he spoke to them as Conall moved off into the woods.

That was the last he saw of them. He grieved at the thought of leaving them, but he had to get back and warn his people.

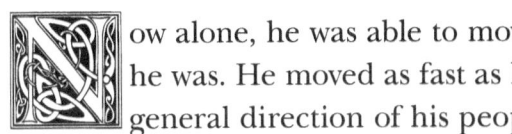

Chapter Thirteen

ow alone, he was able to move as the swift wolf-warrior he was. He moved as fast as he could. He moved in the general direction of his people, but never traveled in a straight line; he was always circling back and crossing over his trail in an attempt to confuse the enemy that he knew would be tracking him.

The terrain was rugged, untamed, and for those not skilled in moving in the wilderness, it was filled with hazards, such as unstable rocks along the steep cliffs, dangerous rivers, and narrow trails along the ledges that with the wrong step, might lead to a fall to injury or death. Conall was moving with ease at a pace that few would ever match.

The forest and the mountains were his home, and he had spent his entire life learning the secrets of these remote places. He knew what to eat to stay alive and what plants to apply to his injuries, but more importantly, he knew how to hunt like a predator. He found comfort and a sense of protection whenever he entered a thick stand of tall sheltering trees; among the trees and the rocks covered in thick moss, he moved in silence and confidence as he climbed higher up the mountain, deeper into the cool moist places that called home. The stillness of Cymru's ancient forests brought to his spirit a feeling of friendship and peace, as he felt both the living world and the spiritual world covering him like a mother's blanket.

Yes, he was with the goddess, and she was all around him.

But there was also urgency, a sense that something was wrong. Conall began moving eastward with all his skill and speed, and soon he recognized that he was in the country. He was back in the territory of the Celtic tribe of the Ordovices and he had to get home; he wasn't going to lead the filth that followed him back to his clan. He had chosen to first travel east, up into the mountains, before turning northward and finally west, back to his beloved Briga.

Now he moved north toward Caer Caradoc and the hilltop fortress of Caer y Twr, one of the strongholds of the Ard Righ. He was hoping he would lead this party right into the hands of Caradoc's warriors.

It hadn't taken the raiders long to send out hunting parties of warriors with their berserker slaves—angry men intent on murdering all those who had escaped. Once Conall had decided to expose his trail, it didn't take them long to find it. Conall had succeeded in leading the hunting party away from the women and children he had rescued from the Luti. The raiders now followed him, while the women and children moved safely away from danger. Soon they would find protection among the mountain people of Cymru.

The Luti who had found his trail were filled with seething anger and hate; vengeance filled their hearts with darkness, and their blood ran hot with a desire to savagely kill anyone they happened upon. Death had become their god, and the screams of victims were the only songs they wanted to hear.

From far behind him, he now began to hear the sound of the approaching enemy. Ahead of the main body of Luti warriors ran the three berserkers, like trained dogs. They would track, find, and destroy anyone who had escaped, and they had gotten close enough to him that he could hear them. He could not smell them yet, but he knew they would stumble upon him if he continued moving as he had been.

Conall was caught between two conflicts: on the one hand, he needed to hurry and warn his clan, and on the other hand, he needed to make sure he diverted the Luti from picking up on the trail of the freed captives. His solution was to rapidly move north and lead the raiders into the hands of Cymru warriors. He was no longer interested in stealth or disguising his trail. If he had wanted, he could have stayed invisible to his enemy, and they would have never found him; but now he was only interested in speed. He knew the lives of everyone he loved depended on his rapid return.

The men from the raiders' camp did not relent. They were filled with hate forged by days of confusion and death, and they wanted blood vengeance—now.

The berserkers found his trail and followed him for the next five days, stopping only when it was to dark to see...

As they followed Conall, he played games with the Luti, often circling behind them, and as one or two would leave the camp for water or to relieve themselves, he struck suddenly from the darkness, making sure he was silent, terrifying, and brutal. Like the wolf, he would only attempt a kill that he could make easily and swiftly; unlike the wolf, which devoured or concealed the remains of its kill, Conall made sure he left a ghastly headless corpse for the raiders to see.

Circling back ahead of the enemy, he would move down the trail for several miles, and in the middle of the trail, he would place the head on a tall, sharpened pole. The head faced those approaching on the trail, so that anyone following him was greeted by the open eyes and open, gasping mouth of the dead raider. Those that followed the Conry Conall soon realized that the same fate would be theirs if they continued to hunt this convel of Cymru.

Conall enjoyed the sport he was making of sending them back to the places of their foreign gods. He found great pleasure in tormenting these destroyers of peace who did not belong in his land.

One night as the invaders rested around the fire, Conall stood in the darkness on the edge of their encampment. Holding the severed head of one of their comrades by the hair, Conall heaved it skyward in a wide, sweeping arch. In the darkness the head sailed until it fell earthward into the firelight, hitting the ground. It bounced several times and rolled to the edge of the fire pit, coming to rest faceup, staring back at the raiders.

Conall watched, amused, from the shadows, as resting men jumped to their feet, pushing and falling over one another in an attempt to distance themselves from the bouncing, rolling head of their fallen comrade. He even had the good fortune to kill one of them as the terror-stricken man ran into the darkness, smack into his waiting blade.

Pregnant, the moon was growing again, adding to its fullness every night. Like his brothers and sisters, the wolves, he enjoyed hunting by the full moon, Conall had the light he needed to move, spot his game and hunt. It was the wolf that had taught him the secrets of the hunt. The idea was to first lead the prey in the desired direction, and then circle around and trail the victim in complete secrecy.

On the next night, as the Luti lay sleeping, Conall walked into the center of their camp, howling like a wolf and shrieking like a banshee, and then killed two of the raiders as they tried to rise from their slumber. He stood defiantly on the edge of their camp, and with a high-pitched squeal like a wild boar, he went running into the darkness to the safety of the woods.

Conall would move ahead of the sleeping camp, leaving a trail for the Luti to follow during the daylight, only to fool them on the following day, when he would circle back while it was still dark and attack the camp early in the morning, before dawn.

Having terrified those who were lucky enough to survive, Conall would find a safe place to rest for a few hours. Once he dozed a bit, he would once again become the wolf, hunter of the sheep. He tracked the invaders and attacked any stragglers whenever he had the opportunity.

For several days now, they'd been climbing higher into thicker woods and deeper snow. It had become an increasingly difficult struggle just to move, and the cold was almost unbearable, even for Conall. He had stopped hunting the enemy and had now begun moving as rapidly as possible north, in the general direction of his people.

As he approached the mountaintop, he estimated he'd cut their number in half. The fear and death were too much for most of them; that morning, as the day had started crisp and cold and cloud-covered, and as icy sleet pellets rained down on them, all but three had decided to turn back. Now he only had to worry about these few who followed as he crossed the mountain ridge into his own lands.

Chapter Fourteen

The way Conall had it figured, the three men following him wanted revenge, as their actions spoke of men intent on blood vengeance—*dìoghaltas* in Conall's native tongue. In truth they'd lost kinsmen to the blades of the wolf-warriors, and they wanted to avenge their loss of honor. Now, with so few of the Luti behind him, he gave up his idea of leading them to the warriors of the Ard Righ. Time was running out; he had to end this pursuit immediately.

He found a suitable place for an ambush and made himself comfortable, waiting patiently as they approached. Conall was growing tired of the chase, and he wanted it to end, so he readied his mind and body for one more attack as he watched them approach. He had selected this place of ambush to give him the greatest possible advantage. The raiders had to climb a steep slope to get to the place where Conall waited, and once they reached his hiding place, they would have to move one at a time past him and down the trail.

The trail was narrow; not far from it, the terrain rapidly turned into a cliff that fell hundreds of feet onto jagged rocks and certain death. The steep slope was on the leeward side of the hillcrest, and blowing snow had dropped a deep drift that had to be crossed to make it to the top of the hill. On the other side, the ground was almost free of snow, as it had rained heavily just recently on this western slope. The ground sloped gently downward into an open area that was a patchwork of snow and mud, and it was just right for the attack that was now the focus of Conall's attention.

The raiders, hampered by the steep climb and the deep drifts of snow, had been forced to spread themselves farther apart; the strongest moved ahead of the rest, but all had labored and were tired. The weakest and most exhausted of the three men walked last in the single-file row of men who were now spread well apart on the trail.

Conall watched and waited. By the time they reached him, they were exhausted from moving up the steep climb and forcing a trail through the deep snowdrifts. They had spread out to a distance of several dozen yards between each man. Now each of the men was helplessly on his own. They would not be able to come to the aid of the other.

Like the wolf, he struck the straggler first.

As the last man walked by, Conall launched himself outward from under the cover of the overhanging snow-covered branches of a tree. He hit him hard from behind, plunging his blade into the man's right side, driving the knife tip and the cutting edge upward. The eighteen-inch dirk blade easily pierced past the man's spine and lung and into his heart.

An eerie gurgling sound came out of him as he fell. The man's crimson blood spurted from his mouth and defiled the snow as his lifeless body fell onto the patch of white-covered ground.

The other two men turned, but it was already too late for the second. Conall had the advantage. He was strong and disciplined in warfare; therefore, he was able to close the distance rapidly, crossing easily on the gentle slope of the trail they now stood on.

He moved so fast that the second raider died attempting to pull out his sword. Conall crashed with his full body into the man standing in front of him, and the force of his attack pushed the raider's sword arm against his body, making it impossible for him to pull out his weapon.

The dirk that Conall held ready in his right hand flashed in the sunlight only for an instant before it pierced the man's gut, ripping him open to the bottom of his rib cage. The dirk's blade was long enough to reach the man's heart. He died before his fingers lost their grip on the hilt of his sword. The light that had reflected from Conall's blade was the last thing the raider saw as he died.

Conall threw the body of the man aside in disgust as he roared in defiance.

The next man stood wide-eyed, looking to his left and right, but there was no place to escape. Again Conall charged down the gentle hill, but this man had time to prepare. A long blade was in his right hand, held and ready.

Conall ran at him with all the fury of a charging wild animal, but only a feet away from his kill, a branch hidden under the snow caught his foot and sent him falling into his enemy. The man's long blade cut deep into Conall's left side.

He lay on top of the man, but the raider wasn't moving. Conall's blade had found its true mark. Twisting and glancing off a rib, the blade had pierced into the side of the man's chest, through his lung and into his heart. Rolling over onto his back, Conall's hand went to his bleeding side.

"Damn lucky, you piece of *cachi*," he growled with contempt at the invader, but he also knew it was his clumsy footing that had helped to inflict his wound. He smiled, thinking to himself, "Once again Danu has preserved my life.

"Thank you, Mother Goddess, thank you once again for my life." He said this out loud for all of creation to hear.

Holding his side and with his fingers pressing hard against the wounds opening, he groaned in pain as he stumbled to his feet. He searched each man's body for anything he could use and found just a little dried meat and some pouches of stone-crushed grain. He would have taken some of their clothing, but all three were filthy and stunk of human excrement aand rancid sweat. He wanted no part of anything they wore.

"I was wrong," Conall said out loud. "You are not animals. Animals are cleaner than you—foul-smelling worshipers of foreign gods." Bathing must not be an approved method of worship among these people, he thought.

As he searched their bodies, he noticed they were crawling with fleas. The fleas had already begun leaving their rapidly cooling hosts, moving onto the snow, seeking any warm living thing they could find and call home.

He smiled as he thought of Briga and how she would have shaken her finger at him, admonishing him in a loving tone, if he had brought home raider fleas; happy that her husband had survived, she would insist that he bathe himself before touching her.

"No, my little friends, I am afraid Briga would not like you," he said as he moved away from the fleas and dead raiders.

Now he had a new and greater concern.

He knew he would first have to stop the bleeding from the wound on his side before he would be able to complete his journey home. He would have to find some yarrow, honey, and spider webs for his wound dressings; he barely had enough dried sphagnum moss and dried woad leaves that Briga had put in his traveling pouch. He knew honey and spider webs would be impossible to find in this cold, so he began looking for the telltale tops of the dried yarrow and soon found what he was looking for.

Chapter Fifteen

t is one of the wonders of creation...

When the Primal One that dwelled at the center of all creation began dividing, it opened itself into two halves: one with all the masculine qualities of creation, and one with all the feminine qualities. As any woman would say, the female mind thinks and works much differently from the mind of a man—as does the mind and the concerns of the good goddess from those of the good god.

Briga would often wonder at the location of Conall's mind, as it seemed to have the ability to disappear even as he stood right in front of her. It seemed to her that as she asked him questions that made him uncomfortable or gave him instructions he didn't like, his eyes seemed to stare into some faraway place, and his mind went blank.

The truth is, it did.

Briga would be the first to say that Conall was very good at disappearing into some distant place.

To avoid discomfort, pain, or severe and cruel situations, men take their minds to different times and places. Briga often wondered what Conall was thinking, since her mind ran at full speed almost all the time, solving the problems at hand, while he always seemed to be in some dream place. If she could have gotten inside her man's head, she would have found that much of his time was spent thinking of the past and replaying his life events—both the very pleasant and the very unpleasant.

In the swirling mists of his thoughts, Conall moved his mind to a place of joy and happiness. When faced with severe conditions, a man simply keeps moving from the past and back to the present as needed. Conall's mind once again was returning to the present, to the sunrise and the downhill slope that he'd been following since he'd been wounded.

Conall was back in reality and no longer yesterday's thoughts...

"Fleas...fleas," he chuckled to himself. "Dogs have fleas, and so did the filthy raider who kissed me with his blade, that dirty, filthy pig," he said sarcastically. He thought about home and swore out loud, as if the forest trees had ears and living things within earshot could understand.

"Briga would have killed me if I'd brought fleas home," he said.

As he walked, he chuckled at the idea of his pretty little Briga being angry at him for bringing raider fleas home. She had such a temper when things did not go her way. The woman he loved seethed with passion and was quick to anger at injustice, and she was easily aroused with desire and sexual passion at his touch.

Conall smiled.

"Yes," he said to the world around him, "my Briga does have a temper equaled only by her lust and passion." His smile grew even larger. "I am looking forward to touching her."

But the thoughts of Briga and the humor he was enjoying were soon replaced by the serious need to return to his people, and to stop the bleeding from his side.

He had to get back to warn them.

On the horizon the brilliant edge of the sun's disk began to move above the mountain ridge that lay to the east, on the far side of the valley he called home.

"Now," he thought, "I will be warmed by the Oak King, and with the help of his light, I will finally be able to move faster than an infant learning to crawl."

The forest trees had been spaced far enough apart that Conall had been able to continue moving down the mountain slope in the deep darkness of the cold night. He had used a walking stick to reach out and feel his way down the mountain. Now it was light enough that he laid the stick back on the earth and thanked it for its help in keeping him steady.

Reverence for all things born by the goddess ran deep in his warrior heart.

Once the sun cleared the mountaintops, it leaped into the sky and quickly reached four fingers above the horizon. The entire world was bathed in light, and Conall believed he could even feel warmth coming into him.

Bright sunlight touched his face, and closing his eyes, he thanked the Oak King for the warmth he now felt on his forehead and cheeks.

As he held his cold face up to the sun in thanksgiving, the call of Bran the Raven, broke the silence. From behind him, back up the mountain toward the cliffs, the call of the raven repeated over and over as the bird moved rapidly toward him.

He turned just as a large, blue-black adult raven flew low over him. As it approached, it called his name: "*Kaaa-nall.*"

To his amazement, it flew right over his head, less than ten feet above him. It called his name again before racing past him toward the valley.

The raven appeared to fly directly into the valley, and then it turned to fly toward the sun before disappearing into the brilliance of the Oak King's light.

As it seemed to disappear into the sun, Conall called out to the raven, "Why, Bran, have you flown here seeking me, and why have you called out my name?" He knew he had to comprehend the vision he was given, and as he walked, he reached into his mind for an understanding of what seemed to be a warning.

Conall was deeply troubled by this omen.

Bran the Raven was his Briga's animal guide and her clan kin in the animal world, just as his was the wolf. Briga had been given the raven's sight, which allowed her to see to the peripheries of reality and into the mists of the future.

She was also a healer and knew about the various plants, having mastered the knowledge of healing practices that had been handed down through many generations of women in her family.

It was Briga who had taught him to use yarrow as a compress to stop the bleeding of a wound and of the antiseptic power of the first year leaves of the woad plant. She had instructed him that when possible, he could slow the flow of blood with the combination of clean spider webs and yarrow; if he could not find the webs, yarrow by itself was the next best thing. It would stop the bleeding of a deep-cut wound, but the wound had to be cleaned daily with urine, and fresh yarrow or dried sphagnum applied each time.

Conall's concern was not with his wound; it was with Briga. To have Bran call his name, fly into the valley, turn, and disappear into the sun was a sign that troubled him.

He was not the best at interpreting signs, but the core of his soul was deeply disturbed. He was much better at sharpening a blade and knowing when and how to use it, but even Conall now felt the forebodings of this omen.

Something was wrong, and Briga was in trouble. Why else would one of her relatives come looking for him and call out his name? There was trouble brewing in the valley below, and somehow it involved her.

Holding his wounded left side, he began to move quickly forward in a hard trot, a mile-devouring gait used by of the wolf-warrior. He moved down the hillside as rapidly as any living creature could, and yet in his heart, he began to believe it was already too late, that he would not arrive in time.

His mind, tired and weak from cold and exhaustion, began to fear the worst. He raced downhill at a trot that soon moved into the run of the wolf-warrior.

For the first time in days, he was running on bare ground again—muddied from the rain, but bare—not the deep snow he had left behind in the fields of the upper slopes. Below him was the familiar ground of home, and when he entered the valley below, he would be in his people's holdings and among the Ordovices. He would soon be running on the game trails and footpaths of his homelands.

Before long he would be in the arms of Briga.

His only thoughts now concerned forcing his body onward in an effort to get back to her as quickly as possible; shutting down his mind, he was only thinking of his forward movement. All his attention was concentrated on this ability to move rapidly forward; his trotting run had broken into a full, loping run as he held his left side.

He forced thoughts of Briga aside with intense focus; his energies were conserved for his body. His mind was emptied of everything as he centered his complete attention on each running step and the terrain ahead of him. He looked out ahead, down the trail, and his mind sent that information to a body that would react to what had been seen long before he reached it; now every muscle in his body moved to that one task and the goal of getting back home.

He chose each step carefully as he ran; he did not want to fall again. He certainly didn't want to twist his ankle by stepping off into a hole. He was a man intent on moving forward, and for what seemed like a long time, nothing else mattered, and nothing else entered his thoughts. Before him was home and Briga. He was running back to her.

Chapter Sixteen

umbed, he kept moving. He thought of nothing but home until he heard the calls of a wolf pack. They must have found his fresh blood, and now they tracked him, just as he'd tracked the raiders. At first he hoped they were hunting the upper slopes, but it was soon apparent that the pack had chosen to run his trail.

Their calls had no rhythm but instead seemed to gather together in an odd harmony that flowed into a series of barks and yelps, which rapidly grew louder as they ran toward him. Their ability to close the distance between themselves and him was far greater than his ability to outrun them, and he no longer worried about falling or losing his footing.

Conall broke into a hard, full run. He was now in a race to survive.

He was alarmed and in dread of the approaching wolf pack. Holding his side, he ran with determination and a clear sense of direction. Conall had never known panic quite like this before, and he was beginning to feel a great sense of trepidation, especially at the thought of experiencing or encountering something as unpleasant as a large, hungry wolf pack.

He moved rapidly as a man and a warrior, intent on staying ahead of an enemy that he knew would be stronger and more powerful than him. He'd no desire to fight a pack of wolves' intent on making him their next meal.

He ran...and stumbled...and staggered, always moving northwest, toward his Briga and those he loved. He was intent on moving in a line that was as straight as possible. His flight soon brought him to an obstacle that stopped his advance: an angry and wild river.

This was a churning, cascading, boulder-filled line of thundering white water, which was saying to the world very loudly, by its very actions of turbulence, "I dare anything living to try and cross me!"

Groaning, he said, "This day I may die." At that moment the lead scouts of the wolf pack spotted him and began to alert the rest of the pack.

Conall saw that far back, under the thick cover of the trees, were a number of wolves, most light gray and a few black in color and of medium build. They watched him from afar. Soon the woods behind Conall seemed to come alive with the howls, barks, and yelps of a very large pack of wolves.

Conall counted over twenty wolves moving about in the shelter of the trees. There were grays, whites, and one very large black wolf. From the size and look of the black wolf, there wasn't any doubt that he was the leader of this horde—the alpha male. Nearest Conall, almost close enough to touch, were seven adults, six juveniles, and three yearlings. Every wolf watched him intently for any movement he might make in an attempt to run away from the pack.

With his back to the river, Conall was now surrounded by a semi-circle of a half-dozen large females that acted as bodyguards to the large, black, dominant alpha male, and there would be no getting past them. The rest of the pack began running back and forth, waiting for a signal from the black male. Some of the smaller males ran with tails tucked between their legs, urinating as they ran. These young males were rapidly turning their heads from their leader back to Conall.

Several of the larger females walked straight toward him, heads down low; they did not take their eyes off Conall. As they advanced, they growled with curled lips that clearly exposed their canine teeth, keeping their heads down and their ears laid back. Conall could see long, slimy strands of drool dripping from their snarling, exposed fangs. Not taking his eyes off them, he spoke loudly. "So, are you looking for a bite to eat?"

He continued. "Are we hungry and looking for an easy meal?" The large female leading the advance stopped and growled deeply—a throaty, deep, long, rumbling sound of disapproval at food that would say something to her.

She hesitated and looked back over her shoulder at the large black male.

The black male stopped and lowered his head, looking straight at the female. He snarled fiercely as she turned and continued her advance toward Conall.

"Now, cousins, do you really want to eat one who is a kinsman?" he asked. "I am Conall the convel, a wolf-warrior." But this didn't seem to impress them.

"I will not be easy to kill," he advised the female advancing toward him, but she kept coming forward.

Unlike the raiders he had faced for days, the wolf generally had no fear as a man would understand fear. Caution and apprehension, yes; but fear, especially the fear of death, was not a feeling any of the wolf pack comprehended, and especially not this female. Conall knew of only one thing that would drive a wolf to hunt a man—a man with a fresh wound that was bleeding. Conall's hand went under his garment and to his side, and as he felt his wound, he said, "Damn." He pulled back fingers covered by fresh blood.

Usually the wolf was very selective about the prey it chose, but in the right conditions and deep hunger, the wolf would hunt men.

It had been days since she'd last eaten, and hunger now ruled her conscience. The sole purpose and meaning of her life had been reduced to only one thing: the need to eat.

The wolf reacted to events and opportunities as it traveled; it pursued the prospects it needed to continue to live. Today's event was hunger and feeding. Conall held the prospect of a good meal, and it was the wolf's deep sense of hunger that compelled her to pursue an opportunity—a man such as Conall—that on better days she might have warily avoided.

Her hunger was a deep pain that filled her mind as her body ached with an all-consuming need to feed. She wanted to taste blood and fill her stomach with meat. She wanted to take away the hunger pains that tormented her. There was no emotion at the thought of killing, just the primal need to satisfy her hunger.

For a split moment, he felt himself a kindred spirit to the wolf; they were so beautiful and powerful. His spirit guide was the wolf for many reasons: they had excellent night vision and keen auditory perception, they ambushed their prey, they mated for life, and their genius lay in the power of the group. However, they also had a couple of inherent weaknesses, including that they were only astute trackers if they picked up a scent of fresh blood.

Conall knew of only one thing they disliked enough that you could call it fear: the sound of stringed instruments. For the hypersensitive hearing of the wolf, the loud vibrations and high notes played on string instruments created a painful and sharp stabbing that sent the animal fleeing and howling.

Conall also understood the wolf had no feelings. There was nothing personal or evil behind her impending attack; there was just a need. He wrinkled his nose with a half smirk and shouted, "You won't be filling your belly with my flesh. No, my friend, you'll not be doing that today!"

Conall was ready, and he knew her next move. She would run at him and leap, attempting to lock her jaws around his neck; she would hope to crush his windpipe and maybe even break his neck. If she could not secure a hold on his neck, she would lock onto his arm with jaws capable of closing with a force of six hundred pounds per square inch. His arm would be paralyzed, and as the bones crushed, she would hold him or drag him to the ground. Once there, the other females would rush in quickly. While he was still alive, the wolves would begin to rip him apart in a feeding frenzy. It would all be over rather quickly.

He stood on the edge. Behind him was the river. In front of him was certain death by the fangs of the wolf pack. He watched her shoulders, jaw, and neck for the first muscle movements that would communicate that her charge had begun. He didn't have to wait long; she exhibited slow and deliberate movements, high body posture, and raised hackles. Her shoulder muscles tensed…

She charged, and to the surprise of the whole wolf pack, he matched it. This was very unusual, and a wolf's mind has trouble with the very unusual. Food never charges back; food runs away. He sprang forward at a full run, rushing her. This startled the rest of the pack; some of the weaker and smaller males ran off into the woods. Many of the lesser females backed away and took up positions behind the big black male and his escort.

The black wolf didn't move, and his escort stood its ground.

As Conall ran toward the charging female, his right hand withdrew from under his cloak the eighteen-inch dirk with its double-edged razor-sharp blade. She leaped at him. He stopped and braced himself, then answered the wolf's leap while she was still in the air. In a graceful arching motion, he caught the she-wolf at arm's length with his outstretched left arm, his hand grasping her by the throat, and using the weight of her own forward motion, he swung her off to his left side while the blade in his right hand flashed up with a forceful, thrusting cut that drove deep into her lungs. Blood gushed from her open mouth as her eyes, now wild with fear, dimmed and closed.

Dead, she landed on her left side just past his left leg.

He stepped back several steps. Still facing the remaining wolves, he knelt beside her and placed his left hand on her lifeless body. "I'm sorry, mother wolf, but I could not let you feed on me," he said with a sadness that came from the lower depths of his spirit. "I have a destiny that does not include nourishing you and your pack."

He stood facing the large black wolf. "Let me go home!" he shouted loud and defiantly. He had hoped his bold charge would discourage the pack leader and the others. He was answered by the charge of the black wolf and his bodyguard of she-wolves.

He'd already made up his mind. There were too many to fight, so he would retreat. Unfortunately, the only direction he could turn now was into the thundering white waters of the river behind him.

He turned, and without a second of hesitation, he ran.

The black male wolf exploded into a full run right behind him, the escort of large female guards following very close. At the edge of the river's bank, Conall thought, "I hate cold water."

He swiftly drew a great deep breath of air into his lungs. With his heart pounding hard and without a second to spare, he leaped out and away from the overhanging riverbank with every ounce of strength he could summon.

Chapter Seventeen

uspended between the two elements of water and earth, he sailed out over the churning river, and for a moment he seemed to hang in the embrace of the air. He was held there for just a split second, and as the air released him, he fell crashing into the violent waters.

Right behind Conall's running leap, the large black male followed, jutting forward nose first; there was no hesitation from the wolf. Two of his females joined him, not hesitating either—following the pack leader over the abyss and into the river.

Conall slammed into the water feet-first, the force of his fall driving him deep under the surface of the turbulent river, down to the rocky bottom.

The strong current tore at his body, forcing him to move in its direction. He fought to keep himself upright; his head was toward the surface and his feet toward the river bottom.

He looked up as bubbles swirled around him, just in time to see three wolves breaking through the shimmering silver water's surface. To his surprise and theirs, they had joined him deep under the water.

Trapped by the water's fury, far under its raging surface, wolves and man lingered, fighting for survival. They tumbled and were driven even deeper by the current. Surprised-looking wolves pawed at the water that surrounded them, seeking with their claws, a means to pull themselves down from above toward the great Conall.

With stinging lungs and death's hand grasping and crushing his throat, he thought, "I have one last chance."

His feet hit the rocky bottom, and once again he mustered every bit of the great strength he had in his legs. He pushed off and shot up past the sinking wolves. Fighting with every muscle, he pulled and kicked against the water as he tried to move toward the river's surface.

The great black wolf snapped at him as he moved swiftly upward. It was almost comical as large amounts of air bubbles escaped past his viciously snapping teeth. The wolf stopped moving his jaws, and his eyes bulged; the last of the air in his lungs was lost in his failed attempt to bite Conall.

Conall watched as the black wolf ceased moving and drifted downward, rolling and turning as he was moved by the current.

Looking up through the water, Conall saw the glimmering bright disk of the sun, its light dancing across the water's surface and creating a mirrorlike reflection just beyond the ends of his fingertips. With his outstretched arms, he reached up and cupped his hand around the sun's shimmering image. Over and over he reached up, grabbing at the sun only to find water in his cupped hands. Drawing down the water from above his head with his strong arms, he pulled and fought his way to the surface. He looked down one more time during his ascent, and as he did, he saw the three wolves tumble along the bottom of the river. Their bodies struck hard against the boulders that lay along their path, and the last of the air they had held in their lungs escaped as hundreds of round silver bubbles.

They soon disappeared into the murky depths as Conall watched them being carried away by the current.

His head and shoulders broke the surface of the water. The loud sound of the rushing water filled his head; it was all he could hear. He was caught in the full rage of the river, and it was carrying him rapidly downstream.

All along the stream's path, very large slate boulders stood above the churning surface, intent, it seemed, on reaching upward to grab him, to drag him back under the surface to join the poor hapless beasts that Conall knew had surely drowned.

Almost immediately he was driven into a wall of rock. Now it was his turn to have the air driven from his lungs by the combined brute forces of rock and water. Trying to catch his breath, he was struck hard against the rocks again and again, and each time he had to fight to break free as the raging water tried to pin him to the side of the rock and drag him below the water's surface.

As he was tossed about by the strong current, the river threw him forward and pressed him along like the head butting of an angry bull. He was no longer able to swim; battered, out of breath, and losing feeling due to the numbing cold, he simply did whatever he could to keep his head above the water. Now he only fought for the air he needed to keep alive.

His body became a limp rag doll. He was at the whim of the water as he tumbled and fell into a narrow gorge of steep rocky walls that briskly descended, creating a river of ever-increasing speed that continued sweeping him along.

As the elevation dropped quickly toward the valley floor, the river turned into a series of rapids filled with large rocks and white water. Conall was soon carried feetfirst through a narrowing channel of powerful water. He was pushed helplessly past bluestone boulders by the combined forces of water, gravity, and sharp elevation changes.

Again and again he struck the rocks. He felt his left leg snap as he was hurled straight into a large slate boulder. Pain exploded into his consciousness, but he only had an instant to think, "I broke my leg." Twice more he slammed up against rocks that knocked the air out of him, leaving him gasping for breath as churning water tried to cover his head.

A loud roaring sound lay just ahead, and Conall recognized it as the sound of falling water. He dropped over a ledge of rock and water, down into a yawning, deep, clear pool. Pushed by the strong hand of the cascading water from above, he was held firmly to the gravel bottom of the pool.

He fought.

Nothing else was in his mind but his battle with the river. Time seemed to come to a halt, and Conall's whole world was now reduced to his fight to free himself from the powerful hand of water that held him to the floor of the river.

He pushed and clawed at the bottom, grasping at rocks in an attempt to pull himself free. His lungs ached for air, and his throat felt a clawing, crushing spasm while his upper chest and neck muscles screamed at him to gulp in air, to breathe. Like a hot rod piercing into his brain, the urge to breathe screamed at him from inside his head.

Conall tightened his jaw and fought the powerful urge to open his mouth and suck in water. Clawing and digging at the gravel bottom of the pool, he pulled himself along until he found the edge, the invisible end of the powerful wall of water that held him down, and then he was able to push and kick with his one good leg out from under it.

His head broke the surface, and Conall took the second most important breath of his life. He forced out the stale air in his lungs and took in life-restoring air, forcing as much new air into his lungs as possible. Not since his first birthing breath had Conall needed a single breath to save his life. Like a newborn's breath, this breath started his life again and saved him from darkness and death's sleep.

The water carried him farther on.

He was broken and weak. Cold and exhaustion had drained the last of his strength; his only concern was keeping his head above water. His arms and legs had become cold and as heavy as stone. He no longer had the energy to fight.

Like a lifeless piece of broken wood, he was carried along, and only one plea left his lips: "Please help me, Mother Danu."

The river's turbulent waves reached out and grasped his limp body with the intent of destroying him, once again smashing his left side into a large rock. The pain shattered him. For the first time in his life, he felt defeated.

Violent water like a cold iron sword pierced his chest. It had done what no living thing, man, or animal could do: it had defeated Conall, the great wolf-warrior of Cymru.

Powerless to help himself, he watched as the force of the water caught him, twisting and turning him around in circles until he went headfirst down the river, straight toward a large boulder.

He was unable to move his arms, now entirely under the control of the water. Headfirst, he slammed into the rock. Searing, blinding pain filled him with white-hot light as his brain began to spiral into darkness. The pain replaced all responsiveness, and he quickly left the world of light and entered the world of an ever-tightening circle of darkness.

He was blacking out.

"I'm going to die," he thought as he began to sink below the waters.

Numbed and unable to move, his mind was falling into the cold darkness of death as his body sank into the depths of the river.

He said only one word as his mind disappeared in the dark: "Briga."

Chapter Eighteen

The distance between Conall's life and death was measured by a breath. Some believe every heartbeat brings you one step closer to death, but for those who walk with Danu, there is no death nor any fear of dying.

For the children of the old gods, each heartbeat is a gift, and it holds the promise of living a moment in time that will add another thread to the great woven mystery on the tapestry loom of the gods. Death, for those who believe in the old ways, may involve the pain-filled release of the soul from one's bodily life, but it is always followed by the joy of knowing that one is returning to the mother of all life—and if one so desires, returning also to the world of flesh and substance in a renewed bodily life. Conall knew this great circle of life, the Cylch Mawr with no beginning and no end, to be true freedom.

The druids had taught Conall that "death is but a short step to a new life." All the people of the Red Dragon knew that as long as the promise was kept by the good gods at the time of Alban Arthuan, the winter solstice, when the Oak King returned his light, all things would be renewed, including the lives of those who had died the year before.

To the people of the ancient faith, there was no death, only renewed life, and this testimony came to them every day in the designs of the world around them and every year in the renewed "circle of the Oak King." Like the Oak King's yearly life cycle, they too would be restored to life, one year and one day after a person died. He or she could return, reborn again into a new bodily life. This was a promise from the gods. They knew with certainty that they would return to once again live among the ones they loved and the people of their clan.

However, there is also the place where a soul may linger, a place of stillness between the very edge of the circle of creation and far from those living on the earth. It is in this place of mindless sleep that the soul rests as the body attempts to repair itself after it has been severely injured.

Neither alive in body nor dead in spirit, the soul drifts, buoyed in the darkness, wrapped in love, surrounded and protected by the Creators. In this place the soul is held against the bosom of the goddess Cerridwen, as she waits until one's body heals or the soul stops fighting death and elects to return, held by the hand of the goddess Fand, to the White Lady Dryad, goddess of the dead, moving on to his ancestors in the Hall of Souls.

This is the place that held Conall. For over two weeks, his soul was in the protection of the good god, and his body—the massive, strong body of Conall, the wolf-warrior of Cymru—was in the hands of children and a young maiden.

As the goddess Cerridwen held his soul securely and safely to her bosom, his body was tenderly cared for by a young maiden and small children. In the design and wisdom of the goddess, children and the Creator are the same. It is taught to all the people of Cymru by Danu herself that "to know the good god, you must be like little children; your hearts must be pure and innocent."

As the soul moves back to the center of the living, it is awakened slowly; the senses of the body awaken before the eternal living mind. Smells and sounds begin to take the mind into the past, and memories begin flooding back into the brain of a soul that has been held in the in-between place.

Out of the darkness of Conall's mind, a warm and wonderful memory began to appear. Slowly he remembered, and as he did, a smile came to his face, which had remained emotionless, without expression, and almost deathlike for days.

He saw himself surrounded by laughing, joyful children. He was a lion, the great Ari of the old Hebrews, who had come to the island generations ago. On all fours he roared defiantly while young children, both boys and girls, pretended to be warriors attacking him as he fought back fiercely.

He was frightening and powerfully ferocious, yet the young warriors persisted in their attacks against this beast. With patient and honed skill, the children played a serious game that they would later play as adults. They had broken into four groups and surrounded the great beast; they all attacked from different directions, some from each side. A couple of the older, more experienced children attacked the great lion's head and snapping jaw, and the smallest children tortured the beast from behind.

Protected by long wooden toy spears and tall play shields, the young warriors struck at the beast over and over, always coordinating their attacks with hand signals and an occasional loud, animallike call from the leader. Soon a battered and mortally wounded lion dramatically rolled over and died.

Into his mind the sweet sound of Briga's voice entered, its crescendo filled with joy and laughter.

"Conall, you are the biggest of our children," she scolded him gently in a voice filled with love, but it was overshadowed with a measure of concern. "Look at you. You are covered in dirt, and the meeting is about to begin."

The great lion Ari opened his eyes, smiled, and rolled over onto his stomach. Before him was the woman he loved, the one whom he would seek in this life and the next. Smiling up at her, he said, "From here on the earth, my beloved, the child within fills you with the roundness of a new life and the beauty of one who will soon bring back a familiar soul to the clan." He flashed a wide, beaming smile up at her, and like the little child he was in his heart, he felt the unspoiled purity of their love; her heart had merged with his that day at the waterfall. He was overflowing with warmth and felt an immeasurable connection to this woman that transcended any sense of time and space.

He loved her more than his own life.

Looking at the swelling of her pregnant belly, he was filled with the wonder and awe a man feels for the woman who carries his child—a child created in the sincerity of love and with the blessing of the gods. Overcome by his feelings for her, he said passionately, "You are beautiful!"

Briga blushed and reached down to grasp the hand of her gentle warrior. "Come, my love," she said. "The Cyngor has gathered in council. They are waiting for you, and Caswallon ap Beli the ard druid is here and wants to speak to you."

╡

Chapter Nineteen

For the first time in days, memories flooded back into his mind, causing the stony mask that had been Conall's face to smile. Memories of happiness and joy brought him back to conciseness, and he laughed out loud, softly, as he returned to the world of the living.

The children around him became excited, their cries filling the cavern that held them with echoes of joy, which became loud shouts of, "He lives! The wolf-warrior lives!" Joining together, the young voices formed *fonn*-like chanting that pulled at him until the world of the living replaced the world of dreams. Conall was moved from the edge of the circle back to the center, back to the world of flesh and blood; he was once again a living man.

Conall opened his eyes and spoke one word in a very dry and raspy voice: "Briga?" The soft touch of a feminine hand lightly caressed his shoulder—at first very softly, then with a strength that caused Conall to open his eyes. The warrior turned his head to look at the hand that had touched him and helped awaken him from the edge of creation.

The index finger was long and delicately formed. At the place where the index finger and the thumb joined, she wore a small tattoo: three small dots of black made of mixture of oak gall, woad, and ash ink, creating a triangle of perfectly placed dots— one below the base of the thumb and one below the index finger, and the third placed toward the wrist. It was the triangle of the goddess. Conall did not need to know any more about this young woman. He knew she was a healer and that she served Danu.

He also knew she was a friend.

Had he known her in some other time—some other place?

He looked at her hand and thought that it was so perfect, so beautiful and pure in its shape, so very young. Without glancing up to the young woman's face, he said out loud in a painful, raspy, dry voice he barely recognized, "You have a beautiful hand."

His glance moved from her hand to the delicate white wrist, up the cloak-covered arm to the face of a now-blushing young girl; and there Conall's eyes stopped.

She was young, not more than fifteen, and so fair. Her cheeks grew crimson red as she blushed, and her eyes shone bright with the miraculous green of early spring. Her hair was long and the color of sun-dried summer barley; it cascaded down in great waves that covered both her shoulders like a golden shawl. She was beautiful, and in her eyes kindness sparkled like the twinkling stars in the heavens.

"Where am I?" he asked.

She moved her hand from his shoulder, and like a mother to her child, she pressed her two fingers against his lips and said firmly, "Quiet. You must rest. I will tell you everything, but for now I must clean your wounds and refresh your poultices. Be still so I can work with the goddess to heal you."

The young girl pulled back the furs and woven blankets that covered Conall. She looked at the bruises, wounds, and broken bones intently, and as Conall watched her, he realized he was completely naked except for his great gold torc and the dressings that covered the wound to his left side and his broken leg.

Still looking at his injuries, she said, "You have a very deep knife wound in your left side, a couple of broken ribs on your right side, and a broken left leg, and there are many lacerations and bruises both outside and inside your body. Your injuries are beyond my skill alone to heal; the goddess and I have not left your side for days."

Touching his side gently and pushing inward with increasing pressure toward the wound's opening, she said, "You are in a cave, and we are hiding from the ones who destroyed our farming village, killing and carrying off everyone but myself and these children. The older boys found you in the river, tangled in some brush along with two dead wolves, one gray and one very large black one. You have been here, held in the dream world, for most of a waxing moon. The moon is now well past full."

She removed the dressing that had covered the wound, and with her fingertips, she pushed on the wound again, this time harder. Without looking up at Conall, she said, "There is no redness and no fever." She leaned over close to the wound's opening and smelled deeply, then smiled and said softly, "Good, there is no more pus. The infection has been driven out. You have lost a lot of blood, and you have been severely hurt. Your injuries have left you very weak, and it is only by the love of the Mother of all the people that you live. You must be thirsty and hungry. Now lie quietly, and I will tend to your wounds and give you water and food."

His eyes told her that he would be obedient and that he would let her care for him. She put one hand behind his head and lifted him up enough to drink from the bittersweet infusion that she now poured past his lips. It seemed to tingle as it passed over his tongue, and his lips began to numb slightly as he drank the soothing medicine. He would have normally protested at being fed like a baby, but now he really didn't have much choice—he only had a thread of strength left to talk.

His injuries and the days of lying unconscious had left him weak, without power, and the muscles of his massive body seemed to have lost much of their command. He felt drained. He was unable to do anything for himself, and for days this young girl would take care of his bodily needs. He was grateful both to her and those around him, who'd kept him alive long enough to make the journey of return from the outer reaches of the Great Circle of Life. Conall knew that if he were to ever find Briga again, his journey would start anew from this cave. He also knew he had been given a second life by the hands of this young woman and the children standing just behind her in the flickering firelight.

Once more he spoke to the young maiden, and then he became silent, as the little strength he had gained faded back under the veil. "I am Conall, a convel, a wolf-warrior of my mother's clan of the *Bona Na Croin*, the family of the undefeated wolf. I want to thank you for saving me, and I swear to you and yours a blood oath to protect, provide, and care for all of you from this day on."

The girl's green eyes sparkled and danced with the firelight as she smiled at him. She spoke with the tenderness that can only come from a woman's lips as she said to him, "We know who you are, Conall Cearnach of the highland mountains; you are the great convel Conry of the order of the Cunobarrus, the husband of the beautiful Lady Briga of Llyn Tegid, the Lady of the Lake, and we know you have come here to save us. Bran the Raven has told us these things."

He started to say more, but once again the young girl pressed her two fingers against his lips, and in the voice of a stern mother to her child, she firmly said, "Now, I won't be having any more of this. I accept your oath, so be quiet and rest."

Behind the two fingers Conall's lips formed a smile, and in a soft whisper, he said, "Yes, my second mother."

Her gentle hands cleansed the deep lacerations that had been ripped into his body by sword and rock. She carefully removed the maggots she had placed on the rotting flesh of his knife wound. They had done their work and were no longer needed, as they had fed upon his bad flesh until it was removed and only the healthy, growing flesh remained. After the wounds had been washed clean with fresh, living water, she covered them with a thick coat of honey. On top of this, she applied new layers of poultices that had been soaked in a tincture of mead, comfrey, thyme, chamomile, woad, and mint; she first applied the mixture to his deep bruises, then to his ribs, and then around his broken leg, which she had set and splinted.

At times her gentle touch found places that caused him to grimace in pain—pain that would have been much worse had she not given him the warm tea of crushed, boiled herbs mixed with crushed poppy seeds. She had applied an even stronger mix of the tea to all the poultices covering the wounds, bruises, and breaks on his body. These bandages were held on with strips of willow tree bark tied in place with thin, braided cords made from the tall dried grass that stays standing, even in winter, under the branches of younger oak trees.

"My name is Marian," she said softly as she tended to him. "My mother's name was Muirgheal, and she was a healer and a daughter of Bran the Raven. Her mother and her mother before her had also known the skill of healing; long ago they had come to this place from the lands to the east in Jerusalem. It was my mother who taught me the magic." As she tended to Conall, Marian spoke and remembered her mother, calling upon her memory to help her now.

"My mother had long, beautiful black hair and eyes the rich, warm brown of the earth. She was of the blood memory of the old Hebrews, but as you can see, I have the look of my father's people and my father's mother, a woman from the land of Erin."

She stopped tending to Conall, and for a moment, it was as if she had traveled far away. When she spoke again, she was deep in thought, and her voice had become much sadder as she said, "She was killed by a fair-colored man from the North, a man with cold blue eyes. I had to watch as he beat and raped her, and while he was still lying on top of her and when he was finished with her, he laughed as he took a blade and with a quick slice, cut open her throat.

"My mother smiled at me as she looked past the man's shoulder toward the place I was hiding, and her eyes did not look frightened. Sadness filled them as I watched her life fade away, and I remember picking up a large stone and rushing out from my hiding place and hitting the man on the head over and over again until he was dead. I rolled him off my mother's body, and I began striking him in the face with my stone, over and over again until he no longer had a face. My mother was dead, but I made sure I would never see that man's face again. I took my mother by her hands and pulled her body into the woods and buried her the best I could. Someday I will find all those who came with him, and I will kill them too!"

Marian sat silent for just a minute or two and once again began tending to Conall's wounds.

Conall said nothing. There was nothing he could say, nothing that would make a difference; he did believe her, and he knew that someday she would kill all those who had come to her village.

Marian finished with Conall's dressings, and with the help of a young boy, she raised Conall's shoulders and head so she could feed him. He had not smelled the broth until it was raised to his mouth. It was only at that moment, when the rich aroma of herbs, barley, and wolf meat reached his nose, that he realized how completely famished he was; he ravenously took in the first warm spoonful.

"This is good, thanks," he said, and Marian smiled.

When the bowl was empty, she said to him, "Now you must rest. You are barely making sense." Once again with the help of the young boy, Conall was gently lowered back down and covered with new wolf furs, one that was very large and very black. When he saw it, he smiled.

In addition to the furs there were clean but old, tattered, coarsely woven wool blankets salvaged from the nearby village, and from the alternating blue and green stripes woven into the design, he knew he was very close to home.

He reached out from under the covers with a large callused hand, and with a gentleness that surprised Marian, he touched her arm, encircling it with his fingers. He grasped with assurance, squeezing firmly. She felt an almost wind-like rush of energy coming from him; it flowed as a great outpouring of love and male spirit energy, and it warmed her deep into every crevice of her being, as he said hoarsely, "Thank you."

Tears of sadness for her formed in his eyes, and a pain gripped at his throat as she leaned forward to kiss him on the forehead. She pulled the coarse woven blankets and the wolf pelt covers up to his chest, squeezed his shoulder firmly, and spoke softly. "Now sleep, Conall." He closed his eyes.

The enchantment in the herbal medicine that Marian had given him did its work, and he fell into a deep, pain-free sleep.

In the darkness beyond the fire's glow, she pulled up the long dress that covered her body down to her ankles. She pulled it up high, past her waist and lower back, well past her naked buttocks, exposing as much of her skin as possible; she wanted her skin to touch his and warm him, to bring his male spirit back to life.

She carefully crawled into the bed and gently touched him, wanting as much of her flesh and her feminine energy as possible to contact his flesh. Conall moaned softly, but it was not the moan of a man in pain; it was the moan of a man in the presence of pure feminine pleasure. As Conall slept, she studied him. She traced the outline of his forehead with her third finger; this finger held the pulse energy of her heart.

From his forehead she moved her hand to his massive chest and made a circle on it, starting at his right breast, moving upward almost to his throat, going down and over to his left breast, and then down to his groin and back up to his right breast—encasing his heart and all his spirit energy. As her hand moved around the center of his energy, she sang a healing chant in a fonn: "Danu mother, Danu sister, Danu healer, and Danu life giver, renew Conall. Restore his well-being and his strength. Danu, perfect in grace and love, heal the wolf-warrior."

Taking care not to trouble his wounds, she placed her healing hands over each energy center of his body, starting with the crown of his head. She then moved to his forehead, then his throat, then his heart again, and then below his ribs to his navel, and lastly to his phallus.

As she brought her front teeth over her bottom lip, she pondered the meaning and the probability of finding such a man as Conall.

"Why has he come to me?" she reflected. As she traced the muscular curves of his arms, her gentle touch on his warm skin caused her to melt inside, and then she felt strange; she felt an ache deep inside her that she had never felt before.

Beltane was only two full moons away; suddenly she knew whom she wanted to walk her into the oak grove on the night of the bright fire. Did she dare ask him when the time came?

Holding him, her body pressed up against the great wolf-warrior, Marian visualized her and Danu's energy spiraling into him and traveling up and down his spine. She repeated her prayer chant and visualization all night while Conall slept.

The food, the gentle, healing touch, and the warmth of Marian's body did their magic. Conall slept soundly—a sleep filled with pleasant dreams and familiar places, and once there, he was filled with joy as he dreamed of Briga.

Chapter Twenty

Briga lay snugly wrapped in the warm bedding and furs of the raised platform bed that Conall had built for her. Quietly she lay in the darkness that now surrounded the home she shared with Conall. She had always felt safe here in this house on the crannog, and her sleep had always been restful, but this had not been true lately; for days now she had wakened during the night's darkness, often after having vivid, disturbing dreams that she had trouble understanding.

Many strange images had come to her in her dreams. She often saw Conall, and what she saw disturbed her: his body was painted in different colors, the blue of woad, the bright red of fresh blood, and the unmistakable dark, almost black color of dried blood. The images she saw in her dreams frightened her, and last night she woke to a nightmare filled with screaming men, ravens calling Conall's name, and even more disturbing sights that she did not understand.

Two nights before, Briga had had a dream that troubled her so much, she couldn't return to sleep. In it she saw four great giants, their arms raised high over their heads as they each held a sword in one hand and a human head in the other. These giants danced around a great fire and chanted songs of insult to their enemies. Huge wolves danced with the four great giants, and both men and wolves shouted over and over again, *"Cymru, Cymru am byth!"*

The giants carried four large bags, and she watched, as they emptied the contents onto the ground. Out of the bags rolled and bounced the heads of men, as well as dozens of hands, ears, noses, and male parts. It had been this scene that had caused Briga to sit up in her sleep, gasp, and awaken.

Briga knew that somewhere many men had been killed.

And they had been killed by wolf-warriors.

But as much as her dreams had been troubled with visions of death, her nights had also been filled with longing for Conall.

For many days now, she had yearned and pined for Conall. As a woman she missed his masculine touch, his male energy, and strength; but most of all, she missed his smell and the warmth of his body nestled with hers under the covers of their bed. She was becoming very aware of just how much she missed being pleasured by him. But more than anything, she wanted and needed his protection.

She sighed deeply as she thought of what little time she and Conall had in the crannog; he had completed their home at the end of that summer and they had only been able to spend a very short time together before the Ard Druid and the Cyngor had sent Conall south towards three rivers.

As Briga lay in her bed, she prayed, "Goddess Danu, please hear my prayer. Please return my Conall to me soon. I ache so much to be filled by him and to feel his body on mine, to taste his kisses and to make love to my Mo Anam Cara."

"*Is tu m' annsachd, Conall…*" She sighed deeply as she lay alone, thinking of him and how, for many nights now, she had been aroused, desiring and needing him in her sleep.

She would wake wanting him.

He would come to her in her dreams and make love to her, and awakened by her burning desire for Conall's deep grip, she would find herself momentarily in the middle of sleep and wakefulness; it was at this in-between time that she often felt weight of his body on top of her and his manliness buried deep inside her, filling her with warmth and pleasure.

It was at these times of burning desire in the early-morning darkness that she would awaken, her senses fully aware of her surroundings and certain that the musky odor of his masculine fragrance still filled her nostrils. There was emptiness deep inside her body that called out to be filled, and it caused her to moan loudly in response to her need. She spoke softly into the darkness around her. "Oh, Great Mother, I miss him."

Briga had had too much time to think and ponder life's enigmas. Conall had been gone too long, and he was late in getting back; he should have been home weeks ago. In her loneliness she had begun to feel abandoned, and it did not help that she had arrived at a place of despondency that had her asking too many questions about her life. With no satisfactory answers, she was becoming sarcastic and pessimistic...

Briga spoke to the goddess and the inky darkness that surrounded her, "Danu was my soul reborn in a different body, or did I emerge from nothing, just to become a thinking person, to have the yearning for life with all its offerings of wonder and joy, all this, only to die alone and unfulfilled? Are we that insignificant to the gods? I have always believed in the gods, but what would my life be if something has happened to Conall? Is our death and rebirth the well-defined straight and narrow path, or is death a greater mystery, a meaningless journey into realm of nothingness...or is it the great circular transition to another body? Why Danu, do I question it now?"

A voice inside her head clearly spoke as the words traveled to her heart, "The thought of death is an insult to my spirit."

All her dreams and longings had begun to fill her with great concern for her husband. Briga sensed something was wrong, and now each day that Conall did not return, her concern was growing into fear—a fear that he might not return, and that she would be alone in giving birth to their child.

Pushing lightly against her left side, the baby inside her moved. It seemed to wiggle with a fluttering that almost tickled, and then came the strong, painful cramp in her groin and inner thigh, followed by pain to her insides. She held her left side as she said, "There is no doubt, my little warrior: you are Conall's son." She smiled, thinking that the baby growing inside her would be coming into the world in three more full moons, maybe less; but then she frowned, thinking of how she wasn't really ready. Conall was still gone, and she did not want to give birth without him near her side; she missed him, and lately the intensity of her wanting him to return had taken on urgency and a deep concern.

Thinking of Conall, she said out loud for all the gods to hear, "He is well past the time he was supposed to be back home to me and our son."

Briga's arms rested above the furs and blankets that covered her, and in the still darkness, she reached through the coverings for her stomach and held it with both hands, whispering, "Yes, my little warrior, there is no doubt: the way you kick, you have to be a boy, and you are nearly ready to meet your mother."

The two dogs that lay sleeping at the foot of her bed stirred at the sound of her voice, but they did not rise from the warmth of the bed; it was still too early to wander off on adventures.

"Yes, you have to be an impatient little boy wanting out now, before your time," she said in the tender tone that a young, expecting mother uses when she is alone. Her hands went under the bedding and her garment until she found the warm, bare skin of her very round and tight-skinned belly. One hand was on each side of her stomach as she began to tenderly caress the restless infant within. "Not long now," she said as a very distinct lump pushed hard against her right hand, so distinct that it seemed to be just under the skin.

"Is that an elbow or a knee, my little warrior? It is much too pointed to be your heel. Are you wanting out or just letting me know that I am keeping you awake too?" She continued to massage her stomach as she sang softly to the son she instinctively knew grew inside her, as she also intuitively knew it wouldn't be much longer before this little warrior would be born. "I hope your father returns soon," she said worriedly, and continued quietly singing with a lump in her throat.

Outside her crannog, the world was waking up, and the morning sounds of the woods and lake were beginning to enter the dwelling. Without looking outside she knew the sky was beginning to grow pale gray as dawn approached. She heard the early calls of birds and the sounds of splashing water as the world began to wake. The cattle began to stir, and soon she would have to get up and take them across the small bridge that connected her crannog to the shore some forty feet away.

Briga almost always felt safe and happy inside the home Conall had built for her. She cherished her home, and she smiled as she remembered how it had been built. They had been married at the summer solstice, and she had asked him to build her crannog shortly after they had joined at Beltane.

She lay in her warm bed thinking of the look on his face when she'd told him she wanted him to build her an island on the edge of the lake. "Yes, Conall, I want you to build me a crannog like my mother grew up in, in Erin." At first he had thought she was joking with him, and he'd had that puzzled look that men get and hold in their eyes whenever they answer a question with a question. "Build an island, my beloved?"

When he had looked into her eyes, he knew she was very serious. As he smiled at her with warm affection, he said, "My darling Briga, are you to become my very own Lady of the Lake?"

"Yes, Conall, and we will live on an island on the lake," she had answered. "I want you to build me an island that will stand on the edge of the lake. It must be on the west side of the lake with windows that open looking eastward over the water and toward the sunrise, so the early-morning sun will wake us, and the trees along the shore will shade us as the sun goes down. I have thought it all out."

Without taking a breath, she went on. "Please, Conall. I must be on the water. I draw strength from its energy, and I want to be near its surface, I want to see the dragonflies dance about the water and watch the moonlight dancing on its suface and I want to see the stars reflected on the waters face. I want to have easy access to the healing plants that grow along the shore. I need to sleep every night on the living waters of the lake so that I may draw strength into my soul and wisdom into my spirit. Please, Conall, let me rest on one of the shimmering gateways to Danu."

Conall smiled at the woman he loved above all others.

"I will build you an island, my true beloved. *Is tu m' annsachd*," he answered. "And you can sit and watch the full moon rise and dance on the waters as I sit with you holding your hand until we are old, gray, and bent over with age."

She laughed and threw her arms around his neck, then gave him a deep, passionate kiss. "I love you, Conall of Cymru, and it will not take so long to build my island that you will turn old and gray. I will show you how."

Her Conall had put on his best "I'm king of the wolves" face. Smiling down at her, he said softly, "Why are women always telling us how to do men's work, as if we can't figure it out ourselves?" He had started building the crannog the next day. With help from his kinsmen, his fellow convel and men he hired from the village y Bala, he had finished it just two months before he had to leave for three rivers. She was filled with sadness at the thought of how very little time they had spent together in the crannog...

Now the world was waking all too early this morning, and this on a day when Briga would have been happy to just lie warm in her bed for hours.

Off in the distance, toward the village was the home of Conall's father's people, the Ordovices. Briga heard the faraway sounds of barking dogs. The two dogs that were her sleeping companions woke, jumped down from the sleeping platform, and pushed past the woven reed covering that hung in the doorway of the dwelling's entrance.

"The world wakes my little warrior all too early this morning!" Touching her stomach, Briga groaned her displeasure as she pulled a cover over her shoulders and followed the dogs out of the bed and past the door covering that separated her from the world outside.

Off in the distance in the direction of the village, she again heard the sound of barking dogs, drifting down the lake—carried, it seemed, on the early-morning mist that floated just above the water. Both dogs heard it too and stopped, looking toward the village and back to Briga. Speaking to the two dogs, she said, "Yes, this should not be happening this early in the morning." Soon the barking dogs were joined by the voices of men; as the dogs barked, she could hear the shouting of voices of angry men.

Something was very, very wrong.

Chapter Twenty-One

Briga dressed as quickly as possible, her heart pounding as she thought, "Is it Conall? Has he returned?" She pushed out of her mind the other possibility, as she did not want the thought to enter the stream of creation; she would not voice or think of what really pulled at her heart and her throat: had something happened to Conall?

Dressed, she once again pushed past the door covering and shouted loudly and impatiently, "Gealach and Grian, come, dogs, come!"

Without waiting for the dogs, she moved to the paddock gate that held the five cattle that she kept on the crannog at night. Two of the cows had given birth late, and the young calves wanted to feed now, but Briga was in no mood to wait. She reached for the long willow switch that leaned against the gate and cracked it hard on the upper rail of the fence.

"Now, girls, we must move now!"

Again she cracked the switch against the rail and yelled loudly, "Gealach and Grian, come!"

This time both of the dogs appeared at the walkway and quickly ran up and into the paddock, past the cattle and the calves. They began doing what herding dogs do best as they pushed the cattle out of the pen, past the gate, and down the narrow walkway to the shore.

Once the cattle had reached the shoreline, Briga whistled loudly and shouted, "Gealach and Grian, pasture, dogs, pasture!"

She knew the dogs would do the rest; they would move the cows and the two calves to the nearby meadow, and they would stay with them until Briga called them home, back to the safety of the crannog.

She headed for the village.

As she walked Briga smiled and remembered how upset Conall had been when she told him that the platform for the crannog had to be larger, "It will need a fenced paddock area and shelter for my cattle Conall."

Looking at her with complete bewilderment he had asked, "Cattle?"

Bubbling with happiness as she watched all the men and all the work that was being done on her new home she smiled broadly and said, "Yes Conall, cattle for milk, so that I might make cheese and for meat and good leather for footware, belts, harnesses and scabbards for my husbands blades. I want cattle like my mother had in Erin."

Conall looked at her in amazement and said, "We are the Ordovices and we raise sheep Briga, not cattle."

Conall had already learned, in the very short time that he had been married to Briga, that when her mind was made up there was no moving her away from her intended direction—like an arrow she would fly straight to her desired goal. He knew she would have cattle and smiling at her he once again asked, "Cattle?"

She replied without hesitation, "Yes Connall, five cows will do nicely."

The voices at the village became louder and her heart seemed to be pounding harder in response; the lump in her dry throat ached as she fought back her concern and her tears. What if something had happened to Conall? Tears filled her eyes as she prayed earnestly, "Danu, my mother, please, please let Conall return to me."

She followed the trail that winded its way from the lake through the trees, ferns, and lush shrubs that grew nearby. Everything seemed greener this morning, washed clean by last night's rain. Puddles reflected the early-morning sun that made its way past the trees, and everywhere the moss created a patch-work of greens and yellow that covered every rock and fallen tree. The earth smelled fresh, the air thick with the musky odor of life and the green, growing things around her. On most mornings Briga would have walked to the village content in the beauty that surrounded her, but not this morning.

Since she was walking as fast as she could, her breathing was becoming labored and her side started to hurt. It had been over six months since Conall and Briga had celebrated the fire festi-val of Samhain, and it was on that night that the mead and the passion had combined, and Briga had become pregnant. Her stomach was now clearly large enough with child that it some-times contracted and gave her pain with each hard-paced step she took; it wouldn't be long before she would be walking with her walking stick and the help of others.

The trail to the village hugged the north shore of the lake and the distance wasn't far from the peace and safety of Briga's crannog. Briga had often counted the thousand paces as she walked along the trail to the village, a distance of less than four furlongs, but today the distance could have been a hundred fur-longs, as time seemed to stand still.

By the time Briga reached the village, the shouting had stopped, as had the barking of the village dogs. As she came out of the trees and into the clearing that surrounded the walled village, she saw that the gate was wide open, and beyond the gate she could see the peo-ple of Conall's village clustered together in the center of the village.

Whatever the shouts had been earlier in the morning, the danger was not so great that the gates had been closed and the walls mounted by warriors; the village gates stood open and the walls empty. As Briga came through the gate, everyone turned to look at her, and it was at that moment that she saw the body lying on the ground.

She began to feel light-headed, and her knees grew weak. She stopped and could not move. She spoke only one word: "Conall?"

Several of the women left the crowd that had gathered around the body, and it was at that moment that Briga saw Gwendolyn. She sat on the ground beside the body, and she was wailing as she rocked Da'ire's head back and forth in her lap. It was only then that Briga realized that the body on the earth was Da'ire. Now she could see the wounds on him; his arms and face had been cut and pierced. He had no color in his face except ash-gray and the black and green of deep bruises. He was lying on his back, staring up at the sky with sunken, blackened eyes, his face a pain filled mask. He looked like a man who had been drained of all his blood. The sight of Da'ire's body and Gwendolyn's grief was too much for the pregnant Briga; her knees melted, and she collapsed to the ground. The women rushed to her, but she had crossed into the safety of the world beyond the light and the living; she was in the arms of the goddess and the arms of the men who carried her into the nearest roundhouse.

It was a burden Briga was too frail to bear.

Chapter Twenty-Two

Sitting on the edge of the sleeping platform was a man. He wore a hooded brown robe made of of very coarse, spun wool. The hood had been pushed back off his head, and in the light coming through the open doorway, one could make out that his long silver-white hair was pulled back into a single braid decorated with interwoven strands of thinly worked pure gold thread. He was bent at his shoulders and upper back, and he was very old, both in body and soul. He sat quietly, his two old and weathered hands gently holding the hand of Briga. He chanted softly, a fonn that he repeated over and over, as he looked at the young girl he knew was the wife of Conall.

After Briga collapsed, she had been carried into one of the roundhouses next to the common square that served as the open market in the growing season. She had been placed on one of the sleeping platforms by the men who had carried her from the commons. Several women from the village had followed the men and sat or stood quietly, watching over the young woman. The old man who now sat with her had entered the roundhouse and politely asked everyone to leave; without a sound, they'd all walked quickly away.

The old man had been in the village hours earlier, when Da'ire arrived, had fallen and lay dying from his wounds. The old man was a healer, a druid, but more importantly he was Caswallon ap Beli, the Ard Druid of Cymru. It was the same Caswallon who had met with Conall and the Cyngor, the council of elders, on the day Conall had been sent west to investigate the reports of raiders landing along the southern coast.

Caswallon had been sent to the village by Caradoc ap Bran, the Ard Righ of Cymru. Caradoc had ordered the reconnaissance that had taken Conall and the wolf-warriors to the coast. It had been two months, and Caswallon had been sent back to the village; Caradoc wanted answers concerning the invaders, and now the old druid had them, but no one would be happy with what Da'ire had managed to whisper to the druid just before he died.

There was concern etched into the deep wrinkles of Caswallon's face, but in his gray-blue eyes, there was tenderness. He looked at the young woman whose hand he held kindly, as if he were her father. He knew with certainty that her world was about to be changed forever. For months his dreams had been filled with deep foreboding and signs of death. Da'ire's dying words only confirmed what the old druid had seen; they were coming, and they were coming here, to this village, to these people.

The Romans with their Luti dogs were coming, and they would kill and steal everything; all the livestock and all the people would be taken back to their stout wooden vessels for transport. They were here for slaves, metals, food, and to make maps for the Romans.

Da'ire had managed to deliver the message that most of the wolf-warriors had died in an attempt to free the hostages. He had also told Caswallon that he had lost contact with Conall and did not know if he was alive or dead. Grasping tightly to the old druid's arm, Da'ire had spoken only a few words before he died: "They are coming, coming here...three rivers." There was no doubt whatsoever in Caswallon's mind that hundreds of Luti had landed on the coast of Cymru, and that they now moved inland toward this village and all the others that lay along their path.

He had to get back to Caradoc with the warning; the Ard Righ had to know, and there was no time to waste. Cruel, merciless death was moving in the land of Cymru, and the people would have to stop it, or it would destroy them all.

Tears came into Caswallon's eyes as he held the hand of the pregnant Briga, and the old words of teaching filled his heart with sorrow: "Woe unto those with child when war comes to the land." He knew it would be the women and the children who would suffer most when war was unleashed on the land. As the old man held her hand he wept silently.

Briga stirred and without opening her eyes, she spoke one word—

"Conall."

Chapter Twenty-Three

Silence surrounded her as she stood in the mist. To her left the mist swirled as if something or someone had passed through it. She thought, "That is not the direction I want to go. Something doesn't feel right." Briga did not know where she was, and she was agitated and a bit frightened. Her heart beat hard and fast as she tried to find her way through the heavy vapor.

Speaking nervously, she said, "What is this presence, and what place is this?"

Looking up she saw nothing but vaporous fog, sinisterly twisting and spiraling upward, so thick that it obscured everything. Into the mist she said loudly, "I cannot see the sun, the sky, or the clouds. Have I died? Danu, help me. I am lost."

She could not remember how she had come to be in this place.

She wanted to make her way back to the world of her people, but this place was so unfamiliar. What she could not yet understand was that this strange place was in her mind. Briga had not yet awakened, and she was lost, but not in the world of the living; she was still in that place found in between the world of the living and the world of spirit. Few ever enter into this place that separates the two worlds, but as cognizant and as aware as Briga was, she was on the outermost edge of the circle, and her mind was fully awake.

She stopped and listened, seeking some sign, some direction in which to move, a way to get home. In the mist she heard a rustling. A light breeze blew and the mist parted, revealing the leaves of an oak. "An oak tree!" she exclaimed. Briga moved rapidly toward the familiar sight of the patterned oak knots, branches, and gentle knoll, and the closer she came, the more she seemed to know this place.

She moved cautiously into what quickly became a grove of huge and ancient oaks. The mist had vanished, and the entire area was bathed in a golden light that filtered down through the leaves and bathed this world with warmth—warmth that seemed to want to ease her fears. She began to feel safer, but she was still consumed and surrounded by the cold, nagging worry that something was wrong; something had happened to Conall.

Inside her mind Briga had made the journey to the oak grove of her ancestors. She had often dreamed of this place, and upon waking she usually forgot most of what she had seen, but now her memories filled her, and she found her surroundings peaceful and soothing.

She knew that she now stood in the oak grove of her people.

The warm, golden light touched her bare arms and face. She looked up, but there was no sun, just the glow that seemed to come from every angle, and it warmed not only her flesh but also her spirit. Briga realized that it was light that radiated from the invisible Beloved Danu, whose life-force is everywhere...

"I'm afraid," she said loudly, "afraid that Conall will never come back."

Something brushed lightly against her cheek, like the soft touch of a parent brushing away the fears of a child, and in her mind she saw Conall walking in silence, very much alive and struggling to move forward in deep snow.

"Where is he, Danu?"

She didn't know if Conall would ever come back. Many warriors never returned from battle, and suddenly she remembered standing in the village. "Da'ire is dead, and Gwendolyn has been left alone." She began to cry. "Will my Conall suffer death too? Am I to be left alone in this world like Gwendolyn?"

A voice came into Briga's mind that did not enter by way of her ears. She was startled as she clearly heard a woman's voice say, "Do not fear. I am here with you." To Briga's amazement, it was her mother's voice, and suddenly Briga found herself standing in the oak grove near her crannog.

Before her was a tree she knew very well and visited often.

As she walked toward the tree, Briga knew it as the place her mother was buried; she knew it by the three knots that protruded at eye length—a perfect triangle. As she placed her lips on one of the knots, she whispered, "Spirits, gods, and goddesses, portal to the otherworld, *màthair*, please help me."

She stopped and just stared with a blank expression for a few seconds. She was hoping to be granted some sliver of inspiration and strength. One minute became an hour. Her thoughts tumbled and turned in her mind, like the wind thrashing the branches of the rowanberries whose thin trunks were part of the sacred landscape among the oaks.

She whispered Conall's name. "Conall, *is tu m' annsachd*."

Then, in a voice loud enough for all creation to hear, she shouted, "*Is tu m' annsachd*. Conall, thou art my best beloved."

Her mother's tree, whose roots went deep into the womb of the otherworld, did not respond. Briga stood paralyzed by depression and despair. In her heart she feared for Conall; if Da'ire was dead, was her beloved also dead? If the raiders were coming to y Bala, she would need to travel into the mountains, and if Conall returned, how would he find her? She wanted someone, something, to make the decision for her; should she stay or travel deep into the mountains with her clan? "How would Conall ever find me?" This was the moment of her greatest suffering—her darkest day, her *Cruaidhghleachd.* "Please, *màthair,* Danu, help me to know what to do."

As a woman in her clan, Briga was responsible for some of the village orphans, and now she was pregnant. As the child grew inside of her, she began to have fears. She had no mate; he was gone fighting battles. Her thoughts kept competing for space in her mind: "What if he never returns? What if he is dead? How long should I wait?"

Still no answer…

Finding another life mate would not be a problem for Briga; the truth was, there were many men who wanted her, but most of them were gone fighting, and the ones who were left were much older than she. She bit her lip as she mused. She was numbed by the thought of sharing the pleasure of her passions with a man she did not love.

She heard Mother Danu's voice as a soft whisper in the wind: "Remember the ancient legend of the Mo Anam Cara, the twin flames."

Briga remembered the teaching that when a soul comes into *y Daearen,* the earth, from the Hall of Creation, it comes here as a complete soul, possessing both female and male traits. It is taught that the soul must pass through through a protective barrier, a barrier provided by the good god and goddess. This barrier surrounds y Daearen and protects it from the lesser gods, which would destroy all created life.

Briga answered, whispering into the warm, gentle breeze, "As a soul enters this protective barrier, it is split in two. The female is ripped away from the male, and two separate human beings are born from the one soul. These two humans will begin a search, in an attempt to come back together, to become 'one flesh.' It is this search that drives us to look for love."

Briga and Conall, were this one soul—a Mo Anam Cara.

Many look to find a mate, a soul mate, their Mo Anam Cara. It is this coming together as man and woman that everyone seeks and very few find. Over many lifetimes people expand their wisdom and knowledge by living many soul-lives; most people try to seek a loved one they have lost in this life or in a prior life, and they will always be restless, empty, having a sense of loss, until they find the soul of the lost one in a new body-life. It is taught that there is only one person that can be your twin flame. The other half of one's soul is the one each of us seeks, your true Mo Anam Cara. We cannot rest until once again we are joined together, as one soul and one spirit. Only united can we find the peace and the total energy and strength we were birthed with at the very beginning of time. Joined together, we will once again have the infinite power of our Mother and Father.

Briga heard Danu's words pass in a soft whisper past her ear, "We are the children of light, the sons and daughters of the good god Daghda and the good goddess Danu."

Then Briga heard her mother's familiar soothing voice: "Do not be troubled, my daughter. Look to the ways of the goddess, which are reflected in every rock, every plant, every insect, every bird and animal, every child, woman, and man; her ways are contained in all things created and never ending. She is the forever fecund being, always fruitful and fertile, birthing life back to even those held in the bony, cold fingers of death's grip.

"She is like your womb, your center, which is full of mystery and hope, a living thing but internally hidden, like the child that you carry. She is immortal in her potency, and she weaves an element of herself within the mind and heart of all beings; that thread is woven in your mind and in the infant you carry and in Conall, and her utterance is *gràdhaich,* 'love.'

"*Gràdhaich* is energy, my beloved daughter, an immeasurable force—the original creation source, found at the center of all things. When the good god gave voice to that which cannot be uttered, creation exploded, the empty darkness was filled, and the One became many that we all shared existence with. Remember, my daughter, that at the very center of every heart is this force we call *gràdhaich*, and those who choose to follow the good god and goddess are touched directly by the Creator—the Creator and the created soul coexisting and sharing the same energy. There is no distance or measurement of time between them, as they are connected by a strand of pure love, unselfish and eternal, much like the umbilical cord between you and your child. They share everything the Creator experiences and everything we experience: every heartbeat, every breath, every choice we make, and the directions we take. The goddess who gives birth and the soul coexisting, coupled with her, are the One. There are footprints from the past left on the forest floor that move toward the present time, and once here, they point in the direction you will go into the future."

"Will Conall come back to me?" Briga hoarsely whispered.

Her mother's voice spoke soothingly as she said, "Remember your promise to meet at the cave of the talking falls—go to Pistyll Rhaeadr."

Suddenly the oak grove disappeared, and she was in darkness. She was not afraid. She felt safe, rested, and all she could think about was the love, the warm *ana gràdhaich*, that connected her to Conall and Conall to her. She felt like he was resting in her bed, but was she dreaming? She knew she was separated from Conall, but her mind went to him. She wanted his touch; she wanted to lie inside his arms, to be held by his muscular arms, and to be joined to him in the world of flesh—she wanted his protection.

As she lay in the darkness waiting for dawn, she groaned for his touch, ached for his smell, and yearned for his love. She longed for him to take her to the stars, as only he knew how to play her body like a skilled musical lover.

The baby inside her moved and squirmed. He seemed to wiggle with a fluttering that almost tickled, and then came a warm sensation to her inside. She held her left side and said the name of the man she loved.

"Conall…"

Two warm hands held her right hand, cupping it, squeezing it with gentle firmness, and a familiar voice far off in her mind spoke softly. "Briga, awaken. You are needed."

Briga opened her eyes, and to her amazement, the Ard Druid Caswallon sat at the side of her bed holding her hand. She said in bewilderment, "Great-grandfather, what are you doing here?"

⊣

Chapter Twenty-Four

aswallon smiled at his great-granddaughter's question, and he was happy she had returned to him and to the waking lands of Cymru. "I was sent by the Ard Righ Caradoc, to check if any news had returned concerning Conall and the wolf-warriors; to my sadness I arrived just in time to comfort Da'ire and speak the words that would open the oak doorway to his ancestor's grove.

"He died, and as I watched, you fainted and fell to the earth, my beloved child; I feared for you as well. You frightened this old man in a most terrible way."

Briga started to say something, but the old man placed his fingers gently on her lips. "You fainted," he said, "and I have sat here by your side waiting for your return. There is no word of Conall, my darling, and I want you to begin thinking of your safety and the safety of the child that grows in you. It won't be long until your son enters the world."

Briga's eyes welled up with tears.

Sitting up on the edge of the bed, she threw both of her arms around the old man's neck and buried her face in his chest and shoulder. She wept. She sobbed for Da'ire and for Gwendolyn, she shed tears for Conall and their child, and she cried for herself—but most of all, she wept for the great change she knew would be coming to all those she knew and loved. Briga moaned in deep grief for her world.

"Da'ire must be buried, and we must leave the village immediately!" Caswallon said. "I must go and prepare the people to leave y Bala, and we must attend to Da'ire and his widow." Looking at Briga, Caswallon leaned forward and kissed her on the forehead. "My beloved granddaughter, can you get up? Can you help me?"

"Yes, Grandfather, I can help," she replied as she returned a kiss to the old druid's weathered forehead. Caswallon helped Briga stand, and together they moved out of the hut and past the opening that served as a door, into the world beyond: a world that was about to change forever.

Without hesitation the body of Da'ire was prepared for his journey. Gwendolyn, Briga, and the elder women from the village washed him and anointed him with scented oils. As these women prepared his body, other women cut and sewed new clothes for him to wear, and the leatherworker Prydwen sewed new boots and the leather bag with a shoulder strap for Da'ire's journey. Other friends would fill the bag with food, flint and steel and silver coins.

When all was ready, the people gathered together, and so began the last journey of Da'ire. His body, clothed in new garments, was resting on two shields joined together and covered with freshly cut yew branches. The shields and Da'ire's body were raised up onto the shoulders of the men of the village and carried with great honor to the womb tomb, the gateway that would start Da'ire's journey onto the dwelling place of his ancestors. The men carried him to the entrance of the cave and there lowered his body to rest on the earth; they dared not enter the tomb, as only the women were allowed to carry his body through its opening.

The tomb had been cut into the hillside north of the village, and the opening faced the sunrise of the equinox. Leading the procession were Caswallon and Gwendolyn. The rest of the women would help Gwendolyn take her husband's body into the chamber within; it was even forbidden for the old druid Caswallon to enter the tomb. The cavern just inside was not the tomb, but a channel that led to the resting place for the body as it decomposed. Surrounded by the women of his life, Da'ire would be made ready and taken deep into the round, inner chamber, to the very heart the womb tomb itself.

Exactly one year and one day from the date of Da'ire's death, the women would return to the tomb, gather up his remains, and wrapping them in white linen and covering them with flowers, they would carry Da'ire to his final resting place in the oak grove.

The outer entrance reflected the outer shape of a woman's birth canal; the rounded shape of the inner chamber echoed the rounded form of a woman's pregnant stomach. Da'ire was taken to the Cave of the Pregnant Woman, her belly well rounded from a nearly complete pregnancy. The outer vertical rocks simulated her vulva and the opening the birth canal.

"You are looking at the entrance to a womb created of earth for the keeping of a human body for the length of one year." Caswallon spoke to Briga outside the tomb, as if to teach the young ones. "The rebirth occurs one year and one day later, when the remains are removed and buried in the sacred grove. Stand inside the narrow birth-canal entrance of the tomb, and look back out into the light—into the world. You are standing in the earth womb, looking out from the birth canal of the Earth Mother, past her opening and into the world beyond."

The women would normally have placed the body inside the womb on the night of the new moon, but they had no time to wait. They had to bury him today, as Caswallon had ordered that the village be abandoned before the arrival of the Luti. Next to the body, they placed Da'ire's sword, bow, his stone wrist guard, a few drinking beakers, and a stone image of a voluptuous female.

Then they placed quartz crystals outside the entrance. "There is nothing male about this structure," Caswallon said. "It is all female, and for thousands of years females have placed the bodies, maintained them, and removed them at the end of one year. One year from today, we will return here to prepare Da'ire's bones for burial at the oak planted by Gwendolyn and Da'ire at the grove of their ancestors."

As the women came out of the chamber, Gwendolyn approached Briga and took both her hands in hers. She spoke of Da'ire's last words to her, which concerned Conall. "Da'ire wanted you to know that Conall was alive at the village, and that he saw him leading a group of women and children away into the forest. He was sure your Conall got away safely."

The two women embraced, and as they both held tightly to each other, they wept, their tears of sorrow flooding freely out of their souls.

After Da'ire was buried, Caswallon wept silently with Briga, for he understood the horrors of war better than most; as a young man, he had fought with Cassivellaunus against the Romans and Julius Caesar. Caswallon knew what evil men did, and he had a great fear in his heart for his great-granddaughter.

After the burial they returned to the village to prepare to leave. Caswallon took Briga back to the hut where she had awakened, and there he spoke firmly to her. "Briga, you must go to the hill fortress at Caer y Twr. I will send my escort with you, and you must leave immediately. There is no time to waste. I want you and Conall's child safe and far away from this place."

Briga stopped crying and lifted her head to look into the concerned and watery eyes of her great-grandfather. She said, "I cannot leave."

The old man started to protest, but it was Briga's turn to lovingly place her fingers on his lips. "I must go to the waterfall of the còmhradh carragh, the talking rock. Conall will know to look for me there; if I go to the safety of Caer y Twr, he may not find me. I will leave for Còmhradh Carragh at first light tomorrow, I promise."

"Briga, my child, when did you, Conall, and the god and goddess conceive the child you carry?" The old man did not try to mask his concern when he asked her the question, the answer to which he already knew.

"Grandfather, it was the night of the great fire of Samhain."

In his most concerned ard druid voice, he said, "Child, the festival of Imbolc has come and gone, and it is almost Alban Eilir. You are too far along with child; you cannot go to the *Còmhradh Carragh* by yourself." Caswallon tried to convince her, but in the end no words of logic or spells of magic would change Briga's mind.

She had made a promise to Conall, and she was stubborn enough to keep that promise. She would wait for him at Còmhradh Carragh.

The old man knew all too well that in Briga flowed the blood of both his wife, his daughter, and his granddaughter, Briga's mother.

"All right, Briga. I can see I am not going to win this fight, so I will support you in your—"

Before he could say another word to Briga, the ard druid stiffened his spine and suddenly sat straighter. He turned his head, as if hearing another voice. His eyes seemed to focus on something that wasn't there. With sternness and authority, he placed his trembling hands on her belly and spoke in a troubled voice.

"The futures of our people are concealed in you—listen to the voice you heard at your mother's tree, the soothing voice of loving words, and the pure *gràdhaich*...the force at the center. We are one. Our communal memory is bound to this child you carry, my beloved Briga. Even amid the bitter grief he will drink, he will walk with Danu. Do not limit him, tangled by your love and confined by your fears for him. His fate is not your doing. Allow him to reside in Danu, give him back to her, and allow him to fulfill our shared memory, so that our future might live on."

The Ard Druid Caswallon, finished with the prophecy and went limp, his chin coming to rest on his chest, and for a moment there was a deep silence that surrounded Briga like the shell of a bird's egg.

Then the old man stirred, looked about the room, and upon recovering, said, "You will take my four bodyguards, trained at the House of Scathach, and you will take a midwife; in this you have no choice. I have already told the people here to leave and go into the mountains of the Cambrian, and I have sent messengers out to the four kingdoms. Word has gone to Caradoc. I have sent for Conall's uncle Caratacus to come down out of the north. We will raise an army, but it will take time; so until we do, my beloved child, we will have to disappear and melt into the woodlands and mountains of Cymru."

Standing beside the old man, Briga saw that he looked older and more bent over than before, as if a great weight had been placed on his shoulders, and she became worried for her grandfather. "I cannot take your bodyguards; you will be defenseless," she said.

Caswallon roared with laughter as he said, "My darling child, this body may be old, but I still have teeth and claws. Danu will be with me, and besides, I will simply shapeshift and walk back to Caradoc as a mouse. The Luti will not even see me; it is you and Conall's child they will seek with blood vengeance. You must be kept safe, and you must leave for the *Còmhradh Carragh* immediately without delay—not in the morning. Will you do that, Briga, for an old man who loves you very much?"

Once again she threw her arms around the old man's neck, giving him a huge smile and looking into his worried eyes. "Yes," she said, "I will be obedient and leave immediately, as you wish."

"Good. Let's go and get you ready to leave, my favorite great-granddaughter."

Briga smiled and whispered into the old man's ear, "I am your only great-granddaughter."

Without another word the old man stood up and said, "*Cymru am byth!*"

Briga also stood and reached out for the old man's hand, repeating his words. "*Cymru am byth!*"

Holding hands, they walked together out of the roundhouse and into a world that would never be the same.

Chapter Twenty-Five

From within the cool, quiet darkness of the roundhouse, Caswallon pushed past the heavy, coarsely woven blanket that hung in the entryway of the dwelling. Briga followed him into the subdued sunlight of a day that held no promise of ending well. All around her the village was filled with confusion; wagons and carts were being loaded by families, while children and dogs moved in slow motion, trying to make sense of what the adults wanted from them. All were engaged in the serious business of hastily leaving their homes.

Just outside the door of the roundhouse stood four exceptionally large and well-armed men—the bodyguards of Caswallon. Caswallon approached an older woman who stood off a short distance from the doorway. Briga remained standing at the doorway, stunned as she watched the disordered movements of people packing to flee their homes before the Luti arrived.

Caswallon spoke quietly to the woman, and as she looked toward Briga, she smiled and nodded her head yes. Without a word she quickly walked away and disappeared out of view of the roundhouse door. Briga knew her; she was Toiréasa, one of the midwives of the village, and Briga knew that when she returned, she would be carrying her birthing bag, and it would contain everything she would need to help Briga deliver the child.

In haste the old druid walked over to the four warriors and began giving them instructions. There was a short exchange, a disagreement between a blond-haired man, the largest of the four, and Caswallon, but it soon ended as all the men looked over at Briga, and the tall man with wild blond hair nodded his head yes and spoke. Briga could read his lips easily as they formed the words, "Yes, my Ard Druid."

Caswallon turned and walked back to Briga with the four men following. Once they reached her, the four quickly moved to surround her, as it was now their intent to protect the young woman. Briga knew that from this moment until Caswallon released them, they would guard her even with their very lives. Caswallon looked at Briga and back at the exceptionally large, wild-haired warrior. Smiling, Caswallon said, "Briga, this is Cuar, and the one standing on his right is his brother Cet. They will go with you to the Còmhradh Carragh, the talking waterfalls and watch over you and the child until Conall returns. Cuar does not want to leave this old druid; he thinks I am too old to wander the hills of Cymru by myself. I have told Cuar of the importance of the child you carry, and he has reluctantly agreed to let me travel alone. He has agreed to protect you and the future that rests within your womb."

Briga looked at the two men whom she had never seen before and realized that indeed they looked like brothers. Cet was a head shorter, but both men had masses of wild blond hair and eyes the color of the cold, deep, gray waters of the Hebrides Sea off the Isle of Skye, the place of their birth. Both men were heavily armed and carried the small yew bow favored by the hunters of Cymru. Quivers of arrows, also made of yew, bristled at their left sides, and covering their backs were notched, oval shields made of limewood and covered with leather. Long and short swords hung at their belts, and in their right hands, they each held an eight-foot spear made with an oak shaft and tipped with a dreadfully large, sharp, and pointed hewing blade. All four of the men possessed the blades, shields, and spears, but only the two brothers carried the yew bows.

While Briga studied the men, Caswallon had again walked away and was now talking to a man who Briga knew was the elder and leader of this village; he too looked toward Briga, nodded yes, and quickly walked away.

In what seemed like a very short time, Briga found herself at the center of four large warriors, the midwife Toiréasa, her grand-father Caswallon, a dozen men, another woman, and one young boy, all carrying bundles and bags packed for traveling. The men, women, and the boy had followed the village elder back to the roundhouse that had become the meeting place for those who would stay to watch over Briga. Briga smiled at the young boy with long, curly, black hair who came to stand next to Caswallon. She recognized that he was Conall's youngest cousin, Odhran; it made her happy to know he would be going with her to the talking falls, and that they both would be waiting at Còmhradh Carragh for Conall's return.

The old druid took the hand of Odhran and walked with him over to Briga. He placed her hand inside the young boy's hand, and encasing both their hands with both of his, he spoke loudly, as the ard righ, for all to hear.

"This man of the house of Conall will now protect and watch over you until the return of Conall. He will care for you until your husband returns, and he will follow all your commands without question."

The young Odhran smiled from ear to ear at the honor the old druid was giving him, and still holding Briga's hand, the young boy knelt down on his right knee while looking into Briga's eyes. He then spoke his first words as a man.

"I am yours to command, My Lady Briga."

With deep affection Briga reached down with her left hand and took the boy's right arm, bringing him to his feet once again. She smiled at the boy who was now a young man and said, "I accept you as my guardian and my champion until the return of my husband."

The young boy seemed to grow taller as his face beamed with pride.

Caswallon turned to the crowd that had gathered and commanded that everyone leave the village before dark. He turned to Briga and placed his forehead against hers, gently holding her head with both of his timeworn, callused hands. In his kindest great-grandfather voice, he said, "My beloved, you will now go with these people to your home. Gather up your things and leave for the safety of Còmhradh Carragh. I must leave immediately to let the Ard Righ Caradoc know that I have sent out runners to call together the men and women of Cymru to battle against the Luti."

The old man continued speaking to her. "Messengers have been sent west to the island of Ynys Mon to Conall's uncle Caratacus, asking that he bring his light horse calvary from the druid hilltop fortress of Caer y Twr as soon as possible." Briga noticed he was looking at her as he talked, but his eyes had a faraway look, almost as if he were looking beyond her. "I must leave you now."

The Ard Druid's words softened even more, and they trembled slightly as he spoke to her again. "Briga, my child, you must not take any chances, and you must not do anything foolish that would harm you or the child." The old man reached out for the young woman with child and embraced her firmly, almost desperately, surrounding her in his arms; he placed his left cheek on her right cheek and whispered into her ear.

"Briga, I will be with you soon. I promise. Know this and believe it with all your heart, but also know that your world will change, that everything you know will disappear, and you will be in a world you have never imagined. I tell you this because you must do everything you can to stay alive, and you must do everything possible to keep the son of Conall alive. This man-child you carry is the future hope of all of Cymru and of the people of Erin and Alba too; he must stay alive as you must stay alive, no matter what happens. And know this, my child: Conall will return to both of you." Briga felt the warm, wet tears from the old man on her cheek, and her tears joined his.

"Grandfather." She wept softly.

The old man pulled away from her, and as he looked deeply into her eyes, he said, "Good-bye, my great-granddaughter." Without another word or without looking back, he walked out of the village gates.

Briga stood silently with her head bowed, softly weeping, knowing deep inside her soul that she would never again see the old man she loved.

Chapter Twenty-Six

It did not take Cuar long to follow Caswallon's orders to get Briga out of the village to the safety of Còmhradh Carragh. Cuar and two of his warriors led the way as the group moved along the trail back to the crannog. Briga walked behind them with Toiréasa on her left side and Odhran on her right. Cuar had given Odhran a bronze thrusting sword with two entangled dragons arising from the handle's end, and he proudly wore it at his side as he walked beside Briga. Behind them walked the other villagers who had been asked to help Briga, and behind them all, walking at some distance and acting as the rear guard, was Cet.

From time to time, the two warriors who walked with Cuar left the group and moved in a rapid, loping run down the trail to scout ahead of the group, only to return to walk again with Cuar. This was the order and manner of travel, and it would remain that way as they traveled from the crannog through the forest, up the slope to the north of the lake, and down into the river ravine that sheltered Còmhradh Carragh.

As they approached the lake house, Briga began calling for Gealach and Grian. Earlier in the morning, she had sent the dogs and the cattle off into the meadow that was a short distance from the lake. It was not long before a puzzled Gealach ran from the woods to the trail and stood with hesitation at its edge, eyeing Briga and her party of travelers. The dog knew it was too early to return the cattle to the crannog for the night, and to find Briga in the company of so many was unusual. She sat at the edge of the trail, ears slightly back, her tail tucked beneath her as she kept her gaze fixed on the large blond man who stepped aside to let Briga walk toward her.

"Good girl. That's my Gealach." Kneeling down to face the dog, Briga began stroking Gealach's head and ears, and soon the dog was standing on all fours, tail wagging, relaxed and happy to see Briga.

"Gealach, fetch home Grian. Fetch home the cattle, Gealach. Home, Gealach, bring Grian and the cattle home." Without another word from Briga, Gealach turned and disappeared into the woods. In the distance she heard the barking of her two dogs, and Briga knew that in a very short time, the dogs and the cattle would be coming home to the crannog.

As the dog disappeared into the woods, Cuar moved up to stand beside Briga. "What are you doing?"

"I am calling in my dogs and my cattle; they will be going with us to the meadows at Còmhradh Carragh." That was the answer that Cuar did not want to hear.

"No! That is impossible, Briga," Cuar sternly replied. "They will not be going with us; they will slow us down, and they will leave a trail to follow that even a blind Luti would be able to find. No, Briga, they will not be coming."

At the beginning of any intense situation in which a group of people comes together, there is a single event that will determine for everyone present who is in charge, and this was Cuar's moment. As Cuar stood on the trail blocking the way back to the crannog, he never saw what was coming next; without a word, Briga stepped in close to the man who towered over her. Her body was almost touching him, and he could smell the sweet flower-like fragrance of her hair. He was looking down into her green eyes when he was suddenly surprised by the sharp prick of a knife blade against his right inner groin—at the place where with one cut, thrusting quickly into the artery, a man would face certain death as he bled out.

In Briga's left hand was a small, black-handled knife with a five-inch double-edged blade that was very sharp; the point of that blade was now firmly held against Cuar's inner thigh. She had placed her right hand on the left breast of his well-muscled chest, as any attempt by Cuar to defend himself would first be communicated through the movement of his chest muscles, which would be a signal in plenty of time for Briga to thrust her blade deep into the warrior's thigh. "Do not move, Cuar," came the stern words from the young woman with sweet-smelling hair and beautiful green eyes.

"Cuar, my grandfather has asked I let you take me to Còmhradh Carragh, and I will honor him, but you will understand this now: I will not follow you. I am the wife of Conall Cearnach and the great-granddaughter of the Ard Druid of Cymru, and you, Cuar, will follow my orders. I do not know you, and I will never follow a man I do not know and who has not proven himself to me."

Cuar stood before the young woman silently as she continued. "We will be taking the cattle and my dogs, as I will not leave them to be slaughtered by the Luti. We will gather up anyone we see along the way, and we will help anyone in need. We will provide for and protect any of the people of Cymru we happen upon as we make our way to Còmhradh Carragh, and we will hunt and kill Luti whenever we get the chance. Do I make myself clear, Cuar?"

Cuar's concerned frown grew into a deep, full smile as he looked into the eyes of the beautiful young woman who held him at knifepoint and said, "Your Conall is a very lucky man to have such a warrior for his woman; I will follow you, as will my brother and the men with me, and I will make sure your orders are carried out, My Lady Briga."

Cuar no longer felt the knifepoint at his groin, and he stepped back and knelt down on his right knee. Bending his head toward the ground, he exposed the back of his neck to Briga and said, "I will serve you, my lady, without question, even unto death."

With this demonstration of obedience from Cuar, before all those who had come with them from the village, there would be no remaining doubt as to who was going to be in charge. He completed his demonstration of obedience by speaking an oath from the ancient code of the warriors of Cymru, loud enough for all to hear: "Never is a man so great and as strong as when he kneels before a woman in obedience!"

Placing her right hand on the wild mass of yellow hair on his head, Briga simply said, "Rise, Cuar, and protect us."

Without hesitation or another word, Cuar rose to his feet, and the group moved rapidly on to the crannog. Briga, with the help of Toiréasa and Odhran, went inside the roundhouse and gathered up the things she would take, including her linen bags of prepared herbs and medicines, and most important of all, the leather bag that had been her mother's healing bag. The bag was marked with three distinct dots forming an equilateral triangle, with one dot at the bottom of the bag and two toward the top. This was the sign of Danu, and anyone who saw the three dots on the bag or the three dots tattooed on Briga's left hand would know she was a healer. She took clothing and her blankets from the bed, and behind the bed she sought and found the small doll that she slept with when Conall was gone.

Unknown to Conall, every time Briga had cut some of his hair, she had saved it, and it was Conall's hair that was the stuffing for the doll; his hair still held the aroma of his body, and she cherished and found comfort in his manly fragrance. She placed the doll deep in her mother's healing bag for safety.

Taking a last look around the house that Conall had built for her, she paused and asked softly for Danu to watch over their home. Turning to Toiréasa and Odhran, she simply said, "It's time to go." Tears formed in her eyes as she moved toward the covered doorway, and they began to roll gently down her cheeks to her chin as she stepped through the opening. Wiping them away with her hands, she looked at Toiréasa and said, "I must not cry. Conall will be back soon, and he will come for me."

She felt a small pain buried in her heart that seemed to grow sharper as she thought of Conall, and she wondered if she would ever be held in his arms or see the crannog again. Under her breath, so as not to be heard by the others, she prayed softly to the goddess for the safety of Conall, her child, and herself, and for their return home.

Odhran held back the door covering, and Briga and Toiréasa stepped out of the roundhouse. Standing just outside the door were two of Cuar's warriors. Cuar and his brother Cet stood guard at the beginning of the bridge that led to Briga's crannog.

Looking past Cuar, Briga saw that the dogs and the cattle had returned. It was raining again, which made walking and herding difficult. She also saw that their party had been joined by two more people from the village: an older man with gray hair who stood very straight and tall, and a strikingly beautiful girl with short, jet-black hair that had been spiked upright and tipped white with lime to evoke protection from Epona, the horse goddess. Both the man and the young woman stood holding the reins of four horses that had been packed heavy with food, tools, blankets, and supplies for their journey; the elders of the village had given the band of travelers the heavily laden horses as ordered by Caswallon.

As Briga came closer, she realized that the young woman was Etaoin, the sixteen-year-old sister of Gwendolyn, Da'ire's wife. Etaoin had chosen to become a warrior; thus she was dressed for combat. She was tall, and over her shoulders she wore a cape closed at her neck by a gold penannular brooch. Given by her warrior mother, the brooch was one of the few prized possessions she cherished; it was comprised of filigree inlaid with gold, silver, copper, amber, and glass colored deep red.

The cape only covered one shoulder and was open in the front; one could easily see how very well this young woman was muscled, and it was also apparent that she wore binding that flattened her breasts. A leather harness woven into braided strands covered both her shoulders down past her waist, much like suspenders, and to these straps were woven three tight-fitting belts that formed thick bands of braided leather, covering her hips, her stomach, and her flattened breasts.

Etaoin wore leather leggings and thick leather boots, and at her waist she carried a Roman gladius, a gift from her grandfather. He had taken the gladius from a dead Roman soldier many years ago, at the time of Caesar's invasion of Gaul. She concealed several other short blades on her person also, and she carried the same short Cymru bow that Cuar and his brother carried. She wore thick leather armguards on both her arms that covered them from her wrists almost to her elbows—every place that skin was visible was painted; blue woad covered her body in signs of protection and symbols of magic and strength, and her arms, legs, and face were covered with tattoos.

Briga looked at both the gray-haired man and Etaoin, smiling at them as she reached the end of the walkway bridge that stretched from the crannog to the shore at the edge of the lake. Both the man and the young woman smiled back. The man said loudly, "At your service, my lady."

As Briga reached Cuar, she said, "Let's go. I want us to be far into the woods before dark."

Cuar was relieved to get moving into the cover of the forest, and he smiled as he said, "As you wish, my lady." Turning to everyone else, he gave a great shout, commanding everyone to follow Briga into the woods. Etaoin handed her horses over to two of the young men who had come along; she wanted instead to help Cet as the rear guardsman. She swept the trail with a bundle of branches after people and animals had proceeded ahead, trying to hide their presence as best she could. Etaoin was clever in many ways, and she was an excellent hunter.

Chapter Twenty-Seven

oving from the crannog to the safety of the talking falls at Pistyll Rhaeadr took a full three and a half days, instead of the usual half day. Their party had grown in number along the way; on the second day, they had found a group of women and children hiding in the woods north of the lake. They had been hiding there since Conall and the wolf-warriors of Cymru had freed them from the Luti. They were thirsty, cold, and ravenously hungry. A couple of the children were bent over with raucous coughs and high fevers. Briga had attended to them and wrapped them in fur blankets. She was desperate to have news of Conall, but at first the women and children were too frightened to speak of the events that had caused them to flee into the mountains. Fear closed their memories and their tongues.

On the journey Cuar and his warriors had led the way under Briga's directions. The rest of the group from the village had walked in a loose line of pairs and small groups; everyone helped one another along the journey to the talking falls. They had trudged on, some limping, while others seemed to trip over their own shadows. Toward the rear of the party walked Meilyr and a group of men from the village, who helped him with the packhorses.

Briga watched as Etaoin appeared and began walking with Meilyr; unlike the others, they were in high spirits. Meilyr could be heard occasionally singing softly to the horses as he and Etaoin walked along the forest floor together, and Etaoin was often heard laughing as Meilyr shared stories with the young girl. The cattle moved at the very rear under the care of Gealach and Grian, along with the help of a couple of older men who had come along from the village. Cet was the group's shadow, often moving off into the woods on either side of the party; he seemed to be everywhere, watching and listening for any sign of the raiders.

Briga and her party would arrive at the waterfall late on the morning of the fourth day, totally exhausted and drenched from the rain. In the meantime Briga was anxious to hear all the details of the women and children's captivity. They all set to work to construct temporary shelter. Briga approached Cuar as he was talking to his two warriors, and placing her hand on his arm to get his attention, she asked, "Cuar, please take one of the cattle we brought and butcher it so we can feed all these people."

A strange look came over Cuar's face as he looked at her hand on his arm and back into the eyes of Briga—he had felt the sudden rush of her feminine energy when she touched him, and it had surprised him. Deep inside his spirit, he felt the very real energy that is generated by the connection of past-life souls that have reconnected. Looking at her differently, he said, "Yes, My Lady Briga," and giving orders to his two warriors, one of the cattle was prepared for the people's nourishment. That night the group rested and feasted along the trail that was just above the pool at Còmhradh Carraghs.

Cuar, Briga, and their whole camp listened as the wandering party told of the cruelty of the Luti raiders, going into as much detail as they remembered. They told how the wolf-warriors had harassed the raiders for seven days, and how the men of Cymru had attacked the camp.

Cuar asked Fflur, a small young woman with long, braided, brunette hair, if she had seen any of the wolf-warriors. Briga bit her inner lip until it bled, and she waited, almost breathless, for the young girl to speak. Fflur's answer caused Briga's heart to race and sent her to thinking of her Conall and the child inside her; she immediately began praying words of protection to the goddess for Conall and all of his convel. The young girl recalled for the group what she remembered of the day of terror. Good men had died that day helping her and the others escape. Dread splintered her emotions as Briga thought of Conall and the other warriors from the village.

Fflur told how three warriors of Cymru had freed them after attacking the evil raiders that had killed her mother and father. Those with her ran to the trees for safety and watched from the dark covering of the forest. "Many Luti warriors surrounded your warriors of Cymru, and the women and children with them." The young girl's eyes filled with tears as she told the story of how the warriors and several of the women who had been freed fought bravely, killing many of the raiders; but in the end, there were too many of the bad men, and they killed everyone: the children, the women, and the wolf-warriors. "Your men died with great honor, and I will always admire and remember their valor."

An older woman from Fflur's party chimed in, as if she heard the pain crying out in Briga's chest. "The last warrior to fall was a massive man, easily two heads above everyone else. His hair was as black as a raven and spiked high on his head and tipped white with lime. He was fierce, fighting like an animal in a rage, but very controlled in his movements and intent. He killed many of the raiders before they finally backed away and brought him down at a distance with arrows."

Briga knew from the woman's description that the man was not Conall. Her heart seemed to take wing and soar in happiness, but almost immediately a wave of guilt washed over her as she realized she was receiving the news joyfully. As if to distract her, the older man who had brought the horses with Etaoin said, "Do'nal, the man's name is Do'nal; he is my younger brother, and it makes me pleased to hear that he died with honor."

The brother of Do'nal had introduced himself to Briga on the morning of the first day of travel, more as a formality than out of necessity, as there really wasn't any introduction necessary. Briga knew the man from the village, where he visited often and entertained at gatherings before the elders and chieftain of the village. He was Meilyr ap' Pwyll, a druid and a bard, and Caswallon had asked him to journey with Briga; unknown to Briga, Caswallon had left a number of instructions and orders concerning her, and he had left them specifically with Meilyr. As the ard druid of Cymru, he knew Meilyr would carry them all out without question.

Meilyr was to be Briga's druid, and as a bard he would entertain the group by spinning stories, singing songs, and offering words of insight. His name, Meilyr ap' Pwyll, roughly meant "man of iron," "son of wisdom," and whenever he sang at the banquet table of nobles, he never tired of introducing himself as the "iron man of wisdom."

As their first day ended and the darkness surrounded them, Briga sat alone before she retired to the shelter that had been prepared for her by Cuar's men. She held on to Caswallon's words that Conall would return to her, and she prayed for him and the protection of the people of Cymru. Toiréasa, her midwife, approached and said, "Briga, it is time, you must get some sleep." Briga rose and took Toiréasa's hand, and together they walked to her sleeping shelter.

The next morning as Meilyr and Fflur walked along the trail together to the river to get water, Fflur asked Meilyr, "Why do you wear the *treskele*?"

There is never a short answer for a druid who has a lot of time to talk, and today Meilyr had all day to answer the young girl. Smiling broadly, he began to speak as if teaching a room full of novice druids.

"I am a druid and a bard; there are female and male symbols, and the treskele is a symbol used for teaching. As you know, some symbols are created to be female, and some of them represent the three-part goddess: maid, mother, and the matronly elder lady of wisdom. The treskele is a tool for teaching, and it does not represent male or female, but instead is both, and as a teaching tool, it can be used to understand the male three-part nature of aging—the young lad, the man of strength and valor, and the elder, a man of wisdom—or the female nature of aging in moving from maid, to mother, and finally to the matronly elder lady of wisdom.

"Wisdom, the way of the goddess, is always viewed as feminine; all wisdom is seen as originating from the goddess. A man can only become 'wise' when he accepts this ideation and realizes that the center of his creation originates in the feminine goddess, represented at the center of the treskele by the triangle that represents the Cruthadair. She is there because she is at the center of all men and women. The triskele is a potent symbol for male energy combined with the energy of the good goddess. Only men who actively serve the goddess can be referred to as wise.

"The triskele is also a symbol for the battle that rages within each man: the battle to choose to become wise or to stay an immature male locked in a little boy's mind.

"The three-part spiral of the treskele represents the created nature of men—that nature that resulted when the One Soul, the Mo Anam Cara was ripped apart and divided into male and female. The male nature is in constant conflict with itself, a current of activity and potentially destructive forces that spirals around the center of the female nature in an attempt to reclaim the separated fullness of its original creation.

"It is this representation that reminds us as men that we are the animal, the human, and the divine. Female nature has also been separated from the original One Soul, but the female half is seen as having been created, from the very beginning, to be constant, nurturing, and life-giving, affirming in all things, directly connected to the Cruthadair, while male nature is seen to be in a constant struggle to find itself, moving restlessly in a three-part battle around itself, between the animal, the human, and the divine."

Fflur touched Meilyr on the arm, a tear in the corner of her eye as she asked, "Meilyr, are the lives we live predetermined by the gods? Did my family and friends have no choice but to die at the hands of the Luti?"

"I wear a treskele, and every morning when I look at it in the image of water, it helps as a reminder to place my day in its correct center; it reminds me that I have accepted the authority of the female nature of creation. I may be under her authority, but I have free will. I know I have the ability to choose to be animal, to be human, or to be divine in everything I do. It reminds me that it is within my ability to control the moment, no action I take is predetermined. In the time of a single heartbeat, all things are centered in myself, and I am responsible for the actions of my mouth, or my words, and my hand through an act that might give life or take life, giving birth or death to another."

Fflur took Meilyr's hand and asked, "Do the gods ever force us to commit acts that we do not want to do?"

"Every second of every minute, every heartbeat is mine to do with as I choose. I am the master of the choices I make. There is no god raising a battle-ax over me, just the feminine power of the goddess, which is greater than I am. There is no negative judgment. I am the sole author of my fate and of the life I will live—simply said I am.

"There are only consequences and results, good or bad, based on my choices. And when a choice is made, the results will bear good fruit or they will bear no fruit. There is never bad fruit: it is just fruitful, or it is not. An act that hurts or harms another has to be made good with replacement, restoration, and full restitution.

The responsibility of every act that occurs, in every heartbeat, is in the sole possession of the individual who creates the thought. Every act and action is our choice. The independent will to choose is a gift from the good god and goddess, and we received that gift at our very creation; from my first breath, I have been free."

Looking at the older man with admiration, she asked, "Is there more to our lives? Everywhere there seems to be destruction and death. Isn't there more to our lives, Meilyr?"

"We have been created to be gods and goddesses. It is our destiny to walk with the gods. We are producing our own soul energy, and that energy is produced and stored within the head. The goddess feeds our spirit, and she is found in our heart; she is the magic that powers our heart. The human body produces two independent forms of energy: one that is completely independent, found in the brain, and one that is located in the heart, that source of energy that is connected directly to the goddess. Each of us must feed our bodies, for the energy that sustains our flesh, blood, and bone comes from the bread we eat; our soul cannot grow unless it is nourished. The soul is complete, and we are complete in ourselves and independent from the actions and demands of the good god. We have been given 'awareness,' but as yet, we are not completely independent.

"We are still connected to the good goddess, as it is her energy that powers our heart. It is her spiritual being that has taken physical form by becoming the world and all living things. I live only because I am surrounded by the womb of the goddess. Space, the void that surrounds the earth, is not capable of supporting life as it exists in this creation. We have a soul—it is ours—but we have only energy to sustain the soul, and we have only a 'body' in the physical form, because we share energy with the good goddess.

"The triskele reminds me that I am mind, heart, and body. I know that the mind and soul, the heart and spirit, and the body are connected as one to the goddess. I am her servant, and she is my protector. I exist because she has given of herself so that I might live. I am a druid and a servant of the goddess Danu."

Looking at the older man, Fflur smiled—she was very happy and in her soul was the simple satisfaction that this man of wisdom was walking with her and taking the time to teach her.

That night after the fire had settled down and its light had diminished, Briga watched quietly from her blankets as Meilyr and Fflur walked together into the darkness of the adjoining forest. Briga did not think anything unusual about the older man and the younger woman walking off into the forest together; in her mind she was sure Meilyr wanted to know as much about his brother's last moments as possible, and he had sought out the young maid to hear more about his brother and to be comforted by her feminine energy.

Briga knew that given the gifts of the goddess, Meilyr and Fflur would give relief to each other in mind, spirit, and body. She thought it would be Fflur's honor and obligation to comfort the man whose brother had saved her life and the lives of all those with her. It wasn't until the first light of the next morning's ineffable light that the two, walking beside each other holding hands, returned to the warmth of the campfire.

Briga and her party had reached the waterfall that Conall and she had named the Còmhradh Carraghs, but to Briga's great disappointment, Conall was not there waiting for her arrival; in the depths of her heart, a dark seed of doubt and fear took root. The day of their arrival came with the early spring rains. The rains were cold, and their garments and all their belongings were soon drenched, causing discomfort and unease among the party. Only the warmth of sun or fire would return them to a place of warmth and peace.

Day after day the damp cold covered Briga with despair, and the gloomy gray skies only added to the speed with which the growing feelings of fear began to spread into her soul. Too many days had passed, and there was no word or sign of her Conall. Where was Conall, and what kept him from her? In her mind the question began to take form: Was he dead?

A sunny morning finally turned into several days of bright, warm, early spring days. Clothing and bedding were hung to dry, and everyone's spirits rose as the people took advantage of the healing power of the sun, basking on rocks around their camp-site. They had energy now, absorbed as a gift from the Sky Father, and strength to improve their shelters and gather firewood and food. The camp exploded into activity as everyone went about working to improve the situation at the temporary camp.

The busy work seemed to help Briga. The friendship grew be-tween her and Toiréasa as the older woman worked beside her, and in the evening, when they went back to Briga's sleeping shelter, Toiréasa became her personal attendant, brushing her hair and washing her feet and legs. Briga relished the gentle touch of the older woman, and she asked her to hold her until she fell asleep.

It was in the darkness of night that Briga was often overcome by her isolation from Conall. In the cold before dawn, when darkness ruled the world, she often wept in the fear that she was all alone.

The days turned into weeks, and soon the entire group began to settle into daily routines and rituals. These kept them preoc-cupied as they moved from building shelter structures to living collectively, and they even began to have leisure time, playing games during the day and telling stories and singing at night. Meilyr the bard was always a favorite in the evening, but it turned out that Odhran had a very pleasant singing voice as he often joined Meilyr in singing ballads of old kings and long-ago heroes.

Etaoin often hunted with the men, and she soon proved her-self to be very valuable, as it was her bow that provided most of the meat for Briga and her entourage. When not hunting for food, she and the men went away morning and night to scout for refugees and raiders. Often Etaoin asked Briga if she would mind if Odhran accompanied her scouting or hunting, as she desired to mentor him; it was becoming apparent that the souls of the two young adults were blooming together. Friendships and kindred spirits grow fast when faced with adversity; the druids taught, "Adversity is the spark that kindles the flame of an un-coiling victorious becoming."

When not participating in the daily exercise of chores, the men and women often huddled in little groups or roamed into the woods together.

Fflur and Meilyr soon became exceptionally secure with each other. They were fast becoming allies and would often be seen taking walks together into the nearby trees.

In addition, some of the men from the village paired up with the women they had found wandering in the forest. The children seemed relaxed as they played together; whatever evil they had experienced was successfully masked by their sense of security. They hid their fears away in the forest with Briga and her people.

Detached from the group, the four warriors led by Cuar seemed focused and intent on guarding the collection of what had become homeless refugees. One of the warriors paired up with Cet as he set out to scout. Cuar stayed with another warrior to guard the camp. The two brothers took turns, as neither really liked staying in the camp but rather preferred to go out hunting for refugees and Luti. Even when the clouds dropped cold rain for hours, they both would rather have taken to the woods; they both disliked just sitting and waiting. When not away from the camp, they would accompany each other along its outer perimeter; but their attention was always on Briga, and they never moved too far from her.

Toiréasa was always at Briga's side. One day Briga almost tripped over her and called her *cysgod*, meaning "shadow" in her mother tongue, and it stuck as a fond nickname. It was not long before the group began referring to Toiréasa as *cysgod y Briga*, or "in the shadow of Briga," as she never seemed to leave Briga's side.

Briga, for her part, kept busy and helped the women collect chickweed and herbs, tree branches, or coal chunks for the small cooking fires. As Cuar watched over Briga picking up chunks of coal, his thoughts turned inward, and he found himself thinking of her as a beautiful woman.

"The men from Rome and the Luti raiders were intent on exploiting Cymru for its coal, shale, copper, tin, and gold," Cuar said as he watched her move about. "Of these things, they want most of all the coal, which contains the magic that changes and strengthens metal. Having faced our superior Cymru blades in battle, the Romans sought to discover the secrets of our smiths. I watched as my father coked the coal that was required to make iron weapons and strong farming tools." The craft of working metal was a magical gift handed down to Cuar from his father and his father's father, and he knew that the true strength of a man in battle was found in the steel of his sword. Cuar often helped Briga carry the coal back to camp, and for short moments, with him at her side, she stopped worrying and smiled, even laughed, as he told her stories and shared time with her. Once they reached her dwelling, he set about building her fire for the evening meal. Cuar was now often seen eating the evening meal with Briga and Toiréasa as friendship grew between the lady and the warrior.

They had found a large vein of coal, and they began using it instead of wood. Coal would make a good hot fire with little light or smoke once it was burning; Cuar allowed Briga and the others to have small coal-warming and cooking fires, but he still watched them like a hawk for any sign of smoke.

Briga continued to help in gathering and preparing food. More spring greens were unfurling every day, and the chickweeds and the dandelions seemed to be everywhere. Plus, it was wet and warm enough for an abundance of mushrooms, if one knew where to look. Meat was not a problem, thanks to the cattle Briga had insisted on bringing and the wild game brought to them by the bow of Etaoin.

But it was becoming more complicated for Briga to move about now, as the child within her had grown bigger, and besides, she was retaining water. She often sensed the child pulsating with the goddess's heart of the universe. She was both anxious and excited, behind a veil of bewilderment.

Nevertheless, she pined inside with loneliness and missed Conall with all her being. But the growing child inside her kept her mind busy, as did her great-grandfather's last warning to her: "This man-child you carry is the *teachd*—the future hope of all of Cymru and the people of Erin and Alba too; he must stay alive." She had fragments of time to occasionally think about the old druid's words, and they troubled the soon-to-be mother.

What would make her son so special, she wondered? She no longer questioned whether it was a girl or a boy; her great-grandfather's word had been very clear: Briga was carrying Conall's son.

The celebration of Alban Eilir and the greening of spring had come and gone, but no sacred bonfire had been set to blaze to celebrate the goddess returning with her whirling energies and resurgent strength.

It was the goddess Danu, the great *màthair-beatha*, mother of all life, who caused the birthing of green plants from the earth following Imbolc, and it was proper to ritually celebrate her with great fires, meats, mead, song, and the joining together of men and women.

Cuar had insisted that no large night fires should be lit, and certainly not a bonfire that would light up the sky and be seen for miles. Briga had agreed, and so for the night of Alban Eilir, the proud people of Cymru gathered together wrapped in pelts and listened as the druid bard Meilyr ap' Pwyll told stories of past celebrations of the goddess greening the world.

Meilyr sang songs of bravery and valor and told stories of great triumphs of war. He even sang the song "Caswallon the Brave," and joined by Odhran's voice, they told a few stories just for Briga about the victories of Caswallon, her grandfather. As the night progressed, his songs and stories changed to warm words of love and the great burning passion and fountain of living flame that men and women feel for each other, and how the good god and goddess celebrate every time people embrace in the vast, living flame of love.

As Briga looked around at each face, she saw auras diffusing and blending into one another. She mused at this spectacle, as it became a sacred moment in her thoughts; she smiled and tingled with life, sensing a glimmer of hope.

As the night grew late, couples began to melt away for the privacy of the woodland darkness. The bard Meilyr and the young maiden Fflur disappeared together.

Even young Odhran took the hand of Etaoin, and together they walked off into the woods to commemorate and secure their bond of life.

That night Briga felt her loneliest—like an utterly emptied chalice, or a cold, empty cauldron. She shivered with tinges of cold despair, left alone with her guards from the Isle of Skye and her midwife, Toiréasa. Briga ached to be held by Conall, to feel his arms holding her in the security of his affection, to smell his aroma, and to taste his kisses.

Toiréasa rose from the ground and took Briga's hand, helping her up and off to bed. Lying in her blankets, Briga said to her midwife, "Please hold me tonight and sleep here with me, Toiréasa. I do not want to be alone on this night."

Toiréasa climbed under the blankets with Briga, and like a nestling bird, Briga was soon asleep in her arms; the older woman's hands rested on the pregnant stomach of the younger woman, and she massaged and held her as a mother would hold and comfort a child. Briga slept that night thinking of Conall.

The following days moved uneventfully in a routine that had become almost mundane. The nights were still cold, but the warm spring sun soon brought comfort and removed the chill of night. The edible greens became easier to procure because life among the sacred whirling energies of the talking falls was blooming with goodness. The water level in the river was increasing with the early spring rains and the run-off from melting snow, and the waterfall once again proved to have a booming, powerful voice.

Briga now found herself often standing on the beach at the pool below the talking falls, staring at the moving water and thinking of that time, as a very young maiden, when she had asked Conall to explore the falls and help her find the source of their voice.

She smiled as she thought of how they had stood naked, cold, and shivering after exploring the cave behind the falls, and she remembered how she had told Conall, "I am cold," and how he had held her in his arms to warm her—and she smiled as she remembered him holding her for a very long time.

It was that day, Briga remembered, when she had made up her mind that it would be Conall who would take her into the forest to lie among the oaks on the night of Beltane and guide her on the path to becoming a woman. She stood now at the edge of that same pool, holding a gold filigree brooch in her left hand, and said, "I miss you, Conall, my Mo Anam Cara. Please return to me." And as she threw the brooch far out into the pool, she said, "Mother Danu, please accept this gift that I cherish; it is the brooch my Conall gave me. Please, Danu, help my Conall to return to me and to his son." Her peaceful prayer was interrupted when Cuar and Toiréasa walked up behind her.

Cuar said without any hesitation or emotion, "Pardon me, my lady, but you must return to camp. Strangers have been taken by our patrols, and the news is not good."

Briga's first thought was of Conall, as was her first question. "Is there news of Conall?"

"No, my lady, there is no news of Conall, but I insist for your safety that you must return to the camp now. I will explain everything."

Without another word, Briga and Toiréasa followed Cuar back uphill and through the trees to the place that had become their new home. Nothing was said as they walked, but Briga had a tangled-up feeling of dread, and she feared the news that was soon to come. Her womb contracted, and she swore she felt the child kick as if in protest. Her stomach and groin area suddenly burned with blunt pins of pain.

Briga's hands held both sides of her abdomen as she tried to walk faster to keep up with the swiftly moving Cuar.

Now the pain grew even more intense, and she realized she had stopped walking; she recognized that floating sensation again, and she could not hear the world around her anymore. It was as if everything were increasingly blanketed in a haze.

Toiréasa was standing in front of her speaking, but Briga could not hear the words. She felt Toiréasa's hands holding her now as a great shadow swooped down on her.

She felt Toiréasa shake her, and this time she heard her voice say, "Cuar, stop! Help me!" But the blackness swept the world away, and Briga left them both. Wrapped in the arms of darkness, she found herself once again standing alone in the oak grove of her ancestors.

Chapter Twenty-Eight

he cold mist descended, and light whispers of rain fell. Then it started getting heavier, steadily drenching everything, including the old man wearing the hooded, heavy, brown wool robe of coarse weave; he was walking alone, following a trail on the wooded hillside, moving toward the rocky outcropping that he knew was at the top of the hill.

The old man's left hand was holding his hip, his fingers cutting into the muscle as if he were attempting to crush the pain; in his right hand, he held an oak staff that he used to help keep his balance as he fought his way up the hillside. He was limping and favoring his left leg; the cold and the wet had caused the old arrow wound in his left thigh to awaken with a vengeance. "How stupid of me to have come alone," he thought.

As if to answer, the heavy gray clouds squeezed the rain into a funnel of ice pellets. Driven by the wind, the cold, sharp pieces of ice struck his face, stinging it while turning his cheeks bright red. There was no escape from their bombardment. Soon his face was so cold, it was numb, and the chill seemed to be spreading into every part of his body. As he walked, he looked only at the ground at his feet. His head was now completely covered by the hood of his robe as he spoke.

"Might I see a rainbow soon, my mother goddess? This son of yours would be ever so grateful if the sun showed his face, as I know he is just waiting behind the clouds to stroke you and me with his warmth. Would it be too much to ask, my Danu, to change this sleet into sunshine? Your son Caswallon is tired and cold; it would be good to see the face of my Sky Father, the sun, and to feel his warmth on my face."

Caswallon smiled as he watched the clouds open slightly, letting through a bright beam of sunlight that seemed to declare, "I am here, and I have heard you."

After leaving Briga, Caswallon had moved steadily northwest toward the druid hilltop fortress of Caer y Twr, on the island of Ynys Mon. It had been his intention to return directly north to Caer Caradoc at Mynydd y Gaer, but he had decided to send runners north to the Ard Righ instead; he was going himself to warn his druid brothers and sisters on Ynys Mon.

He wanted the rest of the druids to know that the Luti had landed, and he wanted to make sure the sacred writings and books at Caer y Twr would be safe, even if they had to move the entire scriptorium across the Irish Sea to Tara.

Once he knew that the old knowledge would be safe, he would raise as many men and women under arms as possible and return for his great-granddaughter. At Briga's village he had sent word out to the four kingdoms to assemble for war, and now all he wanted to do was get to the island of Ynys Mon and return to Briga; he had to make sure she and the child she carried remained safe.

Caswallon now knew that the threat to the people of Cymru could be a volatile and violent invasion. He remembered how as a young man he had faced the Romans under the command of the general who would be known as Julius Caesar. Over fifty years ago, as a novice druid, Caswallon had fought with Cassivellaunus, the Ard Righ of the Catuvellauni, against the Romans.

As the old man limped along in the wet and cold, he seemed to bend forward at the waist, as if anchor stone hung around his neck. His mind returned to the time long ago when he was young and at the battle of the river crossing.

It was in the early autumn when the Romans had come at their barricades with an animal none of them had ever seen. It was a huge beast clothed in sheets of iron scales, and on its back was a tower full of Roman archers and slingers.

The sight of this monster lumbering down into the river, arrows and stones raining down from its back, was horrific enough, but when the creature easily crashed through the sharpened stakes that had been driven into the riverbank as a barricade, it was too much for all but the very bravest of the men and women of Briton; most of the defenders bolted for the protection of forest trees.

Caswallon had watched what had happened as if he were in a dream. The great beast had crossed the river, carrying Roman soldiers on its back. Two legions of Romans ready to cross the river followed the animal.

He knew what he had to do, and he yelled orders to those warriors standing near him. "Torches! We need fire!" He did not hesitate, and he ran yelling toward the great beast. "It must be turned—turned around!" he thought. Running with him were several men, naked, their bodies and faces heavily tattooed and painted in blue woad with circular designs and symbols.

Seeing Caswallon run at the Romans' beast brought courage to some of the warriors, and rapidly more men joined, some carrying torches. They all yelled and waved their swords and spears at the animal. A few threw their spears, and Caswallon watched as the spears and a few arrows bounced off the iron scales. "The torches! Take the torches to his face!" he shouted. "All flesh fears the strength of fire!"

Caswallon took the torch from the man standing next to him, and with a sword in one hand and the torch in the other, he ran toward the animal. Arrows and rocks rained down on the men with Caswallon, and many fell under the Romans' defense of the beast, but Caswallon stood his ground at the head of the great animal, blocking its advance.

The beast trumpeted loudly in protest and began swinging its massive head back and forth. Long, gleaming, white tusks, the tips covered with polished silver, swung within inches of his chest, and like a long arm, the animal's long snout reached out to grab at the druid; he fought off the serpent-like snout with his sword and stood his ground, shouting curses at the animal and the Romans. He was waving his torch in the animal's face when a Roman arrow struck him in his upper left hip; it glanced down the bone into his thigh, the arrowhead coming out just above the left knee.

The pain and the force of the arrow impact at such close range dropped him to the ground in front of the beast, but two of the naked warriors painted in woad rushed in to save their druid. Others joined them, and Caswallon was carried from the battle to the safety of the woods.

The Celts lost the riverbank that day as the elephant and the Romans flooded across the river, securing the ground that had been defended by the people of Danu.

As he walked in the cold and wet, the pain in his left hip was softened as he thought of his hatred for the Romans and the honor he had been given by Cassivellaunus later that autumn, when the Romans had finally sailed away from Briton. In a great ceremony at the hilltop fortress of Caer Caradoc, Cassivellaunus and all the lesser kings of Cymru, along with the druids of Ynys Mon, had honored the young druid for his bravery and for keeping to the old law code that said, "Honor the gods. Do no evil. In the face of attack and adversity, be brave." He had been given the purple robe of bravery and self-sacrifice by the Ard Druid of Tara as the warriors of Cymru and the bards of Ynys Mon sang the new songs of "Caswallon the Brave."

He smiled as he walked along the trail, and he mumbled to himself, "Caswallon the brave, my ass! I was so afraid facing that elephant, and when that arrow hit me, I wet myself." He chuckled as he said, "You couldn't see the piss because of all the blood." It would not be the last time the old man earned the purple robe, but it made for his best song, sung by the bards around the fires at the fortresses and villages of Cymru.

He had now managed, still limping, to move out of the trees; he had almost reached the top of the rock outcropping that capped the hilltop. It was midafternoon before he reached the top and looked down into the valley below, which lay north to south and was surrounded by low mountains, much like the one he stood on. A river snaked along the valley floor, and he knew he would have to follow it, heading north, and cross over the mountains to the next valley.

"Now that I'm walking alone, it seems to be much farther than I remembered," he said as he looked out at the valley. He had begun to seriously regret his decision to come alone, but he knew it was his *annsachd*, his greatest calling, to reach the island of Ynys Mon and warn the rest of his brothers and sisters at Caer y Twr.

He had also seen a vision of the future as he said his good-bye to Briga, and he knew with certainty that his immediate future was in that valley below and that he must face that future alone— looking into the shadows in the valley, he felt strongly that he might never again hold his great-granddaughter in this bodily life.

Far off, toward the south end of the valley, he could see smoke from several fires hugging the treetops. "I'll avoid those," he said out loud to himself.

The clouds had lifted to the west, and sunlight now streamed into the valley below. To Caswallon's delight, a large rainbow hung over the valley.

At heart the old druid was still a child, and even as an old man, he still marveled and delighted at the sight of the rainbow. As he stood looking at the beauty of the world his Danu had given him, he heard the words of the rhyme his mother had taught him many years ago, and thinking of her, he chanted the words, "Rainbows, colors bright and true, clear weather is ahead for you."

The overcast sky had darkened, and the clouds were swollen with moisture after crossing the ocean to the west. Light, misty rain had fallen for the last several hours of the old man's journey. A cold wind blew from the west, pushing the cold rain, whose icy fingers dripped down his neck to wet his back. As the storm clouds moved toward the east, the wind and rain pushed at his wet back, and combined with the cold, caused him pain—they did their work to get him moving off this craggy hilltop.

Caswallon knew the wind was letting him know the cloud cover would move east, and it would be clear and cold tonight. He knew he would have to get off the bare, exposed slope and into the tree cover before dark. Speaking out loud, he said, "I will be spending a very cold and miserable night under the open sky if I don't get to the cover of the trees below before dark."

Turning his face to the wind, he said, "I hear you, my old friend," and he started toward the valley below. The descent was steep and rocky. Everything was wet from the rain, and he had to watch his footing, as he feared he would slip with every step. Puddles lay in the hollows of the rocks, and Caswallon took the time to bend over and sip the water from a hole he found on a large one jutting out of the earth; the rock was covered in the rich tones of multicolored lichen and moss.

The water tasted of earth and was slightly bitter as it quenched his thirst. As he renewed his descent, he slipped on the wet, moss-covered rocks and fell, but thanks to the protective arms of Danu, he was not hurt—just embarrassed and happy that no one had seen his fall.

Even as old as he was, Caswallon still thought of himself as potent, and when in the company of beautiful young maidens, he would even think himself young; such is the mind of a man, even a man that is Ard Druid of Cymru.

He was forced to move more cautiously, and this concerned him, as the temperature was now dropping rapidly. As the temperature dropped, it became harder for him to think, and his balance seemed to be eddying away with his strength. He did not want to spend the night outside the cover of the forest trees. He pushed on; his mind journeyed into the memories of the past. This kept him warm as his body moved slowly, painfully down the steep rocky slope.

Chapter Twenty-Nine

He reached the trees shortly after sunset. The temperature had dropped sharply as the storm moved east. Under the cover of the oaks, very little light made its way to the ground. Daylight was receding fast as the dark swooped in to fill the void. The cold was enough to snap his bones in two, and the old man knew he was ill prepared for a long, frigid night. Caswallon had long lost the resiliency of his youth. He had packed a very small bag for his trip, as he wouldn't need much— not much more than a kit to make a fire, some dried fruit, dried meat, and some crushed barley cakes.

There would be no fire tonight or any night, since he'd seen the smoke in the valley and knew from Da'ire's dying words that the Luti were coming to take blood vengeance on the people of Cymru.

He had his heavy wool robe, but unless he could find a tree hollow or other small natural shelter soon, before darkness swallowed the world around him, he would be spending a nasty night cold and in pain. "Old men and cold ground really are not good bed friends," he said as he moved deeper into the woodland. "Oh, my blessed Danu, what I wouldn't give for a couple of warm maidens to lie with me this night."

His left hip and leg ached bone-deep, and he stopped to open his bag. Inside he had placed fresh-cut willow twigs snapped from a stream on the other side of the hill he'd just crossed. He had drunk from that stream as if he were an empty cavern that hadn't seen water for years, filling his waterskin, and while there he'd no-ticed the willow growing on the water's edge. He had cut a number of willow branch pieces about the length and thickness of his little finger.

One of these he now removed and began chewing on to re-move its outer bark and all of the soft inner bark next to the wood. The old druid removed two more twigs from the bag and stripped them of their bark also. Caswallon knew that inside the bark, the good goddess had placed the magic that would reduce his pain; it would also cool down the fever and reduce the swell-ing he had in his hip and leg.

"Thank you, Danu, for all your gifts," he said softly into the advancing darkness. Then he looked around and said to himself, "This is not good, and it's almost too dark to see."

Wanting to avoid a fall that would result in injury, the old man decided to bed for the night right where he was. He began to collect small twigs and place them under a carpet of moss, which would become a moisture barrier between him and the ground, both for extra comfort and warmth.

He sat down at the base of a massive oak tree; its roots formed a deep, cradle-like depression into which he huddled. Surrounded by the tree, he felt a profound sense of safety, as if securely pro-tected by the tree herself. He covered his feet and legs as best he could with his tunic and leaves and whatever ground debris he could find. He pulled his hood over his head and curled up like a hidden fawn amid the mossy arrangement.

Cold moved toward him in the hope of tormenting the old man, but exhaustion prevailed. The elderly man soon fell asleep.

Caswallon's sleep was filled with many dreams. One such dream was of his youth: a memory of his first Beltane and the older woman, a widow of the clan, who had taught him of the passageway to the ultimate paradise. He also dreamed of being strong and young again, of battles and brave men and the women he had known, strong in combat, soft and warm in love, but always his dreams seemed to return to a place he did not recognize.

Rocky cliffs surrounded a long, narrow inlet on a coastline of land that was covered with conifers; the cliffs reached down deep into the ocean, and in certain places they didn't touch the sea, but instead seemed to disappear into thick, swirling clouds of cold, grayish mist.

There were gentle slopes also, covered by conifer trees that stretched down to the ocean just above the high tide line. Very narrow beaches covered with gray cobbles and pebbles made a thin line between trees and water.

At times angry waves thrashed at the rocks, and salty mists covered the tall trees; the place seemed mysteriously gray and cold. His mind floated above the water and out over the land, but it was all strange and forbidding to him, and he knew it was a place foreign and far away. In his dreams he asked, "What is this place, Danu? Why have you shown it to me?"

As he watched the land below, he saw a great black wolf standing on a rock outcropping. Lying on the rock, at the foot of the wolf, was a large, dead, sea hawk, its head ripped off and one wing missing. The wolf raised its head high and howled defiantly, loud and long. Five times it howled, and then it looked right at Caswallon. "What is this?" the old man asked. "What does it mean?"

The wolf looked away to the valley beyond the trees, and Caswallon saw that a river emptied into the narrow ocean bay, its entrance into the bay almost hidden from those who might sail into the narrow waterway.

Following the river inland, he saw that ships lined the riverbank, and clusters of long, narrow, stone and timber houses stood in neat rows on both sides; smoke rose from the longhouses, and many strange people moved around them and the ships.

As he floated overhead, he saw ships being loaded and men-at-arms making their way onboard. Sails unfurled—tan-colored sails painted with great red sea hawks.

Then all became blurry.

Again the old druid asked the question, but this time he begged for an answer. "Mother Danu, please, what is this, and what does it mean? Why am I being shown this place?"

No answer came.

The old man seemed to float lower, down to the long, rectangular buildings built of logs, rock, and earth below him, and standing in front of one was the black wolf. Beside the wolf stood a boy, his hand resting on the wolf's head; the boy turned his head as if to look toward the wooden doorway of the house, then looked back again straight at the old man, as if he could see him floating overhead. The boy's lips formed words; he was speaking and looking directly at Caswallon, but Caswallon could not hear what he said.

To the old druid's surprise, the ancient and deeply carved wooden door opened, and there stood Briga. She walked over to the boy and put her arm around his shoulder. The black wolf was gone, but the boy and Briga stood together. The boy was talking and pointed up at him as if he saw the old man, and Briga looked up too, slowly shaking her head as if to signal no. It seemed that only the boy could see the soul of Caswallon floating above the village.

Suddenly pain filled the old man's left side, and the world he was seeing below disappeared. Again, sharp pain ripped through his body and his head, recurring over and over. The old druid opened his eyes just as another hard kick struck him in the side.

Standing over him was an angry man, yelling at him in words Caswallon did not understand. He kicked Caswallon again just as another man pushed the angry man aside.

Caswallon looked past the two men. Twenty or more armed men stood around him and next to the oak tree. The man now standing in front of him held an ax in one hand and a round shield in the other; on the shield was painted a red sea hawk.

Caswallon looked at the man and at the shield and smiled. He said to those close enough to hear, "Now I understand the dream, Mother Danu. Now I understand." Beyond the men, standing silently at the edge of the trees and watching, was a great black wolf.

Looking past the men and ignoring their words and kicks, the ard druid of Cymru spoke only to the wolf: "I will join you soon, my brother."

Chapter Thirty

The old man fixed his gray-blue eyes on the man with the shield who now stood above him, barking orders to the men standing around the tree. Caswallon knew by the man's tone and posturing that this was the leader of the party of raiders.

The man leaned in close to Caswallon and spoke again. The old man turned his face away, not out of fear, but because of the stench that came from the raider's long, full-faced beard and foul-smelling breath.

Turning his head back to face the man, his eyes burned with defiance and hatred. The old man said in his mother tongue, "You stink like pig shit, and every word you utter is an insult to creation. Your mother found you in a pile of pig shit. You go away before I hurt you."

The foul-smelling man did not understand the words Caswallon spoke, but he understood the anger and the hatred in the old man's voice and the look in his eyes. He began striking the old druid in the face with his fist, again and again. Caswallon did not turn his head to protect his face; instead, he looked straight at his tormentor, glaring at him as blood began pouring from his broken nose.

His face battered and bleeding, his mouth full of blood, the old man defiantly spit his blood into the raider's face and said, "You *twll tin*."

Caswallon hoped the man would become so filled with rage that he would kill him quickly, but another man pushed his tormentor aside, yelling at him as he pushed.

The man began to speak to him, and to Caswallon's surprise he understood what this man was saying. "Who you...where farms...villages?"

"I do not know. I am lost and confused. I am just an old man lost in the woods," was the answer from Caswallon. The man now in front of him barked out orders, and two of the raiders, including the man who had beat him, roughly grabbed at Caswallon and lifted him by his arms to his feet. As Caswallon now stood held by two men, the raider who had spoken to him reached out and pulled back his hood.

Caswallon's long braid fell out across his shoulder to his chest, and the intertwined fine gold thread caught the morning sun; the raider quickly recognized the gold and grasped the old man by his hair, pulling savagely and forcing him to look high up into the oak tree beside him. Pulling out a blade, the raider began sawing away at the old druid's braid until it had been cut from his head at the scalp.

Putting the braid in a leather bag at his side and replacing his blade, the raider said fiercely, growling, "You druid...you lie."

"I do not lie," he said mockingly to the raider. "I am old."

The raider again growled an order to those standing around the oak tree, and a third man joined in securely holding the old man. This man grabbed at Caswallon's right hand, and holding firmly to the wrist, he pulled the index finger straight and held it outstretched with his left hand, crushingly, viselike. The raider who spoke the words of the people of Cymru said, "Every lie to me...I cut one fingers. You lie."

Without another word the man again pulled the knife from his waist and sawed off Caswallon's index finger at the place it joined the hand. Blinding pain flooded the old man's senses, and his knees buckled, but he did not call out or scream.

Caswallon held firm as the Luti asked again, "Who you… where farms…villages?"

"I am just an old man lost in the woods," replied Caswallon.

The man holding on to the old man's bleeding hand took a filthy rag from a pouch at his side and wrapped it around the bleeding wound left after severing the index finger. This was done not out of any kindness, but only to improve his grip.

Grasping and pulling on the middle finger until it was straight, the man looked into Caswallon's eyes, sneered, and said simply, "You lie." Once again the Luti raider began cutting off one of the old man's fingers, but this time slowly, causing as much pain as possible.

The pain swept into Caswallon's mind. His soul burned, and the agony of his torment flooded into his heart. His spirit screamed out to the gods, and from his body he screamed out in anguish to the forest trees. In unimaginable pain the old man called out, "Danu, please forgive me!"

He would have fallen to the ground if not held upright. Once again he was asked the question, and once again his answer was, "I am just an old man lost in the woods." And once again the Luti cut and hacked away at another one of the old man's fingers, but he would not answer their questions.

The raider who spoke barked out orders, and from the woods Caswallon watched more men emerge, pushing and shoving three captives, two young girls and a man. The man had been badly beaten, his face swollen, cut, and blackened; he was no longer recognizable except for the wolf tattoo on his right upper arm, which identified him immediately as a convel, a wolf-warrior of Cymru.

Caswallon knew this had to be one of the warriors who had left with Conall, but he could not recognize which wolf-warrior was now before him; the man had been beaten beyond recognition. Coming very close to the old man's face and sneering, the Luti said mockingly, "Maybe you like pain, old man. How feel when lies...cut these ones?" The Luti raider pointed to the man and the two maidens and asked, "Druid...who you...where farms...where village?"

"I am just an old man lost in the woods," replied Caswallon.

The raider turned and angrily screamed out an order to the two men who held the beaten man. One of these men was holding a rope that ended in a noose around the neck of the convel— a noose that was intended to strangle its victim—and without a word the raider tightened the noose, harshly choking the wolf-warrior, cutting off his air until the man collapsed to his knees. The other man grabbed at the warrior's hair with both his hands, pulling at him savagely. He forced the convel to look high into the sky, his head pulled back to expose his neck. The raider who held the rope brought an ax out from under his cloak, and holding it in his right hand, he placed it against the throat of the convel.

Once more the Luti raider leaned in close to Caswallon. His foul breath struck at the old man like a fist as he asked, "One time last, druid. Who you...where farms...where village?"

Glaring at the man, Caswallon answered with all the hate and contempt he had for this man fused into the words and tone of his reply. "You *twll tin* son of *cachi*, I have told you everything I am going to tell you. I am just an old man lost in the woods!"

Again the Luti raider roared orders to his fellow raiders, and two more men joined the others holding the wolf-warrior on his knees. Working together, the four held him by his hair, his head forced back to even further expose his neck, and the two new raiders now began grabbing and twisting the man's arms, forcing them in a painful direction while a third man pushed at his shoulders, forcing the warrior to bend at the waist.

They held him down, bent and kneeling on the ground. The warrior of Cymru began to chant softly, and Caswallon knew he was singing his last fonn. As he chanted, he looked straight at Caswallon. His head held firmly by his hair, the convel of Cymru shouted out, "I am Bleddyn!" And before the Luti could stop him, he shouted, "*Cymru, Cymru am byth!*"

The first raider began hacking with an ax at the right side of his neck, near the shoulder. The call of the wolf-warrior was soon silenced as the four Luti held him, and the man with the ax kept hacking away at the neck and head until the head, under a shower of blood, fell to the forest floor. The old man watched as the white eyes of the convel writhed and stopped moving, appearing to have fixed their stare on him.

Tears filled the old druid's eyes; his human heart, the organ of his body that held the essence of the goddess, was ripped to pieces by the death of one of the children of Cymru. A brave man now lay on the forest floor, tossed aside by the Luti like unwanted trash.

Caswallon began to speak softly, murmuring words very low, not really loud enough to be heard. He watched as the black wolf that had been standing at the edge of the forest trees walked into the circle of men and past them to stand beside the old man; it was unseen by all of the Luti, but Caswallon saw him and knew him as a friend—a spirit companion that had walked with him all his life. Thinking to himself, he said, "Do you come to stand beside me now, my old friend, as I face my death?" The druid looked down at his old friend the wolf and said in a voice loud enough for all to hear, "Danu, I am ready!"

The Luti who spoke, turned back to the old man and said, "What you say, old man?"

"I am ready..." The old druid spoke very softly this time. "Come closer. I am ready to tell you everything you want to know, but I am very weak." Caswallon's Luti tormenter glared at him and said, "What say you, old man?" Repeating himself in soft, whispering words, the old man said, "Come near so I can tell you—tell you what you want to know." The Luti who stood in front of him drew closer and spoke again. "What, old man?" Caswallon once again said, "Closer, I am very weak." The man who had tormented him moved extremely close, only inches from Caswallon's face. The old man leaned in even closer to the Luti raider and began to almost whisper, "The farms and villages you seek..."

Like the swift wolf, his teeth and lips snarling, the old man lunged his head forward with amazing speed. Before the Luti could react, the old man grasped the man's face in his mouth, his teeth securely taking hold of flesh, nose, and cartilage. He bit and held on, his teeth piercing deeply, until he tore the Luti's nose off.

Caswallon had been filled with rage as he'd watched the killing of the convel Bleddyn, and with that rage the old man's body had been filled with magical energy; the natural painkillers had worked to mask much of the pain the old druid felt, and now he only wanted revenge on those who tormented him and his people.

He bit the man savagely hard, with all the force and strength he had left in his tormented body. The man began to scream; he began flailing his arms and then striking at Caswallon's head with his fists. The man who had been holding Caswallon's hand let go and began striking at him. With his two hands free, Caswallon placed both hands on the man's face and as his thumbs found his eyes, the old druid began digging deep into the screaming man's eye sockets, blood and eye fluid flowed down the man's cheeks. As Caswallon bit and gouged the Luti's face, his blood mixed with the blood of his tormentor, and he began to growl deeply, loudly, like the wolf that was his spirit animal.

Now yells and screams exploded from all the men standing near the oak. The watching men lunged forward, forgetting about the people held captive, horrified at the screams and the sight of the old man tearing and ripping at the screaming man's face. The young girls ran in terror off into the woodland.

A half a dozen men kicked and struck at the growling, savage animal that was attacking their comrade. Caswallon the old druid had become the *madadh-allaidh*; he had merged with the black wolf, shapeshifting together with his spirit animal.

The Luti became anxious and almost panicked at the sight of the crazed animal that attacked their comrade; the sight and sounds caused a few to cower, but others were full of rage at the horrific sight of this animal-man tearing away at the face of their screaming friend.

The Luti raider who had been holding Caswallon, the same man with the shield painted with a red sea hawk, pulled a long thrusting blade from his belt and with a hard, quick thrust to Caswallon's side, pierced the old druid's heart.

Caswallon's head lunged backward in pain as the blade, glancing off a rib, found his heart. It would be the last pain he would ever feel in this bodily life. Caswallon spit out the man's nose that he'd ripped from the face of the now eyeless Luti raider, and with his mouth, teeth, and face covered by both the blood of his enemy he said, "This old mouse still had teeth."

His eyes closed, and as the last of his blood pumped out of his body from the wound sliced in his heart, his body collapsed, down onto the Earth Mother who awaited him with open arms to absorb him back into the land of Cymru.

But the old man's soul, an eternal gift from Daghda and Danu, swirled upward from the broken, tormented flesh that had been the body of Caswallon, the Ard Druid of Cymru. Floating above the raiders, Caswallon watched in amusement as the scene below turned into chaos; the man with the shield cut the throat of the one who had no eyes to see nor nose to smell, then pushed him to the ground to bleed out.

Still in a rage, the leader turned on the two men who had been guarding the young maidens of Cymru, who had fled into the woods. Screaming in a deafening, riotous voice, he ordered the two men put to death. Stammering and trembling in fear from the horrific events of their encounter, the raiders fell upon their comrades without question, cutting them down like weeds and killing them where they stood.

"Enough of this," Caswallon thought. "I must find Briga." Caswallon's soul turned from the scene below him, and he looked toward Ynys Mon and the druid hilltop fortress of Caer y Twr. "I must say good-bye to my friends, and I must visit Dalgn first before I find Briga." And with that thought, his soul changed direction with the speed of light.

Chapter Thirty-One

fter checking the dead druid's body for valuables, the Luti left him at the base of the oak tree, at the same place the spirit of Caswallon had left his body. Without the embodiment of spirit, the old body that had housed his soul died as the heart stopped. Immediately, the elemental physical magic that had been the old man's flesh would begin its return into the earth, and Cerridwen, the three-part mother goddess of the earth, would waste no time; she would waste nothing of the substance that had formed Caswallon's body.

Insects in the earth, grasses, fallen leaves, and even the air soon found his body; birds and small mammals also found the remains, and they too began nourishing themselves. As darkness fell upon the forest, the scavengers, and even hungry predators like the fox and wolf, would find life-sustaining nourishment in the old druid's corpse.

Even the old man's bones would be crushed by the jaws of animals large and small, to expose the marrow, and the fragmented shards of bone would be chewed into fine dust by rodents seeking the valuable calcium and minerals they contained. In a year there would be very little left at the base of the ancient derw ynn to tell the world, "Caswallon died here."

This is the way of Danu, and this is the way of Cerridwen, as nothing is ever wasted, and even death brings nourishing life to the world of creation. Caswallon, upon looking down at his broken, old body, had smiled; his body was dead, but he knew what all the people of Cymru knew: "Death is the doorway to life." It is natural for life to be nourished by death; it is the Way of the Circle.

Caswallon had not stayed to observe the natural decomposition of his body; now free from the physical world, his soul was unfettered by all physical laws. For the old man, there was no time, no distance, and no limitation like that felt by those who walk the earth in a bodily life. Like his brother the hawk or his cousin the sunbeam, Caswallon could now fly high above the mountains of Cymru.

He was now in the realm of pure thought, and he was free to move at its speed.

Like light itself, Caswallon was moving to illuminate and find the friends he wanted to tell about his death. He wanted to share with the druids of Ynys Mon the name of the woman he had selected as his new birth mother. It was a selection he'd made years before, having waited for the forging together of spirits and flesh and forces at the right moment.

He also wanted to share the dream, the prophecy, and the appearance of the wolf. They were all interconnected, all meant for this moment—for Caswallon's return.

The old man had seen the details of his death months ago; he had always had the gift of forward sight and this ability to tell the future, and even with the limitations imposed by Daghda the good god, his gifts had served him well during his lifetime.

The old man had dreamed as old men do, but Caswallon knew that the dream of the approaching storm that had filled his heart with anguish and fear came directly from Danu. He had been given the vision of a storm with a wall of black clouds, blown toward him by fierce winds; he knew this would be the Luti, and that they were but the first clouds of an even greater approaching storm. Danu had placed in him the knowledge that they had come to scout and prepare the way for the Roman invasion. The Romans would follow like lightning and loud thunder, crashing down in a fury to destroy the people of Cymru and all of Alban.

Knowing his death was near, he had prepared, leaving both verbal and written instructions with the druids of Ynys Mon. Now his soul had to travel to the druid fortress of Caer y Twr, and there he wished to enter the minds and the dreams of his dear ones, to say good-bye and to let them know of the *cruaidh-ghleachd*—meaning "hard struggle" in his mother tongue—that had come upon the people of Cymru.

And he wanted to visit one last time his oldest friend, Dalgn, the druid who would certainly replace him as ard druid of Ynys Mon.

Upon reaching Caer y Twr, Caswallon floated around the rooms and the sleeping chambers of those who lay dreaming, and like a silent shadow, he visited each one by entering his or her dreams.

He spoke to his dear ones with tenderness and love as he thanked them for their friendship and exalted their spirits not to be concerned over his death; indeed, he told them to rejoice, for he was starting a new life.

Only at the bed of Dalgn did Caswallon stand looking down for a long time at his friend and comforter in life. His Anam Cara, Dalgn, was a soul friend that he would dearly miss. At this moment Caswallon felt the deep sadness of leaving this bodily life.

"Dalgn, it is only you I will surely miss among my brothers and sisters, as you are my dearest friend. You have always been there for me, and I will need your loyalty once again; you must carry out one last great duty for me. I will need you to carry a great burden that will be your *cruaidhghleached*—the knowledge of my return. It is only you whom I would trust with this greatest of duties, and I know you will make certain that all that must be done will be done." As Caswallon spoke, his presence penetrated Dalgn's mind.

Dalgn stirred and rolled over to his left side, which faced the apparition that stood at the edge of his bed. He opened his eyes in the darkness of the room only to see a deeper darkness, which seemed to have a form, leaning over him.

"Who is there?" he asked softly.

"It is Caswallon."

"Caswallon, are you dead?"

It was a rhetorical question, as Dalgn knew the answer. Tears welled up in the eyes of the younger man, and he said, "My friend, do not leave me alone in this life. I am ready to join you, and we can start together in new lives. I will end this one now and join you on your journey."

"No, *is tu m' annsachd*, you must not, not yet. There is something I need to ask you to do, and I trust only you to oversee the completion of my returning circle. It will be necessary to watch for my reembodiment, my rebirth, and it is you who will announce my return. I have moved among the minds and hearts of the others on the council, and you will be named as my replacement; it is you, Dalgn, who will be called Ard Druid, instead of me. I trust only you to complete the awakening of my soul when I return."

Upon hearing this, Dalgn bolted up in his bed and looked straight into the dark form that was the sole essence of Caswallon. "How will I know you when you return?"

"Know this, Dalgn," the old man said, "and do not forget it: I will be one who is blind and will see again. When you recognize me, you must make sure that I am taken to the Hill of Afallach.

There the ladies of Afallach will know how to restore my memories; our sisters will ready me for my return, and with the help of the Red Dragon, Y Ddraig Goch, and the blood of the people of Cymru, I will be fully restored."

The younger man swung his legs to the edge of the bed and stood up, his arms reaching out in an attempt to embrace the dark shadow that was now almost touching him. "Please, Caswallon, I cannot bear it; I am filled with *ana ghràdhach*, and I do not want to live without you!" He reached into the mist that was now the spirit form of Caswallon, but that form eased away from his fingertips, always staying just out of contact with his corporeal flesh.

In a voice of concern edged with a determination that could not be missed, Caswallon once again instructed Dalgn. "I will need you to think of nothing but the great cruaidhghleachd I entrust with you, the knowledge of my return. I can trust only you with this greatest of duties, as I know you will make certain that all that must be done will be done."

The shadow in front of Dalgn suddenly intensified and darkened, blocking out all the light behind it. Along the edges of the form, a pale glow began to grow that seemed to come from thousands of fine rays of light that now grew in strength and brilliance.

Caswallon's voice changed and was now almost angry. "Dalgn, the Luti are here. They killed me and the convel Bleddyn whom I had sent with Conall. They are here to do the work of Rome; I have seen this in my dreams, and I have seen the future. The Romans are returning to Cymru, to all of Alban, and they have sent their dogs, the Luti, to kill as many of us as they can before the armies of Rome once again cross over from Gaul.

"Listen to me and do what I command you. Go to our brothers and sisters and tell them that the Luti need to be destroyed.

None must survive to return to their homes and take back knowledge of our people or our land. They must all die!"

The form in front of Dalgn was the spirit being of the Ard Druid of Cymru. He burst into light so bright that Dalgn had to shield his eyes. As Caswallon continued speaking, that light filled the entire room with an intensity that was blinding. "Tell our people they must make haste to the coast and to the ships of the Luti, and they must burn all the ships and kill all of them. Not one warrior is to be taken as a slave; they must all die.

"It is what Cerridwen demands. She insists on a blood sacrifice for the blasphemy that has been placed upon the people and the land of Cymru. Cerridwen insists that this must be done in order to restore the milk to the breasts of Mother Danu. The land will die if the Luti live and the Romans return."

As Caswallon's spirit energy grew in response to his rage, flashes of light, like lightning, began exploding inside the ink-black darkness of his form—flashes so bright and so blue-white hot, they temporally blinded Dalgn, and he fell to his knees and covered his face with his arms.

In a thunderous voice that awakened almost everyone in Caer y Twr, Caswallon shouted, "The land must be avenged! Not one ship is to escape from Cymru, and Cerridwen demands her vengeance. The blood of the invaders must replenish the land!" Everything in the room seemed to disappear into the overpowering intensity of light that was now the anam of Caswallon.

"Act upon this immediately, Dalgn. Do not hesitate as I now go to Caer Caradoc at Mynydd y Gaer and enter the Ard Righ's mind. He will gather up his armies, and they will hunt the Luti until they have all been plucked from the land. In time they will even disappear from the memories of our people."

And without another word, Caswallon's spirit energy exploded from the room and traveled across the sky toward Caer Caradoc.

Those who beheld it in the night sky saw what appeared to be a star, fallen from the firmament above the earth and streaking downward. This bright star flashed across the sky so bright that it revealed the earth below. It moved across the face of the earth and did not stop until it entered the stronghold of the Ard Righ Caradoc ap Bran. There would be no doubt in Caradoc's heart or mind as to what he was to do when he woke the next morning.

Those who saw Caswallon's essence leave the fortress rock of Caer Caradoc that night spoke in hushed tones, of a star that had exploded from the fortress and traveled straight up toward madainn rionnag, the morning star that rested above the eastern horizon. The star they saw was Caswallon, and he was racing east across the sky in search of only one person; he was racing back toward the birth mother of his next bodily life—Caswallon was racing back to his beloved great-granddaughter Briga.

Chapter Thirty-Two

ilence surrounded her as she stood in the depth of a glowing warmth and light that radiated from everywhere and everything. Surrounded by energy generated by the souls of her family that had made the long journey home, she felt contentment and peace. Briga knew exactly where she was, and she was not frightened. She was once again standing at the edge of the oak grove of her ancestors.

This time she recognized the great derw ynn, the oak tree of her ancestors, and she knew this grove of trees held no harm for her—she entered willingly. Her heart beat hard and fast to match her anxiety; Briga was apprehensive about what message she would soon receive. She had a premonition that an ancestor was about to visit her. She prayed to Danu that it wouldn't be Conall.

Nervously, she spoke out loudly. "Mother Danu, why have you brought me here again? What is it that you must tell me this time? Why have the Cruthadair removed me from the land of my mothers and once again placed me here in the grove of my ancestors? I feel so abandoned and all alone."

No answer came into her mind, and her heart began to feel weaker. Looking around, she saw only beauty; everything was fresh and growing, and the woodland was not so dense that light found it difficult to enter. In precise areas touched by the light, grass grew in patches, long and green, and the wildflowers, bright in their colors, grew abundantly. The place was serene and beautiful.

It looked like Alban Eilir, the king of spring himself, had just laid a blanket of refreshed life on Terra Mater, preparing her for Briga's visit. "It is beautiful, Danu. It is very beautiful."

Looking at the stunning landscape did not keep her thoughts away from her precarious life; her thoughts floated along with the wind, and she remembered.

"Yes, I was walking with Toiréasa and Cuar. Cuar had come to take me back to the camp. He didn't tell me anything, Danu, but I knew there was great danger. I can remember his last words to me clearly: 'No, my lady,' he said to me. 'There is no news of Conall, but I insist for your safety that you must return to the camp now. I will explain everything.'"

She thought to herself of how the deep pain to her stomach had come as she'd quickly walked with Toiréasa and Cuar, and she remembered the darkness that had overcome her. Her hands went to her round abdomen as she said, "My child?"

She waited...nothing. There was nothing—no movement.

"Please!" she cried out in a loud and desperate plea for help. Almost immediately her supplication was answered in her mind and her heart: she felt a reassuring force, like a warmed blanket, that surrounded and comforted her completely.

Inside her womb she sensed the movement of the child. As if on demand, the infant now turned hard; there was no doubt that under her right hand, a heel had brushed against her stomach. She held her breath and waited. Once again the child was telling her he was alive and wanted out.

She smiled as she said, "My little warrior is awake, and I am aware that the son of Conall is still within me."

Three times she patted her stomach with her right hand at the spot the child had turned, and three times she said, "Thank you, Danu."

Briga looked around her. Her concern for her child now eased as she began cautiously moving deeper into the oak grove of her ancestors. This was a place of exceptionally large and ancient oaks. As before when Briga had been brought to this place, there was no visible sun, just subdued light.

However, a few bright rays found their way past the filtering branches high above the treetops. Off in the distance she could hear the sound of running water. "I am thirsty," she thought, and she moved toward the sound of the water.

There was silence in the grove except for the sound of the underground spring that bubbled up from within the earth, creating the resonance she was drawn to. The sound not only reminded her of her thirst, but also seemed to be calling her, and she had a strong feeling that it was an ancestor beckoning; the spirits waited to speak.

Through the oak trees, Briga saw a clearing, a meadow yawning with lush green grass and filled with purple wildflowers. Butterflies danced on the tips of the purple centauries and fluttered to the sound of the water that welled up from an unseen source.

A small stream flowed out from the spring around the large rocks that concealed its source; tall birch trees grew there. Their white bark reflected the light with a brilliance that seemed to originate from within, making the green leaves look even greener. The entire area was bathed in a golden light that seemed to come from everywhere, and Briga stopped; she stood in the meadow wrapped in warmth that melted her anxiety. At that moment she felt Conall was alive.

She whispered Conall's name. "Conall, *is tu m' annsachd. Is tu m' annsachd.*" Then she spoke out in a loud voice for all creation. "Conall, thou art my best beloved."

To her surprise there came a reply. "Briga, my child, I thought I had always been your most beloved." Sitting on a large flat rock at the spring was the figure of a man. He was surrounded by a glowing light that outshone even the white bark of the birch tree.

He laughed, and Briga's heart welled up with a deep sense of safety and love.

Great warmth engulfed her inner spirit, and happiness surrounded her as the light of Caswallon reached out and touched her softly on the cheek.

"Come here, my great-granddaughter. It's me." Briga immediately recognized the voice of Caswallon, and holding her stomach with both hands, she began running across the meadow to reach the old man she loved. Like a ray of sunshine, she quickly crossed the distance that stood between her and the old druid, breathing hard. She stood in front of him. She did not hesitate as she reached out to touch him. Gasping for air, she said, "It is you!" There wasn't any doubt in Briga's heart or mind that this was her great-grandfather.

When she reached him, he smiled broadly as she said, "Yes, my love, you are my first and favorite; you are my most beloved, my *is tu m' annsachd*." Before the old druid could speak, Briga began swiftly asking questions.

"Are you dead? How…Did you suffer in your death? What are the Cruthadair like? Grandfather, have you seen Conall?"

The old man's eyes sparkled with kindness, and when Briga stopped to catch her breath, he at last had time to answer. "My child, please, I will answer all your questions, but first give this old man a hug, as I have missed you dearly." He stood up and extended his arms, and Briga melted into the strength and security of his paternal bosom. "Yes, my beloved, I am dead. The how is not important, and don't be concerned, my darling. I only suffered a little, and now I have been released."

Caswallon continued. "A most remarkable thing happened, Briga, as I died. I entered into a long dark tunnel. I still had a sense of form and movement, and as I approached the light at the tunnel's end, I remembered everything about my life. I even remembered the story of our coming here, Briga—what we all must experience when the Cruthadair sends us to live here on earth. It is how we all must arrive when we make the sacred journey by moving through the star gate of our birth mother."

"Let me tell you a story of what I experienced in the darkness that surrounded me, and yet how that darkness was all very familiar. I had known the darkness as part of my life, and I was not frightened by its depth and vastness. But this day would be different, Briga, as I moved from my familiar darkness within the great circle of the Cruthadair. This day I would begin what was the first step on my long journey home. Suddenly I moved with great, unimaginable speed in a direction I had never gone before. I knew my destination; it was a place unique in all creation, and I was very apprehensive."

"I was on a journey and with me was my champion, my advocate, reassuring me that the journey would go quickly. I could not see or feel my champion's physical presence, but he was very near to me. Together we raced to a place that is different, unlike any world created by the Cruthadair. My champion brought to my attention a small point far off in the blackness. This one had made this journey many times with others who had gone before me. The speck in the darkness, my friend told me, was light. As I began to move closer to the light, I began to experience my first amazing wonder on this journey. Then the lighting changed, and as I approached, my friend told me that the marvelous wonder before me was color. Hanging brightly in the darkness was a beautiful orb of blue and white surrounded by a purple haze."

"Briga, I was like a child and I marveled at the changes in my reality and the new dimensions of the creation that I had always known, and at the beauty of what I was seeing for the first time. 'It is beautiful!' I cried out as my soul delighted at the beauty that was now before us. Just as the brain has two halves, so does the soul, Briga, and I was suddenly aware and could feel, both halves of my soul. 'This is nothing,' my champion said to my soul. 'My dear one, there are so many more colors here, and you will get to delight in all their richness!'

"It was only at this moment Briga, that it became clear to me, that my soul was made of two halves—the female and the male—they were being pulled apart as we drew closer to our destination. My champion replied with sadness in his voice, 'You will see so many more colors, and you will dance joyfully at the sight of them. Each of you has your own favorites, but it will be purple that both the male and the female halves of your soul will grow to love; it is for purple that you have come to earth. Before this is over, you will love the color purple, and you will have won the right to wear it. Both of you will share in the learning and the suffering; together you will celebrate the right of return. Together as Mo Anam Cara you will make the long journey home.'

"The color blue became more intense Briga, more mysterious, as we drew nearer and my half of my soul was overwhelmed with emotions of bliss, contentment, and a sense I had never experienced. I was surrounded by a vast sea of black nothingness, which was the void between the spirit and flesh."

"I was told that my soul was about to experience great joy and pleasure in the most unique place in all creation. Our champion said, 'No matter how many times I see newcomers here, or those who want to return, the experience of this place brings pleasure to all who are exposed to its beauty. Some believe, as I do, that the best of all the works the Creators have given us is what we are seeing now.'

"We were very close now Briga, and in front of us, our new home hung beautifully, suspended in the surrounding darkness. Its brightness held my attention, and I could not turn away from its beauty. The blue was rich and arresting, and surrounding the orb was a vale with a mist of color surrounding it. 'That mist, my friends, is purple,' our champion said.'

"My twin half cried out in excitement, 'Oh yes that is stunning! Words fail me. The orb looks as soft as a cherub's breathe, and yet I feel its strength pulling me forward; it touches my soul and makes my spirit quicken, and the purple that surrounds is glorious.'

"Our champion spoke to us, as the scene became more beautiful, 'what you see in that purple aura is the life force of all those who have come before you. It is the barrier of sacrifice that is keeping this place hidden and safe.'

"Suddenly, before we could ask more questions, the darkness immediately exploded into a vast sea of thousands and thousands of points of light. Then a huge, brilliant light pierced the blackness before us; it was so bright that the sight of it hurt our eyes. It filled the blackness beyond the blue orb, and there in the sky next to it was a smaller bright light, hanging in the dark as if it were the orb's twin."

'They have named the smaller lights stars. The larger, yellow light is called Sol, and the white companion that circles the orb is its twin, Luna,' our champion continued. 'You cannot see any part of creation until you are very close. Not until you cross the barrier of protection that the morning star has given this place will you ever see it. Creator Mother calls this island-like place Avalon, a place of healing and protection. She has covered it with a mist, and only those who serve her are allowed to enter, safe and sheltered from one's enemies and the enemies of creation.'

"The orb was very close now, and it changed in appearance. It was no longer just blue; the orb was becoming streaked with colors. There were areas of many colors blending together, forming patterns that were unlike anything in all creation. Even the smaller twin orb, Luna, had also begun to change appearance with shades of dark and light."

"The champion told my twin and me that our new experiences would be coming so fast that we would not be able to understand them at first, but over time we would come to know new and amazing knowledge. We were reassured that we would learn for ourselves the marvels of this creation."

"Many people," the champion said, "never want to return from this place. They find it so wonderful and feel so safe and protected that they are willing to sacrifice everything they have ever known in order to stay here, to tend and care for this very unique place in the center of creation."

"We were both so very excited now, my twin flame and I—the other half of my soul. We were arriving, and we could not contain the burst of emotions we were experiencing. Rapidly we were dropping toward the surface of the orb. As we moved toward the streaks of color, our friend sensed our thoughts and said, 'Those are clouds.' We moved faster, and all manner of sights began to flood our minds.

"Through the clouds we raced at a tremendous speed, but we missed none of the sights that we began to see below us. Passing through the clouds, we moved lower and closer into a creation that we had only heard about in legends. "Oh, such phenomenal landscapes!" my twin exclaimed. "I have never before in all my existence," I proclaimed, "ever had the opportunity to behold a wonder of creation as perfect as this!"

"Our champion's thoughts seeped into ours with the words, 'Land, water, and mountains are drunk with rain. The dark green is forests pregnant with trees. The lighter green is meadows, clothed with a mantle cloak made of grass and wildflowers. And those winding barriers of sparkling, brilliant light are rivers and lakes. This, my friend, is life. This is Mother Danu.'"

"Flying between the land and us were great masses of white birds. 'See Terra Mater in all its glory, and look over there; those are herds of deer, elk, and buffalo that run freely across the great grassland of the prairie.'"

"Our champion was as excited as we were. 'Look at how the great herds move across the land, chased by the shadow of that large moving cloud! Isn't it wonderful?'"

"Together we were all flying sunwise across the planet, over sights so incredible that I was without the ability to speak. My delight was beyond anything I had ever known, as was my wonder. This creation is filled with magnificence, and I was in a blissful state at the fullness of life. We were moving closer to the land, the life, and the wonders of creation, toward our final destination."

"The sun was now at our backs as we moved forward across the land from west to east. Below us now was a vast, shining blue ocean. Looking at the dark shapes on the horizon, our champion said, 'Those are islands. We will soon be in Cymru.' Off in the distance, we saw two islands. The first was the smaller of the two, and suddenly we dropped down to the larger one."

"Below us now was a large, open space surrounded by a wall, and within the wall were roundhouses. Standing at the houses were people warming themselves around glowing red fires. Our champion spoke to us in a rush. 'I have only a short time left before you will enter the world of humankind through the star gate of a woman. It is now that your one soul will be ripped in two; the male part will enter a woman, and the female part another woman in another village, and you both will be given separate bodily lives. You must seek each other out. You must find each other here in this world.'

"I heard my champion's thoughts: 'This will be the last time I talk to you. From now on you are on your own to choose your path. The people down here cannot understand you, and all they hear is a crying infant. They don't understand who and what you are, and most of them wouldn't believe you even if you could communicate with them.

"'But believe this: we all scream and cry out when we enter this place. You are not alone. The Creators hear and feel what you are experiencing. They will experience everything you experience—what you dream of and hope for, what you think—and they will know what you know: every feeling, every fear, all your joy and your pain.' With a great urgency, my friend began filling my mind with as much information as he could in the seconds I had left before the connection between us faded."

Caswallon told Briga, "My companion guide told me I had been separated from my soul twin, my Mo Anam Cara, and that I had been separated from the Creators and the rest of creation, but that I was not completely alone; I was with you, Briga, as is the spirit of truth."

"Danu is here also, and she will help guide you. She will even speak to you through your heart if you listen. You cannot hear her surrounded by the noise and sounds of mankind, so remember: she is always in her natal creation, which can be found in the natural surroundings of this place. And don't forget also that truth is in your heart."

"This is a wonderful vision you have received from the Cruthadair, Grandfather," she said. Briga looked at her grandfather, and as tears filled her eyes, she said, "Grandfather, I feel so alone."

"Now that I have awakened, Briga, you will not be alone, and I affirm to you that Danu, the good goddess, is wisdom, love, and the mother of all life. She is the morning star, and it is her love that protects us. She is with us always, and she is always with you."

"Briga, your spirit is my spirit, and we are all connected together by the spirits of our mothers and fathers. We are all created in their image! You and I are the sons and daughters of light, and we will always be the children of truth."

Briga looked up into the face of her beloved grandfather and witnessed tears welling up in his eyes. Caswallon spoke again.

"Briga, I am coming back. I have volunteered to come here again. When I return in this new bodily life, my beloved granddaughter, I will…enter your womb! The vision I have shared with you, Briga, is of the journey we make to come to earth. We all make this journey, Briga."

"I have much to share with you, and you must listen and remember everything I tell you. I told you I was dead, but I will soon return. By the great love, the *gràdhaich* of the Cruthadair, I am to return to a new bodily life. You, Briga, carry within your womb the child who will be born to receive my essence—my very soul. Briga, you will be my birth mother!"

The young woman's beautiful green eyes welled up with tears of happiness as she smiled, and the old man's eyes brightly twinkled back like dancing stars as she said, "This is the greatest of honors and the greatest calling, my *annsachd*, which you could ever trust me with. Thank you for choosing me. It will be an honor for me to give you new life and to nurture you at my breasts, next to my heart."

Briga's grandfather loved her with the deepest love, and he now spoke words filled with concern. "I have seen two paths that your life may take, and one of those paths is a great cruaidhghleachd, an agonizing and very hard fight for you and the child, but I have chosen you because I know you are hardy and capable of enduring the greatest of hardships and pain. Just remember that regardless of how appalling and confusing your world grows, you and the child must live."

Briga touched the old man's face gently, and in a voice filled with emotion, she said, "I love you, and I will care for and protect your soul even with my life."

The old man leaned into his great-granddaughter and kissed her forehead with gentle affection. "I have also seen into the future with certainty, and I know that you and Conall will be together and happy; remember and hold on to this vision. Conall is alive, and he will find you no matter what journey your life takes. And remember always that you are a daughter of Cymru, and that your son will grow up to be the Ard Druid of Cymru.

"Never be distressed, my dear. Honor the truth inside your soul, and know that Daghda and Danu are always near you. They sleep in every rock and resonate and sing in every living plant and every bird and insect. Their souls stir inside the animals and awaken in women, children, and men. You are powerful beyond belief. You co-create with the Cruthadair just by thinking; they will hear you, and they will guard over you."

Caswallon took the young woman's hands in his and held them pressed together. He looked kindly into her eyes and continued. "I must ascend to our Mother and our Father and to the circle of our ancestors, but for a short time. The next time we hold hands, I will be the infant son of Conall, and you, Briga, will be my birth mother. I have waited for many years knowing this day would come; I celebrate that soon I will be with you, and I know you will love me with the infinite love that only a mother has for her child. Remember, all things created are never ending, and love is the greatest of these eternal creations. And remember, Briga, inside your womb you carry the *teachd*—the future hope of all of Cymru."

The old man continued. "My darling Briga, I have burdened you with a great responsibility and a great honor; you will give birth to the Ard Druid of Cymru. You must protect yourself even if you must submit to indignation and cruelty, and you must keep the child alive; you and your son must survive."

The infant in Briga's womb stirred, and Briga felt great love for both it and the old man holding her hands, and it was at that moment that she fully realized they were the same; her son and the old man would be the same soul. Now her eyes welled up with tears as she asked, "Grandfather, is there a name you wish to be called when you are born of my flesh?"

"Yes, child, you are to call me Weylin, son of the wolf."

Caswallon continued speaking. "When you return to the land of your fathers, you must leave the waterfalls of Còmhradh Carragh, and you must let Cuar and Toiréasa take you to the safety of the fortress at Tintagel. Two young girls have been found who witnessed my death and the death of the convel Bleddyn.

"Cuar and the druid bard Meilyr ap' Pwyll will want to go and recover my body and take it along with Bleddyn's to the druid fortress of Caer y Twr on Ynys Mon; do not let them do this, as the danger to you is great, and everything must be done to get you safely to Tintagel. The Luti hunting parties are now roaming the woods, intent on finding you. They know that the leader of the raid on their camp was Conall, and they even know your name, Briga. They are searching for you with intentions filled with great hatred and minds set on vengeance."

Briga returned the old man's kiss and said simply, "I will obey you."

The old man smiled. "Good. Now I can leave. The next time you see me, your star gate will have opened, and you will have suffered the *cruaidalach* of childbirth. The pain will soon be forgotten as I lay suckling at your breasts. You must tell me stories, Briga, of who we are and who I am. I will have dreams as an infant and as a young child, but I will not have the ability to recall my identity until I reach the age of nine, and Weylin will not be fully Caswallon until he reaches the age of twelve; it is the way, and you must help me make the long journey home."

"I promise, my love. I promise." As Briga spoke, the old man pulled away from her and transformed. He left his human form, and pulsating with the goddess's heart, he became a brilliantly blazing ball of blue-white light that sped rapidly upward and away from Briga, toward the mother goddess who births all life.

The light was so bright that Briga was forced to close her eyes, and when she opened them again, it was the face of Toiréasa that hovered only inches away from hers. "Oh, it is you, Toiréasa," Briga said, somewhat bewildered. Briga looked around and realized she was lying on the forest floor. She had not moved from the place where she'd been overcome by darkness.

She could see a very worried-looking Cuar standing just behind Toiréasa as her midwife said, "Cuar, she has awakened. Help me carry her back to the camp."

Briga looked at Cuar as he reached down to help her get on her feet, and said simply, "I know about the two young maidens and the death of my great-grandfather and the convel Bleddyn. We must leave for Tintagel immediately."

Chapter Thirty-Three

All that evening rain fell—soft, gentle drops that seemed to match the tears that welled from Briga's eyes and rolled down her cheeks. Toiréasa sat beside her, holding the younger woman, her right arm wrapped around her shoulders while she held her hand—the hand of a woman now filled with the deepest grief. She had drawn Briga tightly against her, and Briga rested her head on Toiréasa's bosom and sobbed. She was weeping for the loss of her beloved Caswallon and for the *ana ghràdhach* of her life, the one she loved excessively—her Conall.

Briga had entered the Hall of Cruaidhghleachd, and there she was held in the hard struggle of the agony that filled her heart and darkened her spirit. Well into the dim early hours of the next day, Toiréasa comforted Briga as the debate raged on among those who gathered around her.

She had walked back into their encampment earlier, in the late afternoon, with Toiréasa and Cuar, with the expectation that she would give instructions to leave immediately; she had even given the order to Cuar to make everyone ready to move toward Tintagel. But almost immediately a challenge exploded from Meilyr ap' Pwyll and Cuar's own brother Cet. Soon the entire camp was involved, and this loud, explosive argument only added to the grief that was swallowing Briga's spirit.

"No, we must recover the bodies and move on to Holyhead on the isle of Ynys Mon," Meilyr ap' Pwyll shouted over and over again.

As arguments raged around her by those gathered together in the camp, Briga was told by the two young sisters, Megan and Rhonwen, the details of the death of Caswallon and the wolf-warrior Bleddyn. The savage ruthlessness of her grandfather's death at the hands of the Luti crushed her heart, and she could not stop thinking of the depth of suffering that the gentle old man had endured; she loved him so deeply, and now Briga feared the worst had happened to her Conall.

Briga knew that two of Conall's men were dead, and with so much time having passed without his return, Briga no longer feared the worst—she felt certain he must be dead too. Even with Caswallon's words of comfort that had come to her in the dream, she feared she was now alone.

Her Conall would have returned to her by now if he were still alive. She had watched as Da'ire died in the village, his wife Gwendolyn and Caswallon at his side, and now that the two young girls had shared the story of the brutal death of Caswallon and the cruel murder of Bleddyn, she felt all alone, very weak, and left without a defender.

Briga's heart fell deeply into darkness as she began to mourn the loss of her two beloved men; despair now covered her like the steady rain that had been falling on them for hours.

Cuar had given the order to begin packing for the journey southeast toward Tintagel, when immediately that order had been challenged by the druid Meilyr ap' Pwyll. Meilyr insisted they have the two young girls take them back to the place where Caswallon and Bleddyn had been murdered. "We must return the body of the Ard Druid Caswallon to the druid fortress of Caer y Twr on Holyhead on the isle of Ynys Mon; we must not leave him alone in his death. Caswallon must be returned to Ynys Mon and his body prepared for the great passage and his soul's return to a new bodily life. His body must be laid among the remains of all his brothers and sisters that have passed before him."

Briga had protested, remembering the words of Caswallon. She shouted at Meilyr, "My grandfather told me you would want to go and recover his body and take it along with the body of Bleddyn to Caer y Twr. He told me that I must not let you do this, as the danger to me and all of us is too great, and everything must be done to get me and the child I carry safely to Tintagel.

"Luti hunting parties are filling the woods, and they are intent on finding us. They know that the leader of the raid on their camp was Conall, and they know the name of his wife. Meilyr, we must not hesitate; they are searching for me, and they are filled with blood vengeance. Their hearts are burning for revenge, and we must do as Caswallon ordered. We must leave immediately for Tintagel."

Other voices joined in the argument, and soon shouts filled the night. Among the villagers who had come with Briga were many who knew the convel Bleddyn, including his *brawd*, Drystan. "No!" shouted Drystan. "No, you will not be leaving my brawd's body to be rotting on some forgotten forest floor—not while I'm still drawing breath. If I have to be going it alone, I will, and I will find my brother's body and return him to our home."

Tempers exploded as those who supported Briga and wanted to leave for Caer y Twr joined in to defend her. Shouts of anger went on for several hours as Briga, her head resting against Toiréasa, could only weep. When the piercing and angry words turned to pushing, the child within Briga began to stir. The camp had become clearly divided between those who wanted to recover the bodies of Caswallon and Bleddyn, and those who wanted to see Briga taken immediately to Holyhead and on to Tintagel.

There was nothing Briga could do or say that would make a difference or stop the fighting, as she was now deeply possessed by her grief. Even her dogs, Gealach and Grian, lying pressed up against her legs, could not find a pathway into her heart.

Standing behind Briga the entire evening was a tall, thin young boy with long, curly black hair, a boy who proudly carried at his side a bronze thrusting sword with two entangled dragons arising from the end of the handle. The young lad had had enough and without hesitation he boldly stepped into the center of angry, shouting people and pulled from under his shirt a finger-width carved bone whistle. With all the air he could force out of his lungs, he blew it loudly with a sound so intense and piercing that everyone immediately fell silent.

"I am Odhran of the House of Conall, and I am guardian of Briga until the return of Conall!" the young boy shouted out with an authority and force that carried his voice to all those who had gathered about.

"There will be no more argument, as there is only one solution. We must do both." And the young Odhran looked straight at Cuar and said, "Cuar, you and your two warriors will go with me, as will Toiréasa and anyone from the village who wants to leave with us at daybreak. You will help me care for and guard Briga. We will take one horse with supplies led by Etaoin, and we will move as rapidly as possible toward Holyhead, but we will separate from the party that Cet will lead, and we will turn south and journey on to Tintagel.

"The dogs, Gealach and Grian, will come with us, as they will comfort Briga, but the cattle must stay here, and you will turn them free to graze. Cet and the druid bard Meilyr ap' Pwyll will go and recover the body of Caswallon and the body of Bleddyn, and they will take them both to the druid fortress of Caer y Twr on Ynys Mon.

"Caswallon's body must be prepared for his journey back to Tara; his soul must be provided directions in order that he might find his next birth mother. Bleddyn must be given the honor of a warrior's funeral, and all the druids and novices of Ynys Mon must honor his death; he must be given a hero's burial mound.

"Drystan, you and all those from the village who have kinship with the convel Bleddyn must go with Cet, as will the maidens Megan and Rhonwen, as they alone know the resting place of the bodies, and they will guide you to the bodies of our Ard Druid and the convel of Cymru."

Cuar moved through the crowd toward Odhran and stopped directly in front of the young boy, towering over him. He started to protest, but Odhran would have nothing of it. His right hand reached down to grasp the dragons on the hilt of his bronze sword, and his eyes locked on the gaze of the cold, gray eyes of a much older and lethal warrior.

Odhran's next words surprised everyone but Cuar, and he smiled back at the young boy with a new respect. "On your honor, Cuar, you swore to Caswallon to take care of Briga. As it is my oath and my honor and it is our mutual duty to see her safely to Tintagel, even if we must die in the attempt, there is no more discussion. As the protector of Briga, I insist—no, I order you to make ready to leave for Holyhead at first light. We must get Briga safely to Tintagel as the Ard Druid Caswallon commanded us to do; he made us both promise to obey his last command and we will."

The warrior Cuar, towering over the young boy, extended his open right hand. He rested it on Odhran's shoulder, and still smiling at the boy who had just completed his journey to becoming a man and a warrior, roared out in a loud voice for all to hear, "Odhran, guardian of Briga, it is my honor to add my blade to yours, and if needed to lay down my life besides yours in the protection of the Lady Briga, the Lady of the Lake and wife of Conall Cearnach of Clan Diahad, conry of all of the convel of Cymru!"

Cuar and all those who would protect Briga gathered around her and Odhran. Cuar was giving orders as Cet approached and bowed his head to his brother. "I will obey your orders, brother, and I will go with the druid Meilyr ap' Pwyll to recover the bodies of the Ard Druid Caswallon and the convel Bleddyn, and I pray to Daghda and Danu that we will all meet again soon." The two brothers embraced each other without another word or look between them and began to go about the duties they had been given. The entire camp was busy making ready to leave in the morning. As night fell, the men and women who had formed bonds melted away into the forest to briefly share the joining of their bodies and souls. Briga's shadow, Toiréasa, had disappeared into the woods also. This was one of the rare moments Briga was left alone.

With hot tears rolling down her cheeks, Briga soaked the furs and coverings that had served as her bed. Her emotions took her to places she never intended to go. Rage stole her ability to reason as she felt betrayal; then fear surrounded her and she felt paralyzed—her body went completely limp. Her hands held her belly as the infant inside her kicked. Briga's soul was in deep distress as she wailed out in anger, "Conall, why did you abandon me?"

Standing outside her shelter, Cuar heard her wail and pulled away the covering that blocked the doorway. Stepping inside and seeing her anguish, he asked, "Are you all right, my lady?"

A single flame burned in the oil lamp that lent its light to the gloomy darkness surrounding Briga. Looking up at him, her eyes filled with more irrepressible tears at the thought of another human being who cared.

Cuar immediately sat down next to her, put a strong arm around her, and drew her close, his free hand grasping her hands together. He held them securely but with a gentleness that spoke of deep affection and admiration. Briga felt his warmth and his strength, and looking up into his face, she said, "Cuar, I feel so alone, so cold, and I suffer. I am a lifeless nothing." She laid her head on his chest and continued crying.

Cuar took the inside of his garment and blotted her tears and her nose. Briga responded with a look of complete brokenness. Cuar shot back a look that entered deep into her eyes and beyond to her soul—a look that spoke volumes about this man's wisdom and hidden pain but also of his hidden desire.

Without a word he placed his lips on her forehead, then her cheeks, then her hands. The healing salve of Cuar's lips made Briga want more. She returned his kisses, which set his wolf-beast on fire—he uttered something like an internal howl as his hands and lips freely roamed. Passion exploded immediately with all the pent-up fire and lust that burned inside him for this woman he had grown to respect, cherish, serve, and love.

They removed each other's clothing as they kissed. Cuar's callused and strong hands found Briga's breasts and massaged them gently, with an increasing firmness.

Waiting to be filled by him, she ached deep inside as the warmth of his mouth and his hands invaded her body.

Her hands touched and pleasured him, and then she pushed him onto his back and straddled him as if he were a stallion to be mounted. His hands found the roundness of her hips, helping her position as he gently placed his sword in her sheath. They both were starved to feel alive and loved and desperately wanting sensual touch, she closed her eyes and bathed in the glories of being a woman. The aching emptiness of her body melted as he filled her with wordless wonder that forced away the coldness, the pain, and the suffering.

Her hands reached out, and she leaned forward, resting her hands on his chest. She rolled her pelvis and hips slightly, gliding herself on him until she found new places of pleasure. Wanting this feeling to last forever, she dared not hurry; it had been so long, and she was so very hungry. Like a woman savoring a meal long awaited, she fed on the fullness of his manhood, and her hunger was satisfied by the ever-deepening waves of orgasm that exploded from deep inside to surround her and carry her away with the gods.

She rode the waves, climbing past the mortal to the divine, and gasping, she was consumed by her pleasure until she collapsed onto his chest. He surrounded her with his arms and held her, pressing her to his chest, in a safe place where they both fell into a deep sleep. While darkness still ruled, Briga woke early only to find Cuar gone and Toiréasa sleeping peacefully curled up next to her. In the quiet Briga wondered for a moment if it all had been a dream, but her question was soon answered by the tingling warmth deep inside her.

For long, lingering moments she felt whole, and she knew she could trust Cuar to lead her and the group to safety. She would not worry and pine in her emotional pain again; as she fell back to sleep, she knew what she must do.

By the morning's first light, two parties of men and women began to move away from each other and from the camp of the waterfall with a voice—the Còmhradh Carraghs, the place that had always been sacred to Conall, the place where they had fallen profoundly in love with each other, and now the place where she had taken another man. Briga had only known Conall in this life, and now she had used Cuar to ease her pain—Conall should have come to Còmhradh Carraghs, as he had promised her. At the place the trail dropped down to pass along the pool and the falls, Briga paused. Looking at the waterfall, she said, "You did not come for me, Conall; you have failed me and your son." Lowering her gaze, she walked away from the Còmhradh Carraghs.

Briga, her senses dulled by pain at the loss of Caswallon and by the persistent belief that her husband, Conall, was dead too, didn't feel a thing. She walked on unaware that she was leaving the place of the talking falls for the last time. Two dogs walked along with her, and Toiréasa walked beside her, holding her hand and speaking softly to her. But no touch or words from the physical domain around her could possibly cheer her; she entered the blanket of grief that now totally covered her world. Briga was a woman in mourning over the loss of her grandfather Caswallon. Her grief was also overshadowed by the loss of the only man she had ever loved—her Mo Anam Cara, her twin soul, Conall. As Toiréasa walked beside the grieving young woman, she watched her closely, as it was often the way of the women of Cymru to kill themselves so they would join their husbands and both return to new bodily lives at the same time.

Toiréasa had no way of knowing that the world had changed for Briga when she lay with Cuar; Briga no longer thought of Conall, but now focused on her life and the child within her. Toiréasa was right in watching Briga; normally a young woman of Cymru would have taken her own life when confronted by the loss of the two most important, most loved men in her life. But Toiréasa had no way of knowing the strength of the passion that now burned inside Briga from having taken in the masculine energy of Cuar. Nor could she have known the power of the vision and the force of the words Briga had received from Caswallon's visit.

The old druid's words had been written on her heart when he'd said, "Briga, I have burdened you with a great responsibility and a great honor; you will give birth to the ard druid of Cymru. You must protect yourself, even if you must submit to indignation and cruelty, and you must keep the child alive; you and your son must survive."

Even covered in the darkness of her grief, Caswallon's words brought light into that darkness, and when the darkness was pushed just a little further away from her heart, she would remember all his words; she would remember that the baby she carried would be Caswallon, and in the days ahead, she would remember the old druid's promise—a promise he had spoken to her just before he ascended: "I have also seen into the future with certainty, and I know that you and Conall will be together and happy; remember and hold on to this vision.

"Conall is alive, and he will find you, no matter what journey your life takes. And remember always that you are a daughter of Cymru, and that your son will grow up to be the ard druid of Cymru."

It would be the old man's words in the days to come and his promise to her that would give Briga the strength to endure. Ahead of her was pain, suffering, and fear, but Caswallon's words would empower her; she would live for her child, Weylin. In her heart also grew a seed of anger for her husband, Conall. She was beginning to believe he had died, or worse, abandoned her to an unknown future. She would live for the future promised her by the Ard Druid of Cymru, Caswallon, and son of Cerridwen. She would live for Weylin.

Chapter Thirty-Four

oiréasa's arm was wrapped around Briga's shoulder, pressing her tightly against the older woman's body as they walked. In fact, Toiréasa was doing the walking for Briga as they both moved silently through fine, mist-like rain that turned the woods into a wet, dripping reminder of the tears that had fallen from the grieving woman's eyes just the night before. The tears had stopped, but Briga's body now moved along the trail only because she was guided by the older woman. Her mind was deeply buried in grief and far from her body.

Even the dogs, Gealach and Grian, walked silent and subdued beside their mistress. They both felt the deep emotions that flowed from Briga's soul, and they knew she was in bitter pain. Walking alongside the young woman's right side, Gealach nuzzled her fingertips and pushed her wet, cold nose into her hand. There was no reaction from Briga; her fingers, like her hand, hung unresponsive from an arm that didn't feel. Her body moved because it was guided by Toiréasa, but her soul, the center of her mind, had been guided to a gentler, safer time by her great-grandfather Caswallon, whose soul was now within the infant cradled in her womb. Briga's soul was far from the grief of her body.

Sunlight filtered down to the forest floor as she walked toward Caswallon's hut, deep in the woods, along a well-traveled trail that led from the village. Many villagers had walked along it seeking her great-grandfather's advice, healing, and magic. She was only nine, and she had gone off into the woods to visit her great-grandfather Caswallon; he come to her village from the druid fortress of Caer y Twr and was in the forest hut he had built for the times he stayed at Llyn Tegid. No power in creation was going to stop her from seeing her *hen dadcu*—

He had become, in those formative years, her most beloved teacher and friend. When Caswallon was near, she found every opportunity to steal away to be with him, even if she disobeyed her parents to do so, and this day was no different as she walked along the warm summer trail seeking to visit her beloved great-grandfather.

It had rained the night before, and the world was fresh, washed clean with sparkling water droplets that still held on to the tips of the leaves along the trail. All the ferns and moss seemed to be covered in diamond-like jewels that glistened and reflected the morning light as she walked along the forest floor, and everywhere small pools of clean water rested in all the moss-covered depressions, the bowls of downed trees, and the large stones that seemed to line the trail guiding folks to the old druid's home.

Briga stopped at one large moss-covered stone that held a deep bowl of rainwater, and pushing aside a leaf, she cupped her hands and lifted the clear, cold water to her lips. She loved the taste of the earthy water, and the mossy aroma of the liquid delighted both her sense of smell and taste. The whole world had been gifted this morning with the deep, rich, lusty earth aroma of the goddess; her rain had washed away and made new all the green and growing things of the forest. Everywhere life seemed to have been cleansed with a freshness that spoke of the goddess's love for replenishing and restoring her creation.

As she drank the refreshing water, Briga caught out of the corner of her eye a swift movement, high up in the tree branches. Almost without sound, a goshawk flew overhead, hunting. Briga stopped and now watched the tree canopy; she did not have to watch long. A robin flew across an opening on the trail, and as swift as a thought, the goshawk fell upon the unsuspecting robin, striking it in the air.

Briga yelled out loudly, "No!" and the goshawk, startled by the sound, broke off the attack, releasing the robin from its grasp. The bird dropped toward the forest floor. With a surprisingly gull-like screech of protest, the goshawk flew off into the darkness of the deep forest. Briga watched as the robin fell into the underbrush just off the trail, and she quickly ran to the spot, entered the mass of ferns and shrubs, and began to search for the fallen bird. She spotted the bird's red breast first, in the green of the wet moss and leaves covering the trunk of a fallen tree. It lay motionless.

The bird had landed on its back and seemed dead until the young girl reached out to touch it. In a swift movement that startled Briga, the robin flipped over, got to its feet, and began hopping along the fallen tree trunk, its left wing oddly trailing behind its body. Briga ran along the trunk and quickly reached out with both hands. She picked up the bird as gently as possible. Now cupped in her hands, the bird only struggled for a few seconds, and stopped as soon as Briga started to soothe and speak to the bird.

"My little friend, don't be frightened of me. I am only a little girl, and I won't harm you." Caswallon had taught her how to talk to animals, and as Briga spoke to the injured bird, she formed word pictures in her mind; her words matched those images, as did her feelings, and both thoughts and feelings became a focused beam directed into the robin's soul as she gently spoke to soothe the bird.

She felt the rapid beat of the bird's heart against the softness of her inner hand, and she saw the look in the robin's eyes change from fear to acceptance. "How badly have you been hurt, my robin friend?" she asked as she began to examine the bird. It did not take long to discover that the left wing had been broken in the attack by the goshawk: a small amount of blood was on the wing and on Briga's hand, and a jagged, sharp, white bone pushed out through flesh and feather.

"I must get you to my grandfather," she said, and without delay the young girl pushed back the underbrush, got back on the trail, and began running toward her great-grandfather's hut.

At the end of the trail, almost hidden by the huge oak trees that stood guard on either side of the structure, stood a rough, small building made of stone and timber collected from the forest floor. Moss grew freely on it, and the roof was a mass of joyfully growing things; ferns and bright flowers grew with wild abandonment, and small seedling trees that had sprouted and taken root on the roof now looked like wild clumps of unkempt hair.

A spring bubbled from the rock outcropping to the left of the dwelling and flowed into a series of small pools, seeming to disappear in the thick, lush growth that grew beyond the shade of the oaks.

All along the water's edge were overhanging ferns and beyond the ferns, shrubs grew. Birds, butterflies, and dragonflies seemed to be everywhere, fluttering and joyfully flying about. It was the kind of magical place where one knew the fairy folk could be found on a full moonlit night. Standing near the door were a red squirrel and a pine marten that faced each other as if talking.

As Briga ran up the trail toward the primitive hut, both small animals turned and looked at her; it was as if they knew the young girl and were welcoming her to the home of Caswallon. The red squirrel began chattering loudly, and the door opened. In the doorway was a woman much younger than Caswallon. Her wild, long, blond hair covered her head down to her shoulders, and her smiling, rich, deep-blue eyes beamed when she saw the young girl running toward the hut.

"Good morning, Briga." The woman's voice carried musically across the distance. Turning to look back into the darkness of the hut she said, "Caswallon, Briga is here, and she approaches like the wind herself."

From the shadows inside the hut, a man stepped into the doorway. At first look one would think him old, but he moved and had a presence that spoke of the energy of youth. He stepped beside the younger woman, and she stepped in closer to him, touching his chest and right arm with tenderness. She was much shorter, and he leaned over and gave her a gentle kiss on the forehead.

"Thank you, Vivienne," he said affectionately as he turned to give his full attention to the young girl running toward him. "Briga, my darling child, why do you run so, and what is that you carry cupped in your hands?"

She had run the entire distance, and as she stopped and stood in front of him, she gasped to fill her lungs once again with air. Caswallon's left hand reached out and lightly touched the young girl on the top of the head. "Blessings be, my child. Why have you run so hard and what have you brought to me?"

With her lungs once again filled with air, the words exploded from her in rapid and unbroken succession, in the manner that only young girls seem to have the energy and life force to produce.

"Grandfather, you should have been there. You should have seen it. I was drinking from a small pool of water when I saw it… well, I didn't actually see it. I sensed it like you have taught me to do. It was like a shadow that I felt moving behind me, and I caught it on the edge of my vision. It was a goshawk hunting among the trees, and it swept down from high in the treetops and snatched this poor robin, and I shouted really loud, 'No!' And the hawk screeched or maybe it dropped the robin and then screeched, but anyway, I had to search for it, and I found it, and look at the bone coming out of the wing. Its wing is broken, and I've run here so that you can fix it. It's hurt. Please, please, can you fix it? Please, Grandfather."

The old druid stood looking at the little girl who was his most beloved above all others; she was his greatest soul attachment in this life, his *is tu m' annsachd*, and he would do anything for her, anything that was possible.

"Here, let me look at the wing," he said, and the young girl gently opened her hands and showed him the broken wing. The red squirrel stood chattering at Briga's feet, and the old man said, "You'd better show Bronwyn. He won't stop talking until he gets a look." Caswallon and Briga both knelt down on the earth in front of the red squirrel, and Briga lowered her hands so the squirrel could see the robin's broken wing. The squirrel began chattering very loudly, looking from the bird to Briga and then to Caswallon.

The old man stood up and said, "Yes, Bronwyn, it is very bad. Robin is hurt. Yes, I will let Briga know that Robin has been hurt and may never fly again."

The old druid looked at Vivienne and taking her hand in his, he squeezed it tenderly and said, "Briga, Bronwyn, and I are all going to walk over to the cròmleac and the circle of stones. We'll be back soon."

Looking at the gentle man, the young girl holding the robin, and Bronwyn the red squirrel, Vivienne said, "Yes, I will go in and fix us something to eat for when you return." And without another word, she turned and disappeared into the darkness that lay beyond the doorway of the hut.

"Now, Briga, you and I and Bronwyn will walk to the standing stones, and I will give you a new lesson in magic today, something I haven't shown you yet, but it is time for you to learn." Putting his left hand softly on her shoulder, he walked with her toward the circle of the standing stones. As he walked the old man sang a fonn in a very quiet voice that did not carry beyond the party of four:

> Goddess mother, be with us, walk with us,
> Touch us spirit, soul, and body.
> Goddess mother, love us, nourish us, free us from fear.
> Goddess mother, remove our pain, remember our soul,
> Take what is only yours to give and only rightfully yours
> to take.
> I am the dewdrop found resting on the leaf at sunrise.
> I am the gentle breeze that warmly sways the meadow
> flowers.
> I am your child and you are my mother.
> Love and remember me, for I am.

When they reached the stone circle, the old druid stopped and looked at his great- granddaughter and said, "Come, Briga, sit with me at the great cròmleac that stands at the center of the circle of stones. We must sit facing the north, toward the Druuos star—the firm one that never moves in the night sky, home to all our ancestors."

When the old man reached the stone, he sat with his back toward it. He looked up at the young girl and said, "Sit here, Briga, on my lap. Let me hold you and the robin."

Without a word Briga sat on her beloved grandfather's lap, and the old man wrapped his arms around her and held her close. "Briga, there are things that even the greatest druid cannot do— magic that only the good god, goddess, and Esus can do."

Bronwyn the red squirrel sat on the ground and chattered as if in agreement. He fell silent as Caswallon continued.

"Let me hold the robin, Briga. Let me look closer at the bone break of his wing." The young girl gently handed the bird to him. The old druid now cupped the injured bird in his hands.

Caswallon carefully examined the splintered bone that had once supported the robin in flight. "This is not good, Briga. The bone is all splintered, and there are pieces missing. We cannot mend this bone, and our robin is doomed to never fly again. The break has torn past flesh and feather, and infection, fever, and death are likely to follow such an injury. It would be best, Briga, to return the robin's spirit to the goddess so that he will be given another life next Imbolc, when the robins return."

Great tears of confusion and sadness welled up in Briga's emerald eyes, flowing down her cheeks as she sat on her grandfather's lap and looked desperately into his eyes. "Please, isn't there something you can do? Can you not fix him? Please...please, Grandfather?"

A man's heart over the years becomes hard, tempered by pain and suffering and by the unspeakable acts of war that he must inflict on the enemies of his people. Caswallon had seen much suffering and deep pain, and with his own hands had inflicted unbelievable savagery and death on the enemies of Cymru.

The old druid's heart was like a cold, black stone, except for the warm, bright center, and at the center of his heart, a fiery, brilliant, blue-white light burned freely. It was the light of the goddess and of Briga, and Caswallon had placed them both there for safekeeping. The goddess and Briga could warm the heart of the old man, and the stone of that heart would soften and melt, releasing the love and tenderness that Caswallon felt for the goddess, for all womankind, and especially for his Briga. The goddess melted this stone with one word from her spirit, and Briga melted the old druid's heart with her tears.

As Caswallon's heart melted, he felt pain in his chest, and his eyes too filled with tears that rolled down his cheeks, joining those of his beloved great-granddaughter on his lap.

Caswallon cried with Briga.

Holding the robin in his hands, he smiled at the young girl and said, "I can feel his heart beating very hard and fast."

Looking only into her beloved grandfather's eyes, Briga said, "I could feel it too."

"The robin will never fly again, Briga. The earth is now as close as it will ever get to the Sky Father. It will never again touch the clouds."

"I know, I know," she said in a very sad, low voice.

The old druid brought his cupped hands up close to his face. The robin struggled, and the old man cooed kind words. "It is good, my friend. It is good, the journey home." The bird stopped struggling and tilted his head toward Caswallon. Looking into the bird's eyes, the old man said softly, "Goddess Danu, this is my good friend, Robin, whom Briga has brought to me to heal. He has been badly hurt, Danu, and is beyond my skill. He is in pain and suffers. Please, Danu, come and take away his spirit. Put his soul in your hands and take him on the journey home to the Hall of Souls. Please, Danu, release Robin from his pain."

They sat together watching as the robin's head tilted and fell to its shoulder, coming to rest on Caswallon's hand. The bird's eyes closed slowly, and its beak opened. A very audible breath was heard leaving the bird as its spirit was exhaled, and Caswallon felt the last heartbeat as the bird died.

"It is done," the old druid said very softly.

"Is he with the goddess, Grandfather?" Briga asked in a very soft whisper.

"Yes, my beloved child, he is with the goddess, and all of his ancestors are celebrating, and next Imbolc he will return to once again bring us joy with his song."

Briga sat silent, thinking, as the old man held the lifeless bird in his hands.

"Grandfather," she said, "it is amazing, what great magic you know—to be able to take away life with only your words, and to pray to the goddess, and she obeys you."

The old man leaned forward and kissed the young girl on her cheek.

"Oh no, my beautiful granddaughter, the goddess does not obey me; I always and forever worship and obey the great Mother Danu.

"I am just an old druid, Briga. Any good druid can take away the spirit of life from one who is suffering, but there is only the one druid who can heal those who have no hope of being healed and restore the dead with just the words spoken from his mouth."

Looking at her grandfather in amazement, Briga asked, "Who is the druid that can do such magic?"

"He is Esus, my granddaughter."

Briga inhaled deeply and asked, "Will I ever meet Esus?"

Looking deep into her eyes as if he were looking into the windows of her soul, the old druid said, "Yes, Briga, you will see and meet this druid. He is the Esus, the anointed child of the great Daghda and Danu."

The old man smiled at her and once again softly kissed her on both cheeks and then on the forehead. "Yes, you will meet this Esus; we both will get to meet him. Now we need to bury Robin and place rocks over his body, as his soul is now held safe by the goddess."

Briga and Caswallon stood up, and as Caswallon began digging a small hole, Briga gathered stones to cover the resting place of Robin's body. With tenderness and deep reverence, the old man placed the robin into the earth-womb, and together Briga and Caswallon replaced the earth, then neatly stacked the stones. Bronwyn the red squirrel stood silently watching, and as Briga placed the last stone, he began chattering almost as if he were singing. They all watched as three holly blue butterflies landed on the top stone. They stood facing one another, slowly opening and closing their wings in a fanning motion that kept time with Bronwyn's song.

"It's a good sign, Briga. The goddess is letting us know that Robin will be reborn next spring at the equinox of Alban Eilir. Now, let's go back, as I am sure Vivienne has made us something very special for lunch." And reaching down, the old man took Briga's right hand in his left, and together they began walking back to the little roundhouse.

They hadn't gone far when Caswallon stopped. He turned and squeezed the young girl's hand hard, and his face took on a look of deep concern. In his eyes the look of fear suddenly appeared. At the same moment, Briga reached down and grabbed her stomach with her left hand as pain filled her, and she said, "My stomach, it hurts."

"Something is wrong, Briga. You must go back. You must go back now." And without another word, the old man let go of her hand...

Briga stood with both hands holding her stomach. The child within was vigorously kicking, and she realized that a woman, Toiréasa, was now standing next to her, holding her up. Her arm was wrapped around her, keeping her from falling. The panicked voices of men and women filled the air around her, and as they yelled, the anguished neighing of a wounded and dying horse pierced her spirit. She looked down, and at her feet Gealach lay motionless, dead from an arrow that had stuck in her body.

"What is happening?" Briga asked. She turned back to look at Toiréasa. The woman's eyes were wide open, and surprise and fear filled them completely. She opened her mouth as if to talk, but only frothy red blood bubbled out, and she released her hold on Briga.

Briga fell straight down to a sitting position on the ground and looked up at her midwife. She saw both of the woman's hands reaching for her throat, to the arrow stuck completely though her neck. The arrowhead, clearly visible, was sticking out of the other side. Gurgling sounds came as Toiréasa tried to speak, and then the fatally wounded woman took one step back and fell to the ground, dead, next to Briga.

Briga was now sitting on the ground between Toiréasa and her dead dog, Gealach, and she reached out and touched both of them. She spoke softly. "Danu...why?"

All around her angry voices yelled and screamed. Over and over she heard the deep, raspy voice of Cuar shouting, "The Luti! The Luti are upon us! Fight for your lives! Protect Briga!"

Chapter Thirty-Five

The drums of the Luti beat out a loud rhythm that echoed the frenzied attack on Briga's party. The Luti, known as the people of the North or the Cimbri, came from the coast of Jutland. They now burst out of the trees that had hidden them on both sides of the trail. As they charged, the drums beat faster and faster, and the sound seemed to take control of their minds and bodies, creating a response that matched and set the pitch for the battle. The berserkers charged first into the party that escorted Briga, without regard for fear or death. The battle was united instantly with an animal fierceness.

An old woman dressed in white stood on the path with the Luti. She was obviously an important leader who had traveled with them. With no regard for the forward momentum of the charge or the danger of the moment, she blocked the advance of Briga and her escorts.

Standing with her were two tall warriors with long blond hair and white-blue eyes, twins in appearance, both armed with round shields and tall, long-bladed hewing spears. Briga did not know the words the woman screamed, but had she understood the language, she would have realized the woman was a shaman calling upon her magic and the magic of her namesake, the goddess Freya. She continued wailing and shrieking loudly in a high-pitched, shrill chant to summon the spirit of the bear.

She called upon the bear spirit to materialize and to enter her warriors. She chanted to encourage her warriors to berserk and transform, and as she screamed louder, the drums beat faster. The Northern warriors, led by several men wearing bear skins, appeared to shapeshift from human to bear.

Briga sat on the ground between the bodies of Gealach and Toiréasa and watched all in dreamlike slow motion. Even the beating drums seemed distant and muffled. Screams filled the air around her, as did the calls of mortally wounded men, cursing as they died. Cuar had fallen back to protect her with his two warriors. Dozens of the enemy raiders charged at them as the three warriors of Cymru stood their ground. Briga watched as their blades fought to shield her from harm. Again and again their blades swung high and caught the sunlight, just to descend back downward, cutting away the life of a Luti raider. Soon the dazzling glitter of the men's blades vanished, as the swords, covered in blood, no longer reflected the sun's light.

To the right of Cuar, Briga saw a young woman running at the men, screaming in defiance. Etaoin was loosing arrows as she ran, and each found and claimed the life of one of the raiders. As the last arrow sailed from the young woman's bow, she yelled out "Cymru!" Her black hair, tipped white with lime, was spiked and stood upright, held in place with pine-pitch; it caught the sunlight as she ran, and the white seemed to burst into a bright, glowing crown.

She was tall for a woman, and well muscled, and now running with her sword drawn, she moved toward the woman dressed in white. One of the raider men stepped forward to stop her, and he did so at the cost of his life; she cut him down without missing a step as she continued moving toward the Luti shaman woman. The shaman's guards stepped forward, their spears lowered with the long, cutting blades pointed directly at Etaoin.

The two men seemed to proceed forward in one movement as the young girl ran within range of their blades. One of the men thrust and parried with his spear as the woman attacked him with her sword. The other warrior, his twin, suddenly dropped his shield and grasped his spear with both hands, swinging it over his head in a wide circle that brought the long, sharp hewing blade cutting across Etaoin's neck, just above her shoulders. Briga gasped in horror as the young woman's head was flung away from her body by the warrior's forceful cut.

Briga felt a hand touch her shoulder, and it squeezed hard and firm. A familiar face filled her vision, and a young boy was speaking. "Briga, get up! You must get up!" Odhran stood over her, yelling at her to get up. Suddenly fear appeared in the boy's eyes, along with resolved determination as he spoke again. "For the sake of Conall's child, Briga, get up and flee into the woods!"

Briga, looking past the face in front of her, watched in disbelief as two raiders came running toward them. In a voice almost too hushed to hear, she said, "Behind you, Odhran."

The young boy moved quickly and turned, facing the much larger men bearing down on them. In his hand he held a bronze thrusting sword given to him by Cuar, with its two entangled dragons arising from the end of the handle. Odhran did not wait for the two men to get to him, and he charged the enemy as Conall had taught him to do. Only a few feet from the first man, Odhran's charge exploded into a forward roll; suddenly leaping, his forward motion turned into a somersault. The raider swung his sword at the boy as he went by, but the larger man was too slow, and Odhran swept past his right side only to pop up behind the surprised warrior. Swinging his sword as hard as he could, he slashed the man's leg behind the right knee. The man screamed, grabbed at his leg, and fell to the ground.

Odhran stood up. He seemed to tower over the man who rolled on the ground holding his leg, cursing. Without hesitation, the boy-warrior thrust the blade of his sword into the man's throat. The raider's death was sudden. Odhran withdrew the blade and turned to face the second man.

This time the Luti raider was ready. As Odhran ran toward his enemy, the bear of a man stepped surprisingly quickly to the side. Whatever move Odhran had in mind, it was canceled abruptly as the raider's shield swung around and caught him squarely in the upper chest and face. The force of the blow picked the young boy up off the ground and threw him backward several feet, causing him to land hard on his back. The Luti raider laughed and mocked the dazed boy as he approached him to finish his kill.

Odhran lay on his back, gasping for breath, as blood gushed from his broken nose. Dazed, he watched as the raider confidently approached, sure of making an easy kill. But at the same moment that the man took his final step to close the distance between himself and the boy, Odhran quickly rolled over on his side. Once again the brass blade of the boy's sword flashed, and in a hard, thrusting stab that entered deep into the man's left leg, just below the groin, he completely severed his femoral artery. The raider reeled back with pain at the force of the blow. His left hand dropped the shield he carried and moved to cover the wound, which now freely gushed blood past his clenched fingers, soaking the earth and turning it bright red below his feet.

Odhran rolled several times away from the man and got to his feet, still bleeding from his nose, his sword at the ready.

Holding his wound, the man uttered words that Odhran did not understand, but there was no doubt in the young warrior's mind that this man was angrily cursing. The larger, older warrior took two steps toward the boy and stopped, his head falling backward, as if he were looking high into the sky. The raider's head seemed to be resting at an odd angle on his shoulders as he uttered one final word. His eyes rolled back into his head as darkness swept over him from loss of blood. He swayed and fell, rigid, straight backward, hitting the ground hard with a solid, loud thud—never to rise again.

Odhran moved back to Briga and knelt down beside her. Taking her hand in his, he said, "You must get up, Briga. You must for your sake and the baby's." He began pulling at her arm, trying to get her to move. He stood over her, and using both of his hands, pulled harder, hoping to free her from the grip the earth had on her. In a voice edged with a sense of panic, he began yelling at her as he slapped her across the face. His face only inches from hers, he now shouted, "You must save the child, and you must run! Run into the woods and hide, Briga!"

Briga blinked her eyes and looked at the young boy whom her eyes finally recognized, and suddenly her understanding returned. "Odhran..."

Looking past Odhran, she saw that the two warriors of Cuar lay dead near him, as did all the members of her party, and now only Cuar remained standing. Cuar continued to fight on fiercely with an arrow in his right leg and one in his left shoulder. He stood defiantly facing the enemy amid the dead bodies of dozens of slain Luti and berserker warriors.

Cuar turned only long enough to shout at Odhran, "Get her out of—"

The sharp twang of bowstrings being released ended his words as six arrows struck his body at the same time. The force pushed him back and caused him to fall to the ground. He lay on his back, gasping, fighting now for each breath he took, as blood filled his lungs. Darkness overcame his soul, and the good goddess released him from his pain. A large group of ravens appeared, called an unkindness of ravens by his people, black as the darkest night, and had begun circling above the battle, drawn by its noise and the smell of blood and death. Among them was a raven of the purest white, the goddess Fand. As Briga watched, the white raven flew down beside Cuar and shapeshifted into Fand, a beautiful shield-maiden was now standing over him. She reached down and took Cuar by the hand, and she led him away from the battlefield to celebrate his honorable death with his ancestors.

Just Odhran and Briga now remained.

Briga rose to her feet and stood beside Odhran, and as she touched his arm, she smiled at him.

"Thank you, Odhran, for being my brave guardian and my champion. Conall will be proud of you, and Caswallon as well."

Looking at her, the young boy bowed his head in quiet agony, and in a voice that was barely audible, said simply, "My lady."

The Luti did not rush in, but instead formed a circle around the two. The old shaman woman bent down at the body of Etaoin and ripped the brooch from her cape. She approached Briga and Odhran with her guards and stood in front of them. As she spoke, more men and a young, badly beaten woman appeared from behind the trees. Briga recognized the young girl as Rhonwen, one of the young maidens who had gone with the party led by Cet. This could only mean that Cuar's brother Cet, Meilyr ap' Pwyll the druid, and all those who had followed them in search of Caswallon's body must have fallen at the hands of the raiders.

Speaking to a man who was standing in front of her, the shaman woman spoke quickly and then struck him. The man looked Rhonwen, stepped closer and gripping her arm tightly, he asked the badly beaten woman, "Is this the wife of Cymru's most dangerous man?" Slapping the girl hard across the face, he asked again, "Is this the wife of the wolf-warrior they call Conall?" Odhran started forward with intentions of attacking the man and the shaman, but Briga held him back.

Briga spoke loudly as she looked directly at the man, "Do not slap this maiden of Cymru again, you piece of *cachi*. I am Briga, the wife of the convel Conall, the conry of my people." Sweeping her arm out as she turned in a circle to face all those around her, she continued speaking. "And all of you are dead. The men and women of Cymru will hunt you like rodents and kill every one of you."

As she reached the place where Rhonwen and the traitor stood, she stopped and asked, "What is your name, traitor? I want to be sure that all my ancestors know you, especially my husband and my grandfather Caswallon."

The man mocked her in his movements as he bowed toward her. "Oh, my great *witsio*, the great witch of Cymru and wife of the coward Conall, I am the unfree and one of the thralls. I have no name, and I am considered dead by the Luti, and now, my great lady, so too shall you be." The man turned his attention to the old woman dressed in white and started to speak, but the woman quickly barked orders to the man she saw as less than a dog. The shaman shouted out to the men gathered in the circle, and six men with bows stepped up to stand off to her left side.

The man who was translating had been captured by the raiders from the coastline of Erin. Briga considered the man a traitor, as she believed he should have killed himself before becoming a slave to the Luti. The thrall once again addressed Briga and said, "These two die, and you will come with us." Without another word the coward turned, and grabbing the girl by the hair, he cut her throat; Rhonwen slumped to the ground. Turning back to Briga and Odhran, he pointed his bloody blade at Odhran and smiled.

Briga only had time to shout, "No!" as the Luti released four arrows, and all four found their target in Odhran's chest. The young man grabbed at the arrows with both his hands as his blood gushed out. His eyes wide, he looked at Briga and said, "My lady." And falling to his knees, he spoke only one more word as he fell dead: Meriel, the name of his mother. Briga stood over the body of Conall's cousin; with tears stinging her eyes and with her face toward the sky as if questioning the gods, she spoke loudly. "Is this how life ends, with Conall, Caswallon, and now Odhran all dead?" She was filled with rage as she looked down at the young man. Her vision was filled with the red blood of hate that boiled into vengeance, and she called out to all the gods to join her as she turned to die.

Pulling out her blade, Briga charged the old woman in white, but this time one of the guards did not attempt to kill her. Instead, he struck her on the head with the metal capped end of his long spear. The blow was hard, and almost immediately the world tunneled down to a pinpoint of light, and Briga fell to the earth in total darkness.

Chapter Thirty-Six

It was dark, rainy, and cold; a small shimmer of light bounced off a few glowing coals remaining from the small fire that had been used to cook some meat the raiders had plundered. Briga was lying on her side, rolled up in a ball in a pathetic attempt to keep warm. Her hands were bound tightly behind her back, as were her legs at the ankles, which she could no longer feel. The rest of her body ached from the beatings she had received when they had questioned her about Conall. She felt death was closer than life. During the last three days, she had been beaten repeatedly in an attempt to gain information about her people and other villages in the area, but her enemy seemed most interested in finding Conall.

One of the raiders had even put a knife to her throat, drawing it lightly across her neck and leaving a shallow wound that ran from the left side of her neck around to the line of her spine. He had growled like an animal as he interrogated her. How could Briga answer? She had no way of knowing where Conall was. Not satisfied with cutting her, the animal of a man beat her about the face and head until she lost consciousness. When she finally came to, she pushed back the need to cry as she struggled to set up. Her hands and feet were bound tightly. She managed to sit up and she propped herself up against the oak at her back. Her long black hair had been savagely cut from her head and now covered the ground around her.

Looking at her hair lying in the mud, she whispered a prayer in a hushed, trembling voice to the good goddess Danu. "Mother Danu, they have cut off my hair."

She gasped, her need to cry stuck in her throat like a strong hand choking her. She fought to control her need to cry. All around her was her beautiful, long black hair, her "crown of glory," as Conall called it. It had been trampled and pushed into the mud by the men who had stood around her laughing as they'd sawed it from her head with their knives.

At the thought of Conall seeing her without her hair, she began to loudly sob. She tried to quiet her sobs; she did not want to be heard. She did not want the men to return to torment her. In silence, Briga wept great tears of sorrow mixed with a deep, burning hatred for the Luti.

And once again she asked the goddess, "Where is my Conall, and where, Danu, are you? Why have you both abandoned me?"

They had used willow switches to whip her arms and legs, leaving angry, red welts covering her back and limbs. They had taken great joy in ripping what clothes she had left.

Naked, she lay exposed to the cold, blood oozing from the wounds inflicted on her from her many beatings. But the old woman had insisted that her torture wouldn't include rape, so as to not harm the child within her womb, and for that Briga had felt oddly thankful.

The Luti shaman of Cimbria seemed to have taken an interest in Briga, much like that of a cat watching a mouse. The woman's hair was gray and matted, and she was clad in a white gown that had threads of gold woven into the sleeves and across her shoulders. She wore a yellow-orange flaxen cloak that fastened with clasps made of gold, as well as a girdle made of bronze. She walked about barefooted, her feet blackened by dirt, and she smelled dirty and unwashed. She was missing teeth, and those she had were yellow and ground down almost to her gums—and her breath was foul enough to make Briga vomit when she drew too close to her face. Briga had learned from the thrall that she was one of the high priestesses of the Cimbri of Jutlandand a gifted seer.

"She has great enchantments, and she can kill by speaking magical words," the thrall had told her in a hushed whisper.

The woman's name was Freya. She was named after her fertility goddess of beauty, though she was anything but beautiful. Freya was as pale and blotched as the white-faced birch. Briga had learned much from the man who was thrall to the raiders. This unfree traitor to his people was a translator, and he let Briga know the old woman's name. He also told Briga that he had told the old woman that Briga was a witsio, a witch of Cymru, and a great healer among her people. The old woman, according to the thrall, had taken a great interest in her. Consequently, she had ordered all the men to keep her alive until they reached the ships.

Laughing and mocking, the men had beaten her every day until pain was her only indication she was still alive. The old woman had warned them not to harm the child, so they beat her across her back and buttocks with switches made of willow. As they beat her, they questioned her—they especially wanted to know how to capture Conall. They thought she held the key to capturing the convel alive, and they wanted him alive, as they had plans for him, which included a very slow death. So they had beaten her for hours, all the time seeking answers to the same question: "Where is Conall?"

As she now lay in the darkness, limp as a cloth doll, she was sure her nose was broken. Her left eye was swollen shut, and her right eye was so swollen that she could only see out of a narrow slit. Her face and eyes had started to turn black and blue. Bruised and battered, she was so glad she didn't know Conall's location;

the pain she had experienced in the many beatings she'd suffered over the past few days had been too much for her, and she now lay in utter resignation, weeping, thinking she would have told them if she had known where he was.

Only her beloved Caswallon's words remained her comfort. He was with her now as she felt the infant inside her move. The movement was comforting and almost pleasurable. It reassured her that the infant was still alive, and that as long as she remained alive, the child would be born. She thought, "I have to do everything, anything I can to stay alive for my son and for my great-grandfather."

Feeling the gentle, soothing movements of the child within her, she began to think of the child and of Conall. Exhaustion finally touched her like a gentle hand placed on her by Danu, and mercifully Briga fell asleep. She dreamed of Conall standing behind her, and as she leaned back, she pressed hard into his embrace; his muscular arms wrapped around her and held her secure and safe.

He buried his face into her long, beautiful hair. Pressing his nose and mouth against her ear, he kissed her, warmly, gently, and said, "I love you, my best beloved." They stood together for a long time, watching as a young boy ran laughing with a friend on a hillside planted with flowering apple trees.

Pressed against each other, they watched as the flower petals fell gently like light snow, and Briga smiled as she felt the warmth of the spring sun on her head and her shoulders. But most of all, she smiled at the great comfort and safety she felt, wrapped tightly in the strong arms of Conall. She heard his voice whispering into her ear, "*Is tu m' annsachd*," and she knew he was safe.

She knew he was alive.

She smiled and moaned softly as she slept, unaware that the old woman Freya sat in the darkness watching Briga like a cat watching a mouse. She protected her now, only to save her for the evil she wanted to deliver later on the wife of the wolf-warrior Conall.

Freya was not just a shaman of the Luti, powerful in magic; she was the grandmother of Healtholaf, the leader who now lay near death due to the wound he had received at the hand of Conall.

In her right hand, she held Briga's medicine bag, and in her left hand, she held a small cloth doll filled with light-red hair. She knew whose hair this was, and as she held the doll, she spoke into the darkness a curse on Conall, on Briga, and on the un-born child in Briga's womb. The words came from deep within the old shaman woman.

"May the goddess Hel take Conall into Éljúðnir and never let him see his wife or his child. Let Briga suffer and her child per-ish by the force of cruel hands." With a raspy voice, she prayed and chanted for her people, and she sought from her gods the fulfillment of justice for all those killed and injured at the hands of the wolf-warriors of Cymru.

Yes, she wanted justice, but even more than justice, she wanted revenge. She would keep this young woman and torment her for the rest of her days; she would make her a thrall, one of the unfree among the people of Jutland and Cimbria. The child would be-come an unfree person too and would spend all its days a thrall, a slave to all the Luti. The old woman watched the young girl in the darkness, and as Briga smiled in the warm memories of a woman whose heart is deeply in love, the old hag frowned at the young maiden— Freya's cold sense of hate and need for revenge would remove that smile.

As dawn's pale, gray gloom began to lighten the eastern sky-line, Briga stirred and opened her eyes. Sitting only two feet away was the old woman. "Good morning, grandmother," she said out of a sense of politeness. Any kind words were wasted on the old woman as she stood up and walked away, only to return a few minutes later with the thrall interpreter.

The man yawned as he sat down on the ground next to Briga and said, "Sit up. The old woman has some questions for you." As Briga moved to sit up, the man continued. "She wants you to know she is taking you to Jutland. You will be her thrall, as will your son, and in time your son will be trained to be a berserker. It is Freya's grandson, Healtholaf, the leader of the raiders, who lies near death from a great wound to his back, a wound inflicted by your man, Conall. She believes you have the magic to heal him; she figures her grandson's wound was inflicted by your man, and to heal that wound, Freya needs Conall's woman."

Briga sat up as straight as her pain would let her and looked directly into the deep-blue eyes of the old woman. She said, "Tell her I understand."

The old woman spoke to the thrall, and he said, "She wants you to know that your child and you will live as long as her grandson lives. When he dies, you both die."

Looking deeply into the old woman's eyes, Briga said, "I accept her conditions, and I will use all my skill and magic to keep her grandson alive and to heal his wounds."

Without speaking, the old woman stood up and bent over Briga. She handed her the medicine bag she held in her hand. In her other hand she tightly held the doll. She looked at Briga, watching every detail of her face as she spoke. The thrall looked at the old woman and at the doll held tightly in her hand, and then he looked at Briga.

"She gives you your medicine bag, but the doll, the talisman of your man with his hair, she has cursed and will throw into the fire. The fire will consume the doll and seal the curse that she has placed in the hands of the goddess Hel. You will never see your man again. He is dead to the dead."

Briga wouldn't look at the woman. Instead, she looked past her at what had appeared just as the woman started to speak. A huge black wolf moved out of the trees and stood on the edge of the shadows, almost invisible to her. It was looking at the old woman, and as the old woman stopped talking, it turned to look directly at Briga.

Briga watched as the wolf, still looking straight at her, turned its head to one side, almost placing its ear on its left shoulder. Briga inwardly laughed to herself as she looked in wide-eyed amazement at the wolf. Softly she said to herself, "That is exactly the way Conall turns his head when I scold him."

Like a shadowy ghost, the wolf melted back into the darkness of the trees. Just as quickly as it had appeared, it vanished from her sight. With an icy stare, Briga smiled at the old woman as the old hag walked away and said under her breath, "My Conall dead to the dead—I don't think so, you old crone."

As the old woman walked away, she paused and turned, speaking quickly to the thrall without looking at Briga. When she finished speaking, she turned and resumed walking— entering the trees, she disappeared into the early-morning dark- ness of the forest.

The thrall got up off the ground and approached Briga, hold- ing in his right hand a small dirk-like blade. It was very sharp, and as he bent down, he grumbled at her, "Roll so I can get at your ropes. The old woman has told me to cut you free, both your hands and your feet."

Following the tidal waves of continual misery, Briga was all too happy to conform to the man's orders. As soon as the ropes fell, she started rubbing her legs and hands to get blood moving back into her feet and fingers. Soon they began to tingle, and the pain she felt was a good sign. The thrall watched until hun- ger got the better of him; smoke had filled the air as the raiders began cooking what meat they had left, and the aroma made Briga remember her hunger.

"One more thing, Briga," he said as he turned to walk away. "Freya wants you to know that if you try to escape, she will have the men tie you, spread you out on the ground with stakes, and with her sharpest knife, she will skillfully cut the child from your womb. She will keep you alive to watch as she cooks your child alive on an open fire, and she promises you will live long enough to watch her enjoy eating the tender young flesh. I wouldn't run if I were you, as that old woman will do exactly what she threatens."

The thrall had been holding some dirty clothes, and tossing them on the ground at Briga's feet, he said, "Dress yourself."

Without speaking, Briga dressed in the filthy rags. She followed the thrall toward the small cooking fires in the hope of getting something to eat, all the time thinking to herself, "It won't take long for the warriors of Cymru to find these fools and their fires."

Chapter Thirty-Seven

The next few days went by without Briga experiencing the beatings and humiliating treatment of her first days of captivity. She had been declared the thrall of Freya, and now the men paid little attention to her; most would hardly look at her, and none spoke to her, except the coward who acted as translator for the old shaman woman.

It did not take Briga long to discover just how strong a woman the old crone was, and how completely she controlled the men. Apparently she had made it very clear that no harm was to come to the Cymru witsio. If Briga did approach the men, they would step aside without looking at her, and if she got too close, they quickly moved far enough away that they had no chance of actually touching her. No one dared touch her, as it had become very clear that the word of the grandmother of Healtholaf was the same as a word from Healtholaf.

Briga had not only had her bindings removed, she had also become untouchable, and that was a great relief to her, as she now concentrated on doing everything possible to stay alive for the sake of her child and the hope of rescue or escape.

As the party of men moved rapidly west toward the coast, they met other groups of Luti who had also come deeper inland looking for escaped prisoners from the raid led by Conall. All of these men also wanted revenge, and at every opportunity they plundered, killed, or took as slaves anyone they found. They set fire to homes and buildings whenever they happened upon them, and they stole the livestock as they made their way back to the sea. Once they reached the coast and had a good view of the Sea of Erin, they followed the coastline south, back to their ships.

It was the many fires burning, sending smoke high into the sky of Cymru that gave Briga her greatest hope. She knew that the great billowing clouds of thick gray and black smoke would be seen for miles. It was this smoke that marked the raiders' escape trail to the sea, and it would be the smoke that Conall or any of the warriors of Cymru would follow. She now felt reassured in the most alive place in her heart, where Conall lived. She also had total faith in Conall Cearnach himself, and she had complete trust that he, the victorious, would come to free her from these murderers and cowards who beat and raped women.

She knew with certainty that Conall's uncle Caratacus would have assembled an army by now, and that warriors on foot and light horse calvary would be following the trail of smoke and destruction left by the raiders. It was her hope that the men and women of Cymru would burst out of the woods at any moment, drums beating, war trumpets blasting and screaming, shrieking battle cries with such dreadful sounds that the Luti's courage would fail, and they would be slaughtered to the last man and the last old hag.

A smile came to Briga's face as she walked along the trail. She looked at the men nearest her and thought, "It won't be long before all the heads of the men around me will be atop tall, sharpened poles at Caer Caradoc, the fortress of the Ard Righ Caradoc ap Bran." She knew that once Caratacus and the warriors of Cymru found the Luti, they would all be put to death. Not one would be spared.

Her pain and the suffering of her people and the land would only be made whole by the death of the raiders. Their blood flowing into the earth of Cymru and their heads displayed at Caer Caradoc would do much to heal the land and the people.

The ranks of the Luti war party who had found Briga increased as more raiders joined them and brought along captives, all young women; many of them had been severely beaten and raped. Briga was soon very busy comforting the women, helping treat the wounds and the ugly bruises beaten into them by the Luti raiders. But the bruises beaten into the souls and spirits of the women went deeper than her potions and herbs could reach.

Briga feared for all of her sisters, especially the youngest girl, barely in her teens. As Briga looked at the women, it was hard for her not to scream out in anger at Conall and the men of Cymru. Instead she quietly asked the gods, "When will they come?"

Once the women realized she was the wife of the great convel Conall Cearnach, they gave her great honor and respect. The women knew of Conall, and now they whispered in hushed tones his name, Conall Cearnach of Clan Diahad. Every woman captured by the Luti looked to Briga with great respect and total obedience. All of them had a renewed hope that the great Conry Conall, the "King of the Wolves," would follow and find them; they all felt freedom would be theirs soon.

Briga's bruises would take weeks to heal, but the swelling around her eyes was getting better. She now could see out of both eyes, but what she saw troubled her and gave her soul much grief.

She was safe from rape, but the women who had been taken slaves would have to endure much pain and suffering until they were rescued; each night men would drag them off and abuse them. Briga tried to ask Freya to stop the violence, but it did no good; the old crone had taken to carrying a long willow switch just to strike Briga. The shaman was intent on letting all the men know she was in control of her thrall, and whenever Briga displeased the old woman, she would strike her severely on the back with the switch.

The party of raiders and their captives kept moving south along the coast. The Luti seemed concerned, and every day they sent scouts out in all four directions in the hope that they had not been followed. They pushed the captives, and if they didn't move fast enough, the Luti would beat them and strike at them with the butts of their spears; the pace was hard, and for a few, it was too much. One young woman who had been badly beaten fell to the ground and could not get up. The thrall yelled at the others to keep moving. "Don't touch her if you want to live!" he shouted, and as the women continued down the trail, two men went back to the young maiden of Cymru. They all knew she would soon be dead, and each of the captive women prayed as they walked, begging the good goddess Danu to send the goddess Fand to come and take the young girl's hand, lifting her soul to the hall of her ancestors.

Briga tried to keep time by the moon phases, and she was sure it had been almost two weeks since she had been captured. As the child grew, Briga felt sorrow, as this was a bad time to be pregnant. As she walked along the trail, she counted the months since she and Conall had celebrated the fire festival of Samhain. She felt a deep warmth and love for Conall as she remembered the night they'd celebrated together, and she was certain she had conceived when they'd made love together that evening, when they had returned to the tent they had set up at the lake edge to live in as Conall worked on the crannog on the lake. "Yes," she thought, "it has been about seven months, and I should be at least seven months pregnant."

The child seemed to move more during the day as they walked, and it was often difficult for Briga to walk the rough trails; the other women would often reach out to help her keep her balance. She was only allowed to rest when they settled down for long periods at night. It was during these quiet times in the darkness, when Briga lay down to sleep, that she found her only happiness—dreams.

But she also secretly rejoiced at the gentle fluttering movements as they walked along the trail, and the child's activeness only helped to reassure her that her son grew stronger every day. Surrounded by pain, suffering, and fear, she fought to forget the misery and to think only of her son and her beloved Caswallon.

Her face and broken nose were healing, and the swelling from her earlier beatings was decreasing. Her bruises would remain for many more days—ugly greenish-purple and black-brown reminders of the cruelty of men who do not love the goddess. As she had knelt down to drink from a small pool of rainwater, she had seen her reflection. She had trembled in shock at the image that looked back at her, and she said to the women around her, "I am a frightful-looking hag, and Conall will never recognize me." Briga had held her head in her hands as she burst into tears. Sobbing, she'd trembled in her despair as the other women with her quietly reached out to comfort her.

Her healing slowly continued, and as her nasal airway opened, she realized that not being able to smell had been a good thing. The Luti stunk; no, they reeked. They smelled so bad that if she got close to one of them, she gagged. These men had not bathed or washed their clothing in months. The more her face and nose healed, the worse the stench seemed to grow, until the rancid body odor and the smell of human shit seemed to hang in the air like a thick, nasty fog. As they all walked together, a light breeze gently blew across the men in front of her, bringing with it the full force of their aroma, and it was not good.

"I can't stand the smell," she mumbled, knowing only the thrall and her fellow prisoners would understand her words.

Briga's hand went up to cover her nose in an attempt to stop some of the stench from making its way into her nose. "If the men of Cymru smelled like this, they would have no women, no children, and no one to sleep with except one another or the wild animals." Looking at the women walking with her, she added, "No, the wild animals wouldn't have them." Several of the women laughed softly, while others glared at the Luti and began voicing their hatred of these men. One tall blond woman looked at the raiders, spit on the ground, and between clenched teeth said, "These are not men, and these cowards were born from the shit of their mothers."

Briga heard laughter behind her from several of the women, and she turned around to see who it was. When she did get a good look, she started laughing too, as she saw all the women near her also had their hands covering their noses. For a brief moment, they all giggled and laughed together until the thrall shouted at them to "Shut up or die!"

She had noticed that whenever they did find enough water to wash, all the women of Cymru did the best they could to stay clean by washing; among the Luti, however, only the shaman Freya seemed to know what water was and how to use it.

As evening approached, the men would leave the trail whenever they had enough trees for cover; they would also push the prisoners into the tree cover to hide from the men of Cymru. Moving faster once on open ground, the group would keep pushing forward until they found a suitable hill, and then they would force everyone to the top, where they would settle in for the night. The men would eat, and if they had anything left over, they would throw it at the prisoners; but usually there wasn't enough for everyone. Briga had begun to organize the women, and together they agreed that the ones who ate at night would not eat in the morning, while the ones who ate in the morning would not eat at night. No one had received food both morning and night for days.

The women had also begun to sleep pressed together for warmth, but it was still the nightly fear of every woman that one or more of them would be taken away to be raped and beaten by the Luti pigs.

Only Briga was left unmolested. In their village, the women of Cymru lived and grew old together as sisters of one family, and it made them all pleased that one of their sisters with child was protected, even if the protection was from the old crone hag, Freya.

As darkness covered them, sleep came to everyone in the camp. For the first time in days, Briga dreamed of Conall.

She felt his mouth softly kissing and gently sucking on her neck. She was straddling his hips, her palms on his chest, and her arms supporting her weight as she rocked gently forward. She moved her body and her hips to counterbalance the soft, swaying motion of her upper body. He was deep inside her as she found just the right place that brought intense pleasure with each movement. Briga was transported to a place she wished she could stay at forever. She moaned as she arched her back, and her head turned to look up at the ceiling of the crannog. His hands moved to both sides of her waist, and he helped support her weight as she moved. She was his, and his touch reached deep inside her over and over again, until all she felt were bliss and great waves of pleasure, each washing over her, taking her higher, until her world was one with the goddess. Surrounded by the safety of her lover's arms, she collapsed on his chest and began to fall into a bottomless sleep. She thought as he held her in his arms, "Conall is the only man I could ever love."

Briga slept that night in the safety and strength of Conall's arms.

Her dreams moved darkly across her mind as her lover's face changed from Conall's to the death mask of Cuar; dread filled her spirit with a sense of doom, and anguish spilled from her heart to chill her soul. Before her now was only the reality of her capture and the possibility that she too would become a thrall— one of the nameless slaves of the Luti.

Chapter Thirty-Eight

It had been raining intermittently for the last two days, and the sky had stayed mostly cloud covered, gray, and cold. The women, wet from the rain, shivered as they walked. As they moved, pushed forward by the Luti and their dog, the thrall, they pressed together and held on to each other in an attempt to share their body warmth. All of them had slipped into a numbed, mindless walk—not talking, just enduring. This morning the sun had risen above the Cambrian Mountains along the horizon in a narrow slit of sky that had opened from the cloud cover. Briga knew they were moving south. They had dropped out of the mountains into a valley that had a river flowing in the same direction they walked. The Cambrian Mountains rose on three sides of the river valley, and they moved toward what appeared to be a wide opening ahead; Briga thought they might be following the Afon Tywi.

She had realized days ago that the Luti seemed confused and maybe even lost. It had become apparent that they were looking for a specific valley. They had wandered in the mountains and dropped down into valleys with rivers on two different occasions, and on both occasions the men had seemed confused and frightened. The last time this happened, the raiders had exploded in a heated argument between what were clearly two different groups of men. The argument became so violent that two men died fighting—choking, drowning in their own blood from the wounds that had inflicted. Many others had continued to fight even after their comrades fell.

The belligerent struggle had only ended when Freya, screaming at the top of her shrill voice, had run right into the middle of the fighting men. She'd kicked and struck them with her clenched fists until they stopped fighting. Like dogs that had been kicked by a cruel master, the men had withdrawn.

Briga also watched as the raiders continued sending out groups of six to ten men. They would be gone for hours, and sometimes when they returned, they brought fresh meat; once they brought back a very young girl with long, red hair.

Briga was sure the old crone was ordering them out to look for Conall.

The raiders had also come back twice bloodied and missing men, and Briga guessed that they had encountered men and women who fought. One party of six men had not returned, and the women had taken this as a very good sign. They believed, and rightly so, that scouting parties moving ahead of the army of Caratacus had found the raiders. The women believed that in the hills and trees, the men of Cymru searched for and may have already found them.

Briga was sure that the Afon Tywi was the river the Luti had been looking for, and once they seemed sure they had found it, they refused to send out raiders in search of Conall or even food. It did not matter how loud the old crone Freya yelled at the men; they would not leave. Instead they stayed together and moved as rapidly as they could down the river toward the coast.

When the Luti had first attacked Briga's party, they had numbered over a hundred. Cuar and his warriors, Etaoin, and Odhran had left dozens dead in the woods of the Cambrian Mountains, and the Luti had killed almost a dozen of their own men in the march back to the sea. Several had died as they fought among themselves, but more had died because they had been wounded and could no longer travel. The Luti only enlisted men robust for fighting and traveling; a severely wounded man would be handed his sword as he lay on his back, grasping the blade by the hilt, the point toward his feet as another warrior approached his head and, kneeling, cut the injured man's throat.

Briga watched in disgust as the Luti killed their own, and turning to the thrall, she asked, "Why don't they care for their men? Why do they kill them holding their swords?" The thrall told Briga that these people believed that to die sword in hand was to die in honor, and a warrior who died holding his blade would be taken to the great hall to celebrate a feast in his honor with his ancestors.

Briga was awakened by the sound of the raiders moving around the camp, it was early dawn, and the Luti had risen early; soon all the women had been forced up by the thrall, and he began pushing them in the direction the Luti were moving. About midmorning two other small parties of raiders joined them as they moved back to the coast, and Briga estimated the entire party, including the women taken as prisoners, to number about sixty. Now, sure they had found the right river valley, they stayed together, tightly grouped, and to her surprise, the Luti didn't send warriors ahead of them or even to the rear of their group; they just stayed pressed in a tight ball of men with their prisoners in the middle, pushing the women forward, often beating them, and always moving south, toward the sea.

As they traveled, it was apparent that the Luti had been here. Everywhere the homes and farm buildings had been burned, and the land seemed empty, lacking both animals and people.

Briga was sure everyone had fled or been killed or captured.

The land was utterly desolate. Occasionally they happened on a wandering cow that was quickly killed and butchered, but instead of making fires to cook the meat, they cut thin strips and ate these raw as they walked.

As bare as the land looked to Briga, it also looked empty to the Luti. They had expected to see their own people here along the river, and their absence meant only one thing: they had withdrawn to the coast. Now fear began to enter the hearts of the Luti as they began to think, "Maybe the ships have already left." They now pushed themselves and their captives without mercy, and anyone who could not keep up was put to death. Briga, helping a young girl who had developed a bad limp, wondered if any of them would survive the march to the coast.

The group started to spread out as the stronger, faster men began to almost run as they fled to the sea. Shouts began to fill the air from those at the head of the column of raiders, and soon they all stood on a cliff overlooking a large bay. Briga knew this place as Three Rivers, and she knew they had indeed been on the Afon Tywi. They had reached the estuary of the three rivers at the great ocean bay of Bae Caerfyrddin. The men looked south and started talking with great excitement, and Briga tried to understand what it was they saw.

The thrall came up beside Briga and spoke quietly to her. "It's the dunes, the sand dunes at Cefn Sidan. This is the place they landed their ships, and from here they came inland. They pulled their ships up onto the sand in the shelter of the bay formed by the sandbar. This estuary is the place the three rivers empty into the bay, and where they left their ships. We are close now, almost back to the ships, so tell your women to push and push hard, as they will probably kill all of you if you slow them down."

They moved, following the shoreline of the estuary, and looking across they could see eight wooden ships pulled up on the beach. One of the ships had a long, pitched tent erected along its entire deck, so that it almost covered the ship. Scores of red flags flew from it and from spears on the beach, all of them holding the image of a great black bird. Men stood on the beach and around the ship. Briga and her party, drunk with fatigue, were bent over double, like old farmers under heavy sacks. When they came into view, the men at the ships started pointing and shouting.

The Luti who held Briga and the women of Cymru captive shouted back, and suddenly there was much confusion and shouting as the voices of the men around Briga became harsh and angry. Some of the men sped forward at a full run toward the ships, and even the old crone Freya added her voice to the confusion, cursing through the rain-soaked sludge. The knock-kneed old hag was harshly coughing but still she tried to add her voice to the confusion of sound.

The thrall, still walking with Briga, laughed loudly and said, "They are very angry, these Luti. You see, over there on the sand, there should be twenty-eight ships; instead there are only eight. Four belong to Gundwulf the Good, and the rest belong to Healtholaf; there might not be enough crew to sail two of the langskips. It also seems that their leader, Healtholaf, is almost dead, which is not good news for you, Briga. The other raiders took their ships to sea three days ago and left their leader, a handful of men, and these empty ships for whoever made it back. It sounds like there was a great fight between the two groups of men, as the ones who left abandoned those who stayed with the ships and their chieftain. We are lucky; the men across the estuary have shouted over to us that tomorrow morning they planned to set sail in the ship of Healtholaf. They will be setting fire to any ship on the beach tomorrow that does not have a crew."

Briga's heart fell as the reality of the words sank in. "No, not tomorrow. We cannot leave yet."

The women around her heard too, and they started to talk among themselves. Some even began to cry. All of them slowed, and a few stopped walking.

In a burst of anger and violence, the thrall started yelling, hitting, and kicking the women who had slowed or stopped completely. "You'd better keep moving, you stupid bitches. I am not lying to you! If they have cause to kill one of you, they will kill all of you and me too. These Luti are enraged, and they may kill us all anyway."

Hitting them and swearing at them, the man beat the women until he had them all moving again. Briga looked across the estuary and thought, "I must do something to delay. I need more time. I need more time for Conall to find me."

Walking with the other women, she felt for the first time that she might not be rescued, and that she might be carried away on the ships that sat on the north side of the sandbar at Cefn Sidan. The idea of being taken away by these filthy Luti was too much for her, and she began to cry, softly at first, but soon all the women sobbed as the thrall cursed and beat them, pushing them onward toward the ships.

Briga looked to the only one who could possibly help her now. She prayed, "Mother Danu, please help us. Please save us or show us how we might save ourselves, please."

Chapter Thirty-Nine

As soon as they made it through the estuary to the ships, the old woman started screaming at the men. One large fellow came forward. He had long blond hair and was beardless except for several days of light-blond whisker growth. Briga guessed that he was the leader of the group of warriors who had remained. Freya was yelling at him, and as he was answering her, she struck his face with a loud slap. The warrior did not hesitate to respond, and swiftly he struck the old hag in the face with his fist. The old woman fell to the ground and didn't move.

The women standing with Briga gave out a common gasp at the sight of a man striking the elderly woman of their own people, and the rest of the men stood completely still for what seemed like a long time. Briga could feel the pounding of her heart, and she knew more chaos was soon to follow.

The man who had struck the old woman had made up his mind that he was not going to follow the dying Healtholaf any longer, and he had already given orders to his men to leave in the morning. They had planned to burn all the langskips they didn't need, including the one in which Healtholaf lay near death. Healtholaf's langskip was to become his premature funeral pyre. Plotting the early death of the chieftain was a sign that his men no longer feared or followed him. They had become weary of waiting for him to die, and they reasoned there was no harm in speeding up that death a little.

This man who now seemed to take on the role of their leader began barking orders at the rest of the men, and without any further prompting, most of them began loading what they could onto three of the ships. The man who had hit the old woman walked over to Briga and the other women and started to talk to the thrall.

The thrall listened and turned to Briga to translate as the Luti warrior watched her face. "This is Gundwulf, and he wants you to know that he is a great Luti chieftain with many ships and many men. He wants you to know that he is kinder and he treats his unfree better than the piece-of-pig-shit grandson of the old bitch Freya. Briga, the wounded chieftain's name is Healtholaf, and he was wounded by Conall."

Briga looked into the raider's blue eyes, and she smiled. He smiled back.

The raider spoke again, and the thrall continued to translate. "He is offering to take you and all the women with him and his men. He does not want to leave you here with the old crone. He wants you to know that they have many men who do not have wives, and in time many of you would become good Luti wives. He wants you to know that you will be treated well, that his men will not beat or rape you. He will be a kind man as long as you obey and do not try to escape. He is also fearful that if he leaves you here with Freya, she will have you all put to death."

Without breaking eye contact with Gundwulf, she started to speak. "Tell him this and tell him every word," she said to the thrall.

Briga continued. "I thank the great Luti chieftain Gundwulf the Good for his concern and his kindness, and I do agree with him that if the women of Cymru are left on this beach, the old hag will have them killed. I agree that under the circumstances, your offer may be our best chance. I will let the women with me make that choice. I have to stay, as I made an oath to heal the grandson of Freya, and I stay knowing that if I fail, I and the child with me will surely die."

Gundwulf looked at her, then turned toward the thrall and asked him a question. With the answer to his question supplied by the thrall, he turned again to Briga and started talking once more. The thrall continued to translate. "You are the woman of the great wolf-warrior Conall?"

Looking at him, she said yes and nodded.

He smiled at her and said, "Even badly beaten, I can see that Conall's woman is very beautiful, and she is also very brave. I hope that if your man still lives, he gets to this beach in time to save you and his child. Now, ask your women if they want to go with me and my men or stay here; they must hurry, as the tide has been coming in for some time now, and we must float our ships. As soon as the tide begins to turn, we must leave; I do not want to stay in this cursed land another day, and I will leave tonight instead of tomorrow. The thrall dog with you tells me your name is Briga. I shall remember your name, and I will tell the women of my country of the great beauty and brave spirit of the women of Cymru, and of the wife of the convel Conall. I promise you, Briga, that the maidens of Cymru who go with me will be well treated and protected."

The women of Cymru who stood around Briga heard all the words spoken by Gundwulf translated by the thrall, and given the choice between leaving with Gundwulf or staying on this beach with Freya and her grandson's men, they all quickly, by unanimous decision, voted to go with Gundwulf, thinking their chances of survival were greater with him.

Deep uncertainty was etched on the faces of the women standing with Briga, and a few of the younger women sobbed openly as she embraced them and said her good-byes. All the women gathering around her reached out to touch her with trembling hands and eyes that seemed to shout out the finality of this moment. Some kissed her tenderly on the forehead or on the cheek, and as tears welled up in Briga's eyes, the bitter taste of insecurity and fear clouded her mind. She watched dreamily as Gundwulf's men led the maidens of Cymru down the beach to wait for his ships to be floated. As she watched, Gundwulf paused and turned to look back at her, and for a brief moment, Briga hoped he would come back and take her with him.

As Briga watched Gundwulf, a group of men walked toward him. They were not Luti. From their appearance, she was sure they were Romans. She had often sat at the evening fire at the crannog listening to Conall and his friends talking about the Romans, and she had listened intently as Da'ire had described to her husband the Romans he had fought in Gaul.

Several men in red wool cloaks stood beside a younger man who was wearing a white tunic. His shoulders were also covered by a red cloak. As the younger man spoke to Gundwulf, the Luti looked past the Roman, back toward Briga. He said something to the younger Roman and nodded his head to indicate yes.

The Romans all looked at her and began walking toward her. Speaking to the thrall standing beside her, Briga asked, "Who are these men, thrall?"

Looking past Briga toward the advancing group of men and speaking almost in a whisper, the thrall said, "These men are the reason we are here. They have been sent by Rome to explore and map the coastline and bays of Cymru, and the man in the white tunic is their leader."

The men stopped a short distance from Briga and the thrall, and as the man in white stepped forward to stand in front of them, he said with a broad smile, "Salutis!" The thrall returned the man's greeting, and to Briga's surprise, he began answering the man's questions in the man's native tongue, Latin.

Both men now looked at Briga, and the man in white watched her eyes as the thrall began asking her questions. "This is Gaius Suetonius Paulinus sent to Cymru by the Senate of Rome, and he wants to know if you are the wife of the red-haired warrior who struck down Healtholaf."

Looking at the man, Briga saw he was very young. He was handsome, with sharply cut features and a nose that reminded her of a hawk's beak. His hair was black and wavy like the gentle waves of a calm ocean, but looking deep into his dark, black eyes, she saw there was nothing kind or gentle about him.

Briga turned her attention toward the thrall and forcibly said, "When I answer this man, I want you to speak my words exactly. Do not soften them, and be sure you speak both the meaning and the emotion of my words so he understands."

She turned her attention back to the Roman and held his gaze as she answered, "Tell Gaius that I am the wife of the great convel Conry of the order of Cunobarrus, Conall of Cymru."

With his cold, black eyes riveted on hers, he spoke again, and once again the thrall translated. "He wants to know if all the warriors of Cymru will fight as fiercely as the men who attacked and tormented his camp in the river valley."

If a cat could smile at a mouse as it readied to eat him that would have been the smile on Briga's face as she answered the Roman's question. "Our druids teach us that a brave and honorable death is the only door that leads directly to birth. Yes, Roman, all of our men will fight like the convel who attacked you, as will our women and our children, and if I had a knife in my hand, I would lunge forward and thrust it into your throat."

The fierceness of Briga's look and the sound of her words surprised the young Roman, and he took a step back. For a moment he looked at her, taking in the whole view, and without a word he turned and walked back down the beach toward the ships of Gundwulf.

Pale and shaking, the thrall said to her, "You are either very brave or very mad, Briga of Cymru."

She looked at the thrall and asked, "How many languages do you speak, thrall?"

Both now trembling, they slumped down on the beach's white sand, and the thrall began to speak. "I was captured very young from a village on the coast of Erin. In the first months, those who had captured me did not demand much of me, and I would sit around listening to their words. I have the ears of a rabbit, my lady, and I heard every sound of every word. I would sit by myself and play a game as I softly tried to make the sounds and the words I was hearing. Soon the sounds and words had meaning, and I was able to speak. I discovered that the gods had given me a gift, and I found it easy to learn the tongues of different people. It was by listening that I brought to my tongue the voices of other people."

Briga asked him, "How many, thrall? How many can you speak?"

He looked down at the sand at his feet and said, "Six, my lady. Six. I can understand and speak well enough to be understood by the voices of Erin, Cymru, several of the languages of the Northman, and the Latin of Rome."

Looking at the thrall, she began to see him not as a slave dog but as a young man who would prove to have value. Touching his arm, she said, "Thank you for telling my words to the Roman. I would like to learn the tongues of the Northman and the Latin of Rome. Will you teach me?"

As he looked into her eyes, Briga saw in the thrall a sparkle that had not been there before. He smiled at her, saying eagerly, "Yes. Yes, my lady, I will teach you." Briga and the thrall sat together on the beach, and as they watched the raiders work to float their langskips, the thrall began to teach Briga the tongue of the Luti.

The next few hours flew by as men worked frantically to dig away at the sand that held the ships' keels. They created a ditch that would allow the incoming tide to float and free three of the partially beached ships. Then, at the highest tide, the Luti began pushing the three ships back into the bay, guided by the rhythm of several men beating drums and two warriors singing in deep voices that matched the drumbeats. Soon all three ships rested in the water only a few yards from the shoreline.

Once the ships were in the water, the Luti formed a single line of men to each ship, from the beach shoreline out into the water, until they stood chest deep next to their vessels. The Romans were the first to move along the line of men standing in the water and climb aboard the first of Gundwulf's langskips. In great haste on the beach, other men rushed about gathering food and supplies, and like dutiful ants, they carried them to the men standing in the water. The men who stood in line then began to pass what items they had been handed from man to man along the line, over their heads, until all their supplies were on board the three ships.

When all the supplies were loaded, Gundwulf divided the captured women into three groups and began to move them toward the line of men. One by one, each woman was passed from man to man until she was able to reach up to the ship's side rail and be lifted aboard with the help of warriors on the ship. The men laughed and smiled broadly as they passed the women along their line, and as the last of the maidens was pulled up in the langskip, all the men gave a great shout.

Loaded with their supplies and the maidens of Cymru, all Gundwulf's men climbed aboard their ships and soon tendered them ready to sail with the outgoing tide.

Freya's men had picked her up off the beach and carried her to the place under the tent covering on her grandson's ship. These same men who carried her now set about getting another ship pushed off the beach and into the estuary. They waited to load it. Then they anchored it just off the shoreline, and Briga thought to herself that this might have been done in case they needed to get away quickly. She knew these men expected an attack any moment, and it made sense to her that they wanted to be ready to leave in the event of one.

Briga had sat on the sand watching as all the preparations were made. Emotions flooded her, and she had to fight to keep from crying. As she sat, she thought of the women boarding the ships, and she wondered what would become of them and whether she would ever see them again. She also worried about her child and what would become of him, but she held on to the hope that Conall or others would come for her and save her and the son she would name Weylin. Yet she also felt guilt, knowing that as she sat in the sand hoping for rescue, the other women would be taken far away from Cymru.

Her attention was momentarily diverted as she heard the screeching, high-pitched call of an osprey as it flew out of the trees on the other side of the estuary. It was only then that she noticed the unbelievable number of birds on the water, on the beach, in the grassy marsh, and in the woods of this shoreline world. Great flocks of birds of many different sizes and colors filled the air; sometimes a group would land just to explode off the water, taking to flight.

She was from the inland mountains, and she had never been to the coast. To her amazement, it was an intense place full of life, with so many birds she had never seen before. She recognized the ducks and had heard of the osprey. Birds called all around her with so many different sounds that her senses were overwhelmed. She watched as the osprey flew low across the water and reached out with its talons, snatching a fish from the water; it called out at full volume as it flew back toward the trees.

Good to his word, the ships of Gundwulf now began to glide under the oars of the Luti. It had been over six hours since they had started to get ready to leave, and during that time Gundwulf's men had managed to float and load three of the ships with what supplies they had, including the women of Cymru. Briga heard a loud shout, and all the oars of the three vessels dropped into the water with a splash. With the oars in the water, the men started rowing hard, dipping and pulling to the rhythm of men calling out a litany of chants.

The sound of water splashing and wood creaking was surprisingly loud, and Briga was amazed at how quickly the shallow-draft Luti ships began moving. She watched as they flew across the water's surface, hardly creating a wake. As Briga watched the ships, she was curious to see that creatures in the water appeared to be watching the Luti leave; a family of four sea otters, male, female, and two young pups, stopped hunting and playing long enough to watch the ships begin to move out of the estuary. Briga envied the otters' freedom of movement.

Under the forceful power of the oars, the three ships of Gundwulf moved out of the estuary of Gwendraeth and past the sandbar of Cefn Sidan. Briga watched as the ships moved past the tip of the sandbar toward the setting sun. As the vessels rounded the point, she heard Gundwulf's voice booming out an order that carried across the water; in one motion, all the oars lifted together and were held upright, as if in a salute, and standing at the rear of the lead ship was Gundwulf. He stood tall and as straight as his oars, his long, blond hair blowing in the wind. Briga, admiring his appearance, thought, "What a magnificent-looking man."

As the oars disappeared from sight, she watched as the three ships raised their large square sails, and she noticed that Gundwulf's sails were woven in a pattern of wide, alternating red and white vertical stripes. The wind in the bay was blowing from the land, and it did not take the sails long to be filled to bursting. Like spring clouds driven across a blue sky, the langskips raced rapidly out toward the deep ocean.

Briga watched as the light rays of a setting sun brightly reflected off the ships' sails until they disappeared from her sight as they entered the waters of Bae Caerfyrddin and the great ocean beyond.

She sat alone on the beach, watching until twilight's fading light dulled toward darkness. The thrall had wandered off, and she now sat with her thoughts as company.

She was thinking about what Gundwulf had said to her when she softly said, "Gundwulf, yes. Gundwulf the Good—I should have gone with you."

Briga thought, "I am not brave, Gundwulf the Good. The reason I stayed was to delay going. I wanted more time for Conall, more time so that he could rescue me from this bad dream."

She looked around for the thrall and did not see him. What she didn't know was that now that they had returned to the ships, he was chained again, deep in the storage hold. Much like a dog, the Luti only took the man off his chains when his masters needed him.

Darkness came upon her like an unwanted intrusion, and she hadn't eaten all day. The men had some cooking fires smoldering, as they had already eaten and most had drifted away from the fires to look for places to sleep. She walked up to one of the fires and stood staring down at a man who had several large pieces of meat stuck on the tip of a long-bladed hewing spear.

The man looked at her and without a word, pulled one of the pieces from the spear, flinging it as far away as he could, much like one might do to get a pesky dog away from the table. The hunk of meat bounced several times and rolled on the sand, and by the time Briga picked it up, it was well covered in fine, white sand.

She looked back at the man and said gratefully, "Thank you."

Having her dinner in hand, she walked down to the water's edge and stepped into the cold water until it reached just below her knees; she started to wash and brush the sand off the meat. She was still standing in the water as she ripped the first mouthful away from the chunk with her teeth. Enjoying the taste of salt on the meat, she realized how hungry she was—as she ate, she thought, "This is the most delicious meal I've had in many days." She continued to dip the meat into the seawater as she ate, as the savory taste of the beef was made richer by the salt in the water. Only for a minute did she think of saving some for tomorrow. Her hunger and the wonderful flavor, enhanced by the sea salt, kept her eating until there was none left.

Her hunger pains wonderfully eased, and she looked for a place to lie down for the night. The sand provided more comfort than she thought it could; she found an area away from the others and dug out a hollow to lie in. Once in the hollow, she rolled up into a ball and started to think of all that had happened in the last few days. Her son started moving, sending butterfly-like ripples of feeling across the inside of her abdomen. She smiled, and instead of the usual fragmented thoughts or worried concerns, Briga held her stomach with both her hands and started to tenderly pat her stomach as she softly sang to her son.

Sleep and rest on my breast, my little love, my treasure,
Knowing my love for you is too great to measure.
Sleep, sleep, safe and warm
In my arms until the morn.
Sleep, my child, and be at peace all through the night.
Warm is my breast, my beloved, and to my lullaby
You may surrender in delight as I hold you tight.

It was not long before both mother and son had fallen into a deep and peaceful sleep. Her mind was blank that night, and she did not dream; her spirit and her body rested and healed. In the secret darkness, that place of her deepest sleep, Briga found safety and repose.

She slept well after the sun rose the next morning. Briga tried to stretch in her little sand hollow and moved so that she could peer out at the world. Men once again tended small fires as they started to make their morning meal.

A shrill screaming suddenly broke the morning peace. From the tented ship of Healtholaf, a wailing woman's voice pierced through the morning air, and every man on the beach looked up at the tent. Briga felt disgust as she saw every man's head drop when they realized it was Freya.

Briga looked around at the cowering Luti and said, "Yes, gentlemen, the crone is alive." Briga rose from the confined sand hollow she had been resting in and walked over to the ship. Some of the men watched her, but most just continued to look at the ground. Briga sensed a great deal of hopeless despair among this group of Luti. She stood as tall as she could and shouted out loudly, "Freya, I am here, ready to help!"

As an answer to Briga's announcement, from the ship came screams instead of words. Soon the screaming stopped, and the crone's high-pitched voice started speaking words, followed by commands. The men around her on the beach turned to look at Briga, and several walked toward her, stopping several feet from her. One of them pointed up at the ship's deck. As he started to walk away toward the ship, he turned to wave at her to follow him. Several men helped her climb up and over the ship's railing, and once she was on deck, they all quickly disappeared.

Briga looked about, but she could not see under the tent, so she called out loudly, "Freya, it is Briga, and I am here!"

Briga didn't have to wait long as the old woman, escorted by a much younger red-haired woman who wore a slave collar, walked out from under the tent. The old crone was stooped over at the shoulders, and she was having a difficult time walking as she approached Briga. Finally, Freya stopped and looked up at Briga. Briga could not help but gasp, covering her mouth with her hand, as she reacted to the appearance of the old woman.

The full fist to the face, delivered by Gundwulf, had broken the old woman's nose, spreading it flat across her face like a piece of unleavened bread; her three upper front teeth were also missing. Both of the old woman's eyes were beginning to blacken, and they were almost swollen shut. Her face was very bruised and swollen. Her upper lip was horribly enlarged and discolored. Freya spoke to her, but Briga couldn't understand, so she asked Freya, "The thrall, where is he?" The young maiden holding Freya looked at her as if she were dumb.

Instead of waiting for an answer, Briga started to shout, "You traitor-of-a-dog thrall, where are you? Briga wants you and your tongue."

From below deck came the answer as the thrall rattled his chains and shouted back, "My Lady Briga, I am here below deck! Like an animal they keep me chained in a small dark space, and I am wet and cold!"

The younger woman continued to look at Briga with confusion; Briga pointed to the man's voice that was coming from below deck and said, "Bring me the thrall. Here…bring him here!"

Briga could hear the thrall shouting at someone below deck and several other voices talking, but she couldn't understand what was being said until the thrall called out loudly, "I am coming, my lady! These fools have finally taken off my chains!" And suddenly he stepped up on deck, squinting and sheltering his eyes with his hands. He approached Briga. "I am ready to serve you, my lady," he said.

Briga looked at the man and said, "Serve me you will, my Luti dog, and since you don't seem to have a name, I will give you one. From now on I will call you Grian, after my last dog, and when I want you, I will call for Grian, and you will come. Now tell this old hag that I want to see Healtholaf."

Briga understood men, and she understood her power over men. She had been taught from a young age that women have both great power and authority that come directly from the goddess. She knew that as long as the Luti chieftain lay near death and the old crone suffered from her injuries, there would be little or no authority leading the men left on the beach.

Briga knew that men needed leadership. She knew they would respond to strong will, and she planned on being that strong will; like a mother feeding her infant, she planned on becoming their mother goddess. She would feed them her strength, give them commands each day; she would touch them in a mysterious way they may not have known since they had suckled at the breasts of their mothers. She would give them kindness and love. All men have mothers. In the heart of every man stands a little boy, and within that little boy linger the spirits of his earthly birth mother and Danu, mother of all creation, ready to be awakened by a woman's gentle touch or kind word.

The young maiden, the old crone, and the woman who would soon give birth walked together to the tent, followed by the dog-man Grian. Under the tent, the first thing Briga noticed was the staleness of the air and the putrid smell of human waste. The stench almost made her vomit. She turned to Grian and growled, "Get some men up here."

On the beach, all the Luti stopped and looked up from the deck. They heard Briga command loudly, "Get them up here now!" They did not know what the words meant, but they understood the tone and the weight of the authority the words carried;

they all understood that Briga was a woman of authority and command, and they also feared her as a witsio.

As she approached the bed that held the body of Healtholaf, the smell grew worse. The man was lying on his stomach. Looking at him, Briga guessed that he had to be well over six feet tall. His hair was long, bright red, and dirty, and grew wildly in a nasty, tangled, knotted confusion; he looked unattended to and abandoned. He was naked except for a filthy covering someone had placed over his wound days ago. Briga stood examining the man for several minutes. He was in his late thirties, perhaps, and appeared strong and well muscled, with very little fat on his body. She was sure this would be one dangerous man if he were conscious. He had large jagged scars on his left shoulder and right upper arm. She could not see his front side, and she really didn't care to.

Grian had turned to leave, but Briga reached out and gently grasped his upper arm. Looking him in the eyes, she said, "Grian, I want this tent opened up. I want fresh air in this place. I want this man moved so that his flesh and wound can receive sunlight and moving air. I want cloth, boiled in water and made fresh and clean, brought to me. I want water gathered in clean oak buckets; the water must be living water that bubbles up out of the ground. Find a spring and gather the water at its beginning. I want you to boil seawater and gather the mineral salts that remain, and I want fresh moss, yarrow, and honey. Bring me the clean cloth and fresh clean water immediately. Now, get the men to help me open this tent and move this man."

Without saying a word, Grian disappeared over the side of the ship. Freya had returned to her bed platform and was lying on her back with her eyes closed. The young red-haired maiden stood over her and seemed to be fanning her to keep off the flies.

Looking back at the man and his wound, Briga realized the place was covered with large, black flies. "What kind of animals are these people?" she said as she approached the man. She took a deep breath, and with both hands she started pulling the dressing from the wound; it was stuck, and as she pulled gently, he groaned in pain and started to move. "I had better soften that covering with warm water before I attempt to pull it from your wound, and I must have you tied down; your arms and legs must be restrained, my massive friend."

The area around the wound was red and felt hot with infection; putrid green and yellow fluid had oozed from the area she'd exposed when she'd pulled at the bandage, and when she placed her hand on his forehead, she said, "This man is burning up with fever."

Grian returned with six of the Luti warriors who had been down on the beach, and they began helping as Briga directed Grian.

Soon the men had the tented area open, and a fresh breeze began to blow out days of trapped air that had become foul-smelling and stale. They helped her move Healtholaf into the sun and almost seemed happy to help her bind him facedown, his arms and legs tied and anchored securely at the wrists and ankles.

Once they had him tied down, Briga began bathing him with cold water in the hope she might drive out some of the fever. Grian and two of the warriors helped her, and once his body had been cleansed and cooled, she opened her medicine bag.

Looking inside her bag, Briga was filled with sadness as she remembered that Freya had burned her talisman doll of Conall shortly after she was first captured. Looking over at the old crone lying on her back with eyes closed, Briga said boldly, loud enough for everyone on deck to hear, "You, old crone, will regret having destroyed my love talisman of Conall, and you should never have threatened to cut me open, remove my child, and cook and eat him. You are cursed, old woman! The goddess will seek you out, this I promise." Only Grian understood the meaning of her words, and he smiled broadly at Briga.

Reaching into the bag, she took out what she needed and began mixing herbs that she knew would drive down his fever: ground oak bark and dried chamomile flowers mixed with dried, shredded willow bark were quickly brewed into a strong infusion. Its taste needed to be sweetened with honey to mask the bitter bite of the oak bark, and with Grian lifting the man's head, she trickled as much as she could on the inside of Healtholaf's cheek. The man, still unconscious, resisted, but Briga and Grian worked together. They forced him to drink all of the infusion.

As they worked together on Healtholaf, she noticed that the Luti warriors had been bringing the things she had asked Grian to get for her, and she soon had everything she needed; she began to realize that Grian had a very good memory. He seemed intelligent, with a good ability and a willingness to follow directions. "He could be very useful," she said to herself as she began to think of how this man might serve her in the future.

They boiled clean living water from a spring. As it cooled, she started to work, moistening the filthy dressings that had stuck to Healtholaf's wound. It made sense that they had him tied down. Even semiconscious, he resisted and fought them with the strength of a bear. Briga pulled the embedded cloth as gently as possible, but even so, she ripped festered flesh from the wound. The man screamed out in pain and tried to swing his arms and kick; if freed from his restraints, he would have been very dangerous. As she worked, the stench of his wound, the pus and the rotting flesh became too much for her, and she vomited in a wrenching convulsion that caused the infant Weylin to move in protest.

Several times she had to stop and walk away for fresh air, the stench more than she could tolerate. With a measure of amusement, she watched as one of the Luti men turned and vomited at the feet of his companion; the two had been assigned to fan Briga and Healtholaf, to keep the flies off both. The fanning of the air only helped a little, and Briga moved as quickly as possible to end the ordeal for all involved.

Finally the dressing was off, and she began to drench and wash the wound. They had given her their sharpest blade, and she began cutting away at any rotten or jagged flesh. She shook her head and said out loud, "This is bad—very, very bad." All the time she worked, Grian stood by her side, and when needed he would translate for her and ask if she needed anything.

"Yes, Grian, I need maggots—young, white maggots. I need...maybe fifty. Find the place these men have been dumping their garbage and look for them there. Wash them carefully in cool, clean spring water, and bring them here in a bowl. Do this quickly."

Now that the dressing was removed and the wound cleaned, she took more time to look at the damage that the sword of Conall had done to the Luti leader.

Conall's blade had entered about six inches below the right shoulder. From there it had cut diagonally, across the man's back, to about six inches above the left hip. It was a large, deep wound, deepest as it crossed his spine at his lower back, just above his hip. Having cleaned the wound, Briga could see the exposed and damaged bone of Healtholaf's spine. She shook her head and said quietly, "If I manage to break your fever and reverse the infection, Healtholaf, and you live, you may still have trouble walking again."

This secret she would keep to herself, and she told no one.

Grian returned with a clean oak-wood bowl that was crawling with well-washed maggots. She smiled at him and said, "Thank you, Grian. Those are perfect." The man's smile exploded. He looked like a happy young child. And in a way he was: it had been years since a kind woman had thanked him. The last time had been just before he was taken slave by the Luti at six years old.

Looking at the wound, Briga selected the areas that showed the worst-infected dead flesh, and she began gently laying the maggots on the rotting meat that was once a well-portioned muscle. With the maggots in place, she put moss in the wound and again poured a small amount of living water over the moss; she wanted to keep it moist, and she would check the dressing every couple of hours, day and night for the next few days, keeping it moist and removing and adding new maggots and fresh moss.

With Healtholaf's wound freshly dressed, Briga turned again to Grian and ordered him to construct a bed for her on deck, next to his master. As Grian was about to leave, she added, "Also, bring me some good food, as I am hungry."

That night she slept on the deck next to Healtholaf.

Grian slept on deck near the stern, so that he might be near Briga.

On the second day, Freya got out of bed and started to demand that Briga get Healtholaf ready to leave. But Briga, in complete command of the situation, turned on the old woman, and with the help of Grian and several of the Luti men, she removed the old crone, screaming and kicking, into the hold below deck.

Briga was not about to let the old hag interfere with her plan to buy time for Conall and the men of Cymru. She spoke with force and authority as she told Grian, "From now on, Grian, until Healtholaf awakens and can command, I am in command, and you and all these men will do as I say. Now tell these men and the others on the beach."

She worried about Healtholaf, as she had discovered that not only did he have the massive wound on his back inflicted by Conall, but also a very large bump on the right side of his head, and his head seemed oddly shaped and swollen. Briga believed that the man must have struck his head on the ground with great force when the blow from Conall's sword had hit him in the back, throwing him forward off his feet. Briga was sure his soul was trapped inside his head and that he was deep in a black sleep. She believed he had been summoned to stand at the center of the circle, to appear before the Cruthadair and answer for his evil deeds toward the people of Cymru.

So every day for almost two weeks, she cared for the Luti chieftain.

One day she went down on the beach with Grian and had him set up a tent against the side of the ship. She also asked if the men would make her a rope ladder with wooden rungs, and two men rushed off quickly, finished it, and had it hanging from the side of the ship in a couple of hours.

Talking through Grian, she invited the men to come to her tent, as she would use her healing magic to help them. All that day they came, and she treated them with kindness as she cleaned wounds and applied healing salves and lotions that she had made; she smiled and touched the men with tenderness and genuine affection, and soon they were smiling, joking, and laughing together.

One evening the Luti, grateful for all that Briga had done, cooked a great feast in her honor and brought out mead and fine dried fruit, pickled herring, and salted fish. They ate wild duck, a wild boar they had managed to kill in the woods, and fresh shellfish from the estuary that was exotic to Briga but tasted wonderful. It was a wonderful feast, and they all ate until they couldn't eat anymore. Then the men began telling stories woven with deep threads of laughter. Grian sat beside Briga and said in a low voice, "Thank you, Briga. I have not heard these men laugh with happiness in a very long time."

Even the young red-haired maid climbed down the ladder and joined them on the beach to eat. Briga learned from Grian that the young girl was wearing an iron slave collar because she often tried to run away. "She tries to escape every time we come ashore anywhere near Erin, so they put the collar on her, and they keep her chained below deck with me until she is needed." She was very young, and she had been taken in the same raid that had captured Grian the thrall. "Her name is Cerys," he said, and the girl looked up at the sound of her name.

"Grian, tell Cerys that my name is Briga, and I would be happy if she sat beside me while she eats." The young girl quickly sat next to Briga and ate, but when she finished, she smiled and quickly disappeared back up the ladder with food for Freya.

The day turned into night, and the men built a great fire and continued telling stories. As they drank more mead, the stories became more animated. They began adding gestures in an attempt to help Briga understand the stories, while Grian translated the words as fast as he could. One large man stood up and pointed at another man sitting at the fire, and he began speaking as he continued to point. "I am Ulrich, and I was there the day the bear mated with Bojerik." All of the men turned to look at Bojerik and exploded in laughter, and when Grian translated his words to Briga, she joined in.

Ulrich stood up very tall and raised his arms high, making clawed paws out of his hands. He growled and took a step toward Bojerik, and Bojerik leaped up from the ground and stood facing the bear. The bear roared and started walking, slowly, toward Bojerik, and he turned white, yelled, and ran off into the darkness. The men and Briga all burst into roaring laughter, and Ulrich, smiling, turned and sat back down.

The stories and the mead went on for hours, and at one point a man stood up and pointed to Briga while talking to Grian, who translated, "You are a kind woman, gentle and beautiful. How is it that you are a witsio, a witch of the Cymru?"

Briga smiled and spoke with the tender voice of a mother. "I am a witsio and daughter of the Cymru god of the sea, Dylan. My father loves me to the highest degree and would not want to see any harm come to me. He has taught me to care for all men and women and to use my magic to help the people of Jutland and the people of Cymru."

Looking at all the men, she added, "My father, Dylan, watches over the ships that sail in waters around our island, and he protects those who honor and care for his daughter. It makes me very happy that all of you have given me this great feast. I will let my father know how well the men of the North have taken care of me, and I will ask him to watch over your ships when they leave so they will safely return home."

Every man stood with horn or cup filled with mead and exploded in a roaring chant of "Bri-ga, Bri-ga, Bri-ga," over and over as they drank to her. Soon they began to sing, while drums beat deep, cavernous rhythms and soon the sounds and the strong mead had her head swimming. Briga turned to Grian and said, "I think I have had too much to drink." As the words left her mouth, she slumped down onto the sand.

The men roared with laughter and again called her name over and over again as Grian picked her up and laid her in the tent at the side of the ship. Several men appeared with furs, and Grian covered her and stood outside the tent opening to watch over the witsio of Cymru. Slowly all the men melted away to sleep and dream the dreams of happy men wanting to see their loved ones back home.

That night Grian once again slept near Briga, just outside her tent on the sand, watching and guarding her from harm.

<h1 align="center">Chapter Forty</h1>

onall sat on the edge of his bedding platform and turned to look at the young maiden who was still asleep on the bed. Her long blond hair was draped around her shoulders, and in the flickering light of the waning fires, it glowed like a halo. She was naked, and from the first day that the boys had found Conall down at the river, tangled in brush along the shore, she had been taking care of him. She had also been sleeping with him every night, holding him and giving him her warmth and her pure feminine birthing energy.

Reaching over her bare shoulder, he grabbed a handful of fur on a black wolf pelt and pulling it over her, he covered the young woman. He turned to examine his wounds, which on the outside had healed rapidly under Marian's care and the blessings of Danu. Inside his body, much soreness and deep pain still existed.

He had been in this cave under the care of Marian for over a month. He had not been outside yet, and he longed for the sun.

He stretched, swinging his arms in a wide circle and twisting at his waist. The right side of his ribs felt much better, but the deep knife wound on his left side still ached with a searing pain deep inside that refused to yield to Marian's magic. He looked back at the young maid and was astounded that she had not only saved his life with her healing skills, but had also prevented infection and loss of limbs. He lifted his left leg and made a small circle with his foot; he felt pain, but it was tolerable. He stood up, putting his full weight on the leg, but overtaken by dizziness, he slouched back down. He repeated the ritual again: stepping slowly and purposefully, he moved forward. It felt so good to be alive this morning. He conquered the dizziness and endured the pain with a wincing half smile.

He had been hobbling around in the cave for several weeks, at first with the help of Marian and the children, and then with a makeshift crutch, but in the last few days, he had been walking, slowly, on his own. He had wanted to go outside days ago but when he had tried, Marian had scolded him sharply saying, "When you have the balance and strength to walk without your crutch you can go outside and play."

He had smiled at her and said, "Yes, my second mother."

He got out of bed and pulled one of the blanket coverings around his naked body. He had no idea what time it was; all he could think about was getting outside for the first time. Outside was the wind, the smell of the green world; he was sure the sun was waiting for him if he could just get to it. Conall placed his crutch on the bed beside Marian and slowly made his way past scores of sleeping children toward the opening of the womb-like cave.

When he reached the cave opening, Conall discovered that it faced eastward, and the sun was just beginning to rise. He moved carefully and slowly to the left side of the cave opening, where he found a large, flat gray stone to lean on. A cold breeze filled with moisture and rich forest smells touched his senses as he sat down. He inhaled deeply through his nose and closed his eyes; he enjoyed knowing that he was still alive.

Opening his eyes, he looked out and realized he was high on a hillside that looked out across a valley, with a small river snaking along the valley floor. The view was perfect, and he watched with wonder as the edge of the sun began to rise above the mountains.

Looking out at the rising sun, Conall prayed, "Thank you, Daghda, for saving my life, and bless the maiden Marian for having cared for me and all these children. Danu, bless Marian and all the children and keep them safe."

He sat thinking of home and Briga, and he smiled as he thought, "She will still be in the sleeping platform, snuggled deep in her fur blankets, safe at the crannog with her dogs, Gealach and Grian. And if I know those dogs, they will be up in the bed with their mistress in my absence."

Once the sun's orb had cleared the mountains, it seemed to jump into the sky, and its light began to have warmth. As Conall sat down facing the sun, he opened his blanket, exposing his body the energy, light, and heat of the Sky Father. The sun energy touching his naked flesh, added healing power to the work of Marian.

He closed his eyes to enjoy the Sky Father's warmth.

Sitting there, he thought of the days he had been spending here in the cave. He had spent many hours talking to Marian and telling stories to the children. Marian had shared with him how they had come to be at the cave.

The farming community that was home to Marian and the children had been attacked by a large band of Luti. Her people lived together in a setting of roundhouses and livestock buildings. They had no wall or defenses. They were families, farmers, and craftsmen. Marian had been up on a hillside with a few young girls collecting greens and edible roots. Marian had left her girls safely on the hillside and had crept back to the edge of the village only to watch the murder of her mother. Some of the boys were at the river fishing or out hunting. The Luti had attacked swiftly, overrunning the village. They had killed everyone they found and set the place on fire.

The surviving children and Marian hid for hours in the woods outside the village, until they were sure the raiders had moved on. Marian and the older boys then went back into the village to gather what they could; it was a terrible sight. Conall knew that she and the young boys would have horrific dreams for the rest of their lives from the brutality they had witnessed that day.

Marian had found this cave two years ago while hunting mushrooms, and when she needed a safe place to hide the village's children, she had remembered it. Following the attack, she had searched the woods and brought all the children she could find here for safety. When the boys had found Conall, they had brought him here too.

His eyes were closed, he had opened his blanket so that the sun would touch his entire body. He enjoyed the warm touch of the sunlight on his face. When a shadow suddenly blocked the light and the warmth, he opened his eyes. Marian stood naked in front of him, except for the black wolf blanket wrapped over her shoulders. He smiled at her, gathered his blanket to cover his nakedness, and said, "Good morning."

She sat on the rock next to him, and smiling at him, she said, "Good morning, Conall. You looked very deep in thought and very far away."

As Conall looked northwest toward his home at Llyn Tegid, he said, "I was, Marian. I was thinking of my village and my wife, Briga, and how much I miss them. Now that I am better, I need to get back to both."

"I'm pleased to see you made it out of the cave; your healing will progress faster now." She stood up a little and pulled some of the wolf fur under her naked buttocks, exposing her breasts as she did. "The stone is cold," she said.

Looking at her for the first time in the natural light, he realized just how beautiful she was; her long, wavy, blond hair, more the color of golden honey, reflected the sunlight, and her intense green eyes told a story of maturity beyond her years.

He simply said, "Yes, it is."

"Are you hungry?" she asked.

"Yes, I am," he answered.

"Good," she said. "I will go in and find you something. Stay here and enjoy the sun's warmth and energy. Come in when you're ready, or if I finish making the meal before you come in, I'll bring it out to you."

As she stood up to go back into the cave, Conall reached out to touch her arm, and as his fingers brushed against her exposed breast, he realized how intense his emotions were: he felt gratitude and affection for the young woman. He would be dead if not for her, and with that thought, he said, "I want to thank you again, Marian, for caring for me. You have restored me, bringing me back from the dead; you have given me a second birth. I will always be in your debt and your service. Ask of me what you want, and I will give it to you. I owe you my very life."

Looking at him rekindled the flame that had been lit deep inside her when she had first begun caring for him. It was a flame burning in the cavernous place of her deepest feminine secrets, and when ignited, its warmth burned with an aching, wanting desire. Did she dare wish…Did she dare hope?

Beltane was almost upon them, and would he walk with her to celebrate her first Beltane as a woman?

Looking down at him, she smiled and said, "I will bring you a meal, Conall, and we will sit and talk."

Conall watched as she walked back to the cave. He could not help but notice that as she had turned to look back at him, her face had flushed red down past her neck. She had taken a long, deep breath through her nose as she looked at him, and he had watched as her nostrils flared and her face flushed. As his eyes followed the red flushing down her neck to her breasts, he saw that her nipples had responded to the cold morning as she stood in front of him. She glowed, and Conall realized that this young maiden was profoundly attracted to him; he also realized the depth of her beauty and his own attraction to her. He sat back, opened his blankets to the sun, closed his eyes, and thought of the young maiden who had saved his life.

Chapter Forty-One

ach day he grew stronger, and by the end of the next week, Marian removed the binding from his leg. Once the binding was removed, he started walking, to strengthen his leg and build back his endurance. Often Marian would walk with him, and she would ask him to tell her stories of the world outside the Cambrian Mountains. His stories were always on the light side, filled with humor, and he would soon have her laughing; Conall liked to make her laugh, and he liked to watch her eyes sparkle as he told her new stories.

All the children watched them as they walked off into the forest together, and even the young children smiled and played as the three older girls in the group, nearly adults themselves, whispered and giggled as they talked among themselves away from the boys. These young girls talked about how handsome and strong Conall was, and how fortunate it was that he liked Marian, since it was obvious that she had made her choice for the upcoming fire festival of Beltane.

They got excited thinking about the festival and about how if Marian selected Conall, they would be the ones who would help her prepare. Beltane was only a few weeks away, and the girls had begun to plan the henna designs they would apply to Marian's body on the Eve of Beltane. Usually, older women experienced in the ceremony would help prepare a maiden for her first Beltane, but there were none among these young girls. The girls giggled as they planned for the night, and they had no misgivings, as they knew what to do and felt ready and excited at the idea of helping a sister.

All the older boys and girls watched and accepted the approaching change that would happen as Marian leaped over the "bright fire" to go from young maiden to young woman. Everyone seemed to understand how profoundly attracted Marian was to Conall except Conall. But this is often the way between women and men, as it is often the man who understands his emotions last, and only after the woman makes clear her intention.

As the days seemed to flow rapidly toward the celebration of the night of the bright fire, Conall regained much of his strength, but he still had to rebuild his endurance, and the side of his abdomen and his leg continued to need special care as he went about hunting with the boys; almost every day the older boys and Conall disappeared together into the forest at first light, and they didn't return until the sun had reached its high place.

Conall had wanted to teach the boys his tricks in hunting, but he soon found that these young boys had a few tricks of their own, especially when it came to setting traps for game. The boys had been taught well by their clan and knew how to trap animals with a variety of snare traps, fall traps, and pits capable of trapping animals as large as deer or pigs—or, if needed, raiders such as the Luti.

In the evening he played with the younger children after dark, when they all retired to the safety of the fires within the cave. Conall told stories to everyone, and laughter and song became the new normal in the cave as everybody's spirits grew. With Conall healing and able to help Marian, her life became much easier; they now had all the food they needed, and with the great convel sleeping and living with them, they all felt safer.

Conall had even shown the boys and older girls some very valuable fighting skills, and he had shown Marian how easy it was to kill an evil man who might be harming her or the children. "You do not need a blade to kill. It is easy to kill; a rock the size of your fist, held firmly, makes an excellent weapon. Strike at the side of a man's head, by his eye at the temple, with all your strength, and he will never trouble you again. Sharpen a small stick to a point the diameter of your finger and about the length of your foot, and you have a weapon good for thrusting quickly into the eye of an evil man. Be sure you hold it at your side so he does not see it. Look away into the distance or say to him, 'Look at that,' and when he looks, quickly, with great force, stab him square in the eye with the stick. Be sure to wiggle it hard, let it go, and run. He will not follow you, I promise."

He also taught them about plants and mushrooms that kill, if needed; one can poison a man with just the right amount added to his food or drink. And Conall taught them that even small animals like the badger could be very dangerous or even lethal.

As the days passed, they seemed to be filled with more and more laughter and joy. On one particular evening, Marian stepped out of the cave just in time to see Conall rolling on the ground as all the younger children piled on top of him. One little girl came running up to Marian laughing and joyfully shouting, "Marian, Marian, look, we are catching the lion, the old lion Ari. Watch us catch him, Marian." She turned and screamed at the top of her voice, running and jumping on the panting, out-of-breath old lion.

Marian smiled and laughed with the children as she jokingly scolded Conall. "Conall, if you break your leg again, I am not going to fix it. As for the rest of you, dinner is ready, and Conall and the boys brought us a young doe for dinner, so come and enjoy the meal the goddess has provided with the help of our brave hunters."

The children exploded off of the humbled Conall and ran screaming and yelling toward the cave. The poor old lion was lying on his back looking up at the sky as he said, "One too many.

That last one knocked the wind out of me. I am glad you came along to save me."

Marian walked over to him, and bending at the waist, she reached out a long, graceful hand to help him up. "Here, old lion, let me help you off the ground."

He reached out and took her slender, perfect hand, and she helped pull him upright to once again be Conall the man. Still holding her hand in his, he bent and kissed it lightly as he looked up at her and said, "I thank you, My Lady Marian, for your help and for your kindness." As he looked into her green eyes, he watched as her face and cheeks began to blush a most beautiful rosy red.

He studied her as if for the first time: the way her light blond hair framed her face, emerald-green eyes, full red lips, and blushing cheeks. And he spoke, stating the truth that was found in his heart. "You are very beautiful, Marian."

He stood looking at her, and she stepped so close, they almost touched. Her right hand reached up to touch his shoulder and moved down his upper arm, stopping to rest on top of his muscular bicep. "Thank you, Conall. I need to thank you for so much, for giving us hope and laughter and for giving me feelings deep inside—feelings that let me know I am almost a woman."

She looked up into his face and penetrated his blue-gray eyes as she spoke. "The night of the bright fire Beltane approaches, and I have no one, none of my people, to share my journey to womanhood. I know I am ready. You have shown me that I am ready, that I am a woman, Conall. You have made me grow inside. I have no men left in our clan; all the men are dead, and I have only young boys."

She stepped in close until her firm breasts pushed lightly into his chest, and reaching up to touch both shoulders, she pulled herself up until she was standing on her tiptoes, almost looking eye to eye.

"Conall, I choose you. I choose you to jump over the bright fire, you to help me make the journey with the good god and goddess. I am filled with desire for you, Conall, and I want you to gently take me on the trail that will make me a woman."

She stepped back and held her breath, waiting for his answer...

In Conall's mind a hundred thoughts raced about, but foremost in his thinking was Briga, the woman he loved above all others, his one true Mo Anam Cara. He looked into the young maiden's hope-filled eyes, now eager to hear his answer, and the longer he took to give that answer to her, the more she began to take on the look of someone who was about to experience the biggest disappointment of her life.

Conall looked at the maiden who had saved his life and thought of Briga. He loved Briga deeply, but in his soul he knew he would be dead if it hadn't been for the outpouring of feminine energy that Marian had given him. He was the only man in Marian's life as they approached Beltane; if he were back at his village, he would have redirected her to his young cousin Odhran.

Conall was alone in an uncertain world with a young girl who was ready to make the walk to womanhood. He closed his eyes for a moment and prayed to himself, "Danu, what am I to do? I love Briga with all my heart. What am I to do?"

The voice of Danu moved throughout his soul, spirit, and body as words formed in his entire being. He heard, "You are convel, sworn to protect and obey the goddess and the people. Now serve Marian."

Conall opened his eyes and smiled at her and said, "Yes, Marian, I would be willing to jump over Beltane's fire and walk with you into the oak woodland, to open the oak door between man and woman, god and goddess. The desire of the goddess is my duty, and if you have chosen me, I must not say no. I don't want to say no, Marian. I owe you everything. I owe you my very life, but beyond what duties I may owe you, I think you are kind, beautiful, and filled with compassion and love, and I want you to know that I desire you out of my own free will. Yes, Marian, I will jump the fire with you."

She stood for just a heartbeat, then yelled and took a deep breath almost at the same time. She jumped up into his arms, throwing her arms around his neck, and gave him a full kiss on the lips. Then, just as quickly, she let go and dropped to the ground, shouting, "Thank you, Conall! Thank you!" Turning, she ran off toward the cave.

As she ran away, she shouted back to him, "The meal is ready, my conry, Conall!"

He stood for a moment and thought only of Briga and his sworn oath to Danu, and he knew that his obligation to the goddess went beyond his duty to Briga. He would play out his role as the horned god Cernunnos, the great stag of Beltane, for Marian, but his love would always belong to Briga. He walked into the cave to the sound of laughing, singing, and very happy children.

Chapter Forty-Two

The world around them seemed far away, and all the death and destruction of the recent past was temporarily forgotten as the children laughed and played. The three older girls knew immediately that Marian had asked Conall and he had said yes; they saw it in her face when she walked into the cave, and soon all the children delighted in the knowledge that Marian and Conall the convel would jump the bright fire and go off together into the forest to gather *y naw goedwig*, the "nine woods." They all knew that Marian and Conall would spend the night in the forest gathering the wood that would be used to start the new *angen tân*, the "need fire," the next day.

The girls giggled and smiled at one another and at Marian as the young boys talked about how dark it would be in the forest, and how Conall and Marian would have to find a safe place to sit and wait for the sun to rise before they could make it back to the cave, their arms filled with wood so that they might bring new life to the angen tân.

The children were excited, as they all knew that the fire festival of Beltane was the most joyous and happy celebration of the year. Opposite Samhainn on the great wheel of the year, Beltane was in many ways its very converse. Unlike the fire festival of Samhainn, which was an *ysbrydnos* or "spirit night" that remembered the dead, Beltane was an *ysbrydnos* that celebrated the rebirth of life and the joining together of man and woman with god and goddess. Both festivals were a time when the veil cloth that hangs between the two worlds, the world of flesh and the world of spirit, would be opened by the Cruthadair, and when those dwelling in spirit or in flesh might pass freely between the two worlds.

Four times a year, the people of Cymru celebrated with their gods when they held the great fire festivals—on the days before the solstices and the equinoxes of spring and fall, at Samhainn, Imbolc, Beltane, and Lughnassad. It was on Samhainn that the druids called for all the fires to be extinguished throughout the land, plunging the people into darkness the night before the great festival day. The people would then wait for sunrise, when once again the druids would light the angen tân at the center of every village. The female head of each household would approach the angen tân, and placing a birch twig bundle into the fire, she would light it and return home to rekindle the fires of her family's home. So it was that the druids renewed the fire that burned between Daghda and the people, and womankind renewed the fires of every home and every family.

For the children Beltane was a celebration filled with joy and singing, dancing, and feasting; for the adults it was also a night for drinking *melheglin*, mead infused with the sweet-smelling herb, woodruff. It was a night that celebrated the joining together of men's and women's souls and the rebirth of the land. All the people, of all ages, rejoiced at Beltane as they celebrated the renewed greening of the world and the birthing of the livestock, other animals, and birds of the forest. It was the great feast of fertility, when the Sky Father was wedded to the Earth Mother, and when Brighid the daughter of Dagdha and the children of Cymru rejoiced and were glad to be alive.

Above all the wonders, mysteries, and joyous celebrations, it was a day of hope and a night when requests could be taken directly through the veil to the Cruthadair by the sons and daughters of the earth; anything that could be dreamed or desired could be placed before the Cruthadair with the hope that the Creators would grant the request of the worthy.

All the children had been taught about the circle that represents the year; they knew that life in the world and the Oak King died every winter solstice, and they knew that the Cruthadair at Alban Arthuan was renewed and born again. They understood that their lives and the Mother Earth were one, together in all things, and they knew that the wedding at Beltane of the god and goddess Brighid meant the world would grow lush and full of life, and there would be copious amounts of food, plenty for all. So when Marian and the children looked up and saw the full moon that announced the arrival of Beltane, all their pain and sorrow vanished, and hope filled their souls and their spirits. They knew that death had been overturned and replaced with the promise of renewed life. Beltane had arrived.

Conall also stood with Marian and the children as they looked up at the full ripeness of the moon. He looked at Marian and said to her in a whisper, "It is time for us to prepare for the joining together of the horned god Cernunnos, the Sky Father, and Brighid, the exalted daughter of Daghda."

Marian smiled and took Conall's right hand in her left. Turning to look at him, said, "I am ready for you to be my Cernunnos, and I am ready to be your Brighid." She held his hand with a warm firmness that sent a pleasant tingling dancing down his spine, and as Conall looked at the maiden in the bright light of the Beltane moon, he wondered why the Cruthadair had ordained the events that had brought him to this cave and to this young maiden.

He wondered at the meaning of it all and at what future threads would be woven from the actions of his and Marian's lives, and how all of these threads would fit into the great tapestry that was forming on the loom of the gods, as they wove the story of his life with Briga. It was not uncommon among the people of Cymru for a man to have more than one wife or a woman to have more than one man, but Conall had never been a man who wanted any other wife but his beloved Briga.

Looking at Marian in the bright, full moonlight of Beltane, he was again struck by her beauty and the great wealth of kindness reflected in her eyes, and as he held her hand in his, he looked past the portals of her eyes, boring into her soul and beyond into the spirit that dwelled in her heart. He penetrated her very being with his soul, looking into the depths of the young woman for answers from the goddess Brighid, but what he found was kindness and love, and the love he saw was directed at his soul.

He now held her hand in both of his and said, "You are very beautiful here in the moonlight, Marian, and I have seen that the center of your spirit is filled with beauty. Briga will be happy to know you and will be grateful to you for restoring her husband and helping him return to her. She will welcome you in her home and declare you her friend and her sister."

Marian stretched up on her toes and reached to kiss Conall on his cheek. "Thank you, Conall," she said. "It will mean so much to me to be a sister to Briga. My family is all dead at the hands of the Luti, and I have no one left; it would mean so much to me to have a friend, a sister, and a home filled with love and joy. I thank the goddess Danu for the day the boys found you washed up on the riverbank, and I thank Brighid for the hope that someday people will not fight one another and take lands, but will come together and love one another."

She kissed him one more time on the cheek and then said loud enough for everyone to hear, with anticipation in her voice, "Come, everyone. We should go to the cave and sleep, as we have much to do tomorrow to get ready to welcome the joining of Cernunnos and Brighid."

They all retired to the cave to sleep and dream; Marian's dreams were filled with thoughts of Conall.

Chapter Forty-Three

The next morning, the excited children woke up early, and Conall watched as the young children, especially the boys, went about gathering the rocks that would be used to form the circle for the Beltane fire. There was laughter and singing as the children worked to prepare for the night. This was one festival in which the children always helped the adults, and all across the land of Cymru, they had the honor of preparing the great fire.

Conall resisted building the large bonfire outside—he was worried it might be seen by the raiders—but Marian had stepped in and persuaded him, telling him that the children needed the fire of hope and renewal, and in the end he had agreed, but he insisted that the fire be kept small. She had smiled and said, "Well, certainly, silly. It will have to be small, as we don't want Conall hurting his leg again jumping over a big fire."

The children near her who heard the conversation laughed and ran off shouting, "We are building a fire! We are building the fire of angen tân!" It was at that moment that any illusion Conall had had of control over these children disappeared; like magic, they just ran off and disappeared into the woods, looking for rocks in the nearby streams.

Once they had built the fire circle, all the children disappeared again looking for wood; children always seemed to want the fire to burn for hours. The older boys and most of the younger children searched the woods for hours, looking for as many of the nine sacred woods as they could find for the bonfire. They would be looking for birch, oak, ash, hawthorn, and willow. If they could find those, they would also bring back yew, hazel, elm, and the most difficult to find, alder.

Marian and the older girls prepared the food for the Beltane festival, and later these girls would be Marian's attendants, helping her prepare for the great transformation during the ceremony of joining.

There was really nothing for Conall to do but slip away into the woods and prepare himself and the bed of Brighid. He went back into the cave, and when he came out, all the furs and bedding that he shared with Marian were piled high in his arms; on the very top was the large, black wolf pelt.

A week ago he had helped her carry all the cloth bedding to the river so it could be washed. At the river he'd stood in water up to his knees, pulling and working at the bedding in the water and twisting it tight to get out as much of the water as possible. "You do that like you have washed clothes before," Marian had said. "Maybe you should come to the stream with me again, as all the children's clothes need to be washed."

Every time he'd turned to bend and put a blanket in the water to wash, she'd playfully splashed him. Finally, as he was washing the last blanket, he'd stood up and turned toward her, starting to walk out of the stream, intent on throwing her into the pool of water in which he had been standing—knowing he wouldn't, for the waters were much too cold.

Marian had looked at him and perceived the mischievous look on his face. She'd yelled out, "Oh no, you don't, Conall!" Holding wet blankets in her arms, she'd laughed and run back toward the cave, shouting back at him as she ran, "Conall, please bring the blankets back to the cave, and I will hang them to dry!"

With those same clean blankets now piled high in his arms, Conall started to walk off into the woods, but as he did, one of the young boys, named Rhun, ran up to him with a big smile and slipped a small ax into his hand.

"You will need this, Conall," he said as he ran off to join the others.

He spent much of the morning hours searching for the precise place among the forest trees and ferns. With fixed eyes, his gaze fell on strangely curved boulders covered with moss; instead of being covered just on the north side, they were covered only from the east side. Perhaps this was his omen that this was the right place.

It was an oak grove that formed the great circle, and Conall had found not only the perfect place of oaks, moss, and ferns, but also a place in which he felt an invisible presence. Looking around the circle of oaks, he said out loud, "This has to be a place of one of my ancestors, or one of the spirits that live in the forest, older than humankind.

"The circle, the great Cylch Mawr." he said slowly and audibly to himself, staring at the ground. "The cycle of conception… birth…growth…death…and rebirth. The cycles of time and nature are the seasons of one's life. This is perfect; this is the place." As Conall smiled, he said out loud, "It's great to be on the living end of the great circle of life."

In this grove of oaks that formed a somewhat irregular circle stood a massive, ancient, gnarled, and twisted oak tree; there was no doubt in Conall's mind that this was the ancient *derw,* the great mother tree of this oak circle. "Hmm, the tree of life," he mused in his deep voice.

He located the sunrise side of the tree and began preparing a soft bed of leaves, fronds, moss, and soft plant material that he would cover with the wolf furs from the cave. He would make this place sacred by building a fire and performing the ancient rituals.

He removed the soft duff from the forest floor until he came to the mineral earth and placed the duff in the area that would be his and Marian's bed. After he was satisfied that the padded area was thick and soft enough, he filled both his hands with earth from the fire pit, and facing the east, he raised his two hands to the sky.

"Daghda, I invite you to join us tonight, and your daughter, Brighid, the Earth Mother."

Slowly turning to the south, his arms and hands still raised high toward the sun and the great Sky Father, Cernunnos, Conall said, "Danu, please join us this night." Still moving in his circle sunwise, Conall stopped, facing west next to the massive old oak, and with raised hands he said, "My brawd Esus, my brother among the stars, please stand guard and watch over us this night."

He then continued his circle, and facing north, he stopped and said, "Great hall of my ancestors, home of my family and my war band and all those who have come before me and stayed, choosing not to return nor walk again among the people of Cymru, I invite you to join us this night as I walk Marian down the pathway to meet Daghda and Danu at the very center of the Cruthadair."

Pausing for a moment, he lowered his outstretched arms and placed his fists still full of earth against the thick muscles of his chest; three times his fists struck his breast with a loud thump, and three times he said, "Briga, *is tu m' annsachd!*" Turning once more toward the east to complete his circle, and facing the Sky Father, he said, "Thank you for joining us this night, Sky Father Daghda."

His fists still at his chest, Conall turned to face the oak and the bed he had made. Moving toward the bed, he stood over it and began lightly sprinkling the earth from his hands over the leaves and soft forest growth. As the last of the earth left Conall's hands, he said, "Mother Danu, you are invited into our bed. Please enter and join with Marian this night. Please bless her with fullness and new life."

Moving back to the pile of furs he had carried from the cave, he began placing them neatly on top of the forest padding he had constructed.

He saved a large, black animal fur for last; it was the wolf pelt. He smiled as he placed the great black wolf pelt on top, and when it was arranged just right, he stood and said out loud to the forest, "Well, my old friend, who knew when we entered the river together, we would end up here tonight, celebrating Beltane with Marian and the good god and goddess?"

Next Conall began searching for rocks, and about ten feet from the edge of the fur bed, he began building a five-foot circle of stones with a three-foot raised backstop on the sunrise side. When he finished, he stood back and smiled at his work. "There, that should be a good backstop. It will reflect the warmth of the fire back to heat us and chase away the night chill."

Then the great convel of Cymru set about collecting wood for the fire. Once he had all the wood he needed for the evening, he set about placing the tinder and kindling in the fire pit, and with it he formed a three-foot triangle. He would light the firewood later that evening, when he returned with Marian.

Eyeing the oak and the bed that awaited Marian, Conall smiled and said, "Fit for a queen or a goddess. Yes, this should do nicely." Giving the area one last look, he turned and headed back to the cave.

He stopped at an inviting deep pool in the stream he had crossed earlier, where he stripped down and stepped into the water. "It is much too cold," he thought. His long red hair was braided in the style he liked to wear when he went into battle. Removing the braids, he washed his hair and every inch of his body. He scrubbed his skin using sand and horsetail ferns, and when it was red and clean, he rubbed crushed mint and fragrant herbs on his arms, legs, and chest. He had also brought his sharpest blade with him, and leaving only his mustache, in the manner of the Gauls, he shaved the whiskers from the rest of his face.

From the bag he carried, he pulled out a shirt and pants that Marian had secretly made for him. Putting on the clean clothes, he picked up the small ax Rhun had given him as he'd left the cave and set about clearly marking the trail with blaze marks that he cut in trees along his route. It would be very dark when he returned with Marian, and he knew he would have to mark his trail; he selected trees he knew would have white wood under their bark, which would make a blaze mark stand out as they walked along holding a torch. He would carry bundles of torches made from birch branches under his left arm, and he would light the first bundle at the bright fire of the angen tân that the children would have burning. He knew that as the children gathered wood for the fire, they would also gather and tie bundles of birch twigs, making all the torches he would need for his walk with Marian.

Looking at the sun, he realized it was well past noon. He was hungry, so without delay he set about blazing his trail back to Marian and the children at the cave.

Conall spent the rest of the afternoon at the cave, playing with the younger children and telling stories to keep them busy. Meanwhile, Marian prepared herself for the night of Beltane and her great transformation that would forever move the young girl into the circle of women. The three older girls had accompanied her into the cave to help her prepare; they washed her hair and the rest of her with warm water sprinkled with scented lavender oil that Marian had in her medicine bag. The girls had helped her sew the gown she would wear from cloth they had salvaged from their village; they'd also made adornments for her to wear, which included a wreath made of wildflowers, ivy, and slender birch branches all woven together to form a crown that she would wear as she walked with Conall into the woods.

But before she dressed, the three girls began applying thin lines and rich swirling designs using a black dye made of woad and henna. Oak galls, sometimes called oak apples by the children, were the base for the henna ink; they had been ground to a fine powder that would cover much of her body.

The sacred rune symbols and designs covered her arms, legs, breasts, and buttocks, but special attention and time was spent on the design that covered her stomach and thighs. The spiral circle and lines all pointed to the entrance of Marian's womanhood, her star gate, and the great spiral circles started at her belly button and rotating sunrise, circled her stomach until the line reached just below her breasts. These magic symbols were intended to speed the connection between Conall's male energy and Marian's female energy; if the magic was done right, Marian would be open to receiving a new soul from the Cruthadair. She would birth Conall's child and open the way for her mother's soul to return. Even her face had special marks, mostly in the form of dots made into sacred patterns. The three young girls stood back and admired her face and body—the transformation of the goddess Marian.

If the village of Marian hadn't been destroyed and all the older women killed or taken by the Luti, she would have been attended by the women who had borne children, because they possessed the magic that brought new life into the world. It was possible to pass this magic on to the young maiden on her first Beltane night; the magic was in the designs applied by these older women.

The young girls talked and laughed together, happy to have been able to help Marian. They giggled often as they asked

Marian questions about Conall, especially questions that concerned his body and the scars he'd incurred in battle. They talked about the wonder of male and female love and the joy and the blessing of becoming pregnant, and they especially talked about the honor that was given to a woman when she delivered a child, a returning soul, back to the clan family.

The laughter changed to seriousness when another young girl entered the cave and said, "The sun is setting. It is almost time."

Chapter Forty-Four

er time of great transformation had arrived, signified by the triskele pictogram. She would be transformed from maid to mother and eventually to matron. The triskele represented the spiral of life that every Celtic tribe recognized as the unlimited universal force—the feminine doorway to life.

As soon as it was twilight, the children wanted to light the fire, and Conall let them, hoping they would burn up their supply of wood much earlier in the evening; but looking at the pile of wood the children had gathered, he laughed and just shook his head.

The moment the fire was burning bright and furious, the three girls, Marian's attendants, came out of the cave to announce that the night of Beltane, the spirit night of the joining of the horned god Cernunnos and the Earth Mother Brighid, had begun. Turning, they reentered the cave.

Almost immediately they came back out of the cave, but remained in the darkness while the eldest girl announced, "Behold, the bright fire burns, and Brighid has overcome Cailleach, the Hag of Winter, and now she searches for the shining one, her bright fire that will open her loins and bring to the world the season of fertility, rebirth, and growth."

The three maidens and Marian all advanced into the firelight, forming an equilateral triangle with the oldest girl at the point, Marian in the middle of the triangle, and the other two girls forming the base. The girls escorted Marian slowly toward the great fire, holding in their arms great bundles of herbs, wild-flowers and slender oak and birch twigs.

As they walked, the firelight danced with shadow and light, and this only added to the mystery and magic of the night. When they all reached the bright fire, they stopped, and the eldest girl announced to everyone, "In the light that drives away darkness, in the light that restores life, Brighid searches for Cernunnos."

As Marian stepped out of the triangle and into the full light of the fire, everyone saw the magic runes on her face, hands, and bare arms. The runes seemed to dance down the insides of both her thighs to her ankles, and down her neck to her exposed breasts.

Standing in the glory of radiant light, Marian spoke. "I am Brighid, the mother of the earth, and I search for my lord. I search for Cernunnos, the horned god of light. I am the doe to his stag, and I have made myself ready for him this night. May the good god Daghda and great goddess Danu join me as I search and as we celebrate the defeat of the hag, Cailleach, and the great trans-formation ceremony of the joining of male and female energies."

As Marian moved toward the fire, all the children looked her way. The older girls were heard saying, "Marian is beautiful," and the younger children could be heard saying, "Marian looks like the goddess." Everyone was in awe at her transformation from maiden to Brighid, especially Conall.

Marian was holding in both hands a crown woven of holly and oak twigs, with flowers and oak galls spaced evenly around the circle of the wreath. Leaving her attendants to stand at the fireside, she began to search for her Cernunnos, first by walking slowly around the great fire circle earth-wise, the direction that the earth moves under the heavens, and then sunwise, the direc-tion the sun moves across the day sky.

Having moved in the two directions of creation, first the feminine followed by the masculine, she stopped directly in front of Conall, who was sitting on the bare earth, and boldly she announced, "I have found my Cernunnos." Bending at the waist, she reached out with both arms and placed the crown on Conall's head. As it came to rest there, all the children exploded with yells and joy-filled songs and laughter.

Conall stood and raised both of his hands, and the children fell silent, knowing what would come next as Conall announced, "I have found my Brighid, and she has found her Cernunnos. Let the feast begin."

Looking into Marian's smiling face; he reached for her hands and grasped them firmly. He drew her close to him, looking at Rhun as he did so, and said, "The joining has begun."

Rhun moved to stand by the fire and announced, "The joining has begun!" The children jumped up, this time without speaking. The girls began walking around the circle earth-wise as the boys moved sunwise, all of them, female and male, stopping to acknowledge and thank Brighid and Cernunnos for defeating Cailleach and restoring life to the land and the people of Cymru.

When they had finished honoring Marian and Conall and the gods, most of the young girls and Marian's attendants ran off into the cave and brought back food in abundance. The first to be served was Marian, and then Conall, followed by all of the youngest children. From the shadows a young boy approached with two horns filled with *metheglin*—mead flavored with the sweet-smelling herb, woodruff. It was Rhun who held a horn in each hand and gave them to Marian and Conall as he announced in a loud voice, "For the goddess Brighid and the horned god Cernunnos."

Marian and Conall thanked him, and they raised their horns, crossing their arms together. Marian took a long drink from Conall's horn as he completely drank hers. The feast began, and Rhun rushed off to join the other children as they all celebrated Beltane.

The children merrily ate, filled with a spirit of happiness and peace. They sang and before long began to dance around the great fire. The older boys showed off by jumping naked through the flames, and all the girls screamed in response to their daring leaps that conquered the hag, Cailleach.

The children celebrated for several hours until the youngest, happy and exhausted, began to settle around the great fire. Marian sat next to Conall, and leaning over, whispered into his ear, "Conall, I am ready." He stood and looked around the fire, watching the children falling silent as he announced, "It is time, and we must go into the forest to search for the nine sacred woods to feed tomorrow's fire."

Disappearing only for a moment, Rhun returned, stood next to the firelight, and ran up to Conall, holding several bundles of birch twigs tied together in his arms. "Here, Cernunnos, take these bundles of birch twig and light them at the need fire so that you will have torchlight to guide you in the darkness." Conall, smiling broadly at the young boy, took the torches and put all the bundles but one under his left arm. He walked toward the need fire at the great circle, igniting the single torch in the fire. Holding the brightly burning torch high over his head, he announced loudly for all to hear, "Thank you, Rhun. Now I will have light in the darkness."

Conall held the torch high above his head and began walking around the great fire sunwise, so that all saw the light he carried and that he completed his great circle of life. He returned to Marian and stopped to face her; she looked up at him and announced as she stood facing Conall, "My Lord Cernunnos, I am ready…"

As the older children watched Conall, Marian, and the torchlight disappear into the darkness of the woods, a great roaring cheer went up toward the stars as all the children rejoiced. They continued celebrating for hours, many of the youngest falling to sleep around the fire as the singing and dancing continued. In time the wood for the fire ran out, as did the children's energy, and they fell into a restful sleep with their bellies full and their hearts and souls filled with hope for tomorrow.

High above the land of Cymru, the Cruthadair, the Creators of the great circle of life, watched as thousands of Beltane need fires burned below them on earth. All over the forests, the believers of Dagdha and Danu carried their birch twig torches from their need fires as they walked in pairs into the great woodlands of the earth. The gods watched in delight as each man set fire to his joining fire, and it burst into flame. As more fires ignited, the Cruthadair's beloved earth appeared to reflect the stars of the heavens above, as tens of thousands of fires burst into what looked like, from the heavens above, tens of thousands of stars. It was only at Beltane that the stars of the earth seemed to reflect the stars of heaven.

Chapter Forty-Five

Marian walked at Conall's left side as he held the torch high above his shoulder with his right hand. They had no trouble following the trail Conall had left earlier in the day. The blaze marks he'd cut in the trees were four feet from the ground and highly reflective in the torchlight. As she walked, she thought of all that had happened since young Rhun and some of the other boys had come running into the cave, excited and yelling about the man they had found tangled in the brush at the river.

Many times in the past months she had asked herself, "Why have the goddess of fate, Aerten, and the goddess of the river, Coventina, worked so hard together to join Conall and me on this night of Beltane?" The day after Conall had said yes, she had gone back to the river, to the very place they had found him tangled in the brush at the edge of the water. She'd wanted to thank Coventina and to make an offering to her and to Brighid.

Standing with one foot on the earth of the riverbank and one foot in the water, she had pulled from her medicine bag a jeweled brooch of silver and amber that she treasured. It had been her mother's.

As she spoke, she had thrown it out into the middle of the river, saying, "Coventina, goddess of the river, hear me now. I give you this offering for the magic that you have always done and the magic you will do for Conall and me. Thank you, Coventina."

Pulling her foot from the water and standing firmly on the earth, she had again reached down into her medicine bag, pulling from it a small object wrapped in white cloth. As she'd unwrapped the object, the sunlight had found the round shape and smiled upon the gold ring; the ring had also belonged to Marian's mother. Kissing it, she had knelt down on the earth at the edge of the river and had dug a small hole. "Brighid, daughter of the good god Daghda, goddess of healing skills and fertility, Brighid the Exalted One, I thank you both for your help in healing Conall, and I now give you this gold ring in thanks as an offering for the future. Please, Brighid, I pray that when Conall takes me to the bride's bed, I will be open to him, and that his seed will be planted deep within me, that it will take root and grow. Please, Brighid, hear my prayer. Accept this offering of my mother's jewel and ring, and let the soul of my mother, Muirgheal, return to me in my womb." Marian had put the sacred mistletoe in her mouth, and in a muffled voice, she had said, "Let it be so." As she removed the small twig of mistletoe form her mouth, tears rolled down her cheeks as she whispered to the waters and the earth, "Please grant my prayer."

Walking now beside Conall, Marian was smiling—she finally understood why the goddesses Aerten and Coventina had conspired together to bring Conall to her. She prayed that on this night, her star-gate would open, and the soul of her mother, Muirgheal, murdered by a Luti, would return to her, to dwell and grow and be born once again into the clan.

Looking at Conall, she said, "Thank you."

"We are almost there, Marian," he said without looking away from the trail they were walking together. "Here."

As he held the torch high over his head, she saw the massive, ancient derw, the great mother oak tree, and she knew that the oak was the headpiece of the bride's bed, and that the foot of the bed was facing east—because in the morning, the Sky Father would rise to welcome her into the world forever changed. She would be a woman of the clann the next time she saw the sunrise, and she hoped with all her heart that she would also have within her mother's soul.

"Stay here as I light the joining fire," Conall said.

Taking the torch that had been set ablaze in the bright fire at the cave, Conall went to the neatly stacked wood he had placed in the stone fire circle earlier in the day. Setting his torch at the base of the stack of wood, he hesitated only a moment and stepped back, leaving the torch to add its fire and light to the pile.

As the kindling and wood began to crackle, he said, "I invite you, Daghda and Danu, to join us tonight as Marian becomes my Brighid and I become her Cernunnos."

The fire was burning brightly as Conall stepped back to Marian.

Standing directly in front of the maiden, he smiled. When he looked into her green eyes, he saw the longing and love she held for him. He watched her eyes as they now danced with eagerness in the firelight. "Will you be Brighid to my Cernunnos? Will you be the sacred white doe to my stag?"

She stepped in very close to him and placed both her hands on his chest. "I submit to you, Cernunnos," she replied as she looked into his gray-blue eyes.

He smelled clean and fresh, while at the same time his body emitted warmth and an energy that was purely masculine. Marian found that she was becoming aroused by the feel of his chest under his shirt. She wanted more, and she moved her hands under his shirt and felt the energy grow between them as her bare hands came into contact with his naked chest. As her hands moved toward his neck, they found his well-defined muscles.

Near him, touching him, warmth spread all over her body, and she felt a tingling sensation that urged her to press against him harder. She knew how big a man he was; she had tried to put her hands around the muscle of his upper arm one day when he was sleeping, but her fingers hadn't been able to close around his well-formed bicep.

She had cared for him, washed him, and slept with him, her naked, feminine body pressed tightly next to his to give him warmth and her curative female energy, and she had held his erect phallus in her hand while he slept.

She knew every inch of this man. She had longed for this day: this would be the day he would take her on the journey to womanhood.

She stretched up on her tiptoes to kiss him, and he moved to meet her lips and kissed her, softly at first, and then with increasing pressure and passion. His tongue wanted into her mouth, and she yielded to his penetration, for the passion of her kisses became the fire that was burning hot in Conall's loin; her kisses gave life to his manhood. She met his tongue with a moan as her hands squeezed his hard pectoral muscles.

Kissing him, she felt weak in her legs, and strength seemed to be rushing out from her. Tingling energy consumed her with desire; her body sang out, "Please pull me into your arms, please fill me with your manhood." She felt an intense emptiness inside that needed to be filled, and places deep within that hid the center of her fertility wanted to be touched. She tightly contracted the muscles of her upper legs and pulled them together. Her female parts responded, sending tingling pleasure flooding into her groin.

She stepped away from him and stood trembling as she said, "Now, Conall, please."

The dress she wore was sleeveless and pinned at each shoulder. Conall removed the pins and watched as the dress fell from her shoulders, past her breasts, to come to rest at her feet. The firelight danced invitingly on the runes that covered her white breasts, the light exposing her hard, erect nipples, letting him know she was ready for her Cernunnos. He reached out and cupped her breasts in his hands; they were as soft as the pelt of a ewe, but they held the firmness of youth. Holding her close, he kissed her breasts while moving his hands down her back, then farther down to feel the roundness of her hips, where he stopped. He held her hips, pulling her firmly into his swelling manhood, his hands moving down to cover and cup the firm roundness of the cheeks of her arse and squeezed firmly—she moaned with agonizing delight.

Hungrily kissing her as he swooped her up in his arms, he carried her to the bride's bed. He kissed her neck, then moved his mouth to her nipple. He gnawed and sucked her nipples as she tingled inside. Moaning, she dug her nails into the skin at the back of his head.

"Oh, Conall," escaped her lips as she was overcome by feelings that she'd never felt before. "Conall, I am very much going to like being a woman."

He looked at her and smiled as he laid her down on the bride's bed, atop the great black wolf fur blanket.

Standing over her, he undressed, and she could not help but notice that when he untied the rope holding up his pants, he had to help them down past a very large erection. She giggled and placed her hand over her mouth. Delight danced in her eyes, and she couldn't hold back the giddy happiness that filled her.

She was filled with excitement as she realized that she would soon have the pleasure of his phallus deep inside her. She moved over to make room for him on the bride's bed, and as she did, she said, "You are amazing, Conall."

He joined her on the fur, and they lay on their sides, at first facing each other. For a short time, they just touched, his fingertips moving over her body as hers explored his. They kissed, and at one point he rolled to his back, and she laid her head on his chest and just said, "I am so happy, Conall, that you are my warrior. I feel safe in your arms. I long to feel safe again."

The horn she'd drunk with Conall back at the bright fire had been filled with *metheglin*, and the mead was now doing its magic, as her mind and body were now ready to be opened to the pathway that would lead her to Daghda and Danu.

He placed his thick, callused hand in her hair and combed through it gently; at the same time she leaned her head back and opened her mouth to his, and they kissed. She moved to lie on her back, and his hands made their own path on her body. They stopped at her breasts, holding them as if each one were a prized chalice. Then they traveled slowly down her torso, gently passing over her ribs to her narrow waist and hesitating there. He held her firmly as his lips began kissing her, following the path his hands had found.

Her body was the mountains and valleys of his beloved Cymru, but in fact she was Cymru, and she was Danu, and her body was the earth goddess Brighid. Marian was becoming all of these at once. Cymru and Danu merged together, as did Brighid and Marian, and they all became one soul and one flesh as Conall's passion for her increased, and as hers rose to match his caresses, his kisses.

Marian's hands held firmly to Conall's massive shoulders, her fingernails cutting into his flesh as her wanting of him grew; she ached deep inside her body to be filled by Conall the beast, Conall the warrior.

With her eyes closed, she groaned in cavernous pleasure as her breathing became a mix of short gasps and heavy spasms. Marian was transported to the stars; she was in a world without words.

She was on fire inside, and she wanted him, the beast, with all his wildness to join her lusting. She gasped as his mouth passionately worshiped her breasts.

Deep inside her womb, she felt hungry spasms and a call from the primeval animal that growled, "Ravage me, and devour me."

She placed both her hands on his head and pulled him up; matching her mouth to his, she began kissing him passionately. He returned her kisses with greater intensity as his right hand moved down her side and found its way to her center. His fingertips walked on the pathways of her flesh; he knew every inch of her skin from memory, as she was the goddess, and she was every woman he had ever joined with at Beltane, and she was Briga. He knew her every secret, completely, even if it was his first time with Marian. Her voice was thick with aching as she said, "I want you, Conall!"

His hand moved around her mound to the delicate, hot flesh that was the entry to her inner womb, her star-gate channel to Daghda and Danu. His fingers found that her body had responded to his lovemaking, and she was ripe with nectar, ready for him to sow her field.

He wanted her to experience very little pain, as it was his duty to introduce her to pleasure, and fortunately he knew exactly where and how to touch her to complete her journey to the stars. Conall reached with his left hand over to a small basin at the edge of the furs and reached in, covering two of his fingers with an ointment that Marian had made for him of *dwale* and crushed, boiled poppy seed that would reduce and deaden the surface pain she would feel as he entered.

His fingers, now well coated with the ointment, gently began working their way into her innermost sacred place. She was moving in a world that was both physical and spiritual, as both her body and her mind journeyed toward the center of all creation. Conall's hands and mouth had completed their preparation for her journey to becoming a woman.

She was now ready to be the sheath for his sword. Conall rose up. All his weight was now shifted off Marian to his knees and his left arm; for the rest of her journey, he would hold himself above her, over her, and merge with the flower and fragrance of her beauty like a cloud floating above a meadow. His mouth found hers, and each kissed the other hungrily; her mouth opened to his tongue, and he entered and touched inside her lips and then danced with her tongue.

Marian gasped and bit down on Conall's tongue as his phallus entered her, and he glided deeper so that she might wrap his complete length in her sheath.

The muscles of his neck and shoulders tightened, as did his buttocks, but Conall held off his passion and continued moving in a controlled motion that allowed Marian time to catch up with him. Marian began to feel waves flowing over her body, small at first but growing with intensity, and as Conall continued to move, she rose higher in her ecstasy.

Not making a sound, she bit Conall's upper arm just below the shoulder, hard, and her fingernails dug deep into the flesh of his back as her body contorted in spasms of indescribable, never-before-experienced pleasure. Every cell in her body and all creation felt it with her.

Deep inside her body, Conall released his seed, after realizing she was now with the Cruthadair, he stayed deep inside her and held her close as he rolled to his side. She had bitten him hard enough to draw blood, but it didn't matter, as he didn't feel anything but warm, beautiful pleasure. His masculinity had been completed by her femininity as they had joined together to be one flesh and one soul. The god Cernunnos had pleased Brighid, and hopefully now Cerridwen, the Earth Mother, would burst forth new life and prosperity for the people of Cymru.

Holding on to each other, they fell into a much-needed, rest-filled sleep.

⊣

Chapter Forty-Six

olding both his hands outstretched toward the horizon, the four fingers of one hand resting on the four fingers of the other, Rhun counted the fingers that lay between the horizon and the sun. "Eight. Eight fingers," he said to himself. The sun had been above the horizon for some time, and the need fire had burned down until only gray ash covered the hot coals that remained. Standing by the circle of stones, the young boy waited and watched. His attention was on the path into the woods that had taken Marian and Conall away looking for the nine sacred woods.

Most of the children remained in the cave sleeping. It had been an extremely long and late night for them, and now, in the darkness of the cave, they remained warm and without a care. They all knew that today was the first day of Beltane's great transformation; they knew that the goddess Brighid and the god Cernunnos had finally come together, and that Cerridwen, the Earth Mother, would now burst forth with new life and prosperity for the people of Cymru.

Rhun knew the stories too, and he knew that Brighid and Cernunnos had defeated the Hag of Winter, Cailleach, and in defeating her, had restored life to the land; but he also knew that with the completion of the great transformation, Marian and Conall would now return, and so he watched for them.

The boy waited in silence.

As he stood peering intently into the dark, inky shadows of the forest, a doe stepped from the woods into the clearing. Rhun, standing very still, observed her as she moved deeper into the sunlight of the clearing and closer toward the circle. Her head was bent down, and she was grazing as she slowly came toward him. She was only a few feet from the young boy when the doe stopped and looked up; her large brown eyes looked past Rhun and toward the mouth of the cave. Stepping from the cave, Eigra looked toward Rhun, and as she did, she saw the doe turn and in a bounding, bouncing, leaping run, disappear back into the woods.

Eigra looked at Rhun and said, "They haven't returned."

"No, and I have been watching for some time," he answered.

Eigra was the eldest of the three girls who had helped Marian get ready for the Beltane ceremony, along with her two cousins, the twins, Iseult and Nia. Now she was the oldest remaining female at the cave, and she naturally assumed the leadership of the small group until Marian's return.

"Do you think we should go looking for them?" she asked Rhun.

"No," he replied.

She shrugged her shoulders and said, "I will prepare something for us to eat." As she turned to go back into the cave, she paused and asked Rhun, "Do you think they got lost last night in the darkness of the forest, and that is why they are so late in returning this morning?"

"No," the boy answered, adding, "Not Conall. He would not have gotten lost."

Eigra nodded her head yes, and turning, continued to walk away, disappearing into the shadows of the cave.

Continuing his vigil, Rhun peered into the forest, searching for the first signs of the return of Marian and Conall.

She woke just as the sun's orb had first shown a thin sliver of bright light on the eastern skyline. The orb's disk, pregnant with light, became more intense as the sun rose higher above the horizon; she watched until the light began to hurt her eyes. Her head rested on his chest, and she rose up slightly on her elbow so that she might look at him better. She touched his chest and felt his heart pulsating in a great cosmic beat.

Softly she said, "Goddess, thank you for bringing Conall to me, and thank you for last night. You are the wise mother of all life, the great *màthair*. Thank you for the miracle of the great transformation. Yesterday I was a young maiden, and this morning I awoke a woman, and I feel the tingling of life in my body, spirit, and soul. I know I will never be the same after last night, and I am so grateful it was Conall who took me inside the Hall of the Cruthadair."

She was so amazed and dripping with delight at how wonderful the journey to womanhood had been with this man. He had known every right place to touch and the perfect way to move, bringing to her pleasure beyond anything she had ever experienced before. Conall had been a god last night, the horned Cernunnos, and he had awakened inside the chalice of her desire, filling her with an intoxicating liquid of pleasure and craving. She knew it was a liquid fire that would burn all the days of her life; it was the need fire that existed deep within a woman, and it could only be lighted and fanned by the penetration of a man.

Marian felt the fire.

They had made love three times during the night. The last time had been just before dawn, and they had fallen back to sleep in each other's arms. The sun had risen above the horizon when she next awakened in the wonder of all that had happened. As she thought of him, her fire grew until all she wanted was to be filled by him. She had ignited her soul in his living flame, and that flame of passion had tempered the maiden into a woman.

Now she just watched him and thought to herself how very perfect he was, and how much she didn't want the night to turn into day; with the day, she would no longer be Brighid to his Cernunnos, and she would return to being Marian and he Conall—and he would return to his Briga.

Marian would have made love to him again except for the presence of the sun.

The sun's orb was now three fingers above the horizon, and Marian knew that the magic of Beltane was past; she knew Conall was now Briga's, and Marian would not ask him to make love to her again.

She knew they might not ever be together again, and there was sadness in her spirit, but there was also great joy in the knowledge that Conall was her first man. She smiled as she looked at him and said softly to herself, "And what a man, in every way possible."

Conall had reached deep into the soul of Marian, and he had planted a seed that would grow for many years; he had awakened in this young woman the gift of sexual pleasure, and in the years to come, she would enjoy many more Beltanes.

She leaned to kiss him tenderly on the lips, and as she did, she squeezed his shoulder as she softly said, "Conall, it is dawn, and we must return to the cave."

Opening his eyes, Conall looked into the face of a young woman.

"Good morning, Conall. We need to gather wood for the need fire, and we should return to the cave before the children begin to think that we got lost." She kissed his lips one last time and said, "Thank you, Conall."

As he looked at Marian, he saw a change that was part of the magic of Beltane; the young maiden seemed to have transformed during the night, and now speaking to Conall was a young woman. Conall said to her, "Marian, you look beautiful."

She blushed and said, "Thank you, my Conry." She got up from the bed to stand over him. She was naked, and the morning sunlight fell fully upon her, turning her skin golden while her yellow hair shimmered in the morning light. She wanted him to share her nakedness and to remember always what she looked like on this morning.

Conall saw that there was blood on her inner thighs from his penetration. He knew that she would proudly wear this blood, the red of Cymru throughout her first day of womanhood. It would testify to all that this was her first day as a woman of the clann. His gaze was fixed on her thighs as she said, "You are my first Conall and I will never forget you are the wonderful night you have gifted me—thank you my Conry."

She stood looking down at him, and he looked at her. His eyes were warm and filled with deep appreciation for the young woman who had saved his life, but they also burned with passion and with the clarity and admiration a man feels when he looks into the eyes of a kind and beautiful woman.

Looking up at her, he said, "You are beautiful, Marian," and he got to his feet and faced her. He leaned down and gave her a kiss on the forehead, and once again he said, "You are very beautiful, Marian, and I am so honored that you chose me, and I will forever be grateful to you for saving my life. You will come to know that my family, my clann, will always be there for you; my people will be your people, Marian.

"Now, we must return to the cave and get the children ready to leave today for my village. I must go home to Briga." And he turned away to start dressing.

Marian hesitated for a heart beat as a sadness touched her spirit but she quickly joined him in getting dressed.

Now clad in everyday cloths, they walked back toward the cave. Marian collected firewood as they walked, and she began stacking the wood in Conall's arms, higher and higher until he could barely look over the top of the stack he carried.

Smiling at him she said, "There, now you look like a pack-horse carrying wood back to the cave."

She continued picking up wood until her arms were also loaded. As they walked together, Marian talked about the children and what they would need to do to get ready to leave, but suddenly she stopped on the trail and looked at Conall. "Conall," she said, "please tell me about Briga."

As they continued walking, Conall began to share with Marian the story of when he and Briga had first discovered the *còmhradh carragh*, the "talking rocks" at the four-part falls of Pistyll Rhaeadr. He spoke of building the crannog at the lake and how he had thought she'd lost her mind, but how after they had come to live in the crannog, he'd loved hearing the sound of rain falling on the lake, and he'd loved holding Briga in his arms as they watched the full moonlight shimmering on the lake's surface.

"She sings, my Briga, and when she does, the birds stop to listen, and my heart is filled with warmth much like that of the summer sun touching my arms. My favorite time to be with her is in the morning, when the world is fresh and new, and we lie together in our bed, just listening to all the birds sing outside our crannog as we hold each other and talk…just talk."

He continued speaking as they walked. Marian listened, and as she listened, she also thought of the two great secret desires she placed undisclosed in her heart to be held safely by the goddess. Marian had prayed to Aerten, the goddess of fate, and to the good goddess Danu.

As she walked beside Conall, she dared to hope that her prayers would come true—that she would be accepted by Briga as a sister wife in her crannog, and that Danu would have opened her womb to the seed of Conall. Marian hoped with all her wanting desires that she was now with child, and that the soul who would come to her would be her mother's. Marian prayed as Conall talked, and she hoped with all her strength that her mother, Muirgheal, had returned in the great ceremony.

Looking through the trees, Marian saw the clearing ahead and could even make out a young boy standing very still near the fire circle. She smiled as she realized it was Rhun. Still talking about Briga, Conall seemed to be unaware of the world around him, so Marian touched him on the arm and said, "Conall, we are back."

Rhun had been standing, watching, since early morning, even before the sun had completely risen above the horizon. Now it was midmorning, and even young Rhun had begun to worry. He stood in silence, watching and waiting.

He heard them coming before he saw them.

Conall's deep voice carried past the trees and into the clearing. Rhun strained to look into the shadows of the forest to see them, but not for long, as he caught a glimpse of Marian and Conall approaching. He turned and ran back toward the cave and yelled loudly to those inside, "They are back! Marian and Conall are back!"

Turning from the cave entrance, he ran toward the woods. As he ran, Marian and Conall stepped out of the trees and into the clearing. Rhun ran right to Marian and reached out for her armful of firewood. "Let me help you, Marian," he said. She smiled and gave the boy her armful of wood, and as they walked back toward the fire circle, he said, "Marian, you don't look any different."

She laughed gently and smiled at him as she touched his shoulder and said, "I have changed deep inside, Rhun, and I am no longer a young maid, one of the children; I am now a woman, and from this day on, I will always walk with and be counted among the women of Cymru."

As they got to the edge of the fire circle, Rhun placed his armload of firewood on the ground and turned, throwing both his arms around her waist. He gave her a hug and said, "I am happy, Marian, and now we all have a mother again." And slightly red-faced, he smiled up at her and let go, running back toward the cave shouting, "They are back! They are back! Everyone, wake up!"

It was not long before all the children came out of the cave; everyone was laughing and talking. They had remembered what Marian had told them the day before: "When Conall and I return, we all must be ready to leave. Be packed and ready to leave after the morning meal."

The children had become so excited and eager to begin their journey when Marian had told them they would be leaving the cave to start the long journey to Conall's home, to live among Conall's family. Working together, they had finished packing that morning as they waited for the return of Marian and Conall. Looking much like the ants of the forest, the children now formed lines and carried their meager belongings from the cave to pile them neatly, ready for travel.

As the children worked to get ready to leave, Conall and Rhun worked to bring the need fire back to life, and Eigra and the twins, Iseult and Nia, helped Marian prepare food for everyone. As Conall and Rhun sat on their haunches feeding the firewood, they both watched as the girls whispered and giggled, looking toward Conall.

"Conall, I think they are talking about you," Rhun said.

Conall stood up, looking down at the young boy, and smiled broadly. "You are most likely right," he said. "After we eat, Rhun, get a couple of the boys, and we will all go back into the woods and get the blankets and furs I left there. You can all help me bring them back."

Jumping up from the fire, Rhun ran off to find the help Conall wanted. "I know just who to get!"

When the food was ready, everyone once again gathered around the fire circle and ate as Marian told them stories of old teachings handed down to her. All the children stared at her with awe and respect as she spoke to them as a woman.

"As the vaporous mist in a cloud creates many raindrops, the spirit of the good god Daghda created many souls. These souls have been with the Cruthadair since the very beginning. The druids teach us that the source of creation has been with us from the beginning; it is here now, and we are within its embrace. We stand at the very center of the circle of creation, and it is connected to the very center of our hearts. This is the place from which all things have come into being. It is the Cruthadair who have filled the earth with love and given us wisdom. Daghda is the light, and wisdom is the goddess Danu; together they joined with the Cruthadair in creating the world and the people of Cymru.

"Today is a new day, and we will leave here, and we will leave all that is in the past behind. We will go to a new land, among a new people, to make a new world filled with the returning souls of our families and friends. We are going home with Conall!" There was a great shout, and everyone talked at once as excitement filled the air around them and the caverns of their little souls within them.

Conall stood and said, "I have words from a poem that my uncle Caratacus shared with me as we both sat around a fire one evening." All the children fell silent and gave their attention to the great conry as he began to speak.

"It was on the anniversary date of the death of my father when Caratacus shared these words with me, and now I want to share these words with you." The great Conry of Cymru looked around the fire circle at the children and older boys and girls who would soon have to take their place among the adults, and he began to recite the words repeated many times among the families of Cymru:

> I am the great derw ynn, the oak tree that will fall
> with the advance of the winter winds.
> Cold will be the hand of winter, and with vengeance, strength,
> will Cailleach, the Hag of Winter, pull me down.
> She is angry, as I have abandoned her forest, removed my roots from her lands.
> Her heart is cold and unforgiving, and she will seek to destroy me.
> Her strength she will proclaim at my falling,
> but she is foolish, for she has no power over me.
> I have chosen to fall.
> I have removed my roots.
> It is better that I crash to the earth to rest on the breasts of Cerridwen,
> than to die in darkness, thinking I grew in a forest of light.
> I will crash with great force and loud thunder,
> hoping, praying that my falling will scatter my seed out and away
> into a land of warmth and sunlight, a place my seed can grow in peace.

Conall looked around the circle of the bright fire of hope and renewal, and he said, "You are all the seed of your mothers and your fathers and of all their ancestors before them. You are the land Cymru, and it is time we leave this place to go and grow in a new place filled with warmth, sunlight, and love. Today you become part of my clan; all of you are the children of Conall Cearnach of Clan Diahad. Now let us finish packing and leave this place."

The children cheered and danced about, filled with a happiness and hope they had feared would never be theirs again. They all ran to Conall and buried him in an avalanche of hugs and loving embraces.

Marian looked at Conall, and she was filled with deep love and admiration for this man who was so much more than a man; and the children, understanding the words Conall had spoken to them, knew they would never be without family, as they belonged to the Clan Diahad, and now Conall's family was their family.

Unlike the men from the North or the Romans, the people of Cymru were instructed by the druids, and they believed that every human body contained a soul from the Cruthadair, a soul whose value was above all the wealth and material goods of the earth.

The people of Cymru had no orphans, widows, or beggars, as everyone who lived among them became family and found a home among the people. Conall's adoption of the children would not be questioned by Briga; she would embrace them completely, as would all members of Clan Diahad.

Marian and the children set about completing the final packing as Conall, Rhun, and some of the older boys went into the woods to collect the blankets and furs that Conall had taken out to the great oak circle yesterday. As Conall picked up the great black wolf blanket, he said, "Old friend, you are going home with me to meet Briga."

Blankets and furs in hand, the boys and Conall returned to find Marian and all the children ready and eager to begin their journey—a journey home to Briga and the Clan Diahad.

Looking at the children and at Marian, Conall, the conry and great wolf-warrior of Cymru, said, "*Cymru am byth!*"

Marian and the children joined him in a great shout that rose above the land: "*Cymru am byth!*"

Standing beside Conall, a young boy with wild red hair took the first step home. Rhun reached over and took Conall's hand as if he needed to pull on Conall to get him started. "Let's go home, Conall," Rhun said.

Chapter Forty-Seven

onall had spent weeks preparing the children for the march back to his village at Llyn Tegid. As he'd prepared the children, he'd thought of the words Caswallon had taught him long ago: "All experiences have value, but not all experiences are valuable." Looking around him at the children, he had thought, "I will need to make all their experiences valuable in the days ahead."

Conall had started their training from the very beginning, as he lay in bed still confined to the cave, by telling the children stories of great heroes and noble adventures. Later, in the woods, he'd played games with them—the same games he had played as a child when he was training to become a convel, a wolf-warrior. They'd all played together in the woods, and the children had grown to love the hide-and-seek games—games intended to teach them how to be like the animals of the forest, especially the wolf. Howling keeps the pack together as they range over a vast stretch of land; each wolf has a distinctive howl. Conall had taught the children to listen and practice the different pitches until their own howls became uniquely their own. The children had become very accomplished at disappearing into the shadows and melting into the concealment of the forest undergrowth. They'd learned to slither under the brush and through the tall meadow like *neidr*, the grass snake.

Conall had also given them instructions on how to blend into their surroundings when crossing the bare, treeless hilltops.

"Remember, when you are in the open, watch the skyline all around you, and see the enemy before they see you. Once you see them, fall to the ground and don't move. Become the timid mouse that can hide from the hawk by holding very still, in a small ball, so that he becomes a rock. Become a rock, and the hawk will not see you."

He'd made games of the teachings, and Marian would often see the children and Conall crouching or crawling about as they all pretended to be one of the forest creatures of Cymru. She'd heard him say to them, "The wolf-warrior convel is taught to shapeshift and change his appearance; this is simple and easily done in the changing light of early dawn or the twilight at evening, when the physical world slides into the dark spiritual world. It is at this time, at the edge of darkness, when we can become like one of the *Cucullati*, the hooded flesh eaters, one of the enemies of the goddess."

Suddenly Conall had raised his arms high over his head and shouted, "I am one of the Cucullati, and I am hungry!" And he'd begun a slow, limping run across the clearing, laughing, chasing the screaming children fleeing the clearing. The comical scene had soon had Marian laughing too, and she'd called out to Conall and the children, "Fearsome Cucullati, your food is ready! Come and eat the lunch I've made instead of the children of Cymru!" The children had rushed past her as Conall had limped up to stand beside her, and she had reached out and taken his hand. "Come, my mighty, terrible flesh eater. Let me help you back to the cave."

The discipline with the games had paid off as Conall, Marian, and the children now attempted the dangerous task of moving across open land, knowing the enemy was also moving in unknown locations. The group walked silently, with each of the youngest children walking beside an older child. The very youngest children walked in the center of the group while the oldest children walked ahead and behind them. The two oldest boys operated as the rear guard, just as Conall had taught them; they followed at a safe distance behind the knot of children who walked tightly together, as Conall had also taught them. Conall walked far ahead of the group with one of the older boys and Rhun.

"Rhun, will you walk far ahead with me and watch for Luti, and if we see them, will you run swift as a wolf back to Marian to warn her and the children?" Conall asked the young boy.

Rhun smiled from ear to ear, and he seemed to grow inches taller as he answered, "Oh yes, Conall, I will run like a wolf that has the great black raven Bran chasing his tail."

They walked all the daylight hours of that first day; it was not raining, and Conall kept everyone moving until it was almost dark. By the end of the day, the youngest of the children had to be carried; Marian, Eigra, and the twins, Iseult and Nia, each carried a child on her back as she walked.

Conall had picked up a large stick and was using it as he walked to take some of the weight off his left leg; he was now limping, and he was ready to stop and rest.

It wasn't long before Conall spotted a thick stand of trees with heavy brush. He turned to Rhun and said, "Go back and tell Marian that we will eat and sleep under the cover of the trees just ahead. Let her tell the children we are going to rest for the night." By the time Conall had gathered everyone together to rest for the night, he was wearily limping with his left leg, and as Marian approached him, her concern showed clearly on her face.

"Conall, your leg—you have pushed too hard today. We must stop, and you must let me look at that leg." As Marian stood beside him, she touched his shoulder and said, "Sit down, my convel. You have taught us well. Let us take care of you before the darkness of night fills the world."

Conall was exhausted, and the pain of his leg overshadowed the physical world. Without argument, the great conry sat and was cared for by Marian and the children, who now saw him as their father. Fed and with fresh poultices applied to his leg to deaden the pain, Conall was soon asleep. Rhun and the other boys stood watch all night, while the wolf-warrior of Cymru rested and his soul journeyed into the past.

Sunlight passed between the tree branches in beams filtered by the great oak leaves, and each time the light breeze blew, it seemed to dance in golden patches across the face of the young boy and the old man as they sat together, surrounded by the great forest.

The young boy looked at the old man sitting beside him on the rock and asked, "Do you ever regret, Grandfather?"

Caswallon ap Beli, the Ard Druid, looked at the young boy with deep affection and said simply, "Wrongdoing is the act that casts the shadow of regret over the days of your life."

Puzzled, the young boy looked into the wrinkled face of the old man and asked, "What does that mean, Grandfather?"

"I am covered by the light of the Sky Father—it means that I have no regrets, my dear Conall. As I move forward toward the center of the circle, I can look back and see the past. The choices and decisions I've made in my lifetime have always grown seedlings of good that have developed into a strong forest of hope."

The old man placed his hand on the boy's shoulder. "You are one of those seedlings, Conall."

"You will grow to understand that this is one of the cornerstones of belief in the old way: you must never let regret overshadow your life. The times when you think you have failed will haunt you for your lifetime. A seedling of hope never grows in the darkness; to be such a seedling, you must grow in the light. Only when you allow your heart to be overshadowed by darkness and give up, do you fail. Darkness, Conall, will enter your life the day you refuse to trust others.

"This bodily life is about you...your actions. You must always remember that the life you live is yours and yours alone. You are unique in all of the great creation of the Cruthadair, and every choice you make must be made from the center of your soul, your Anam.

"For me life is simple. I have no desire to influence or control others. My concern is about my journey back to the center. When I arrive, I will review the life I've lived with all of my ancestors in attendance, and if the love outweighs the evil, I will advance and return to Cymru to live another bodily life, to experience again the wonders, joys, and pain of a life housed in a body of flesh, bone, and blood.

"It may help you, Conall, to learn and memorize the Samhainn prayer that we always say at the great fire festival. Remember this prayer, and you will not regret:

> On behalf of all, we should have thought, but did not think.
> On behalf of all, we should have said, but did not say.
> On behalf of all, we should have done, but did not do.
> May we be granted the time in which to think,
> to say, and to do what we have not done!
> Let me always do good works.

"You too will grow to understand that this life we live is about your soul, and about the choices you make between good and evil. You are Conall Cearnach of Clan Diahad, and you are of my house, Conall. You will choose to do good, and you will live a life free of offenses."

The old man looked intensely into the young boy's eyes and almost spoke the secret truth that he, Caswallon, was his father, but the druid hesitated. "No," he thought, "it is not yet time for him to understand the meaning of my words."

"You will live a very long life, Conall, and you too will look back and see behind you a forest of strong seedlings growing toward the future—physically, powerfully strong with hope. Now, my grand-son, let's go see your mother and get something to eat. I am hungry."

The young boy looked at the old man sitting beside him, and beaming with affection, threw his arms around his neck and said, "I love you, Grandfather."

=

Chapter Forty-Eight

soft touch on his shoulder stirred him as he opened his eyes to look once again on the delicate hand that had saved him from death. Marian's face drew close to his, and the warmth of her breath touched his cheek as she spoke to him. "Conall, it is time. The sun rises soon, and madainn rionnag is fading with the coming light of Daghda. We must go. I can smell rain in the air. It will be upon us soon, so we must go."

Conall reached for her hand and stroked it in his. "I was dreaming, Marian," he said. "I was a young boy sitting with Caswallon. He spoke to me about choices and told me I must choose the superior way, and that by doing so, I would live a life free of offenses. I did not understand the words when I was a boy, Marian, but now I do, and we must teach them to Rhun and the other children. He told me I would live a long life, and when I looked back on it, I would see a forest of strong seedlings growing behind me, and those seedlings would be filled with hope for the future."

She smiled at him, much like a mother would smile at a child very dear to her heart, as she said, "Yes, Conall, I am very happy that the old druid told you that you would live a long life. I would like that very much, and perhaps as we walk today, you can tell the children about Caswallon. And when we arrive at Llyn Tegid and your people's village, you can teach us all how to grow strong like the derw ynn of the great forest."

She touched his chest with both hands in the dim light of early dawn, as if making sure he was real, and asked, "Does your leg hurt this morning, my convel?"

He pulled himself up and sat with his back against the trunk of a large maple tree.

"I'm in pain," he muttered, barely loud enough for her to hear.

"And the cold rain that is coming won't help much," she said.

She reached for the cup and brought it to his lips. "Drink this, my conry. The herbs will ease your pain and help restore you as strong as a wolf."

He tilted his head back as she poured the bitter-tasting infusion past his lips until every drop was gone from the cup. She put the cup back into the bag that was hanging at her side, held in place by a woven leather strap that crossed her right shoulder. Reaching in the bag, she searched for what seemed to be a round ball wrapped in leaves. Carefully she removed the leaves. In her hand she held a barley cake that she had made with boiled barley, dried fruit, and honey all pressed into a round ball. Handing it to Conall, she said, "Breakfast."

Smiling, she leaned forward to kiss him on the forehead.

"Now," she said, "we really must go." She stood up and offered him a hand, which he took, and as he rose to his feet she added, "Take us home, my conry."

The children, eager to leave, didn't have to be told. They had already gathered up their belongings and stood in small groups, ready to once again move toward Llyn Tegid. As soon as Conall stood up, Rhun approached him and said, "I will lead today, conry." And without making a sound, he disappeared into the morning's half-light with three of the older boys. Once again they began to make their way north.

Soft, steady rain began to fall, cold and filled with the promise of a wet morning. Dark clouds hung low over them. The children huddled together as they walked, looking for warmth from
one another. Marian thought to herself, "At least the air is still
and there is no wind."

Marian stayed close to Conall, walking at his side, and as they
traveled together, she carefully watched him for the first signs of
pain. It wasn't long before a dark shadow appeared that dimmed
the light that burned in his eyes. She touched his arm and stopped;
she moved close to him and spoke softly. "The pain is back, isn't it?
Today will be different, Conall, as I have made something stronger that will help release you from the pain of your healing leg."
As she spoke, she handed him a ball of beeswax about the size of
an acorn. "Chew on this until you no longer taste the bitterness,
as it will help ease your pain, my Conry." She watched his face and
his eyes for signs of pain, and from time to time, she handed him
another small ball of beeswax that contained crushed seeds whose
magic made the pain almost disappear.

Aided by the healing magic of Marian and the natural magic
of the goddess Danu, the pain in Conall's leg became less with
each day, as the walking strengthened both muscle and bone. As
they walked together, he told stories interspersed with laughter,
and the younger children followed closely so that they could hear.

Marian watched with wonder this man who had the power
and strength to kill, but a heart as gentle as a lamb's when it
came to children and women. Her great admiration for him
grew daily, and as it grew deeper, it became an eternal love. She
knew he would always be her *annsachd*.

As she watched him, she said softly to herself, "*Is tu m' annsachd*." She stopped briefly and touched the earth with her open
left hand and said, "Cerridwen, know that Conall is my best beloved and that he will always dwell first in my heart."

They continued moving along the forest and hillsides that ran west to east, forming the first low mountains. For two more days, they followed the river valley of the Wye until they reached the waterfall at Rhaeadr Gwy, and there they stopped for an early meal and to rest for the night.

That day, shortly after noon, Rhun and the young hunters had managed to kill a young doe, and Conall made a fire—the first one since they had left the cave. The young girls had gathered greens and mushrooms from along the stream as they'd walked along the trail.

Working together, the boys and the young maidens prepared a fine feast of venison, wild greens, and mushrooms roasted over the fire. The drippings from the meat fell on the vegetables as it roasted. It was a grand feast, and everyone filled his stomach.

Now thoroughly relaxed, the children and Conall sat around the warmth of the fire as Marian and the twins, Iseult and Nia, sang ballads of the old legends of the people of Cymru. Marian noticed that the heads of the youngest children, as well as Conall's, had begun to nod as sleep began to sweep away the day from their minds.

Marian whispered to Iseult and Nia, and they all rose up and stood together around the fire. In a loud voice that startled the youngest children who had dozed off, Marian announced, "The new-moon goblins, the *Ellyllon*, have haunted the oak groves and valleys of Cymru since the time of the never-ending winter, when the snow and ice covered all the earth and never left, driving away the green of spring from all the land. This is their song, and it is the story of how the Ellyllon hunt for the disobedient children of Cymru."

Marian and the twins sang of the twisted, grotesque bodies of the yellow-skinned moon goblins, and of the black hooded robes they wore as they searched the land for the three things they loved most: toadstool mushrooms, fine, brightly colored cloth, and the disobedient children of the people of Cymru.

As the twins sang, Marian danced around the fire. Iseult sang the words of the ballad as Nia moaned and wailed, louder and louder, and then she too began dancing around the fire.

Now, as Marian and Nia danced, Iseult sang, telling the children how, when the goblins found what they wanted, they reached out with their great, pale, yellow hands to snatch away the children; held in the grasp of their long, bony fingers and sharp, claw-like talons, none of the children they grasped ever escaped.

Wailing in a trembling voice, Iseult sang of the three passions of the Ellyllon, the three things they sought most, the disobedient children of Cymru. As Marian danced about the fire, her arms raised high above her head, her hands outstretched and ready to grasp the disobedient, the twins continued singing their song. In the shadows beyond the firelight, Eigra had moved quietly behind some of the youngest children. As Iseult finished the song by telling how the Ellyllon carried the human children off to be slaves on tiny islands in the cold gray sea, Eigra rushed in and grabbed two small girls. Screams and laughter filled the camp. Conall roared, and Marian laughed so hard, she had to hold her side.

Keeping the fire as free of smoke as possible, Conall kept it hot and burning until long after dark. They all sat around telling stories and singing songs until the smallest children began to once again fall asleep.

Marian looked to Conall and said, "It is time, Conall."

Looking about at all the children sitting around the fire, Conall could only think of his Briga's surprise at how much larger their family would be when he returned to the crannog on Llyn Tegid. Smiling warmly at the children, he said, "It is time to sleep so that we can begin our journey home again at first light."

Everyone moved about to lie down, and Marian moved closer to lie next to Conall. He reached out and drew her next to him, pressing tightly against her back, and as they lay together, he whispered in her ear, "Thank you, Marian."

The next morning, as they all left the falls, they turned north and moved along the Wye Valley, following the river. They followed the valley all that day and most of the morning of the next day. The sun had not yet reached midday when Conall spotted the pile of rocks that was the trail marker telling him he was near the place to leave the river and move into the woods. Soon they were all moving up into heavy woods and steep terrain, into the mountains toward the northeast.

Conall knew they had to cross over into the next valley, and he knew that finally, home and Briga were very near.

For the rest of the day, Conall pushed the children on without stopping, until it was almost too dark to see; he was now very anxious and very near his people and his home at y Bala. Before it became too dark to see, as they crossed the barren ridgeline, they all looked down into the valley below; Conall knew it because he had hunted in it often.

If he had been alone, he would have pushed on through the darkness, but he knew it would be too dangerous for the youngest children. Putting his arm around Marian, he announced to all the children, "This is my land, and we are almost home."

Too weary to do much talking, they all moved silently in the darkness of twilight. To the north they could see Druuos, the unmoving star, and back to the east, Gealach, the moon, was rising; she had waned to a bright crescent that gave them a little light to see by as they moved among the loose rocks and stone outcrops that rose sharply up out of the steep slope.

They continued moving down the slope until they reached the safety and cover of the trees. Farther down into the valley beyond,

Conall knew they would find the Afon Severn. This was the valley with the headwaters of that great river, which flowed all the way to the sea, east of the black mountains. Conall also knew that the Afon Tryweryn would join the Afon Severn at the end of this valley.

As they approached the tree line, Conall announced, "We will rest here for the night among the trees and continue on at first light again." The children and Marian, all too tired to talk, ate silently and quickly, and then found beds among the ferns and trees. They seemed to collapse and melt back into the earth of Cymru, and soon everyone was asleep.

It was another three days moving northeast, crossing the wooded valley and following the river. At times they had to move back into the bare low knolls and hillsides as the forest became too dense along the river, or as the riverbank became too steep to walk. Whenever they crossed into open ground, everyone watched the horizon for raiders, hoping to see friends.

By the end of the third day, the moon had disappeared from the night sky, and it was now too dark to move much after twilight. Now, whenever they stopped, Conall did not build a fire. It was a cold, damp camp that evening as a mist surrounded them in the swallowing darkness. They ate dried meat and fruit and the last of the barley cakes, and once again everyone found a place to lie down among the trees.

Conall had begun to feel that something was wrong, and he had become concerned by what he did not see; by now they should have come across some of his people from the lowlands and the mountain villages.

On the morning of the fourth day after they had entered the valley of the Severn, Conall found himself standing, looking at the steep, tree-covered hillside to his left and at the river fork far below. Now in front of them was a great, flat, open valley, covered in trees and open grassland. Conall knew he was almost home.

Soon they would soon reach the fork of the Afon Tryweryn, the river that flowed from the lake at Llyn Tegid. He knew he had to turn and follow the river upstream, first to the east and then back to the south, and finally back toward the north and west.

They would enter the valley below only to leave it and climb back up steep, rugged terrain that was heavily wooded, until they reached his village at y Bala. He would soon be at the crannog. He would soon be holding Briga in his arms.

Looking at Marian, he said, "One more valley, and we will climb up to Llyn Tegid, to the lake near my village at y Bala. You will soon meet Briga, and she will be so happy to meet the young maiden who saved her Conall."

Looking deeply into Conall's eyes as she touched his bare arm, Marian answered, "I am nervous, Conall. I fear that she might not like me."

Conall reached out to put his arm around her shoulder and said, "Don't be afraid, Marian. Briga is kind. Her heart will be open to you, and she will call you sister.

"It is likely that most of the children will find new families in our village, and it would not surprise me if you and the twin sisters came to live with us. I have already made up my mind that I will have Rhun come into our home as my son, and knowing my Briga, she will not have the twins separated."

Conall leaned toward the young girl and placed his forehead gently against hers. "I know Briga will hold such gratitude in her heart for what you have done, Marian, that she will reward you with a lifetime of love and affection. I know she will offer you a place in our home too."

Her forehead was still touching his, and with her eyes closed, she whispered, "Thank you, Conall, and thanks be to Danu and to my sister Briga. May she be blessed and protected by the Cruthadair."

They continued on and made their way into the valley below. They passed by several circular hut dwellings, the homes of farmers and keepers of sheep. Several of the settlements were large enough to be walled, but they saw no one. The land seemed empty and uninhabited; even the livestock were missing.

Conall walked silently, and it was easy to sense that he had become dark and brooding as he continuously scanned the skyline around him as they walked.

Finally they reached the river fork and stopped.

It was almost dark, and once again everyone found a place to lie down. It was a cold camp again that evening, without the cheerful light and warmth of a fire. They all ate the last of their dried meat and the last of the barley cakes in silence, and everyone sensed that something was wrong.

Sensing Conall's concern, Marian and the children began to sing a song, soft and sweet, of coming home and the love and warmth of a house and hearth too long abandoned by a traveler's journey. After the song she moved among the children and kissed each good-night, whispering to them, "In two more days, we will be with Conall's people, among his clan, and we will be home."

Smiling, the exhausted children fell into a sleep filled with dreams of warmth, love, and laughter.

As Marian lay down facing Conall, she pressed up tight against him, and she brought her face close to his and kissed him softly on the mouth. "I know you are troubled, my convel," she said.

In the darkness that now formed the blanket covering them, he returned her kiss and held her closely, wrapping her in his arms as he said, "This land should be full of livestock and people, and there is nothing. My people will move out of the valleys to enter the high, secret places in the mountains when an enemy invades; something is very wrong, Marian. I fear for Briga and for you and the children."

Marian found an opening in his shirt and placed her hand against the warm skin of his chest. She easily felt the strong beating of his heart as she said, "Do not have worry, my lord. We are with the Cruthadair, and they watch over us."

As they held on tightly to each other, sleep and dreams from the Creators soon wrapped them in peace.

Chapter Forty-Nine

onall watched silently in the darkness as lightning flashed angrily far off to the north. He had awakened long before dawn and sat next to Marian, his mind racing as he fought the urge to get up and head down the trail, leaving the children and Marian behind. He wanted to run, to run as fast as he could to y Bala and on to the lake-house crannog he had built for Briga. Conall wanted to dash up the plank bridge to the front entrance and throw back its covering; he wanted to rush in to find Briga safe. He wanted to put his arms around her and shout loudly, "I will never leave you again!"

Instead he sat shivering in the cold and the dark.

He sat waiting for the first pale glimpse of dawn's earliest light on the horizon.

As soon as it was daylight, he would wake everyone, and they would leave at once. He felt that something was wrong. He knew he must get back to Briga.

Inside his heart he felt an emptiness that gave him the greatest concern; he was missing something essential, and it was eating away at him. Under his breath he whispered, "We should have seen people by now; we should have seen farmers and hunters in the woods and the fields."

Conall realized that the emptiness he felt in his heart was the emptiness in the land of Cymru. The people were gone, and the land was as empty as the feeling that gripped his heart like a clenched fist.

Conall was deeply worried…not for himself, but for Briga and for Marian. He was worried for the children with him, and he knew he would not be able to protect and care for all of them without the help of his clan.

Conall waited.

Far off on the horizon, the lightning tore open the sky. He could hear at a great distance a lone wolf calling out, howling with a long and drawn-out, mournful call, making a sound that seemed somehow to be connected to the emptiness in his heart.

Peering into the darkness, Conall did the only thing he could do: he began to pray to the goddess Danu.

"Mother of all life, the great *màthair-beatha,* please open your heart and hear the words I speak. Reach out your hands and take hold of my Briga and keep her safe. Place your arms around her as I cannot; hold her and protect her from harm. Mother Danu, help me. Protect these children with me, and please, Danu, bring back the people to fill the land of Cymru with your love and their happy laughter. Show me the people of Cymru; return them to the land of *màthair-beatha.*"

He sat with his back against the trunk of a young birch tree. The white bark of the tree stood out even in the darkness of the early twilight. His knees were pulled up to his chest, his arms forming a circle around them, and as he prayed, he held on to his forearms with his hands. When he finished speaking, he laid his head on his knees and closed his eyes.

"Conall." The voice was a thought at first, and far away.

Marian's hand rested on the mass of Conall's light-red hair, and once again she softly said, "Conall, you must wake up. We must leave." She knelt before him and looked into his face; she clearly saw the darkness of worry shadowing his eyes as he opened them to look at her.

His mind was still far away; he did not seem to recognize her, and in a bewildered, questioning voice, he asked, "Marian?"

He looked beyond her and saw the children standing, ready to leave with Rhun. The young boy stood nearest him, waiting for his orders. Conall turned to look at Marian, and it was only when he looked into her eyes that he realized he was awake again. He had been dream-walking, and in his dream he had been visited by Aerten, the goddess of fate.

As Conall looked into Marian's eyes, he spoke in a low, somber tone. "The goddess Aerten came to me, Marian, and took me by the hand. She spoke in a language I did not understand, and as she did, we both shapeshifted; our bodies changed into the form of *gwdih* , the owl. She spoke to me not through my ears, but inside my head, and told me to follow her, and in the darkness we became great black shadows as we flew south. I knew the place well, as we flew above the valley of the Afon Tywi. We flew until we reached the great ocean bay to the south; to the place called Three Rivers, and there, in the bay, I saw the ships of the Luti. Again Aerten spoke and said, 'Remember the way, Conall.' I followed her as she turned back north, and we flew to y Bala. It was in ruins, Marian, destroyed and burned to the ground."

He had spoken quietly so that only Marian heard his words.

"Maybe your journey while you slept was just an *aisling*, a dream, Conall," she said as she took his hands and helped him to his feet. "You are awake now, and we must hurry to y Bala to see what is real and what is dreaming."

Looking directly at the young boy, Conall said, "Rhun, take the oldest boys and girls to form an advance and rear guard with flanks far out on each side. Move as if the enemy were here among us; move like a cysgod, a shadow among the trees, blending into the darkness of the forest shade to be one of the unseen. Follow the river upstream and stay on the south bank as we move toward the lake; the ground is easier to traverse along the south bank."

Looking directly into Conall's eyes, Rhun answered without questioning. "I will be the shadow among the trees, my conry, and we will stay to the south bank." Quickly, Rhun selected a dozen of the older children, and just as quickly, they all seemed to disappear into the forest around him.

Looking to Marian, Conall said, "We must move along the river as swiftly as possible, and we will not stop until it is dark."

Marian picked up her bags, and turning to the children, she said, "Everyone pair up and take care of one another. We will move, and we will move as fast as we can. Do not fall behind. Today we are all wolf-warriors, and we will move like the convel move—no sound, always watching and always listening for the enemy, and we will not stop."

Without another word, the children paired up, and as Conall took Marian's hand, the children reached out to grasp the hands of those who stood nearest to them. Silently as a cysgod, they all moved swiftly into the woods along the Afon Tryweryn.

The terrain soon became steep, and the river ran swiftly in a series of rapids and steep drops. After several hours of walking and struggling through the woods, they began to slow down; the heavily wooded, steep ground proved too much for several of the small children, and Conall and Marian took turns carrying them.

The children helped one another over fallen trees and past steep slopes that dropped off to the river below. The trail narrowed into a game trail that at times ran along the very edge of the white water churning along this stretch of the river. Conall watched them carefully and felt a deep sense of pride in these children as they worked together to move along the trail—always the older children reaching out to help the younger.

All that day they made their way along the river. Every few hours scouts sent back by Rhun returned to report to Conall. "We have not seen anyone, conry," was the report, and as the day went on with each report of an empty land, the shadow that was a deep frown on Conall's face grew deeper and darker.

They stopped to rest at midday for a short time, and everyone sat quietly. Marian sat next to Conall, and all she could think to do was reach over and touch his bare upper leg; she squeezed the muscle, and as he looked toward her, she smiled and said softly, "They are all here for you, Conall; all the children are here to help you. Do not worry about us, and as we near y Bala, if you want to move ahead of us, don't concern yourself about us. You have trained these children to be like the wolf-warriors of Cymru. We will follow the river, and we will find the village."

Conall looked at the young woman who sat next to him and smiled. He leaned forward, kissing her firmly on the forehead, and said, "You truly are a woman of Cymru. Blessed are you among women, my beautiful Marian. Know that my heart aches with love and concern for you and the children. Thank you, but I will stay, as it is my desire to make sure you and the children are safe. I have faced Daghda, and I have sworn a blood oath to protect you and these children; I will only leave you if I am killed in battle, and that, my beautiful Marian, is highly unlikely."

Standing up, he reached down to give her a hand, and with a broad smile, he said, "It is time we move again."

They traveled until almost dark. The young scouts returned, and Rhun reported that all they had seen were a "few stray cows with calves wandering in meadow areas of the woods."

They had not seen or heard of anyone all day; it was if all the people of Cymru had disappeared.

With the darkness came a steady rain.

The heavy cloud cover made the gloom around them thick, and the eye could not penetrate very far into the advancing shadows of twilight. No stars shone in the heavens above. They were cold, wet, and encircled by a thick black mantle of gloom filled with strange noises both near and far.

Marian knew the youngest children, already cold, would suffer greatly this night, as combined with the power of the dark, the rainy forest sounds would be distorted and transformed into fingers of fear that would reach deep into their young hearts and minds.

From the look of the sky, it was clear that this would be a rain that would fall steadily all night. There was no shelter but the canopy of trees they would huddle under, and the semblance of sleep would only entertain their minds. Marian placed the youngest children in the center of what was to become a sphere of bone and flesh as they all held on to one another, hugging and pressing together to keep as much warmth in their bodies as possible.

As Marian moved the smaller children to the center, she talked to them, saying, "Remember the wasp. When the cold of Cailleach, the Hag of Winter, comes to Cymru, you will find our brothers and sisters *gwenyn meirch*, the wasps, all huddled together in a tight ball for warmth and protection from her. Well, tonight we will be like the wasp, and we will hold on to each other and share our warmth until the sun returns."

Instead of warm blankets, Marian gave the children hugs and soft kisses and whispered to each that she loved them. Marian and Conall would not sleep holding each other this night. They would instead sleep apart, at the outer edge of the children, and they would wrap their arms and share their warmth with as many of them as they could reach; tonight they would be a blanket for the children.

When all the children had settled together, Marian turned to Conall and stepped in close to him. She looked up into his face in the dim light. He leaned into her face and kissed her on the lips. She had been cold, but the feeling of his lips and the warmth from his breath sent a glow throughout her body. From her lips deep into her very core, she was warmed by the touch of this man.

"Good-night, Marian," he said, and as she turned to move toward the children, Conall gave her bottom a playful pat; it was too dark for him to see her face, but she stopped and turned back to look toward him. She smiled as only a woman who desires her man can. She went to sleep that night warmed by her memories of Beltane and the horned god Cernunnos.

The next morning the sun returned, and with it warmth.

The clouds had waited until sunrise to leave, and when they did, the sun seemed to be warmer than it was the day before. The fire Conall made and the sun worked as allies to dry wet clothing; they rested longer in camp, as Conall knew they were very close now, and he wanted the children dry and in good spirits when they entered the village at y Bala. Late that afternoon they continued to move upriver, and once again the children's excitement grew, as did their good spirits.

Once again Conall sent out Rhun and the older children as scouts and paired all the other children up as they continued to move along the river. Marian stepped in beside Conall and took his hand. She had dreamed that night.

Marian had vividly relived, in great detail, every word, every touch, and all the feelings of the night of Beltane. As she walked with Conall, warmth grew deep inside her, and a joy filled her heart. In her dream Danu had stood beside her as she lay on the Beltane bed with Conall. As Conall slept, holding Marian in his arms, the goddess had moved closer and knelt down near Marian's head, and she had whispered like a soft breeze into her ear, "You are with child, and you will give birth to Conall's only daughter. You will call her Muirgheal, after your mother, but you are not to tell Conall, not until you see Bran the Raven sitting on the back of a horse."

As she walked beside Conall, she was smiling, thinking of the dream. She warmly squeezed his hand and thought to herself, "I carry within me the daughter of Conall and the soul of my mother."

They ate as they marched, and the scouts returned at evening to report; this time Conall went out with them, and together with Rhun, they ranged far ahead of their little party of refugees. Together they scouted the trail almost to Llyn Tegid, and when he returned to Marian and the children, he said, "We will be in y Bala before sunset this evening."

Hearing the report, young voices whispered in excitement, and several times Conall overheard a happy child say, "Tonight, tonight we will be home."

Standing very near Conall, Marian smiled, and while she touched his strong bicep and shoulder, she said, "It will be good to be home." She now felt the energy inside her growing all the time, and she was sure that the child who grew inside would indeed be the returning soul of her mother. This thought gave Marian great joy, and as the child in her grew, so did her love for Conall.

The last part of the climb was steep and heavily wooded.

The trail followed the river to its source at the lake, and they approached by way of its north end, where the village of y Bala sat. The lake was narrow and about four miles long, sitting in a great rift valley that extended all the way to the Eireann Sea. Conall had not wanted to build Briga's crannog near the village and had chosen a place almost at the far end of the lake, in a cove on the west side near the spot that the Afon Llafar flowed in. Briga had approved the location, noting, "From this circle I will be able to see the moon rise across the lake, and with the stream entering here, we will always have cool, fresh water."

The ground leveled out as they came into the valley, and the woods fell back behind them, creating the opening that was the lake. Conall stopped and stood silent, looking at the scene in front of them, as they all could now clearly see smoke rising from y Bala. It was clear to all those observing the scene ahead that the village had been burned and was now deserted. No one said a word, but a very audible, painful moan went out from many of the children. Marian and the children continued to walk with Conall in silence as they approached the smoldering ruins of the village stockade and houses.

Conall did not speak, and as they approached what had been the gate to the village, Marian watched as tears welled up in his eyes. Standing there, he reached out and held on to the charred post holding one side of the entrance gate. As he looked past what was left of the wall and into the burned remains of the homes that had been his clan's, the convel of Cymru said, "I should have been here."

Marian looked too and said, "There are no magpies or ravens here feasting on the dead, Conall, and I see no bodies. Everyone must have sped away before the raiders burned the village."

From the only building still standing in the village, an old man and a young woman appeared and slowly walked toward them. The old man was bent with great age and walked only by the aid of the woman and the thick staff he held. They stopped directly in front of the convel, only inches away, and the old man leaned forward to study the face of the wolf-warrior who was in front of him.

Conall felt the man's breath on his face as he finally said, "You are Conall. They came here five days ago looking for you, but they did not find any of us. We had all fled many days before they came; most went deeper into the mountains. I am Aodhan, and this is my wife, Vala. The Ard Druid Caswallon ordered us all to leave this village and flee into the mountains, but I am no longer able to walk, so Vala stayed with me, and we hid in the trees until the raiders left. No one was captured or killed here, and Briga was sent off by the orders of Caswallon with a party to care for her, to the place of the talking falls at Còmhradh Carraghs. She left the village many days before the Luti arrived."

"You are sure of this?" Conall asked with the hope that it was indeed true. "And are you sure that you heard that Briga left to go to the waterfall at Còmhradh Carraghs?"

The younger woman who helped support the old man looked at Conall and at Marian and all the children. She smiled warmly and said, "Yes, Conall Cearnach, the words of Aodhan are true. You all look very tired, and the children look hungry. We have food that we have saved from the village, and we would be happy to share it with you, the children, and the lady. Please let us offer you shelter."

Looking to Vala and Aodhan, Marian said, "I am Marian, and these children are now my only family. We had no warning at our village, and it was destroyed by the raiders. We are all that is left, the only survivors. We would be very grateful for your generous offer of hospitality and food. We have struggled many days in the open, and all of us would appreciate the warmth of your hearth and the covering of our heads by your roof."

"Yes," Conall said. "Yes, we would be very thankful. Marian and these children saved my life, and they are now my family and your family. We are all very tired and very hungry. We will gladly accept your kind offer tonight, but tomorrow we must push on to find Briga at Còmhradh Carraghs."

"It will be so," said the old man. "Let us move into shelter, as the evening air is filled with the promise of rain." And as he spoke, he turned and with Vala's help began to walk back into the village.

Suddenly they all stopped and turned to look toward the far end of the lake, where the sound of war trumpets filled the air. Over and over again, they sounded as they approached. Aodhan paused only long enough to say, "The army of the ard righ returns." Without saying any more, he continued moving toward the shelter of the only roundhouse in the village that had escaped the torches of the Luti.

"Take the children to shelter and food, Marian," Conall said as he turned and walked back past the village wall to wait for those who approached, whose war horns declared loudly, "We are coming! Prepare!"

He did not have to wait long. On the trail hugging the lake, a group of riders appeared, with the black raven flags and banners of Caradoc ap Bran, the Ard Righ of Cymru. And still farther behind them, the trumpets continued to sound the approach of the main army.

Twenty mounted men rode without hesitation to the village and stopped, forming a half circle that faced the convel Conall. One of the riders leaned forward in his saddle to have a better look at Conall and said, "I am Pwyll, and I am the leader of the scouts of the army of the Ard Righ Caradoc ap Bran. The army approaches and will stay here tonight."

Facing the men, Conall announced so that all might hear, "I am Conall Cearnach of Clan Diahad."

Pwyll looked surprised, and his face betrayed both awe and fear as he looked at Conall and said, "We had feared you dead and had given up hope of ever seeing you again." The man turned in his saddle to talk to the man next to him, and this man quickly turned his horse and raced off at a full run back toward the main column of the approaching army.

"I have sent this man to announce to the commander of the army that Conall lives. The army's chieftain will be very happy to hear that you are here, Conall, as this army is led by your uncle Caratacus. He will have much to tell you when he arrives." And without another word, he turned his horse away from the village and with his men continued to move north along the pathway that served as the village road.

Conall stood waiting for the approach of his uncle Caratacus, and as he did, he thought, "Now I will start searching for Briga."

Chapter Fifty

onall did not have to wait long, as the army of his uncle Caratacus quickly approached and was upon him before the dust of Pwyll's horses had settled back to the earth. The leading riders approached Conall, and like those who had just left, formed a semicircle around where he stood. The rest of the army split into two columns, one moving to the north and the other to the south of the burned village. It was their intention to put up their marching camp in the open ground outside the walled village.

As the riders rode past, Conall watched as a number of very large wolfhounds ran alongside the horses. Many of the men on horseback carried spears with brightly colored flags that flapped as they paraded by. To the rear of the horse riders was a long line of chariots, each carrying two men. One man drove the two horses that pulled the chariot, and the other warrior stood at the ready to fight. These men held long spears from which colorful yellow flags with the image of Bran, the Raven vigorously flapped in the wind, and hanging on the woven-branch sides of each chariot were additional weapons, shields, arrows, and a short Welsh hunting bow. Behind the chariots came the baggage wagons, filled with the supplies that supported the army of the Ard Righ Caradoc ap Bran.

Well-armed men wearing light armor walked on both sides of the wagons. Most carried tall rectangular shields, swords hanging from their waists, and long spears held upright, the points reflecting the late-afternoon sun. A dozen men walked along, carrying over their right shoulders the *carnyes*, the large bronze war trumpets of the people of Cymru. Each was shaped in an elongated *S*-shape almost as tall as the man holding it, and each was polished to a brightness that reflected the slightest sunlight and even moonlight. A mouthpiece was at one end of the long straight horn, topped by the head of an animal, its mouth gaping open. Held high above the army, the horn produced a haunting sound that directed the army and built up its courage while at the same time filling the enemy with fear.

It was an impressive and colorful sight as men, dogs, and horses collaborated together under the direction of the army's commander, Caratacus. Looking with pride at the men and the horses moving as one, Conall thought to himself that it was no wonder the people of Cymru honored the horse, for in all of the creation of the Cruthadair, only the horse was a true ally in battle; the dog would run away, but the horse would often die on the battlefield alongside his rider.

Conall looked back toward the semicircle of men and horses that had formed to face him. A straight-backed young man sat on a horse at the center, the man's broad shoulders carrying a sense of strength and authority. He was tall even among the men of Cymru, and his deep voice boomed loud and clear.

"Nephew, it is good to see you still alive!"

As the man leaned back in his saddle, he swung his right leg up in an arch, over his horse's head, and dismounted; without hesitation he walked straight to Conall and flung both his arms around his shoulders.

"It is so good to see you, Conall. We had feared the worst, what with the death of Caswallon and most of your convel, and worse, the capture of Briga by the Luti." The much younger man who held Conall in his embrace had no way of knowing that all of this was news to Conall, but as he spoke the words, he felt the wolf-warrior became as rigid and as cold as the cròmleac stones of Cymru. Caratacus took one step back and held Conall's arms just below his shoulders.

"You didn't know?" he said.

Conall stood looking at his uncle, unable to speak, but knowing in his spirit that every day of his life before this moment had just been ripped from his heart. He knew the sorrow that now began to grow inside him was the beginning of his greatest *cruaidhghleachd*; his life would be filled with agony and hard struggle until he once again held Briga in his arms.

The words Caratacus planted in Conall's heart took root, and in a single heartbeat grew into his greatest suffering. With the next heartbeat, tears welled up in his eyes as a terrible unseen hand seemed to grasp at his throat. He struggled to speak, but the pain was too great, and as he looked into the eyes of the younger man standing in front of him, he was not sure he had the strength to endure. With the third beat of his heart, his legs melted away.

Helped by his uncle, Conall came to rest sitting, squatted down. His left hand rested on his knee and as he leaned forward, his head bent sharply to look down as if seeing into the depths of the underworld. If he had not been supporting himself with his right arm, he would have fallen over to lie on his back. The words of Caratacus had been as deadly as the mighty blows of the one-eyed god Balor.

Caratacus knelt down next to Conall and put his hand on his shoulder. He looked at the fallen man and said, "I am so sorry, Conall, that I was the one who told you of these losses."

Marian had heard the army's approach and had stood watching from the doorway of the roundhouse. She could not hear what was being said, but she clearly saw Caratacus step back and Conall collapse, to sit dazed on the ground. She wondered to herself what news could have brought the convel Conall to descend onto the ground. And from her heart quickly came the answer: something had happened to Briga.

Running toward him, she shouted, "Conall!"

The children, Aodhan, and Vala had all come out of the roundhouse too at the sound of the army. As Marian ran toward Conall, she was quickly followed by Rhun and the twin sisters, Iseult and Nia. Vala stopped the rest of the children from rushing forward with outstretched arms and softly spoken words: "Children, let us wait here for Conall."

As Marian reached Conall, she fell to her knees beside him and reached out, touching him on his left arm, and said, "Conall, we are here."

Rhun and the twins stopped to stand behind Marian, and Rhun reached out to touch Marian and said, "We are all here, Conall."

Looking to Caratacus, she said, "My name is Marian."

Conall turned his head to look at her. She could see his great *cruaidhghleachd* as the tears filling his eyes began to move down his cheeks. Marian watched as one tear trickled down his left cheek to rest for a moment on his chin before falling to the earth. She could see that he was softly saying something, and she leaned toward him to hear.

"I should have been here," was the anguished thought that quietly poured from his heart.

He repeated the sentence over and over again, as quickly as the last one ended.

The man kneeling next to Conall said, "Marian, I am Conall's uncle Caratacus. I told him that Caswallon was dead, that most of his convel had not returned, and that Briga has been captured and taken south by the Luti. I didn't know that Conall had not heard any of this; we all thought he was dead too. I am so sorry, Marian. Will you stay here with him while I give my men orders? I will send two men to help you."

Stunned by the news and looking from Conall to Caratacus, Marian stammered out the words, "Yes. Yes, I will stay with him. This is so terrible…"

As he rose, Caratacus touched Conall's shoulder with his left hand and said, "We will do everything we can, Conall, everything possible to return Briga to you and to avenge your convel warriors and the druid Caswallon. This I swear to you with my oath of blood."

Reaching for the blade at his waist, he drew it from its sheath, and taking his left hand from Conall's shoulder, he drew the blade's sharp edge across the palm. Almost instantly blood left the wound and fell to the earth. Once again Caratacus reached out and rested his left hand on Conall's shoulder, squeezing hard enough that Conall looked up at him. "This I promise you by my oath of blood, Conall—by my word and honor I promise you."

Looking at Marian, Caratacus said, "I will send you some help and food for all of those with you." Without another word he walked toward his men; the wound on his hand left a trail of blood spots as he walked. Reaching the raiders, he spoke to two men, who dismounted and handed their reins over to the riders next to them, then turned and walked quickly with determination toward Marian and Conall.

The two men, well seasoned in their appearance, approached Marian and stopped to stand in front of her and Conall. As they both looked directly at her, the larger of the two said, "I am Einion the Anvil, and this is my brother, Morthwyl the Hammer. We are here to serve you, Lady Marian."

Chapter Fifty-One

orking together, Einion, Morthwyl, and Marian managed to get Conall to his feet and started walking him toward the roundhouse that Aodhan and Vala occupied. As they all approached the village gate, a rider approached and stopped. "Caratacus, chief of the army, has ordered that a baggage wagon be assigned to the Lady Marian and the children, and that tents and food be prepared for all of you and the convel Conall." Without another word the man turned the horse and rode back to the column.

Vala had placed a bench outside the door of the roundhouse, and it was on this bench that they sat Conall. As Marian sat next to him, Vala handed her a flagon filled with melheglin and said, "Help him to drink this, Marian. It will soften his sorrow."

Holding the flagon by its handle, Marian raised it to Conall's lips and encouraged him to drink. "Please, Conall, drink. It is melheglin, and it will help the gods ease the *cruaidhghleachd* that grips your heart."

Rhun, the twins, Iseult and Nia, and Eigra had gathered the children together and all disappeared into the woods. As they all ran off together, Rhun could be heard saying, "Let's go into the woods for firewood, and let us find as many of the nine woods as we can for a new need fire."

Soon a baggage wagon arrived, along with a dozen or more men who went to work setting up four tents and an area for cooking. One fellow almost as wide as he was tall approached Marian and smiled broadly, saying, "I am Maddock the Generous. My friends call me Ithel, which means 'generous lord,' and I have been assigned to be your cook. You are very lucky. As you can see by my generous girth, I am a very good cook and very generous." Bowing to Lady Marian, he added, "I am to serve you, my lady, the children, and the convel Conall, but I do not think the great conry will be with us long, as Caratacus has instructed me to let you all know that he prepares warriors to join Conall in his search for Briga. Now, my lady, if I may have your leave, I will go and prepare food for all of you."

Looking at the rotund man, Marian forced a smile and said, "Thank you, Ithel."

Soon another man appeared in front of Marian, bowed at the waist, and said, "My lady, I am Prydwen the *Rheolwr*, the commander of the detail that has been assigned to take care of you. We have made ready a tent and bed for the conry of Cymru. It is the largest tent standing to the right of the other three tents, my lady. I hope you and Conall Cearnach will find your accommodations comfortable and to your liking, and if you need anything, just ask for me. The two tents next to this tent are for the children, one for the girls and one for the boys. The fourth tent holds the kitchen supplies, food, and bedding for you and your party. My men and I will accompany you, Lady Marian, as you and the children move under the protection of the army of Caratacus to the fortress at Caer Caradoc."

Marian thanked the man, and he bowed again, turned, and abruptly walked away in the direction of the tents. She watched as he appeared to give orders to two men standing there. Later Marian would notice that these two men had been placed in charge of a dozen armed guards that stood around their tents—tall men with long, oval-shaped shields and long spears with hewing blade points.

Marian, sitting next to Conall, who was still dazed, turned and looked at him, touched his arm, and stood up. As she leaned over him she reached down and said, "We are going to take you to the tent, Conall, so that you may rest and recover your spirit."

Turning to Einion and Morthwyl, she asked, "Will you please help me get Conall to the tent and into bed?"

The two men answered yes, and together they helped Conall stand up from the bench and walk to the tent. Soon the great convel was in bed and the melheglin, blended with sleeping herbs and his emotional exhaustion, carried him away to the land between the physical and the spiritual, to the delightful plain Mag Mell. He fell asleep.

Sitting on the ground with his back against the trunk of an ancient oak, the old man looked at the young boy standing in front of him. He smiled at the boy as he saw the mark of the Red Dragon of Cymru on his forehead, which matched exactly the one on his. Caswallon was delighted to see that his ancient bloodline had been passed on to this child. He began to speak and teach the young boy.

"Those who do not teach the truth live a lie, and they condemn the innocent to a life lived in darkness."

"The weak stand alone! The strong are the many, standing together as one."

"Smile and rejoice! For blessed is the man who hears the laughter of children and the sweet voices of women singing. His indeed is a life filled with great wealth and riches beyond gold."

"Life is to be lived in the daily devotion of loving one another!"

"Fear profits a man nothing, nor does it increase the length of his life."

"A foolish man turns away friendship; a wise man honors friendship while nurturing respect among his enemies."

The young boy shook his head and said, "Grandfather, my heart is not in the lessons today, as I am greatly troubled, and I feel lost. This feeling of loss I have is growing; I seem to remember someone who has been taken from me, Grandfather." The young boy looked down at the old man sitting in front of him and added, "Help me, Grandfather. I am filled with the bottomless feeling of missing someone, and there is emptiness inside me. I feel like a dried-up spring."

The old man's face formed a deep frown as he studied the young boy, and reaching up for the boy's hand, he said, "Help me to my feet, Conall."

Standing next to the boy, the old man put his arm around his shoulder, and in a firm, forceful voice said, "Conall, we are not here. You are a dreamer, and you must leave this place into which you have traveled to avoid the weight of suffering; you must return and find Briga. She is in great danger!"

The old man leaned toward the young boy that was his son until his face was only inches away, and as he looked straight into his eyes, the druid Caswallon repeated the teaching: "Fear profits a man nothing, nor does it increase the length of his life.

"Now go, Conall, and find Briga."

Conall pushed aside the woven blanket that served as the only door into the crannog. He smiled as he looked around the home he had built for Briga. "This is my most happy place, Briga," he said as he paused. "Yes, this is the place I want to be above all other places." Looking around the large room, his gaze went toward the empty bed against the far wall. Stretching, he mumbled and said out loud, "Sleep is what I need now—sleep and rest. Whatever I have to do can wait until tomorrow, as for now I just want to sleep."

Walking over to the bed, Conall fell exhausted into the raised sleeping platform. He smiled as he remembered building the bed under the very specific direction of Briga. It was a box on a raised platform, filled with soft animal furs and brushed woven-linen blankets and many pillows of different sizes stuffed with goose feathers. In the bed he rolled to the left side and buried his face deeply into the blankets.

He thought, "This is the side of the bed that Briga always sleeps on." Conall breathed in deeply through his nose, and as a reward, the deep, rich fragrance of herbs, oils, and the phero-mones left by Briga flooded into his mind. He deeply moaned and spoke into the darkness that now surrounded him. "Briga, my beloved Briga, I will never leave you alone again."

A sound from the far side of the room caught his attention, and he rolled over to seek the source of the noise. An oil lamp burned in the far corner of the room, its flickering flame creat-ing shadows that danced along the walls.

Lying on his left side, propped up on his elbow, he was de-lighted to see Briga standing in the dancing lamplight, and he watched her intently as she dried herself with a large cloth towel made of soft-brushed linen dyed yellow.

As he watched her, she smiled back at him and said, "Do I please you, my lord?"

Once more he felt the awed inspiration that warmed his heart whenever he watched her, and he said, "Yes, Briga, you make me very happy. *Is tu m' annsachd*, my most beloved."

Standing upright, Briga dropped the towel she was holding, and with her eyes fixed on his, she said, "Why, Conall? Why have you not come for me?"

Standing naked in front of him, her face, neck, shoulders, and arms began to change. Black and green bruises grew to cover her arms and shoulders, while angry welts and raw red skin appeared at her wrists and around her neck. Conall had seen such marks before left by ropes secured too tightly, and he audibly gasped as he looked at her face.

"She has been savagely beaten," he thought. "Her nose is broken and smashed, flattened against her bruised and battered face, and she is covered in blood. Both of her eyes have been blackened, and her beautiful long hair has been cut into ragged clumps."

As he looked at her in shock and disbelief, she began to fade backward into a tunnel of swirling mist. Shouting after her, Conall yelled, "By the power of the gods, what has happened to you, Briga?"

In a panic he jumped from the bed and shouted again, "Briga, what has happened to you? Stop, stop, please! Do not leave me, Briga!"

"Conall." As the mists swallowed her body, her voice entered his mind. "Conall, we are not here in the crannog. You are dreaming, and you must leave this place of your suffering and return to the land of the young. You must come for me, Conall. They are taking me away...they are taking me away..."

Bewildered, Conall looked around the crannog for Briga, but she was gone. In disbelief over the last words she had spoken to him as she melted away into the mist, he asked, "What do you mean, they are taking you away?" Frantic, he looked around the room for her, desperately hoping that he was dreaming and that nothing he had seen or heard was real.

Convinced she was no longer in the crannog; Conall accepted that he was alone. "She is gone," he said as the only image of her that now came to his mind was her beaten and battered face.

Suddenly, he looked around the room in desperation, confusion, and disbelief as he realized he was no longer in their crannog but instead standing inside a tent. When he pushed open the doorway of the tent, bright sunlight momentarily blinded him; he was overwhelmed with both the light and the active sounds of a military encampment. Standing at the tent's opening in the harsh sunlight and squinting his eyes, he continued to look around outside the tent for Briga. Convinced she was not there, he called out her name as he walked out into the sunlight and the world beyond the tent.

The brightness of the light outside the tent momentarily blinded him. It was painfully bright, and he raised his right hand to cover his eyes. As he waited for his eyes to adjust to the harshness of the light, he realized that he was surrounded by people all going about the busy activity of an army camp at high noon. Looking around, he saw that several cooking fires were burning, and several men were working at the pots that were hanging from tripods. Armed guards with spears and shields stood at the ready, and near him were Marian and the children. Bewildered, he began walking in their direction. As Conall approached Marian, he realized that she was sitting on a bench with Caratacus, and she was busy wrapping Caratacus's left hand with a clean, fresh bandage.

Conall's mind seemed to clear upon seeing Marian and Caratacus, and he realized he was back among the living—

"I am back," he said. "And I have returned from my dream-walking."

Several of the children, including Rhun, had heard and seen Conall as he approached, and now they all began shouting at the top of their voices, "Conall, Conall is awake! He has risen from his sleep! Conall is up! Conall is back!"

All shouting at once, a dozen children ran at Conall, with Rhun at the lead; they ran straight for the convel, forming a circle that surrounded him. Here they stopped, only a few feet from him. As they hesitated, they all looked at him with questioning eyes and a touch of doubt as they wondered, "Is this really our Conall?"

Looking at the faces of the children, he realized they were holding back, and he said, "It's me, and I'm here, no longer lost but once again with all of you."

All the children rushed to embrace him once they realized Conall was awake, both in body and soul, and the great wolf soon found himself under a pile of cheerful children. From the center of the ball of celebrating children came Conall's pretend cry for help.

"Marian, please save me!"

Marian and Caratacus stood and walked in the direction of what was becoming Conall's greatest defeat at the hands of happy children. As she stood over Conall and the happy, laughing ball of children, Marian said, "Children, we should let Conall get up, as I am sure he is starving after his long sleep, and I'm sure he has many stories to tell Caratacus, the army's commander."

The children helped Conall to his feet, and with final hugs and many kisses, they all melted away to play until they would be called by Ithel the cook, who would let them know it was time to eat the midday meal. Now standing alone, Conall felt a little unsure and lost, but this did not last long, as Marian rushed up to him and surrounded him with her arms in a hug that spoke a thousand words. Caratacus also stepped in beside him and grasped his shoulder, saying, "We are glad you have returned to us, Conall. It has been three days, and we were worried that you might have been happier as a dreamer in the other world."

Marian took Conall by the arm, and as she walked him toward the benches and the table to get some food, he started asking questions. "What has happened? How long have I been sleeping, and what has become of Briga? I have had a most terrible vision, a dream in which Briga was terribly beaten. Does anyone know where she is?"

As Marian sat down with Conall, Caratacus joined them and began speaking. "The news is not good, Conall. Briga has been captured, and most of those who accompanied her from the village here at Llyn Tegid have also been captured or else killed. A large war party of Luti swept north and intercepted her before she could make it to Tintagel. We believe everyone in her party was killed, including your cousin Odhran."

An animal-like groan, throaty and deep, escaped from Conall's spirit as he looked down at the ground and slowly shook his head from side to side. Caratacus continued to speak, "We do know that she has been captured and is alive. Wolf-warriors followed the Luti who took her, even killing a few of them from the shadows, but they never got the chance to free her. Briga was taken back down Afon Tywi to Three Rivers and the Bae Caerfyrddin. She is with their ships that are beached at the sand dunes of Cefn Sidan. Your convel brothers are watching her, Conall, and will take a chance to free her if they can, but there are still ships on the beach and several hundred Luti."

Caratacus reached over the table and touched Conall's arm. "Nephew," he said, "as soon as I heard that the Luti had moved north, I rode from the fortress at Caer Caradoc with the army of the Ard Righ. We pushed day and night to the coast, only to miss the war party from Jutland. When my scouts informed me that we had missed them by five days and that they had already reached the great ocean bay, I ordered the army to double back, and we rode directly here to Llyn Tegid in the hope that we might find you or some of your convel alive."

Conall looked up at his uncle and said, "I have to follow her and get her back. I cannot leave her with the Luti. Please help me, Uncle."

"It's already done, Conall," Caratacus said. "I have sworn an oath of blood to help you, Conall—to help you get Briga back, no matter what it takes or how long. We will get her back; this I promise. Now, let's eat, and after the meal, we will make ready for you to ride south."

Caratacus waved his hand over his head toward the pots cooking over the open fires, and quickly several men started their way over carrying bowls, pitchers filled with drink, and steaming hot pots. A very large, rotund fellow boomed out in a loud voice as he approached, "Lord Caratacus, I have an excellent venison stew cooked with red wine from Gaul and with barley, wild onion, turnips, and mushrooms!" As he placed a large bowl in front of Caratacus and Marian, he turned to Conall and bowed deeply. "I am Ithel the Generous, my lord, and if you need anything, Conall Cearnach of Clan Diahad, I will gladly supply it for you in abundance."

Acknowledging the man, Conall said, "Thank you, Ithel," and turning to Caratacus, he said, "As soon as I eat this, I want to leave to travel south so that I can find and return Briga to our crannog here at Llyn Tegid. I will search for Briga until I bring her home, or I will draw my last breath in this body trying!"

Caratacus and Marian both looked at Conall, knowing that no words could be spoken that would delay his search for Briga. As they both looked at him, Caratacus said, "I will give the order, Conall." Caratacus looked at both Marian and Conall and added, "Do not worry about Marian and the children, as I will take them all to the safety of the fortress at Caer Caradoc. I will watch over them and provide for their needs until you return with Briga."

Conall smiled and said, "Thank you, Caratacus. It will be a great relief knowing that Marian and the children will be safe." Turning to look at his uncle, he continued. "I'll journey back south along the coastline of the Môr Iwerddon, following the last reported route of Briga and the raiders, and as quickly as possible, I'll make my way to the ships that are beached at the sand dunes of Cefn Sidan. I would like to leave this afternoon."

Turning back to look at Marian, Conall bent and kissed her on the forehead. "Marian, I owe you my life, and when I have rescued Briga, I will return for you, Rhun, and the other children. Together we will all start a new life together here at Llyn Tegid. I promise you that I will return." As Marian looked back at Conall, she felt a strange stirring deep inside her soul as the spirit of Danu moved within her, and in that moment, she knew that Conall would return and that she was pregnant with Conall's daughter.

Filled with a joy that she kept to herself, she smiled up at him and said, "I will wait for you, Conall, and for Briga." Full of the warmth of the goddess spirit, Marian listened to the plans Caratacus and Conall made for the trip south. Her hand rested on her lower stomach; she sensed that it was Muirgheal, her mother's soul, inside her body.

"A dozen other men will want to go with you, Conall," said Caratacus, "men who have also lost their wives or daughters, and who, like you, are intent on saving their women or getting revenge. I will give you my horse and twenty-four of my best mounted warriors to move as speedily as possible back south and to the coast. The men will be under your command, Convel Conall, but I will also send along two of my most trusted, Einion and Morthwy, as advisors. Listen to them, as they have saved me time and again. Now let's make ready your journey."

As Caratacus and Conall walked off toward the main camp, Marian watched them while sheltered in a dream; suddenly she'd thought of her mother, and as the vision of her mother's smiling face filled her mind and her heart, she felt a warmth deep inside that spread outward until it covered her with a layer of peace, much like a silken shroud. She was enclosed in a deep feeling of serenity and a reassurance that her mother's soul, her Anam, was returning to her as a gift from Danu and the gods. Danu had touched Marian's soul and she knew that she carried the daughter of Conall inside her womb. As Marian thought of the child growing inside her womb she knew it was the anam of Muirgheal, her mother, and now Marian, filled with a sacred knowing, was overcome by a feeling of awe; she patted her stomach as she thought in wonder to herself.

Rhun stood nearby, and he watched her as a smile came over her face—a smile that glowed like a shimmering golden veil as she softly said, "Welcome back, my mother."

Chapter Fifty-Two

During the hours of darkness, under the radiance of a waning moon, the men had been working, burrowing in the sand that held the langskips. They battled with time and each grain of sand as they raced the incoming tide. Briga could not sleep over the scuffling of the men; the bellows and barks and clanging were enough to wake the dead. The air was filled with chaos as they prepared to embark. The idea of leaving struck chords of panic, sending vibrations of angst that hollowed her gut completely. The prisoner Briga cried all night as her guard, the thrall Grian, watched over her in the same way Grian her dog would have held vigil; he sat at her feet on the sand and protectively watched with his back to her.

The Luti were making ready to sail, and there was nothing she could do to prevent them. Conall had failed to rescue her, and shortly she would be whisked away to a foreign land infested with heathen gods and heathen men.

Her gods had failed her, as had Cymru's greatest wolf-warrior. Everyone she'd trusted had failed to rescue her; even her beloved grandfather Caswallon was dead. She was alone and hollowed out inside. She felt the edge of the sharp blade of fear begin to dismember her piece by piece.

As she sat up, she gasped, her hand clutching the breast piece of the rude thrall tunic she wore. "Grian, I'm afraid."

Looking at the man sitting tamely at her feet, she said, "What will happen to me, and what will happen to my child?"

Grian turned to face her and gently reached out and took Briga's hands in his. As he did, he stared through her. The moon pierced through the cloud formation above and appeared as a profile of a wolf head. The moon's light didn't touch her face but revealed his. The pale light that fell on his face was too bright to hide the tears that ran like rivulets, cutting channels down his gaunt cheeks, falling silently from his chin to the earth below. His eyes turned dark.

He spoke in an ancient tone, as frightening as a midnight howl. "You will be taken back to Jutland, as these Luti are of the Cimbri, and once you are there, you will become a thrall like me, Briga, a slave to the household of Healtholaf. Your life will be harsh, cold, and filled with pain and fear, and you will work hard all the remaining days of your life. You will have hope ripped from you, and your spirit will turn from light to darkness. Your child, if it is born a male, will be taken away from you at the age of six and given over to be trained as a berserker. He will be taught to fight without feeling or remorse, and he will know no fear or love; he will only learn to follow the commands of his handlers and to kill.

"For your sake, I pray you have a daughter, as she might have the opportunity of becoming a warrior's wife, bearing his children and taking care of his household. You may want to end your life, Briga, by throwing yourself into the sea as we sail back to Jutland, as I have seen many others do since I have been Healtholaf's dog."

Numbed by what she'd just heard, she gave Grian a frozen stare and answered, "I cannot end my life, Grian. I promised my grandfather Caswallon I would keep the child inside me safe, as he is the hope and future of Cymru."

Grian tightly squeezed Briga's hands as if to seal her vow. "Never speak these words to anyone, Briga. Trust no one and tell none what you have just told me about the child you carry; I promise you that on that day, you and the child will die."

Lost under the surface of feeling, the two sat together on the sand, waiting.

They did not have to wait long, as two groups of men now walked past them to Healtholaf's ship. The men climbed the ladders that rested at the side of the horizontal wood planking of the ship's hull and disappeared over the rail. It did not take long for thunderous shouting and cursing to be heard coming from inside the thin hull as the men began fighting with Healtholaf's bodyguards. The shrill, screaming voice of the old hag, Freya, slashed through the air like a battle-ax on an anvil stone; it dominated the men's voices and the clashing sound of metal being set free onboard the ship.

In a hushed voice, Grian whispered to Briga, "Some of the men want to leave Healtholaf on his longboat; they want to set it on fire as a funeral offering, burning the vessel. They hope to appease the gods of Cymru as they sail away from this cursed land."

Surveying the ship, Briga and Grian suddenly saw Freya's young, red-haired maid, Cerys. Two men held her unresisting body tightly as they approached the railing. Hoisting her over the railing, they dropped her down the ladder, and she collapsed upon the sand. Briga and Grian watched as she quickly shot up, refusing to look back at the ship, and ran straight for them. Her body went limp as she dropped to her knees in front of Grian. The arms of the thrall were as welcoming as the presence of Danu.

Between stuttering and parched lips, she stammered, "They are going to kill Freya and burn the ship!"

A womens shrill screaming and the deep voices of angrily shouting men, rose from the depths of the ship, sounding much like disembodied spirits entering into the darkness of the surrounding night. It overpowered the sound of the men working to launch the beached vessels; they stopped to walk toward the boisterous ship just as half a dozen men appeared at the railing. Two of these men grappled with the belligerent, screaming shaman woman, Freya, who was hastening her death by cursing and spitting at the men.

As the men seized the old woman, they barked orders down to the men who had gathered next to the ship. Still cradling Cerys, Grian leaned very close to Briga's face and whispered, "Be prepared. Make no sound, and especially do not yell. These men are planning to sacrifice Freya to your god Dylan. By leaving her body here on the beach, they aim to please you and your god. Watch your words and be prepared, as they will summon you to entreat your father Dylan for protection on the voyage home."

No sooner had Grian spoken these words than the men hurled Freya like a rag doll above their heads and over the railing; she landed with a solid thud, like a rucksack of barley. Three of the men walked over to the twisted, moaning body of the old woman. She screamed in pain as one of these men grabbed her by her arms and lifted her to a sitting position; a second man grabbed a fistful of hair and sharply pulled her head back as the third man, without saying anything, pulled his knife from his sheath and swiftly cut the old woman's throat.

Thus Freya from the North became the legendary Cyhyraeth, the ghostly spirit that announced death in the land of Cymru, its disembodied, moaning voice groaning like someone deathly ill and always sounding three times—growing weaker and fainter each time—just before waning to silence as a person expired. It was the death of Freya at the mouth of the river Tywi that originated the legend of Cyhyraeth.

Briga's words flew past her mouth as she gasped, "By my mother's gods, what kind of men are these?"

In quick reply Grian strongly grasped her hand and said, "My lady, please say nothing more. Do not speak. These men are coming over here to stand in front of you, the daughter of Dylan, the god of the sea. They believe you to be a great healer, a witsio, and they believed you when you told them that your father was Dylan, *gud af havet*. If you want us to live, smile, stand to greet them with great happiness, and show them favor by declaring Dylan's blessing on all the ships and all of them."

Disturbed by what she'd just witnessed, she wanted to escape, but was too pregnant to run into the darkness. Her body took a different direction; amid the warring of disgust and self-preservation, she stood up to face the smiling, laughing men walking toward her. The hard-faced warriors were pensive as their tall frames hunched over hers and waited.

Grian and Cerys remained cowering at her feet. In a very low voice, Grian said, "Please, Briga, say something and smile."

The men, smiling broadly, invaded her comfort space, their collective stench assaulting her nose and eyes. The largest burly fellow stood in front of the others and bellowed, "*Min dame Briga, binge os held.*"

Fighting the urge to heave all over the men, Briga forced a fake smile and waved her arms at the sea toward the ships, mocking them with a soothing voice. "What brave warriors are the sons of Jutland—indeed strong and brave when it comes to raping mothers and young virgin maidens, butchering children, and killing old women. I am sure that my father Dylan, *gud af havet*, will reward you all with exactly what you deserve." Smiling broadly at the men in front of her, she added, "May Dylan, the god of the seas, drag all of you, in your dragon ships, down into the ocean's watery abyss."

Smiling and satisfied with the "blessing," the men bowed slightly at the waist, and as they walked away, they shouted, "Tak" over and over; which means 'thanks' in the tongue of the Luti. They returned to helping the other Luti to shoulder the work freeing the ships.

Now a cluster of men appeared at the deck railing with a couple of Healtholaf's guards. The origin of the rumble below deck materialized as the men rigged a rope chair to lower Healtholaf to the beach. Briga watched as an icy finger crawled up her spine. As she watched her worst nightmare appeared as the men began to lower Healtholaf from the ship down to the sand. Healtholaf the beast had regained consciousness three days ago, and Briga's life had been teetering on the brink of death ever since.

Every day Briga had climbed the ladder to tend to the beast, and every day she had been beaten by the old hag, Freya. Healtholaf had awakened and had become aware that the wounding blow to his back had cut off the feeling pathway to his legs; he could not walk, and he savagely blamed her and her husband. She wasn't sure how much longer the two would allow her to live. Horrified at the cruel manner in which Freya had been murdered, Briga was pleased that the evil old hag now lay in a broken, twisted mass while the hungry sands of Cymru lapped up her blood. The old crone would no longer be a danger that threatened her child.

The Luti were calling her *min dame* Briga, "My Lady" Briga, out of respect for all the kindness she had shown them when treating their wounds and ailments. Confused, Briga sat down next to Grian and Cerys and asked Grian, "What is the meaning of *binge os held?*"

Grian's answer felt like a club that beat to death the last threads of hope she held. "They were asking you to bring them luck, Briga. It is time you learn their language, as you will be speaking it for the rest of your life."

Stunned by his words, Briga was paralyzed.

Too pregnant and weak to draw her knees to her chest, she placed her legs carefully in front of her, as if she were placing sticks on a fire. She watched the men working in the firelight as her thoughts stayed stuck in a numb, cold, and dark world. She wondered about her future and if she would ever live to see the birth of her child. Exhausted, Grian and Cerys held each other and drifted to sleep.

Briga sat alone in silence, her internal agony difficult to hide. Her greatest cruaidhghleachd was upon her. She let her breath out with cursing words toward the lesser gods, and to Danu and Daghda, she said, "You have abandoned me and my child! How can I worship you and believe that you are gods above all other gods?"

Pounding the sand with a militant fist, she unleashed her rage. "I will give you the complete honor you deserve. I will measure that honor by the depth of your protection for my child, and if you do not protect him, I will not honor you!"

Something on the water startled her and caught her attention. She noticed a white haze outlined with an eerie purple glow moving toward the beach. As the haze found its way to the place where earth met water, it stopped. To Briga's amazement, from within the haze, a figure seemed to appear and set foot on the beach. A second figure appeared on the beach, not a man but a very large black wolf, and the two walked past the Luti feeding the fire—the two now walking towards her only seemed to be visible to Briga.

As they approached Briga, the man and the wolf were partly silhouetted by the fire. Briga could not see the man's face, but once she heard his voice, the infant inside her quickened. "Don't be afraid," he said. "It is Caswallon, your great-grandfather."

Her jaw unhinged in disbelief. Slowly the sand spilled out of her fist. The old druid suddenly appeared sitting beside her on the sand, with his hand holding hers. The strange black wolf rested at their feet. Looking at his granddaughter, Caswallon smiled and said, "Be encouraged. I am within you; my soul is housed by the child who grows inside of you. I will return to you as your son Weylin, and you, Briga, will be my mother."

He paused and moved toward her, softly kissing her; the kiss felt like a feather that lightly brushed against her cheek. Up close, Briga could clearly see his face and his eyes. He seemed to glow like the white florescent mists she had sometimes seen appearing at night in the forest.

Touching her arm, he said, "Your time of childbirth will come soon. Within days you will give birth, Briga. Before the new moon comes and the waxing begins, your son will be born; you will hold your child and me in your arms, and it will be up to you, Briga, to nurse me and keep me alive. Most importantly, it will be up to you to teach me and to bring me back to my new flesh, my old soul."

Looking past the old druid's eyes, Briga said, "I am filled with dark anguish, Grandfather, and I fear for the life of the child within me. Healtholaf will surely kill us both soon."

He put his arm around her shoulders and drew her close. "Danu has heard your cry of anguish," he said, "and you're cursing of the gods. She has sent me to comfort you and to let you know that she will never abandon you. Briga, you have the promise of Danu that she will protect you and your child for all the days you are away from Cymru, and until the day you return, she will walk beside you."

Kissing her on the forehead, he pulled back and looked into her eyes. "Remember, my granddaughter, that the feather that falls from the nest is fortunate if a gentle breeze lifts it up and carries it away, extending its life by preventing it from falling to earth."

As if a great breath had been exhaled, a light breeze suddenly blew across her face, and as Briga looked at the old man, he began to fade before her eyes. Smiling at her, he said, "I have to go now, but believe this, Briga: from this day on, Danu and I will be with you, as will the spirit of the black wolf."

As Briga looked at him, he faded and changed form; he was now floating near her, and he appeared much like a bright blue-white star does in the night sky. Suddenly that star moved toward her and into her belly. The baby within her turned, and Briga felt the child's arms and fists push against her sides; there was a strong kick, and she knew that the child inside her was filled with the soul of Caswallon.

Holding her belly, she said, "I am happy you have joined me, Weylin."

Exhausted, Briga curled into a fetal ball on the sand and fell asleep.

"Min dame Briga."

"Min dame, *skal du vågne.*"

Briga opened her eyes to two large Luti warriors standing in front of her, smiling like two children. The largest one looked at her but avoided contact with her eyes. He said again, "Min dame, *vi skal forlade.*"

Behind these men she could see Grian and Cerys standing beside each other. Confused, she called out, "Grian, what do these men want, and what are they saying?" As she looked to Grian, the haze that had held her mind started to clear, and she realized that it was now daylight, and the sun was at least eight fingers above the horizon. Looking past all the men, she could see that three of the langskips now rested quietly on the water; one was drawn up close to the shore, but the other two were farther offshore.

Grian spoke quickly as he said, "*Skal du vågne* means 'please wake,' and *vi skal forlade* means 'we must leave.' They are waking you to leave, Briga, to leave this beach! The boats are loaded, the tide is turning and going back out, and we are leaving now. The only things left to load are the thralls and you, min dame witsio. Please, Briga, do not protest or resist, as these men have orders to cut all our throats and leave our bodies on this beach if you fight!"

Her attention was fully directed to the two men in front of her, and as she studied their faces, she realized she knew these two; it was Ulrich and Bojerik, the men who had run from the fire when the story of the bear was told.

Briga smiled at the men and stood up. She said to Grian, "Tell them I am happy to see Ulrich and Bojerik, and I will be happy to go with them."

Broad smiles covered their faces as Ulrich and Grian carefully lifted Briga. Bojerik picked up Cerys and in one fluid motion lifted her over his shoulder. The two men carried the women on their shoulders as Grian walked beside them towards the boat resting in chest-deep water. As they reached the boat, eager, smiling faces looked over the railing, and hands appeared to sprout from the side of the langskip as men reached down to help the women on board.

Standing on the deck, Briga was surrounded by smiling faces, and she heard men telling her *tak, tak*. Other men touched her lightly on her shoulders as they walked by, smiling, and as they moved away, she heard them say, "*Bringe os held*, min dame Briga." She did not need Grian to translate what they said or what they were doing; she had become their good luck charm, and she was sure *bringe os held* meant, "Bring us luck."

Looking at the beach, she could see all the debris left behind—dead animals, a few human bodies, including Freya's—and she watched as Ulrich and Bojerik set fire to Healtholaf's boat and the other langskip that did not have a crew to sail it back to Jutland. As soon as the boats blazed, the two rushed out into the water and climbed aboard the waiting langskip.

The boat was coming alive with activity, and everywhere men began to take their places as other men gave orders. Grian was now beside her, and he pointed to the back of the boat at a very large man holding the rudder. "Briga," he said, "we need to move to the stern. We won't be in the way standing behind all the oarsmen at the rear of the boat."

All along the sides of the boat, men stood and lifted long wooden oars skyward; with the oars standing upright, their white bleached wood reflected brightly the morning sun, like some branchless forest. For only a moment, they stood in formation, and with a barked order, the men dipped their oars into the sea. As quickly as they touched the water, another order was issued, and the men, still standing, began to pull their oars back toward their chests, the oar blades pulling deeply against the water. Another man stood by the mast, and as he spoke in a rhythmic cadence, he beat the blade of his sword against his wooden shield. This was echoed by a man who beat on a large cowhide drum. Each time he hit the shield, the men in one movement lifted the blades of their oars out of the water, the long handles almost resting on their legs. As the drum was beat, the men once again lowered their oars and pulled at the ocean with all their might. This was repeated over and over, like the routine cadence of walking.

To Briga it sounded and looked like a strange, coordinated, ritualistic male dance as she watched their oars and listened to the men sing to the double rhythm of the shield and the drum.

It wasn't long before they had moved the boat a long distance from the sandbar at Cefn Sidan.

Briga stood near the stern along with Grian the thrall and the young red-haired maiden, Cerys, and together they all watched as they entered the mouth of the yawning ocean.

Grian suddenly pointed back at the distant shoreline and said, "Look, Briga!"

As Briga, Grian, and Cerys watched, a large group of riders appeared on the beach. Ahead of all the other horsemen, a single rider pushed his horse hard to reach the sand, and as he reached the point from which the ships had disembarked, he quickly dismounted. The horseman was a tall warrior, broad at the shoulders, with long, red hair. He ran to the water's edge and stood in the place where Briga had stood just moments earlier. Suddenly he dropped to his knees.

The distance between the ship and the shore was increasing rapidly, but Briga was sure she saw Conall.

Warring for space in her mind were emotions of panic and rage. She looked at the man kneeling on the beach, then turned her back to him and looked out into the barrenness of the ocean. She wore a mask of hardened steel that said, "You have let me be taken by other men, Conall, and now I am on my own; now I will make my own life for myself and my son, Weylin."

From near the mast, one of the Luti shouted out loudly, "*Sænk sejlene!*" and Briga watched as the sails were raised. As soon as they were filled by the strong seaward breeze, they seemed to burst into a plump firmness that pulled tightly at the ropes holding them to the sides of the boat. Almost immediately the slender ship began to swiftly cut through the water like an arrow sailing through the air. The Luti vessels had began their voyage back home to Jutland.

Refusing to look back at Cymru, Briga turned to Grian and Cerys and said, "From this day on, I am Hervor, the shield-maiden of Jutland." In her heart she felt Briga had died on the beach at Cefn Sidan waiting for the great wolf-warrior Conall Cearnach of Clan Diahad. "Yes, Conall the Victorious, the great convel warrior of Cymru who let his wife and child be carried away to a distant land, Briga is dead…"

Without another word the shield-maiden Hervor found a place out of the wind, and lying down, went quickly to sleep.

Chapter Fifty-Three

onall and the riders with him left the village at Llyn Tegid late in the afternoon and rode west along the lake past the crannog. As the crannog came into view, he felt as helpless as a wounded stag brought down by the archer's arrow. In his heart grew an overpowering fear for his beloved.

"Where is she?" he thought.

As he rode past the home he had shared with Briga, he bowed his head. Pressing his chin to his upper chest and pounding his chest three times with his left fist, he called out to Danu, "Goddess, please, cover my beloved Briga with your love and protection until I can free her from the Luti!"

The men who rode near him heard his words and followed his grieving gesture, and soon the entire company was heard pleading for help from the good goddess Danu.

Eighty-five determined men rode west without talking; they rode hard and fast, unburdened by supply wagons or men on foot. They knew theirs was a race against time, and each man was resolute, intent only on the rescue of loved ones and the destruction of the Luti who had dared violate the sacred earth of Cymru.

They carried everything they would need, and all had agreed to ride each day until it was too dark to ride safely. Once the curtain of darkness fell, they stopped and made a cold camp, one without fire or comforts of any kind; after taking care of their horses, they ate the same grain and dried fruit they fed to them.

Conall and the men who went with him were soon riding hard west, toward the coast of the Sea of Erin. Once there, they turned south along the coastline. They continued riding south until they reached the cairn that marked the trail inland to three rivers and the beach at Cefn Sidan. The convel had tracked and followed the Luti and their captives along the coast and sent back runners to let the army of Caratacus know their path of escape.

Conall followed the trail that had been the reported route of Briga and the Luti raiders. From the information they'd received from the convel, they estimated the distance they had to travel was some ninety or more leagues. The Celts measured a league as the distance a man could walk in one hour, and this often varied with the terrain and the plant cover. The Romans used the *leuga gallica,* or the league of Gaul, which they measured as they marched by counting their paces; three thousand, one hundred, and sixty-eight military paces roughly measured one *leuga gallica.*

By pushing the horses and men and stopping only at high noon and dusk, Conall was hopeful they would cover forty or more leagues each day. With determination he figured on reaching the beach at Cefn Sidan in two or three days. "If only I had the black wings of Bran the Raven, I would fly to my Briga," he thought. "I would be with her before sunset."

But he did not have wings—only his horse and the men with him.

In the company of the men who rode with him were twelve who were fathers and husbands who did not belong to the army of Caratacus. Like Conall, they were men who had lost their wives or daughters to the Luti. They now followed Conall in the hope of rescuing their loved ones; no one knew how many women had been taken as slaves by the Luti, but everyone was intent on freeing the captives and killing the Luti.

Along with the men who had lost family members and the riders of Cymru who had volunteered to accompany Conall, his uncle Caratacus had sent along two of his most faithful warriors as advisers to guide Conall: the twin brothers Einion the Anvil and Morthwyl the Hammer.

Scouts had been sent out ahead, to both sides, and to the rear of the swiftly moving line of horses and men. The scouts continuously searched for Luti stragglers, men who may have gotten lost on their way back to the ships. Any such raider was rapidly beheaded.

On the first full day of riding south along the coast, a scout came riding fast and furious toward the head of the column, straight for Conall. Einion and Morthwyl were riding at the head of the column with Conall, and when the rider got close enough, he shouted, "We have found a group of men—ten, maybe twelve, Luti heading south with half a dozen captives!"

Conall, Einion, and twenty riders rode off with the scout to track and hunt the Luti. Morthwyl stayed with the column and continued advancing south along the coastline.

The riders of Cymru caught the Luti on an open hillside where there was no cover to approach unseen, so all the riders pushed their horses hard to cover the distance between themselves and the enemy. Once the horsemen of Cymru were seen by the Luti, they all panicked. Two of the captive women began hitting and beating the men who held them captive, and this unexpected attack gave the women the advantage, as they broke free and ran off toward the riders. Three of the women, too beaten, weak, and dazed, fell to the knives of the Luti, their throats cut and their bodies thrown aside as the cowards who murdered them attempted to run away.

The riders made it to the Luti raiders in time to save one young dark-haired girl before she fell under the knife of the cowards from Jutland. Howls and war cries pierced the air as the riders of Cymru hacked at the heads, necks, and shoulders of the Luti from atop their horses. As they did so, they called out the names of their swords: Neck Biter, Skull Cutter, and Death

Dealer. The names rang out with each blow as judgment and death rained down on the raiders from Jutland.

Their screams of fear filled the air, and in the hope of being spared, a few of the Luti threw their weapons to the ground. But the riders of Cymru, filled with blood vengeance, took no prisoners; those who tried to run away were tracked and killed, their heads brought back to be placed in a barren, cold cave for safekeeping.

It was soon over. The ground was littered with the dead, a Luti feast for Bran the Raven. Conall looked about him at the dead Luti, remembering the words of teaching he had received from Caswallon: "The war is not over until Bran the Raven eats the eyes from your enemy."

Conall was relieved to see that Briga was not among the women killed by the Luti, but at the same time, he grieved deeply for the three young women who lay dead. He turned to Einion and said, "Prepare these women to be taken home, along with the captives who are alive."

As he looked past Einion, he noticed a young maiden with a vacant expression standing among the bodies. She looked dazed; her hands hung at her sides as she looked down at the ground.

Conall rode over to the young dark-haired girl. He extended his hand to her and smiled reassuringly as he looked into her hazel eyes. "My name is Conall, and you are safe now. We will take you home." From his horse, he gestured for her hand. "Let me help you up on my horse."

The girl looked at Conall and at his horse, hesitating only for a moment. Then with outstretched arms, she inched toward him, too traumatized to cry.

As their hands touched, Conall said softly, "You are safe now." Firmly grasping her hands, he lifted her up in one fluid movement onto the horse, placing her just behind the horse's neck. She grabbed a fistful of mane as she prepared to hold on.

"What is your name?" Conall asked.

"My name is Rhona," she replied.

"Do you have any family, Rhona?"

She touched Conall's arm and replied, "No, my family is all dead."

With reassurance he told her, "We will take you north with us, Rhona, to a new home and a new family. You will be cared for and safe."

Among his people, there were no orphans, widows, or widowers. Families grew as others had need, and no one grew old alone.

The other two women were helped up on horses also, and the party of riders turned and quickly headed back toward the column led by Morthwyl. Evening once again stalked them, and they would be forced to take shelter before nightfall.

They reached the column as the first stars began to appear; Morthwyl and his riders had already stopped for the night and moved into the shelter of a grove of trees. Conall talked with Morthwyl, and it was decided that since they now had the three young women, they would make one small fire to warm the maidens. The riders shared their grain, gifting the young women with food, water, and blankets for warmth, and when any of the men would approach one of the maidens of Cymru, he would bow at the waist, honoring her as he would honor Danu.

They attended to the maidens of Cymru first that night, before taking care of their horses, as this was the proper order taught to the men of Cymru: "A man is never as strong or noble as when he kneels before a woman." Next they attended to their horses and last to their own needs; once again they ate the same grain and dried fruit they fed their horses, while sharing some of the dried meat with the young women.

The men watched over the young maids that night, keeping the fire burning, and as they kept watch, they thought of their own daughters and wives.

The next morning the camp came alive at sunrise. Ten riders were chosen to take the three maidens north to Caer Caradoc, the hilltop fortress of the Ard Righ Caradoc ap Bran. As the horsemen prepared to leave, Rhona quickly ran over to Conall and threw her arms around his neck; she tearfully thanked him for saving her life. Conall kissed her softly on the forehead.

"Seek out my uncle Caratacus and a young woman named Marian at Caer Caradoc, and tell them I want you counted as part of the family of Conall and Briga."

She returned to the horse and rider that waited to take her to safety.

Conall and the riders of Cymru watched as they rode away, thinking about their own loved ones and praying to the gods that they all would return safely home.

Morthwyl mounted his horse and shouted, "*Cymru am byth!*" The other riders quickly mounted their horses as they too all shouted, "*Cymru am byth!*" And once again they all rode hard and fast south, toward the birch-white sands of the beach at Cefn Sidan.

By midmorning they had traveled as far south along the coast as they needed, and then they turned southeast and rode inland, knowing they would find Three Rivers. The three rivers emptied into the channel known as Môr Hafren. This was the large channel that emptied into the bay that opened to the sea.

The first river they would cross would be Afon Gwy, the River Wye. Once they crossed the Afon Gwy, they would have to ride hard to make it to Afon Hafren, the River Severn, which was the largest river in Cymru.

Reaching the Afon Hafren, they would then be forced to search for a safe crossing; if they could not find a place that was shallow enough to ford on horseback, they would have to swim, and then it would take time to search for a place that was slow and calm enough for the men and horses to traverse.

They rode hard all day, not stopping at high noon, and as darkness approached, they had managed to cross two of the three rivers; the goddess had blessed them, and they had found a place to ford the Afon Hafren on horseback. They knew they would have to wait for morning to cross the third river and push on to the estuaries of Three Rivers, then on to the beach at Cefn Sidan.

Conall knew he was only a hard half-day ride from Môr Hafren and the beach at Cefn Sidan, but he also knew the men and horses were exhausted. Einion rode up beside Conall; he knew what the man was going to say, so before it was asked, Conall said, "Yes, Einion, we will stop here for the night."

Soaked and shivering, Einion asked, "Conall, the men's legs and feet are wet from the river crossings, and it has not been warm enough to dry out; we will need fires to warm and dry us. We will keep them small and not light them until darkness covers our smoke. May I tell the men to gather wood once we have taken care of the horses?"

Conall looked at Einion and then turned in his saddle to look back at the wet men riding with him. "Einion, you have all ridden well," he said, "and pushed farther and harder than any men I have ever been with; I am proud of all of you. The men have earned the warmth of fires. As you tell them, let them know that I am forever grateful, and tell them that no matter what happens tomorrow, I want them to remember the words of Caswallon: 'There is never failure if you attempt a task with all your strength, and it is not accomplished. There is only failure if you never try!'"

As darkness overcame them, the men settled down and lay near the small warming fires. The men soon dried, and as warmth returned and filled their bodies, dreams of home and loved ones filled their souls. Danu reached into the spirit of each man that night with renewed strength.

Conall too fell asleep, but his mind was walking in a vision, and he was troubled by what he saw: great mountains of blue ice covered with white snow floated on the open ocean under gray and white clouds that raced above a solid red sail. Conall stood behind a tall woman with long, blond, braided hair; her shoulders were broad and covered with a coat made of the pelts of silver fox and white wolf. She wore a helmet made of gold, and her chain-mail armor shone like well-polished silver. Armguards made of gold covered her forearms from her wrists almost to her elbows, and at her side hung a great blade. She did not speak but looked out into the distance in silence. She was young and very beautiful. As the early-morning sunlight touched her face, her skin turned golden. She turned her head as if looking at someone and smiled. Her eyes, the pale blue of the robin's egg, pierced deeply into Conall's heart.

Once again the first pale light of the rising sun brought the camp alive. There would be no delay this morning as the men prepared to leave. Conall mounted his horse and looked at the men as he gave out a loud shout. "*Cymru am byth!*"

Mounting their horses almost at the same time, the men turned toward him. As if in one voice, they joined him in a loud echo of "*Cymru am byth!*" Together they crossed the last river and covered the distance to Cefn Sidan before high sun.

As they arrived, they all saw what Conall saw: three Luti langskips under full sail had slipped away from the beach. The langskips' sails were gray, and for a moment he caught a glimpse of a great red sea hawk on the langskip that was ahead of the other two.

Riding hard, Conall reached the beach and dismounted.

Black billowing smoke rolled skyward from two burning ships that had been set afire and abandoned by the Luti. The acrid smoke burned Conall's eyes and paled the sun's light, casting an eerie yellow shadow across the beach.

Standing beside his horse, he looked in disgust at the soiled white sands of Cefn Sidan. His loathing for the Luti only grew stronger as he realized that all about him on the beach was human excrement left unburied. Litter and debris were thrown about everywhere, and several swollen, dead bodies lay rotting in the sun—among them the body of an old woman wearing a filthy white gown woven from flax and heavily stained with blood. She was twisted and bent, and to Conall she appeared to have been cruelly cast aside by her slayers.

The stench of rotting animals and human waste was overpowering, as was the acrid smoke that rose from the piles of burning garbage and the two beached langskips. The Luti had set fire to everything that would burn as they left the beach.

Conall fought the urge to vomit as he walked to the edge of the water.

Three ships moved rapidly away from him, and he knew that on board one of them, the Luti held Briga and Conall's unborn child. Overcome with a sense of failure, Conall clenched his fists, raised his arms over his head, and shouted out in a fit of rage.

Defying the very gods, he yelled, "You gods of Cymru have failed Briga, and you have failed my unborn child! No longer will I be your blind and obedient servant!"

No sooner had he said the words than a voice rose up in his heart and said, "No, Conall, it was not the gods who failed Briga."

Standing at the edge of the sea, he dropped to his knees on the sand; while he faced the ocean, hot tears burned down his cheeks as he spoke in a loud, deep voice, edged with pain. "The gods have let me know, Briga, that it is I who have failed you."

He didn't move or speak again as he watched the langskips move farther out to sea. They seemed to disappear from view as if swallowed by some sea monster, blending into a great gray fog bank rolling toward the coastline. As the great fog bank rolled closer, the world around Conall, the overcast sky, and the ocean blended into one formless, gray mass. Conall listened to the waves that broke along the beach; he heard the clatter of broken shells and small rocks as they were pushed up on the sand and rolled back to the sea with each wave.

No man dared approach him, and the men who waited for him did so silently, knowing that his time of great suffering had just begun.

Conall stood at the edge of a world that he knew nothing about. Before him were the ocean, the Luti homeland of Jutland, and the mainland continent. Across the sea was another world far different from the world of the Cymru, and Conall the wolf-warrior would be almost helpless in that world.

Taking one step forward, he placed his right foot into the sea that touched those distant lands while keeping his left foot firmly planted on the sands of Cymru. He now stood at the center of the sacred in-between place, with his left foot on the shore and his right foot in the water.

Without hesitation Conall pulled from his scabbard a blade given to him by Briga, and as he held the knife in his left hand, he cut deeply across the top of his right arm, between his elbow and wrist—three cuts that quickly sent blood running down his arm and into the sea. Switching the knife to his right hand, he repeated the cuts on his left arm—again three times across the top of the arm between the elbow and the wrist, the blood once again running down his arm, but this time Conall made sure that his blood fell freely into the sand.

While Conall stood with his arms at his sides, blood drops fell both into the water and onto the earth. After a moment of silence, Conall raised his head skyward and shouted loudly to Daghda, declaring to all the gods a blood oath.

Standing on the silky white beach of Cefn Sidan, Conall had been forced to watch as Briga was carried off in one of the Luti langskips. Rage once again filled his soul as Conall declared *dìoghaltas* to the gods. "Blood vengeance." He would now forsake everything that was his life yesterday and set out to restore Briga to Cymru; he had reached that place within himself that does not fear the gods or men. He would bring Briga home.

Shouting again, he declared to Danu and Daghda, "I will find you, Briga!"

Without asking for the help of the gods, he declared, "I tell all of you gods that you and I have both failed Briga. Witness now my oath: I will not return to the hills of Cymru until I have found Briga and safely returned her and our child home—home to Cymru!"

He turned back to his horse and saw a group of men waiting for him. Among them were Einion and Morthwyl.

As he approached, Morthwyl asked, "Our convel Conall, what do you need us to do now?"

"Nothing," Conall said. "You have done your duty to me, and I release you and your men."

Looking at Conall with tears in his eyes, Einion said, "We failed you, Conall, and your Lady Briga."

Conall shook his head. "No, Einion, you did not fail Briga and the other maidens of Cymru; you and your men did everything possible to save them. I am the one who never tried; I waited too long at the cave with Marian and the children. I am the one who left Briga alone."

As Conall looked down at the ground, Einion and Morthwyl saw the tears that welled up in his eyes; they alone were close enough to see his grief.

Conall raised his head, looking into the eyes of Einion. "I am no longer a convel, nor any longer Conall Cearnach of Cymru. Until I find and return Briga and our child, I am lost to my people, and I will have no name. I will live as if I am in an *aisling*, a dream. I will be lost until I have turned my failure around and brought my family home to Cymru."

Morthwyl and the other men said nothing, as there wasn't anything to say.

Conall looked at them and said, "I am heading for a port city on the east coast, a city where I can hire a trader's *knörr* or a langskip from Gaul to sail and follow the Luti. I will follow them all the way to Jutland, and I will not return unless I have my wife and child. Those who want to come with me are welcome to follow, but I am leaving now. Morthwyl and Einion, take the riders back to my uncle Caratacus, and let him know what has happened."

Stepping forward with a black leather poke, Einion quickly said to Conall, "Your uncle Caratacus gave me this bag of gold coins and precious gems. He feared our journey would end thusly, and that you would continue on, and he wanted you to have the resources to help fund your journey. He gave me instructions to tell you: take what horses and weapons you need, and sell the horses once you have found your pram."

Conall pulled himself up onto the back of his horse and took the poke from Einion. "Thank my uncle."

Conall bent forward at the waist to place the leather poke in a bag made of wolf hide at the right side of his horse. He sat upright, and as he did, his hands reached up to his neck to remove the gold wolf-head torc that he wore around his neck.

As he handed the torc to Einion, he said, "Please give this torc to Caratacus. It is the torc that belonged to my father and my grandfather, and I do not want to lose it in a land far from Cymru. Let Caratacus know that I want him to hold it safely for me until I return with Briga."

Reaching up to take the torc, Einion said, "I will deliver this torc only into the hands of Caratacus."

Still remaining around Conall's neck was the finely braided leather cord that held the talisman medicine bag given to him by Briga when he had left her at the crannog. Grasping the leather bag in his hand, he looked out at the vastness of the ocean and said under his breath, "I swear, Briga, I will bring you home."

Morthwyl stepped up to the horse and touched Conall's leg. "What name will you take? What name should I give to your uncle and Marian? They will want a name that they can speak to the gods when they pray on your behalf or offer gifts at the wells."

Conall hesitated for a moment and said, "I have failed to save my wife Briga and my unborn child—until I can return them both to Cymru, you can call me Drystan, for I am full of sorrow."

Without looking back, Conall rode off, shouting over his should, "Those of you who want to join me, follow now, or you will be left behind."

A dozen men mounted and raced after the man now called Drystan.

Morthwyl, Einion, and the riders of Cymru watched as they rode away, and when they could no longer be seen, Einion gave the command to mount up. The warriors of Caratacus began their long journey home, back north to the fortress of Caradoc ap Bran, the Ard Righ of Cymru, the son of the Raven.

Gaelic, Early Irish, Old Irish, and Welsh Words

Aerten—goddess of fate

Afallach/Avalon—female religious center of the goddess for all of Cymru and Erin. The Ladies of Avalon teach the pathway to the stars, on which stars and souls become one as the *anam rionnag*. Both the ard druid of Ynys Mon and the *penarddun* (Pendragon, the head dragon) ard righ of Cymru are followers of the old way and the word as taught by the Ladies of Avalon.

Afon Tywi—one of the Three Rivers. The valley in which the Afon Tywi flows is the location where the wolf-warriors fought the Luti.

aisling—dream

aislingiche—a dreamer

Alban Arthuan—the winter solstice
Alban Eilir—the spring equinox
Alban Elfed—the autumnal equinox
Alban Hefin—the summer solstice
angen tân—need fire, the fire at the center of the village that supplied fire for the villagers

annsachd—the greatest attachment; best beloved object

anam rionnag—the joining of the human soul to the stars
anam—soul, spirit, the breath of life

ana ghràdhach—loving excessively

Ard Cyngor—high council
Ard Druid—High Druid represented by Caswallon of Cymru
(Caswallon ap Beli)

Ard Righ—High King represented by Caradoc ap Bran (son of
Raven)

Balor—the one-eyed god who had the power to strike dead anyone who looked upon his eye

beithe ynn—birch tree

bleddyn—like a wolf

Bona na Croin—the unconquered wolf

bran—raven

brawd—brother

Brighid—daughter of the good god Daghda. Brighid and
Cernunnos defeat Cailleach at Beltane and restore life to Cymru.

Bronwyn—fair beast, used as a man's name

cachi—crap or shit

Caer y Twr—the druid hilltop fortress on the island of Ynys Mon

Caesar (Julius Caesar)—led an exploratory force to Britain in 55 BCE and in 54 BCE. Julius invaded with around 25,000 legionary troops (Legio VII and four other legions), unknown numbers of cavalry forces and transports, and a war elephant (the first ever seen in Britain). Caswallon, the novice druid, fought with the Celtic ard righ Cassivellaunus, a warlord from northern Britain, at the battle of the crossing of the Thames. Fighting with the Romans were the Celtic Trinovantes under Mandubracius, king in southeastern Britain in the first century BCE.

Cailleach—the Hag of Winter

Caomai—the armed king; the constellation Orion

Caratacus ap Cunobelin—chief of the Catuvellauni; son of the ard righ Caradoc ap Bran. Caratacus is the uncle of Conall.

carnyx (carnyes, pl.)—the Celtic war trumpet; a wind instrument of the Iron Age Celts, used between 200 BCE and CE 200. It was a type of bronze trumpet with an elongated *S* shape, held so that the long, straight, central portion was vertical and the short mouthpiece section and much wider bell were horizontal in opposed directions. The bell was styled in the shape of the head of an openmouthed boar or other animal. It was used in warfare to incite troops to battle and to intimidate opponents. The instrument's upright carriage allowed it to be heard over the heads of the participants in battles or ceremonies.

Cassivelbunus (Cassivellaunus)—British chieftain who led the defense against Julius Caesar's invasion in 55 and 54 BCE

Ceile De—servants of the good god and goddess and Esus

Cerridwen—the Earth Mother

Cernunnos—the horned god of Beltane

Conall—strong as a wolf, used as a man's name

Conry—king of the wolves

convel—wolf-warrior

Còmhradh Carragh—the talking rocks at the waterfall of Pistyl Haeadr

corricle—little round tub of a two-man boat made of animal hides
Coventina—goddess of the river
crannog—artificial island dwelling found on lakes in Wales and Ireland
cròmleac—ancient standing stone

cruadalach—hardly capable of enduring deep hardship or pain

cruaidhghleachd—agony, hard struggle

Cruthadair—the Creators

Cunnobarrus—the order of the wolf head, the highest ranking convel

Cyhyraeth—the ghostly spirit that announces death. Its disembodied moaning voice groans like someone deathly ill, always sounding three times, growing weaker and fainter each time, until waning to silence just before a person expires. The legend of the *cyhyraeth* originated at the mouth of the River Tywi.

Cymru am byth—Wales forever

Cyngor—Council

Cucullatus (Cucullati)—the hooded ones; the flesh eaters of the goddess Cailleach, the Hag of Winter

curyll hebog—the hawk
cylch mawr—great circle
cysgod—shadow
Daghda—Father God; the Sky Father; the sun
Danu—Mother Goddess; the earth
derw ynn—oak tree; the tree of life

dìoghaltas—blood vengeance
Druuos—the firm North Star; the star that never moves in the night sky
Drystan—old Celtic name meaning 'full of sorrow'.
duir—oak. *Dair* is the Irish name of the seventh letter of the Ogham alphabet, ⫣, which is related to the Welsh *derw*.

dwale—the herb banewort

Dylan—the sea god of Cymru

Ellyllon—the faeries that haunt the groves and valleys. Ellyllons' favorite three things are toadstool mushrooms, fine, brightly colored cloth (silk), and human children, which they take away to their small islands in the gray, cold North Sea.

Einion—anvil; used as a man's name

Eryri—the Snowdonia Mountains, source of Welsh gold

Fond—the goddess Fond often appears as a raven. On the battlefield she will change into a beautiful maiden who takes the souls of brave warriors who have fallen to meet the gods.

Fonn—a chant or song delivered as a prayer and sung usually in a 1:3:9 rhythm

Gealach—Briga's female dog; the moon

Grian—Briga's male dog; the sun

gwdihŵ—owl (pronounced "goody hoo")

gwenyn meirch—the wasp

hen dadcu—great-grandfather

Imbolc—the emergence; one of the great fire festivals, occurring about February 2

Is tu m' annsachd—thou art my best beloved

Ladies of Afallach—the ladies of the hill of apples above Glastonbury; the druidesses of the Order of Avalon

leirsinneachd leigheas—healing chant sung in a fonn while holding a beaded paidrean

Llw gwaed—oath blood; a blood oath that involves drawn blood to secure a promise

Llyn Tegid (y Bala)—the lake at Conall's and Briga's village; the village of y Bala at which Briga had the crannog built

madainn rionnag—morning star, the planet Venus
Mag Mell—plain of stone

mam—mother

Màthair-beatha—the mother of all life, Danu

Mamaidh Danu—Mother Danu

melheglin—mead infused with the sweet-smelling herb, woodruff

Mo Anam Cara—soul twin

mochyn daear—badger

Môr Iwerddon—Irish Sea

morgrugyn—an ant of the forest

Morthwyl—hammer used as a man's name

mynydd du—black mountains
neidr—snake; grass snake
paidrean—prayer necklace
pen blwydd—birthing day

Rheolwr—the commander

sêr—stars

Tad-cu—grandfather

thrall—slave

Tír Na Nog—land of the young

tur-chaochladh—shapeshifter
twll tin—asshole

Wyneb Duw—an oath to face God (Daghda)

y Bala—Conall's village at Llyn Tegid

y Daearen—the earth

y Ddraig Goch—the Red Dragon; the land of Cymru that holds the blood of all our ancestors, the land is holy; the land is sacred.

y aw goedwig—the nine woods of ceremony for the fire festivals: birch, oak, ash, hawthorn, willow, yew, hazel, elm, and alder *y tân ymuno*—the joining fire of Beltane

y Saith Seren Siriol—the seven cheerful stars of the sisters of the great star god Caomai, the armed king (the constellation Orion and the Seven Sisters)

Ysbrydnos—the spirit night. Both Samhainn and Beltane are Ysbrydnos spirit nights.

witsio—witch

Conall speaking to his Briga at Pistyll Rhaeadr; the talking falls of Cymru.

"Mo Briga, far an d'ung thu an Còmhradh Carragh le ar gràdhaich."
(My Briga, where you anointed the talking pillar with our love.)

Biography

Alan Roy Johnston

Alan Roy Johnston is a retired administrator and former business owner residing in Eastern Oregon with his wife, children, and grandchildren. Mr. Johnston enjoys working in his garden at home, writing, and sharing his time and his stories with his children and grandchildren. His ancestry is Welsh-Irish and Norse, and his interest in Celtic spirituality was inspired by the family stories and traditions told to him by his mother and grandmother. He is a practicing druid of the *Ceile Dé*.

Researching his genealogy with his older brother, Don, and working with Ancestry.com, he has been able to trace his family's history and DNA ancestry back hundreds of years in Wales, Ireland, Denmark, Sweden, and Norway. His twenty-fifth great-grandmother was Gwenllian verch Gruffydd of Cymru, while his thirty-second great-grandfather was one of Ireland's kings, Brian Bora (Brian Bóruma mac Cennétig). Mr. Johnston's thirty-sixth great-grandfather was the Viking Ragnar Lodbrok, whose father, Sigurd Hring, was king of Sweden. Mr. Johnston's thirty-fifth great-grandfather was Ivarr Ragnarson (son of Ragnar) the Boneless, king of the Norsemen of all Ireland and Britain and founder of Dublin. Mr. Johnston has always loved all things Celtic and Norse, including pagan ideology and theology—especially the deep Celtic beliefs regarding the sacredness of all life on the earth, which today might be described as ecofeminism.

He chose a lifetime of education and a career in horticulture and arboriculture, the landscaping industry, and ranch and estate management as a way to keep a close connection with nature and the feminine creative spirit. He would tell you, "History is in the blood, and as a father and a grandfather, I have sought a way to keep the old stories alive. *Desire's Tempest Journey: The Saga of Briga of Cymru and the Wolf-Warrior* is my attempt as a story telling bard to create a window into the Celtic world of pre-Roman and pre-Christian history."

He hopes you will enjoy reading this first book in the Long Journey Home saga as much as he enjoyed researching and writing it.

Biography

Ena Brennan

Ena Brennan has taught in the field of education for twenty-five years. Ms. Brennan has taught primary, secondary, and postsecondary education, including GED and ESL. She learned to love all things Celtic while she was studying for her master's degree in Celtic studies and Celtic theology in Wales, and she has taught classes in Celtic spirituality.

Her education experience includes the following: PhD candidate in education, Oregon State University; PhD in social justice theology, Edwin Mellen University; master's degree in Celtic theology, University of Wales; Bachelor of Science in history and political science, Eastern Oregon University.

She was the associate editor for *The Apostolic Bible: Polyglot*, a Greek-English interlinear research and reference Bible published in 2006, and has two books forthcoming from Edwin Mellen Publishing Company in 2014: *The Five-Thousand-Year Search for the Feminine Nature of God: A Study in the History of Language* and *Changing the Rules: The Crisis in American Higher Education.*

www.ingramcontent.com/pod-product-compliance
Lightning Source LLC
Chambersburg PA
CBHW051544250626
47157CB00001B/171